Voyages

Jackson Peoples-Rosenblatt

ISBN: 069261415X
ISBN 13: 9780692614150
Library of Congress Control Number: 2016911713
ESC Press, San Diego, CA

For Cap
And,
As always, for L.C.

Author's Note

Voyages is a companion volume to my earlier novel, *The Current* (2014). For the most part, it fills a gap in chronology which occurs between Parts Four and Five of that book. In addition, the section of *Voyages* titled "Cooper Luxemberg: May, 1979" overlaps with the *The Current,* Part Five. Finally, the concluding section of *Voyages* can be read as an epilogue to *The Current.* I provide this information here not to suggest that the books must be read in any particular order or that understanding one depends on reading the other but merely to clarify the relationship between them for readers who find such things interesting. The two books may certainly be read independently. They were intended to be, and are written as, separate works.

Many of the characters in *Voyages* are making "encore appearances" in these pages, having been originally introduced in my earlier books. I hope readers will enjoy encountering them again. A **Directory of Recurring Characters** appears at the end of this volume.

Cooper Luxemberg:
October, 1977-February, 1978

"It's the biggest regional bodybuilding contest in the western United States," Big Steve said. "One of the biggest in the country."

"Historically, it's been a stepping stone to the Mr. America," Matt nodded. "It certainly was in my case. A win at the Western States meant I went into the Mr. A with the judges already regarding me as a serious contender. Perhaps a thing like that shouldn't matter, but inevitably it does. I believe it had a lot to do with how they eventually placed me. My win there really was a turning point in my competition career. So Big Steve and I think that a couple guys we all know should consider entering this year. To position themselves, right? They might not be thinking of the Mr. A right now, but that could change in the future. Somebody's going to win the Western States. Why not one of our guys?"

From the mid Fifties through the late Sixties, Matt Duckworth had competed regularly in the Mr. America contest. Always a top contender, he placed as high as third on three different occasions. As far back as Cooper's grade school days, he'd seen Matt on magazine covers. He still had copies carefully stored away, bought with his earnings from working in his parents' store after school and on weekends. They were autographed now. Even as a third grader Cooper held aspirations, and that's how his journey started, reading every bodybuilding magazine he could get his hands on and dreaming of looking like the guys on the covers. Matt was one of the guys he wanted to look like when he grew up. Now this long time idol of Cooper's was encouraging him to take the next step in his journey, this time in person and as a friend. It was dizzying when Cooper thought about it that way.

"You know who you are," Big Steve said.

Cooper understood that this remark was directed at him. His heart skipped a beat. T. wouldn't need any encouragement. He always did what Big Steve told him. That's the kind of husband Big Steve was. But Cooper had no husband to answer to and a mind of his own. His high placing at last year's Mr.

California—at the ripe age of twenty-one—seemed to point to even greater accomplishments in the future. But he wasn't sure he was ready for this. Still, Big Steve and Matt were far better judges.

"They've realigned the classes for the contest this year," Matt said. "They're still based on height. But the new upper limit for the medium class is seventy inches instead of sixty-nine."

"Meaning that T. and Cooper," Big Steve said, "just speaking hypothetically, you understand, and not ruling out anyone else we know, would compete at the top end of the medium class instead of the bottom end of the tall class as would have been the case last year."

"Which could be a real advantage," Matt said, "in terms of a class win. Being at the top end of a class in terms of size is always preferable to being at the low end. It doesn't determine the placings definitively. There are plenty of other factors to consider as well. Proportion. Conditioning. You name it. But size definitely matters."

"To coin a phrase," T. laughed.

"No question about it," Matt said, "size gives you a certain edge. The overall standings are always a crap shoot. But a class win would be significant in a high-profile contest like this. All the big contests are organized by classes these days, and class winners get almost as much attention as the winner of first place overall. The downside is that if past seasons are any guide, the medium class will be the most competitive of the three."

"Still," Nick said, "it's something to think about."

Big Steve and Matt didn't compete these days, but Nick did. He'd nearly won the tall class at the Californias last time. Cooper had been waiting to hear him weigh in. His opinion always carried weight, though Cooper disagreed with him regularly.

"That's right," Matt nodded.

"In any case," Big Steve said, "it's just over twelve weeks out. So a decision has to be made soon."

"It's almost too late already," Nick observed.

* * *

Three years after meeting Nick Romanovsky, Cooper was still nursing a low grade crush on him. That in itself was unusual. Cooper was never "low grade" about anything. This made the phenomenon baffling, and Cooper was rarely baffled. In addition, he seldom had crushes in the conventional sense.

Whatever he had in lieu of them he consummated as quickly as possible. That a genuine, old school one might persist for such a length of time was nothing less than troubling. It made Cooper reluctant to examine the matter too closely. But at the same time, it meant that Nick was always on his radar screen. They had dated exactly once, and the occasion turned out to be one of the few anticlimaxes of Cooper's life. Contrary to his expectations, and for that matter, intentions, they didn't have sex that night. Nick didn't ask him out again, and Cooper, uncharacteristically for him, was too shy to suggest a rematch. Cooper's buddy, Stone, who had dated Nick once himself, offered a hypothesis for the fiasco, but then as now Cooper wasn't sure that Stone's experience could be generalized from. Hustlers were a law unto themselves, even on the rare occasions when they were working *pro bono*. Still, the possibility of sex seemed to glimmer in the background whenever Cooper and Nick encountered one another. That Sunday afternoon, for instance, as brunch broke up and the gang headed off on their individual pursuits.

"You going to do it?" Nick asked, as they trudged down the block. Somehow his BMW always ended up parked in front of, behind, or next to Cooper's aging but pristine Jag. Surely that meant something. Except if it didn't.

"Do what?" Cooper asked, although he knew what Nick was talking about.

"Enter the Western States," Nick growled, swinging his motorcycle helmet like a club. He sounded like what he was, a prosecuting attorney. But did that make Cooper the defendant or a friendly witness?

"You think I should?"

"You heard Big Steve," Nick said. "And Matt. It's pretty clear what those two think."

"But what do you think?"

"Does my opinion really matter?"

Yes, Cooper thought. That was the point. Nick always deferred when those two offered an opinion. His reverence for Big Steve was the only thing that kept the whole situation from blowing up, and God knew what would happen to the gang if it did. Cooper had been observing closely for a long time, and he'd finally figured it out. The reason Nick had never settled down was as plain as the nose on your face. T. was taken, and by the one man Nick refused to go up against.

* * *

T.'s unavailability didn't mean that Nick stayed home nights pining, however. Nick might be obsessed, but he wasn't neurotic. His exploits had made him a Castro Street legend and were ongoing. Cooper saw him later emerging from a club just down the block from the Castro Theatre with a pair of go-go boys hanging off him, obvious trophies of his night's hunt. Chilly as it was just days before Halloween, they were half naked, sweaty from their exertions entertaining the patrons of the club.

"Hope you left something decent in there for me," Cooper said.

"Don't worry," Nick grinned. "There's plenty more where these two came from."

"Yeah, Cooper," one of the boys laughed. "You won't go home empty handed."

"If you go home at all," the other boy leered.

* * *

In the shower later, while the pair of go-go boys he had bagged slept it off, Cooper considered Big Steve's proposition. He didn't want to enter the contest unless he felt confident of making the final six in his class. But this was a big show and there were no guarantees. No matter how hard you worked, how carefully you prepared, you were never sure when you stepped onto that stage what the outcome was going to be. Mostly it was a question of who else showed up to compete—a crapshoot, in other words. How many other meatheads were out there with the same dreams as yours? And, perhaps, blessed with better genetics? Or more determination? Guys who had logged several more years in the gym than Cooper, for instance. And like it or not there was always the question of drugs. Big Steve insisted on his proteges competing clean, which put them at a noticeable disadvantage. In a contest at this level, it might be too great a disadvantage to overcome. Cooper wasn't sure he saw the point of all that work and trouble for a tenth or eleventh place finish. But Big Steve had spoken, and Matt was authoritative, too. Hell, Matt was definitive.

* * *

"It's not so bad for you," T. said the next morning at the gym. "You have a choice. I'm entering no matter what."

The gang would be celebrating T.'s thirtieth birthday in a few more weeks. In Castro Street years, that made him middle aged and Nick, at thirty-seven, practically a grandfather. Here at the gym, however, things were judged differently. Bodybuilding was the great equalizer. Matt and Big Steve, for instance, were in their forties. But that didn't make them geriatric cases. Because of the iron they pumped and the diets they observed, they were more like gods. And T., regardless of what the queens who thought they ran everything gay might have to say on the matter, was one of the half dozen hottest guys in the city. You could allow yourself to be middle aged at thirty, but it wasn't inevitable.

"Do any of us really have a choice?" Cooper asked, pulling his sweatpants up over his quads. "I mean, I know Big Steve's your husband. But for the rest of us he might as well be our commanding officer."

"I don't remember you ever being in the military," T. grinned.

"Signing on with Big Steve as your trainer," Cooper said, "is like enlisting. Everybody knows that. I didn't get it at first, but I sure do now. And by the way, this boot camp never ends."

II

Big Steve rented a couple of vans. That's how most of the gang was getting to Denver. But all those hours on the road wouldn't do the two competitors any favors. Their condition would suffer, if only the slightest bit. Big Steve wouldn't hear of it. Matt was an airline pilot. He arranged cheap tickets for T. and Cooper. When they got off the plane in Denver, the whole gang was waiting for them.

"Room assignments," Big Steve said, checking his clipboard as they all piled out of the vans in front of the motel. "The married couples bunk together, of course."

That meant not just Big Steve and T., but J.B. and Scott, and Matt and Dr. Ashby.

"And I booked single rooms for Nick and Cooper. The rest of you divide up however you want in the other four rooms."

"Sounds like orgy time to me," Ashby said.

"Right, Dr. Sainte Claire," Kirk said. "Except believe it or not, a couple of us are actually straight."

"Straight in California maybe," Nick snickered. "God knows what you are once you cross state lines."

"At least we'll know where to go if any of us end up needing medical attention," Evan laughed.

* * *

"Coop," Big Steve said, "I'm putting Nick in charge of your final preparations. Any objections?"

Cooper had been expecting that. It seemed pretty obvious that Big Steve was still holding out hopes of marrying the two of them off to each other. He didn't give up easy. But even without that motivation, Nick, with his extensive experience as a competitor, was the obvious choice.

The rest of the crew went off to dinner, but Cooper wasn't sure he had the will power to be around all that food. Ordinarily it wouldn't have been a problem, but twelve weeks of rigorous dieting had taken a toll on his emotional state. The next twenty-seven hours would be the hardest of all. He watched the vans pull out onto the street in front of the motel. Then he closed the drapes.

Cooper opened a can of tuna. He peeled four boiled eggs he'd cooked the night before and brought on the plane with him. He threw the yolks down the toilet. He would eat the whites only. His body was screaming for pizza. It was all he could do not to grab the phone book in search of a pizza joint that delivered.

* * *

He stood in the bathtub. After he finished shaving all over he rinsed off the remaining lather under the shower head. Then he moisturized, wishing someone would make a product that cared for the skin appropriately but didn't smell so girly.

The guys weren't back yet. Everything on television annoyed him. He pulled on clothes and went for a walk. It was freezing outside. There was nothing interesting about the part of the city surrounding the motel. He turned back after only a few blocks. He didn't have the energy, and the altitude, which Big Steve had warned about, made him short of breath.

There was nothing to stay up for. An early bedtime couldn't hurt.

T. was lucky, Cooper thought. He turned out the bedside lamp and pulled up the blanket. He had to be just as hungry, anxious, and miserable as Cooper was, but he had his husband beside him. If Big Steve had his way, every gay man on the planet would be safely coupled. Cooper got the concept intellectually. But he couldn't figure out the emotions of it. He supposed you could come up with some sort of marriage of convenience if the feelings involved were more than you could handle. But where did you find a guy that would agree to it?

* * *

Cooper heard the key turn in the lock and was immediately wide awake. He knew Big Steve had given Nick the extra key to the motel room.

"Just me," Nick announced from the darkness.

"What is it?" Cooper grunted.

"Bed check," Nick laughed. "You know Big Steve."

"I'm here," Cooper said, "and you can tell him I'm alone."

"Right," Nick said. "I'll say goodnight then."

III

"How did you sleep?" Nick asked, staring down at him.

"God," Cooper yawned. "I didn't hear you come in. Sound asleep since you left last night."

"Ashby's here, too," Nick said.

"Morning, Coop."

They both looked ridiculously cheerful. Cooper figured they had ingested five or six times as many calories as he had over the last twenty-four hours. That probably accounted for their mood. Cooper had dreamed of food all night. And when he didn't dream about sex, something was seriously wrong in his universe.

"I'm going through your gym bag," Nick said. "O.K?"

"Sure," Cooper said.

"Just to make sure we're not forgetting anything important."

"Right."

"Not that you would, of course," Nick said.

"I get it," Cooper said. "Big Steve's rules. Each contestant must have a baby sitter."

"Stop talking, you two," Ashby said. "I need to take Cooper's blood pressure."

"Right," Nick nodded.

"Low blood pressure can be a warning sign of dehydration," Ashby said as he pumped up the cuff. "You guys never drink enough water during the last twenty-four hours. You're afraid it'll smooth you out. Please sit still."

"Two of everything in here," Nick said, rummaging in Cooper's gym bag. "Good boy."

"Belt and suspenders," Cooper grunted.

"He's a real Boy Scout," Ashby laughed. "Even though he says he never was one. Always prepared. Now, Coop, I know you're not feeling anywhere near normal this morning, which is to be expected under the circumstances. You're half starved. You slept in a strange bed, or at least tried to. And God knows when you had sex last. A little lightheadedness isn't anything to be worried about. But actual dizziness or irregular heartbeat, have Nick call me backstage immediately."

"Roger," Cooper said.

"There's always a doctor on duty at these things," Ashby continued, "but God knows what kind of drunk or lunatic it will turn out to be today. You should hear some of Matt's stories."

* * *

Prejudging always seemed like an anticlimax, but Cooper knew it was really where the crucial decisions were made. The evening show was just that—a show. It would feature the top twelve contestants from each class, who would parade across the stage briefly prior to full scale posing routines presented by the finalists. The evening show didn't determine anything except the final order among the top six in each class and the overall placings, and even then the results rarely varied from the preliminary placings the judges had agreed to that afternoon. Prejudging, then, was where you staked your claim to a spot in that magic six, qualifying you to appear on stage with the other finalists in your class and perform your posing routine for the evening crowd. So as tedious and boring as the proceedings seemed, you had to maintain your concentration at all costs. You had to give it one hundred percent effort.

* * *

"Don't check out the competition," Nick said as they walked from the van into the high school gym where check-in was taking place. "Half of them won't look as good as you, which will make you overconfident, and half of them will look better than you, which will psych you out. Remember that your only real competition is yourself."

"Right," Cooper nodded. He recognized this wisdom, though uttered in Nick's voice, as originating with Big Steve—always the brains of the operation.

Should T. and Cooper stand side by side in the prejudging lineup? Big Steve, Matt, and Nick discussed the issue over and over. Next to each other, they'd be able to provide moral support, spoken or not. But standing next to each other might invite the judges to compare them more with one another than with the other competitors. It was feasible that one of them might knock the other out of contention for the top six. In the end, the three "experts" decided that optimally they should stand close to each other in the lineup but not actually adjacent. This meant they had to avoid being assigned consecutive numbers at check-in. In the line at the table, Cooper made sure there were two medium class guys behind T. and ahead of him.

Cooper knew what to do once they got to the pump room, but it was easier to let Nick take over, directing him through what amounted to a workout of moderate intensity which would get the blood flowing into his muscles and pump them up impressively. Nick's baritone yelp focused and motivated him as his body warmed up and the adrenaline started flowing. Across the room, Big Steve was putting T. through the same sequence of exercises, his basso rumble unmistakable amid the din of dozens of bodybuilders pumping up.

* * *

"Good boy," Nick said blotting the sweat off Cooper's chest with a fresh towel. "Got a really nice pump going. Big Steve says they'll be calling the class onstage in about five minutes, so we're right on track."

"Roger," Cooper said.

"Here," Nick said, handing him a pair of headphones. "I'll load the tape. Time for you to listen to this loop of your posing music. It's not too early to focus on tonight's show even though prejudging hasn't started yet. Help you visualize your routine. Remember the drill: eyes closed and concentrate on your breathing. Focus on the music and empty your mind of everything else."

* * *

Part of prejudging took place with contestants in "relaxed" posture. If you were truly relaxed, however, your muscles might appear to sag slightly or you might "smooth out", calling your overall condition into question. On the other hand, if you flexed too obviously the judges were required to lower your score. They might even disqualify you. That had happened to a guy at the Mr. California the year before. Cooper was next to him in the lineup. He hadn't forgotten it. He was determined never to let it happen to him. T. and Cooper had spent hours practicing and perfecting their "relaxed" stance. As Cooper took his place in the lineup onstage, he could only hope that the advice of their coaches was correct.

* * *

The hours dragged on as the judges examined the lineup in minute detail, then called trios and pairs of contestants to the front of the stage for comparisons. Whenever he was "on", Cooper could hear Nick in the audience calling out encouragement and advice—a constant stream, really, which helped keep him in the game despite his fatigue and hunger.

* * *

"Gentlemen," the head judge said, "first of all, the Medium Class contestants placing twelve through seven. These individuals will not perform posing routines in the evening show but will appear onstage during the contestants' parade."

Cooper could feel the tension in the room. Next to him, T. was ready to jump out of his skin.

"They are: in twelfth place, from Butte, Montana, Philip Winchester; in eleventh place, from Boise, Idaho, Terry van Meter; in tenth place, from Salem, Oregon, Isaiah Jackson; in ninth place, from Carson City, Nevada, Rudy Escamillo; in eight place, from Spokane, Washington, Larry Laxton; and in seventh place, from Phoenix, Arizona, Michael Forrest."

"We're either finalists," T. muttered, "or we'll be sitting in the audience tonight."

"Bite your tongue," Cooper said. "You know it's not either/or. We're definitely in the finals."

"And our six finalists, in no particular order, are contestants number forty-seven, number fifty-six. . ."

"See," Cooper said, "that's you."

". . .number fifty-seven, number fifty-nine. . ."

"And that's you," T. said.

* * *

"Tuna," Big Steve said. "Egg whites."

They were in the van on the way back to the motel. It was hours yet until they had to report for the evening show. Filet mignons were doing a conga line in Cooper's brain.

"Don't forget to eat a banana," Ashby said. "Got to make sure your electrolytes don't go haywire."

"That's an order," Big Steve said. "Hear me, gentlemen?"

"Aye, aye, commodore," T. snickered.

"And a nap," Nick said. "You both really need a nap. I'll come by and tuck you in, Coop."

Cooper decided that Nick wasn't capable of opening his mouth without sounding dirty. He wondered how that played in a courtroom.

* * *

Nick's hands were huge, powerful, and perfectly manicured.

In preparation for the evening show, Cooper and T. had returned to the pump room as soon as it opened. The atmosphere was completely different from before prejudging that morning. And with most of the contestants already eliminated, the room was far less crowded and chaotic. It was no less tense, however.

Cooper had imagined Nick's hands on him lots of times. The reality was different. Non-sexual, of course, except for what was going on in Cooper's imagination. Non-sexual but at the same time nearly overwhelming, oiling him up. Preparation to go onstage, sure. But just as surely a kind of benediction.

"Listen to me," Nick said. "It's almost time. They'll call your class on-stage in two or three minutes. There's nothing more I or anybody else can do to help you."

"I know."

"You've never been bigger. You've never been harder. You've never been more ripped. You know all that."

"Right," Cooper grunted.

"Your only real competition is yourself," Nick continued, "and you've already won. Your condition proves it. Whatever happens tonight, you're a winner."

The rest of the room seemed to have vanished around them. There were only the few square feet they occupied. As Nick spoke, his hands continued to work. Strong, firm, businesslike, spreading the oil, smoothing it onto Cooper's skin.

"Did you hear me?" Nick murmured. "You're a winner. Anyone looking at you can see it."

* * *

"Medium height contestants, line up please."

The guy was holding a clipboard. He had a beer gut the size of one of the smaller American states, but his shoulders and chest were enormous. Cooper wondered how long it would take him to get into reasonable shape.

Nick grasped Cooper tightly by the shoulders and gave him a crisp nod.

"Numerical order, please, contestants."

A vise-like handshake from Big Steve, who'd been preparing T.

Fire blazing in T.'s eyes.

The twelve medium class contestants filed down the long, dimly lit corridor to the backstage area. The smell of baby oil was nearly sickening. Cooper heard mutters. One guy was repeating the Lord's Prayer, another the Twenty-third Psalm. It always surprised Cooper how popular God was backstage at bodybuilding competitions. He could hear the audience out front. He could almost feel their anticipation.

* * *

One by one, as their names were called, each contestant walked onto the stage, found his mark, hit a single pose, and exited on the opposite side.

"Number fifty-six: Tristan Bentley."

Cooper held his breath. There were all kinds of ways to screw up even as simple a maneuver as that. He counted his heartbeats. He counted his breaths. He listened as two more names were called. Then—

"Number fifty-nine: Cooper Luxemberg."

One step after the other. Lights. The wooden strips of the stage floor against his bare feet.

It was like a dream, Cooper thought, re-entering the shadowy wings.

* * *

The six semi-finalists left. Their evening was over. Cooper and the remaining five men were called back onto the stage. At the prompting of the emcee, they moved through a series of compulsory poses. Front double biceps. Side chest. Side triceps. Rear lat spread. . .

"Contestants, thank you," the emcee said.

They filed back into the wings.

Then one by one each man moved onto the stage to perform his solo posing routine. Cooper listened to their music. Two of the contestants had the same tune to pose to: not as much of a coincidence as you might think, since guys seemed to go for the obvious choices. One man's tape failed and he had to do his routine in silence. The crowd tried to encourage him, but Cooper could only imagine how his concentration had been destroyed.

* * *

"From San Francisco, California, contestant number 56, Tristan Bentley."

Cooper watched from the wings as T. found his mark, took his position, waited for the music to start. Aaron Copland: "Fanfare for the Common Man." There were no words to describe T. Cooper was enthralled. Earlier, he'd mentally placed T. fourth in their class and himself either fifth or sixth. Now he wasn't sure. T. might take the whole thing.

* * *

"Next," the emcee announced, "contestant number fifty-nine. From San Francisco, California, Cooper Luxemberg."

Cooper took a breath and stepped onto the stage. His posture was perfect. He found his mark. Took his position. Faced the audience, heard the applause. Waited for the music.

Thank God for T. In addition to his other accomplishments, he was an aficionado of classical music. He had chosen the perfect posing music for Cooper, "Adagio of Spartacus and Phrygia," from the Kachaturian ballet, *Spartacus*. Cooper had posed to it at the California Championships the year before and he believed its inspirational tone had brought him good luck. There was no need to choose something new. As the melody soared in its fervor and exultation, he hit his poses like the hero of the legend.

Cooper had never felt more alive. He was like a tuning fork vibrating to the heartbeat of the universe. Every set and every rep had led to this moment. Every slice of pizza and scoop of ice cream not eaten. Every baked potato and piece of popcorn not buttered. Every cookie lusted after but ultimately rejected. People couldn't understand it. They thought he was crazy. But none of them looked like this. When they saw him in the bars, when he took them to bed, when he left them afterward to go home, they could only wonder what it felt like to go through life in a body like this.

He knew this because they said so, even if not in words. It was in their eyes. In the way they touched him. In their whimpers and sighs. But it was none of these things that kept him going. He didn't do it for the sake of being desired or worshipped.

It was this feeling. Hitting these poses.

Until he met a guy who made him feel something analogous, there was no use thinking about a relationship.

* * *

"Results for the Medium Height Class," the emcee intoned, the sound system on the cusp of a major attack of feedback.

"In sixth place, from Missoula, Montana, Rocky Fredericks."

The beauty queen simpered across the stage with the trophy. She handed it to Rocky and he gave her an awkward kiss on the cheek.

Next to Cooper, T.'s teeth were chattering.

"In fifth place, from Tucson, Arizona, Enrique Cardenas."

"Top four," T. muttered. "We made the top four."

More awkwardness with the girl and the trophy. This heterosexual posturing was the part of the competition that drove Cooper crazy.

"In fourth place, from Olympia, Washington, Leonard Petrucci."

"Oh, my god," T. said.

Cooper was speechless.

"In third place, from San Francisco, California, Tristan Bentley."

"Jesus, Cooper," T. said. "You're in the top two."

"In second place, also from San Francisco, California, Cooper Luxemberg. And our winner, from Oakland California, Orlando Jefferson."

* * *

The last of the tall class contestants left the stage. There was lackadaisical applause. He wasn't very impressive either as a poser or a physical specimen. Cooper was surprised he'd even made the finals. But it often was the case that the tall class was the weakest one.

The judges filed out, heading off to finalize their deliberations.

The first guest poser was the reigning Mr. Europe, a ridiculously handsome Frenchman. Cooper couldn't help but be impressed.

"This is an object lesson," Big Steve said, "in how impressive a man can look at five feet nine and two hundred pounds."

"Is that all he is?" Ashby asked.

"He may be two hundred ten right now during his off season," Matt said. "But you're right, he looks substantially larger than that."

"Less is more," Nick said.

"It's about two things," Big Steve said, "proportion and overall conditioning."

The second guest poser was the holder of the 1976 Mr. America and 1977 Mr. Universe titles. When he strode onto the stage, the audience went crazy.

"He's exactly your height, Cooper," Nick muttered into his ear. "And his overall shape is uncannily similar to yours. That's what you could look like in another couple of years."

"Jeez," Cooper marveled.

"Not as handsome as you, of course."

"I don't know," Cooper said. "I'd definitely fuck him."

"At the Universe a few months back he competed at two-twenty five."

"He looks much larger than me," Cooper said.

"That's because you've never seen yourself the way you're looking at him. You're not as far off that as you believe. Not nearly."

* * *

The finalists from the three height classes, eighteen bodybuilders in all, filed onto the stage. This time, with nothing to lose by doing it, Cooper and T. stood side by side.

"And now, ladies and gentlemen," the emcee said. "I'm pleased to announce the overall placings. In tenth place overall, representing the Short Class, from Los Angeles, California, Rory Edelstein."

The girl with the trophies, again.

"He placed second in that class," T. murmured. "That means there are only two short class guys in the top ten."

"Our odds just got a lot better, in other words," Cooper said.

"In ninth place, representing the Tall class, from Santa Fe, New Mexico, Hector Concepcion."

"Second in that class," T. said. "That means all six of the finalists in our class are in the top eight."

"In eighth place, representing the Medium class, from Missoula, Montana, Rocky Fredericks."

"That doesn't tell us anything," Cooper said, "does it?"

"No."

"In seventh place, representing the Tall Class, from Artesia, Colorado, Clifton Armitage,"

"Jeez," T. muttered.

"In sixth place, representing the Short class, from Compton, California, Riley Jones."

"That's it, Cooper. You and I just took second and third places overall."

"I can't believe it," Cooper muttered.

"Believe it," T. said.

"Congratulations," Cooper choked.

* * *

"Thanks, Cooper," Lance Garrison said, advancing the film in his camera. "I know you're exhausted right now, but those are some great shots. We'll get together in a couple of weeks and look them over. As many free prints as you want, of course."

"Thanks, Lance," Cooper said.

When Cooper wasn't nursing his *is this really a crush?* on Nick, he was nursing his *is this really a crush?* on Lance. And Lance wasn't available, either.

* * *

It had been annoying having Nick breathing down his neck all day. If it had been anyone else, Cooper probably would have blown his stack. But it was necessary. He understood that. And it served its purpose. The combination of annoyance and—it had to be admitted—security Nick's presence provided made a signal contribution to Cooper's performance. Cooper knew exactly how much he owed his success to it.

The minute they were back in his room, Cooper grabbed Nick and kissed him hard. Nick kissed back, but without any noticeable commitment. After a moment, he pushed Cooper gently but firmly away.

"Wouldn't be fair to take advantage of you when you're overstimulated like this," he said.

"Take advantage?" Cooper said. "What are you talking about?"

"You're half dead from hunger and fatigue. You hardly know what you're doing."

They looked at each other for a long moment.

"Patronizing bastard."

"You know that's not true," Nick smiled.

Cooper took a breath. This wasn't how the scene was supposed to play. There was nothing for it but a strategic retreat.

"Sorry," he said.

"Nothing to apologize for," Nick smiled. "It's an occupational hazard on a night like this. Everybody's testosterone is raging. Don't worry. You'll fly home tomorrow morning and less than twenty-four hours from now you'll be on Castro Street making new friends. But it's definitely time for me to head back to my room."

"Listen," Cooper said. "I'm sorry for getting out of line. Really. Thanks for everything. I couldn't have done it without you."

"Sure you could," Nick said. "You're a champ. No question about it. And anyway, you'd have done the same for me. Next contest, it might be your turn."

"Anytime," Cooper said.

* * *

"Gentlemen," Big Steve growled, wrapping the trophies in blankets and stowing them in the back of one of the vans, "mission accomplished. Second and third places in the medium height class and in the overall standings. We salute you."

"Your taxi to the airport is here," Nick said, an arm around each of them.

"You have your tickets?" Big Steve asked.

"Aye, aye, sir," Cooper said.

* * *

"You really gave Nick something to think about last night," T. said as the plane pulled back from the gate.

"He told you," Cooper said, wincing.

"Told me what?"

"Never mind."

"So it's like that."

"It isn't like anything," Cooper insisted. "What do you mean?"

"It's a better placing than he's ever managed," T. said. "That's all."

"So what?" Cooper asked. "We're not in competition with each other."

"You and I aren't competing with each other," T. said, "but Nick's in competition with the whole world. It's who he is."

"But we're his friends," Cooper protested.

"Everybody in the world," T. insisted. "Really. It's the main reason why he's still single."

"I don't follow," Cooper said.

"He has to dominate," T. said.

"I'd think that would be easy for a guy like Nick," Cooper said. "Plenty of guys are into that role playing stuff."

"It can't be like in a game," T. said. "It has to be real. And it only counts if the other guy is a worthy competitor. When you're Nick, finding a worthy competitor isn't easy."

"How the hell is a thing like that supposed to go?" Cooper asked. "It makes no sense whatever."

"You know that and I know that," T. said, "but we're talking about Nick."

"You said I gave him something to think about," Cooper said. "What about you?"

"He's already got me pigeonholed," T. said. "You're a different matter. After all this time he still doesn't know quite what to make of you."

* * *

Cooper had thought that their experience together at the contest might turn out to be a turning point in his relations with Nick. He supposed he should have known better. Afterwards, Nick was as remote as ever. He was always perfectly cordial in the gym, at their favorite bars, or even at brunch. But at the same time, he remained essentially a stranger.

The new trophies took pride of place at the center of Cooper's hoard, which lined the top shelf in his tiny den.

Nick Romanovsky

When Nikolai Romanovsky, Esquire arrived in San Francisco, he got hooked up with a group of young men more or less exactly like him. Too numerous and disorganized to be described as a gang or a crew, they were just the guys. They were all under thirty, especially the few who weren't and went to whatever length necessary to look and act as if they were. All of the men came from good, meaning at the very least comfortably upper middle class, families. They all had good jobs as measured by that arcane standard which is an amalgam of income, prestige, and respectability. It was impossible to tell from observing them which ones had trust funds and which ones didn't. It was far easier simply to assume that they all did.

They all got the same haircut—with minor adjustments for growth pattern, texture, and cranial shape—from the same barber. They bought their suits and accessories from the same shops. They drank the same brand of whiskey in the same bars, where, in urbane, gentlemanly succession determined by unspoken but universally understood rules of precedence they picked up the same stewardesses, secretaries, dental hygienists, and nurses. They mostly drove boxy little B.M.W.'s or sporty Alfa-Romeos, though there was one Morgan in the fleet and one Citroen cabriolet. There were also a Lotus, two Porsches, and a gaggle of Jeeps. Nick's B.M.W. had only two cylinders and two wheels. This and his carefully trimmed mustache were his signature unconventionalities. They were the sort of nonconformities which were permissible—simple, manly eccentricities comprehended by everyone and immune from real censure, whatever jests they might give rise to. The tail end of the Swinging Sixties might be swirling around Nick's crew, but except for musical matters and a few accommodations to fashion they mostly ignored the phenomenon, thinking of it as kid stuff.

Outside of working hours the men roamed the city in twos and threes. They generally dined in fours, fives, or sixes. Pairing off at meals was permissible at lunchtime, because work schedules and local geography dictated it, or at other times when certain confidences had to be shared. Any other circum-

stance made a threesome obligatory at least, and odd numbers were always preferred to even ones. They attended sporting events in packs of whatever size
accumulated. When they ran into each other at the opera or the symphony,
they acknowledged the meeting with brisk nods and firm handshakes but never
spoke of it afterwards. Escorting women to cultural events was an accepted
duty for young men like them, but those venues were not their preferred stomp-
ing grounds.

They never discussed the relative merits of their various fraternal affiliations. This would have been bad form. They worked out those rivalries on
the squash and tennis courts. That they had such affiliations was a given. They
scrupulously observed and maintained the mores of what one of their number
jokingly referred to as "that great frathouse in the sky." Some found this quip
disturbing because it seemed irreligious, but to a man they subscribed to the
sort of platonic ideal it implied.

A few of them had fiancées. A somewhat larger number had steady girlfriends. These were all young women from good families. They had graduated
from good schools. They would eventually make exactly the sort of wives young
men of this type would be expected to equip themselves with. Meanwhile, it was
an article of faith that the existence of these relationships posed no obstacle to
the men's sporting activities with the ubiquitous stewardesses, secretaries, nurses, and dental hygienists. The differing species of females, virginal or "sporty",
were considered to inhabit parallel universes. The young men would have been
shocked had they known how much overlap there was between the groups.

A fairly large proportion of the men was unattached. Nick often wondered how it felt to be free of entanglements. Though he'd never have admitted
it, he envied them.

* * *

Nick's westward migration occurred as a result of what Joanna persisted
in calling their trial separation. As an attorney, Nick objected to her use of the
term. They hadn't been married. They hadn't been engaged. They had never
so much as discussed the possibility of spending their lives together. When he
thought about it, which wasn't much or often, he assumed that they would eventually end up married. But eventually can be a long time. He had assumed that
Joanna held the same assumptions herself. Calling their current situation a trial
separation made the relationship seem much more official than it had actually
been. It implied that this was a breakup, which it certainly wasn't.

Still, Nick insisted to himself that he was devastated. But the more he repeated this the less he felt it. What he actually felt was relief, though he couldn't imagine why this should be the case. Explicable or not, however, it was undoubtedly relief he experienced, mixed with some guilt occasioned not so much by the end of the relationship as by the degree of relief he was experiencing.

Even the guilt fizzled out pretty quickly once he left Chicago. Each time he talked with Joanna long distance, her cheery anecdotes made it impossible to imagine that he had somehow ruined her life. As for his own—well, his firm was only too happy to grant his wish for a transfer west. They were expanding their activities in California, and as grandson of one of the founding partners and son of one of the senior ones he was just the man to have on the spot. He met, or perhaps exceeded, their expectations by passing the California Bar Exam on his first attempt. He found a Nob Hill apartment he could just about afford, and he pretended to put on a brave face with regard to Joanna. His family and associates seemed to appreciate this last effort especially. Their concern about his emotional state in the aftermath exacerbated his sense of duplicity.

* * *

For members of the gang it was de rigueur to have a gym membership, and Nick met this expectation as conscientiously as he did all others. But there was no associated expectation that any of the men ever went to the gyms they were members of or actually worked out there in the case that they did happen to drop by. A gym membership was just another facet of their social life, and the most the majority of Nick's pals ever did was use the steam room, because all their gyms had steam rooms. Nick, however, not only went to his gym, he went regularly, and he used the facilities as such facilities are intended to be used, and the more he used his gym, the more his condition and size clearly indicated that he did so. Within just a few months his musculature was obvious enough to his cohorts that it, rather than his mustache and his motorcycle, became his signature unconventionality. This was embarrassing at first because it called unwelcome attention to him. He always preferred to be the tall blond one in the background, silent and even a little inscrutable. But at the same time he secretly found the realization that he had a better build than any of his friends extremely gratifying. It seemed much better to be known for something like that than Miller's stamp collecting, for instance, or Wilson's bizarre obsession with ornithology, or Franklin's encyclopedic knowledge of baseball statistics. Still, in the back of his mind he knew that as distinguishing characteristics went it was a potentially dangerous one. It went far beyond the limits of permissible eccentricity and laid him open to a kind of censure that other, more conventional, eccentricities never would have. He knew that he was suspected of looking at his naked body in the mirror from time to time and taking a certain pride in what he saw there, and he admitted to himself that the suspicion was correct. Though he saw no harm in this, he knew that his crew would be—or would at least claim to be—repulsed by the idea. He was quite certain that in actuality it was something all men his age did whether they admitted to it or not. And whether, indeed, they had good reason to. But the degree to which his physique apparently made the whole thing seem somehow titillating certainly increased, if not actually necessitated, its objectionableness. Still, he was able to convince himself that as long as his putative narcissism was a rumor he wasn't required to acknowledge having heard, he didn't have to care what his friends thought about it. And he saw no reason to alter his habits.

He was tall. He was unusually broad shouldered. He had always been fit but now he was making a transition from "lanky" to something he wasn't sure there was even a name for. But it wasn't merely that he was impressed with his new look. He had fallen in love with everything involved in his transformation. The workouts and self-discipline seemed to focus him, to sharpen his thinking. He quit smoking and at the same time realized that he was drinking less and enjoying himself more. He didn't just feel strong, he felt alive in a way he hadn't known was possible. He felt as invincible as he had at eighteen, but now he had something tangible to back it up with. It was hard to understand why his friends didn't want to feel and look like he did, but he had the sense to keep this sentiment to himself. Talking about it would amount to a demand that they stop pretending to ignore it only to talk about it behind his back, and that was the last thing that he wanted.

* * *

There were two constants in the life of Nick's crowd: promotions and engagements. Someone in the group was always in the throes of one or the other. Frequently both. Because promotions and engagements were interrelated in a complicated yet totally predictable way. Men of their sort didn't generally consider marriage until they had reached a certain level of success in their careers. It wasn't the thing to ask a woman to marry you unless and until you were sure, and your certainty could be seen to be demonstrably correct, that you could support her in an appropriate manner. There were feminists around who de-

cried this sort of thinking as outmoded. Nick's friends wouldn't have thought
of dating anyone like that, though many of them had sisters and female cousins
who expressed such sentiments at inappropriate moments, such as in the middle
of Thanksgiving dinner at Gran and Pop's house. And those sisters and cousins
always reconsidered their positions, or at least moderated their expressions of
them, as soon as the right man, invariably the fraternity brother of a brother or
male cousin, showed an interest.

At the same time it was difficult, though not impossible, to advance beyond a certain point in one's career without being married, or at least without
being understood to have the domestic aspects of one's life well in hand. An
actual engagement wasn't an absolute requirement as long as it was generally
recognized that a man had a clear understanding with some young woman or
other to the effect that though an engagement might not be imminent it was
certainly on the cards at some point. This was thought to indicate that the man
in question was "responsible" and "solid", which were code words indicative of
a general understanding that he could be relied on to behave respectably in the
social realm and honestly in the professional one. Behaving respectably was not
by any means the same as being respectable. This was well understood without
actually being discussed.   You could sleep with as many stewardesses as you
liked, for instance, as long as you didn't get caught or as long as getting caught
bore no more than the usual domestic consequences. These entailed the rituals
of confession and the bestowal of expensive gifts in token of atonement, and,
after serving a suitable period in the doghouse, being granted forgiveness. For
its part, professional integrity was always a moving target, mostly having to do
with whatever the traffic would bear in any given situation. Nick sensed that
in reality the terms "responsible" and "solid" were so flexible as to have almost
no intrinsic meaning. Their true significance lay more in what they did not
refer to than in what they did. There was something else lurking in the background, something everyone seemed to understand though no one ever spoke of
it. Something so unthinkable—though paradoxically, it was thought of almost
constantly and apparently was believed to possess powerful attractions or why
else would such a taboo be necessary?—that any and all other infractions of the
code could and were overlooked as long as that one retained its fearsome power
to ensure absolute observance.

Steven Randolph, the group's self-appointed historian and statistician, asserted that among their number there were, year in and year out, eight point

seven marriages for every ten engagements announced. Everyone seemed to take this at face value. No one questioned it. Obviously, of course, not all engagements led to weddings. But enough of them did that there was almost never a time when some man or other wasn't involved in one, whether he was in feverish preparations for the proposal itself, or caught up in the drama of buying the ring, or in the stage which Nick thought of as "along for the ride". This basically consisted of the period between the presentation and acceptance of the ring and the beginning of the honeymoon, during which the man himself seemed almost superfluous. The smarter of Nick's friends quickly learned that it was a time to smile a great deal and say as little as possible, particularly when being asked their opinions about anything having to do with the wedding or setting up the household. That was women's work. Nick's gang would no more have interfered in it than they would with a surgeon performing an especially delicate operation.

All this affected Nick only to the extent that he was frequently pressed into service in some capacity or other. Hardly a wedding took place in which he wasn't a participant. Ushers were always needed, for instance. And it quickly became general knowledge that he had a certain expertise and more than a little panache when it came to planning a bachelor party. He was a better than pass-able dancer and a charming conversationalist. He could be relied on to make sure that aunts and grandmothers were sufficiently entertained at the rehearsal dinner or reception that afterward they told anyone who'd listen what a won-derful time they'd had and who was responsible for it. And he was certainly photogenic. There were a great many brides who liked the idea of having a man of his appearance in their wedding photos no matter how peripherally. His height, also, was an asset. There was never any worry about how tall a particular bridesmaid might be as long as Nick was available to escort her. Best of all, he could be depended upon to perform whatever services were asked of him without making a nuisance of himself. What this meant was that he had an unerring instinct for correctly identifying which members of the wedding party wanted to be seduced and which didn't. Many of the other men were oblivious to this distinction, and the minor scandals resulting from their misadventures were just embarrassing enough to make them fodder for drunken hilarity on the part of their peers. At the same time, these "escapades" elicited profound disap-proval from the women generally, resulting in the men concerned being quietly and often permanently stricken from various and sundry rosters of the elect.

Paradoxically, Nick's tally of conquests was as long as anyone's, and the assumption regarding this was that his charms were so notable and his techniques so perfected that no woman had or would ever turn him down. For the women, however, his sensitivity and tact were his most important qualifications.

* * *

It was not only for weddings that Nick found himself in demand. Women of a certain class quickly discovered that he had plenty of additional uses and spread the word among their friends. He knew the difference between Rossini and Puccini and would sit uncomplaining until the stage was littered with the requisite number of corpses or adorned with sufficient exultant lovers, whichever happened to be the outcome. He could stay awake for Chekhov, Ibsen, or even, God forbid, Shaw. He never looked bored with Rogers and Hammerstein or made faces at Lerner and Loewe. He would never embarrass his companion for the evening by applauding between the movements of a Brahms symphony or Beethoven string quartet. He would never embarrass himself by making crude comments about the male members of the ballet company, no matter how astute and/or piquant those comments might be. He was conversant with all of the major, and a surprising number of obscure, schools of painting, watercolor, sculpture, and architecture. And he never, ever suggested or implied that his companion for the event might help pay for the taxi, split the restaurant check, or provide the tip for the cloakroom attendant or the parking valet. He was attentive to the women he escorted to all these events in a way that they were not generally attended to by their husbands, whether living or dead, current or former. Not to mention their brothers, sons, or nephews, some of whom were heard to opine that he rather spoiled things for members of his sex just a little less perfect than himself. His irreproachable manners and immaculate grooming made him an ideal escort at gallery openings, galas, cocktail parties, receptions, charity auctions, and all manner of other social events, and his wardrobe was equal to any occasion. Given his ever increasing lean muscle mass this entailed no little expense, but he didn't begrudge a bit of it and the tailors of San Francisco rejoiced. The photographers for the society pages found him always willing to oblige. Standing next to him any matron, no matter how bleary eyed or weathered, could be made to seem almost glamorous. He was, in short, the toast of the city. And though he would have been embarrassed to admit it to himself, he basked in his particular brand of pre-eminence.

* * *

He didn't date in any conventional sense of the term. What he did was score. He might be escorting society "gals" to functions thee, four, five nights a week, but the remaining nights didn't find him at home drafting his memoirs. He was a legend and byword among the "swinging singles" of the city. Stewardesses sang his praises on every continent where they landed. Their interludes with him made the term "layover" an especially apropos double entendre. Their colleagues new to the San Francisco routes made a point of looking him up as a sort of local attraction. Nurses found him indispensable for "medical research". Secretaries stood in line to "take dictation". But it wasn't just career girls who were his fans. Debutantes ditched their dates of record for just long enough to book future assignations. Young marrieds slipped their wedding rings into their clutches and went in for the kill. He might appear "musclebound", but the proof of the pudding was in the eating. His technique was prodigious and his staying power the stuff of legend. The orgasms he gave women ended dozens of engagements and several marriages. The degree to which he was the subject of gossip would have astonished his buddies if their girlfriends, wives, sisters, and female cousins hadn't been scrupulous in the extreme about shielding his notoriety from male ears and awareness. It was, one former sorority president quipped, like protecting national security.

He was the archetype of the playboy but would have cringed to hear that term applied to him. The playboy was a species little more substantial, or respectable, than the gigolo. He considered himself far too serious a proposition than that. He was, he believed, elemental. And over time that belief became self-fulfilling.

* * *

When he wasn't at work, he was at the gym. When he wasn't at the gym, he was escorting some woman to some event or other or attending someone's bachelor party, rehearsal dinner, or wedding and reception. When he wasn't doing any of those things, he was socializing with the gang, and when he wasn't with the gang, he was in some bed somewhere. In other words, he was busy. He was so busy that his busyness itself became the subject of talk. People wondered when he found time to sleep. People wondered if he slept at all. People spoke guardedly of burning the candle at both ends, but since his control over his health was firmer than his control over his observers, he just laughed at their concerns.

* * *

It all made the time pass quickly. He was shocked one day, upon receiving yet another wedding invitation, to realize that he had been in the city for three years. He only registered this because of the return address on the envelope. Chicago. It was Joanna's wedding he was invited to.

II

There was no question of Nick's staying away. That would have been to admit that Joanna's marriage mattered to him, and it didn't. Honestly. He had, as a matter of fact, pretty much forgotten they ever entertained such an idea in the first place. They couldn't have been less suited to each other. That seemed perfectly obvious now. Perhaps this occurred to Joanna sooner than to him. That might explain her serene acceptance of his departure. He'd been baffled by it at the time. When he thought back on it, it was still with relief that nothing had ever come of it their whatever-it-had-been. Relief mixed with a tiny bit of chagrin that he'd ever considered such a thing in the first place with such a girl. He had to admit to a little embarrassment at the memory, and he couldn't have called attention to it, to whatever past they had shared or might still be thought to have shared by people they knew, by staying away. Joanna's family was close enough to Nick's that pretty much everyone he was related to would attend the wedding, and he'd never live it down. So he arranged to take a week's vacation from work and he bought his plane ticket.

* * *

It wasn't Nick's first visit to Chicago since moving to San Francisco. Far from it. There had been trips each Christmas, trips for christenings, trips for the funerals of a couple of aged relatives, and trips for several other weddings. He was far from being out of touch with either friends or family. But somehow this time when he arrived the city all those people and places seemed to have changed in subtle but unmistakable ways that made him feel almost like a stranger. His mother, for instance, had left his boyhood room untouched all during his years at university and law school and since his move west. But sometime in the last few months she had completely redecorated it. He had no idea what she had done with his old things. It wasn't that he wanted them. He had no idea what he would do with all that stuff if he had it. But it bothered him more than he would have expected not to know what had become of everything. He couldn't even ask her. She and Dad were in the Caribbean—*the Caribbean in June?*—and would return just in time for the wedding.

But the transformation of his old room and the obliteration of his past that it seemed to signify was the least of it. His father had forsaken his annual Cadillac sedan for a Mercedes roadster and his golf clubs for a tennis racquet and a set of free weights. The golden retriever had been replaced by a pair of West Highland Whites. Nick knew that Rex had been put down due to cancer but he never imagined that his father would agree to the acquisition of those two tiny yet deafening fuzzballs.

It was like visiting the home of strangers. Or being a spy in enemy territory.

* * *

His first morning in Chicago, Nick caddied for his grandmother. Lyudmila Vladimirovna was an early riser. She had left word for him to meet her at the country club at seven o'clock sharp. For Nick, still on Pacific Time, this meant five a.m., which he thought was asking a lot of a man on vacation. But it was Grannie, so there was nothing to do but comply. Her maiden name was Sikorsky. She was distantly related to the man who had invented helicopters. She never tired of explaining just how illustrious a clan her people were, how much they had lost in 1918 when they had to leave Russia. Nick considered it highly ironic that the Menshevik Romanovskys and the Czarist Sikorskys all had to flee their homeland and ended up intimately connected in the new world, though he had never shared this observation with either of his grandparents. Back in Russia, a girl of his grandmother's background would never have married a man like Grigori Romanovksy. Here in America, no one comprehended, much less appreciated, the sacrifices she had made in the name of love. When Sergei Grigoryevich, her golden, perfect baby Seryozha, married a middle class Polish girl, of all things, the decline in Lyudmila's fortunes seemed tragically irreversible. But soon enough came the birth of her first grandchild, Nikolai Sergeyevich, and all was forgiven. Or at least almost all.

Even while golfing, Grannie chain smoked. And she eschewed golf carts. Mensheviks and Czarists alike had despised the bourgeoisie, and what was more bourgeois than a golf cart? Nick lugged her clubs around the nine holes through ever increasing temperature and mugginess while listening silently to her ruminations, delivered in that gruff whiskey baritone which was one of the more distinctive memories of his boyhood. Her life was perfect, she said. Her sons had married extremely well—contrary to her advice and despite her strenuous protests, but well nevertheless. Which was a lesson to her, she supposed, though she suspected herself of being too stubborn to benefit from it. Her grandchildren were flourishing—mostly. Nick grasped fully the significance of that qualifying adverb, emphasized as it was by her skeptical glance in his direction just prior to her tee-off stroke. After it, she went on to say that her great-grandchildren were an unmitigated joy. Nick assumed that this was because none of them actually spoke in complete sentences yet but didn't say so. Her sole regret at this stage of her life—this was punctuated by another glance at Nick—was that there were not more of them.

And by the way, did he remember her friend Yelena Borisova Gradov's granddaughter, Kate Sudbin? Kate had recently returned to Chicago from Montreal after completing her residency in pediatrics. Really, Kate was a lovely girl, charming, funny, beautiful. . .

* * *

Nick lunched with his mother's sisters, Yulia and Liz. They filled him in on all the Krakowiak gossip. His cousins and their spouses were in fine form, apparently. Their offspring were exceptional children. Life was a dream come true. For the Krakowiak tribe collectively, the glass was invariably half full. Nick remembered they had always been like that. His mother was the sole exception.

By the way, his aunts wanted to know, did he remember Marcia Patterson, the daughter of their old schoolmate, Alicia Glienicki, and her second husband, Reg? Marcia had just finished her M.A. in art history at Northwestern. After getting her B.A. *summa cum laude* in three years. How about that? Such a beautiful girl. And so smart. Beautiful, but tall—it was true. Her height was probably the reason she was still single. That was the only possible explanation for it. But surely there were a few tall men around who hadn't settled down yet. Then came the sly glances at Nick, just to see if he'd gotten their hint.

Oh! And had he heard about Darya Korsakov's girl, Mary Margaret, who had just broken that national sky diving record? Now there was a girl who would never bore her husband. There was a girl who wouldn't jump screaming onto the sofa at the sight of a mouse. What a woman. What a mother she would make. Someday. Why didn't more men appreciate her? It really made no sense.

And before they forgot, they simply had to tell him. They had just run into their old friend, Janice St. Vincent, whose daughter Nick probably remembered meeting at June Wyszocki's daughter, Alannah's, wedding in December. That's right, Rachel. Well, Rachel's flatmate, Peggy Finkelstein, had opened her own art gallery recently. Everybody said it was highly successful. Wasn't that amazing? Wasn't that a clever thing for a young woman to do?

Nick knew that since one of the Nowitzki cousins had recently married a Jewish girl that particular taboo was a thing of the past. The young woman had invented something or other, sold the patent to a major corporation, and pocketed a cool two million. It was exactly the kind of thing they all expected a Jewish boy to do of course, so none of the relevant stereotypes had been totally banished. But the fact that the marriage had taken place without bloodshed resulting was nothing to turn your nose up at.

And don't you know what they found out when they went to the opening of Peggy's gallery? Peggy's mother turned out to be none other than Gracie Aronoff from the old neighborhood. They had all been cheerleaders together. It was such a small world, when you thought about it. . .

* * *

He visited Nanna Krakowiak for afternoon tea, by which she actually meant cocktails. They sat on her terrace, which had an expansive view of Lake Michigan. A pitcher of Mai Tais sweated onto the marble table top between them. Nanna was in a particularly loquacious mood. Nick hardly had to speak. She slurred her words occasionally, but that, presumably, was testimony to her sincerity.

She had lived such a wonderful life. There was so very much to be thankful for, as she had told Father Smolinski after Mass just last Sunday. She had been married for years and years. Nick noticed that she carefully avoided saying exactly how many years or describing the marriage as happy. Her children had grown up to be beautiful and successful. Her grandchildren had brought her much joy, and her great-grandchildren brought her even more. Really, she could hardly think of anything that could make it all more perfect.

She was a far better poker player than Grannie Romanovsky, who had the subtlety of a combine harvester.

Nanna had just had a call from her old friend, Marie Tomasecki, whose daughter and granddaughter sold real estate together. Hadn't Nick gone to school with the boy? What was his name? Bobby? That didn't sound right somehow. Was Nick sure it was Bobby? Well, anyway, the daughter and granddaughter, Shirley and Cecilia Rizzo, had recently signed a listing on a property that just might be a Frank Lloyd Wright house. Wasn't that interesting? Cecilia was researching it to make sure. Cecilia was such a nice girl, so pretty and industrious. It was such a shame about that fiancé of hers, that pilot who had been shot down over Hanoi. Eighteen months now. Her mother and grandmother were hoping and praying that some nice young man would take an interest soon. And why not, since Cecilia was such an outgoing personality and such a good tennis player? Father Smolinsky always said that God believes in second chances.

* * *

There was really no reason Nick should have been invited to the rehearsal dinner. He wasn't one of the groomsmen, he wasn't dating one of the bridesmaids, and he wasn't related—except by an intervening marriage or two—to either the bride or the groom. But being a single professional man under the age of thirty-five had propelled him onto the guest list. This was no surprise. Weddings and their ancillary activities constituted, he knew, a prime marketplace where eligible persons might come into contact, however inadvertently, with other eligible persons. The individuals involved didn't actually have to consider themselves eligible. It was enough that someone concerned in the planning of the event did. Nick understood this and RSVP'd in the affirmative because he had no interest in facing the nagging and complaining if he declined.

This was part of the price Nick had known he would be paying when he accepted Joanna's wedding invitation. And really, there was no point fighting it. That would be energy wasted. Far better to ignore the immediate reality of the situation and rely on time and geography to obliterate any troublesome aftereffects of his attendance. Passive resistance a la Gandhi was far more effective in the long run, as alien as it might be to his own inclinations and the current context. There was apparently an inexhaustible supply of smart, beautiful, highly accomplished single women in the Greater Chicago Metropolitan Area. It was as if war or natural catastrophe had decimated the ranks of correspondingly gifted males. Nick could feasibly return to San Francisco having acquired an entire harem, should he feel so motivated.

He came face to face with Joanna only once in the course of the evening. Kissing her smooth cheek he almost laughed out loud at her elaborate show of casualness. It was far too perfect to be genuine. The time she must have spent rehearsing it couldn't be overestimated, while at the same time he found himself a little surprised that he had ever thought himself romantically interested in her. Pulling back from the brief embrace, he saw her fiancé, Mikah Nazarian, winking at him. It was not the gesture he would have expected from the guy who got the girl. It was, instead, the unmistakable signal of a co-conspirator, a comrade in arms.

Mikah Nazarian was a commodities trader. The Nazarians were mostly in banking, though Nick knew of a couple of cousins who were doctors. Mikah had been a fraternity brother of Stan and Spencer, two of Nick's Krakowiak cousins. That was how Mikah ended up in trading, the preferred turf of the huge Krakowiak-Nowicki clan. The commodities traders Nick was familiar with reminded him of the more rakish element of his own crew in San Francisco. With their fast cars, extroverted neckties, and hyper-fashionable haircuts, they gave the impression of eternal fratboys. They owned speedboats rather than yachts, and the married ones who didn't also have mistresses merely hadn't gotten around to acquiring them yet. As a group, their ostentatious flouting of conventions was legendary, but Nick recognized that it was actually as ritualized as an Orthodox Mass. Mikah himself was dashing. There was no other word to describe him. That sleek raven hair, those dimples, that jawline. He had a glint in his eye that confirmed what Nick had heard about him. He was a real hell raiser. Joanna was going to have her hands full. If she even cared. She might not. She was old enough now that she couldn't afford to be too particular. Mikah, Nick estimated, was at least five years younger than her.

As bachelor parties went, the night left nothing to be desired. Nick, an expert at staging such affairs, would have done it differently of course, largely with a view toward classing it up, but that was a matter of taste rather than substance. Since he well knew that the secret to drinking people under the table—a specialty of his—was to disguise the strict limits he placed on his own intake, it was easy to position himself as a careful observer. In this crowd, that was child's play. He had forgotten just how hard-drinking Chicago men were. It was one of the primary reasons they aged so badly. It was also, he realized, one of the strategies employed by their womenfolk for keeping them under such tight control. Incapacitated was disarmed. The whole evening and all evenings like it, he suddenly understood, were calculated to celebrate loudly and elaborately the masculinity of the participants while behind the scenes their balls were quietly being snipped off and spirited away without so much as a by your leave.

Exiting the party, he was nearly overcome by a feeling of profound sadness at the thought of how quickly all these handsome young men would go to seed. He knew about this from observation. He remembered men five, ten, and fifteen years older than this crew, and he had witnessed their sorry declines. These guys would be no different. Their stomachs would expand and sag, smoking and drinking would ravage their complexions and dull their eyes, their conversation would lose its edge and their jokes would grow stale and increasingly coarse. Their wives would exploit and disrespect them and their mistresses would grow bored and petulant. And vice versa. It was not just a question of the men's lack of commitment to preventing all that. They were oblivious to the possibility of it. This was inexcusable given the lessons of history. The whole thing baffled Nick. It shouldn't have worked but it did, time after time. The entire social context seemed intent on their decay as the most efficient way of taming them. Untamed, they might get up to God only knew what mischief. Tamed, they would father children and support them and their mothers financially, and beyond those functions nothing else signified, not a powerful set of shoulders, a smoldering pair of eyes, an exquisitely cleft chin, a head of glossy, luxuriant hair.

* * *

"You're not getting any younger, Nick," his mother said, sitting across the breakfast table from him and lighting what he knew wasn't her first Pall Mall of the day. His parents' flight from the Caribbean had been delayed. They arrived from the airport just as he was rolling in from the bachelor party. His mother had taken one of her migraine pills earlier, and their initial greeting was consequently subdued.

"What's that supposed to mean?"

"I wouldn't have thought," she said, brushing a lock of hair off her forehead, "that a statement of that nature required clarification."

"Ah, but everyone around here seems to consider me particularly obtuse."

"It's not funny, young man," she grimaced, "this act of yours. You're thirty now. You should be thinking about settling down."

"I think about it all the time," Nick lied.

' "You should be making definite plans, then."

"To do what? Climb Mount Everest? Devote more of my time to helping the poor? Mind my own business?"

"Nikolai!"

"Sorry, Mom," Nick grinned, "but doesn't running everybody's life around here keep you busy enough? You have to run mine too?"

"I have no idea what you're talking about," she insisted. "I just want my children to be happy."

"And we are, Mom, we are. Every last one of us."

"I don't see how, Nick. A single man? If you're not careful you'll wake up someday and you'll be your father's age. And alone."

"Mom, take it easy."

"Just tell me this. Did you meet anyone nice at the rehearsal dinner?"

"Mikah Nazarian seemed interesting."

* * *

To his mother's annoyance, Nick left the reception with her and Dad. It was far too early, she insisted when he got up from the table to accompany them. She and Dad were only leaving because they were still jet lagged, she said. Nick refrained from expressing skepticism that jet lag was even possible after a flight between Aruba and Chicago, but she read his mind and changed her tack, pointing out that his grandparents were still "cutting a rug" and might well be for hours yet. And she and Dad were quite capable of driving themselves home. Her gin-perfumed protests occasioned a general clamor on the topic of his proposed departure which made Nick's mind up for him. Public outcry to the contrary seemed the best possible reason to make his exit. In the car, Dad snored in the back seat and Mom nursed her fury almost silently. Thank God she wasn't the kind of mother who went in for prolonged histrionics. Once the cause was lost, she generally let it go. Nick had long since learned to ignore stewing.

She had apparently abandoned Cadillacs at the same time as Dad. Her Mercedes had a roof and four doors. Nick lounged behind the wheel basking in the darkness and silence. Nobody went to more weddings than Nick did, and they were all fundamentally the same. Today, as always, no effort whatever, not an iota, had been expended on making the ceremony interesting or appealing to the men present. And except for the food and beverages provided at the reception, it had been the same there. Men, for all practical purposes, were only props at these functions. Part of a woman's outfit, like her shoes and purse, except requiring somewhat more maintenance. Even on the dance floor men were only there for the benefit of their partners. There seemed to be an unwritten rule in force. Feed them and get them drunk and they'll be fine. This is only about the girls, anyway.

Well, fine, Nick thought, except it seemed to indicate a disregard for his gender in all matters domestic. Except in the men's offices and on the golf course, women called the shots. That's how marriage worked. Any notions to the contrary were stupid. The myth of male domination was transparently false. The feminists were deluded on that score. The only possible salvation for a man was learning the art of subversion. Nick's fellows might be too stupid to realize it or too lazy to act on the knowledge, but that was their lookout. He had always been his own man. There was no reason to change.

* * *

"I don't know what you're trying to prove," Nick's father said, handing him the keys to the Mercedes-Benz roadster, "always playing hard to get. But I wish you'd stop. Mom and Szylvya are after me constantly about it. I don't appreciate being crucified for your sins, old man. Especially not by my mother and my wife."

"So I should get married just to make them happy?"

"It's the only reason any man ever does," Dad said. "To get his female relatives off his back. I'm surprised you don't know that."

He looked extremely hung over. But this was exactly his usual brand of cynicism.

"I bet that's not true, Dad."

"How much would you put down?"

"Seriously. Would you get married if you were me?"

"Son."

"No hedging, Dad."

"Nikolai, a man wants to have sons. That's what it is. You'll pay whatever price you have to for that. You don't let yourself think about the rest of it. You just do it."

"And then you spend the rest of your life telling your sons how disappointed you are in them," Nick said.

"I guess that's a fair criticism. Your grandfather talks to me the same way, you know."

* * *

After escorting his still disgruntled mother to Mass and grabbing a quick lunch with the housekeeper, Nick joined his generation of Romanovskys on Grandpa's yacht. In deference to the generally hung over state of the party they didn't actually take the boat out onto the lake but stayed in the slip. Nick thought this decision reflected well on the emerging maturity of his brothers, whom he generally suspected were lacking in either substance or judgment. Maturity was a two edged sword, however. Mikhail was sporting the beginnings of a paunch, and Piotr was, incredible as it seemed, already going gray at the temples.

The next generation of Romanovskys hadn't yet gotten past the toddler stage and was thus left in the custody of nannies, grandmothers, aunts, and grandmothers' and aunts' housekeepers for the afternoon. It was a resolutely adult party, complete with plentiful alcohol, half a dozen joints handed around with pretentious "cool", and substantially more topless sunbathing than Nick would have expected in the Midwest. His relations had even laid on female companionship for him in the form of the sister of a sorority roommate of the wife of one of Mikhail's tennis buddies. She was, as befitted Nick's karma, a stewardess with American. Well before sundown it was apparent to Nick that he only had to say the word. But he eventually decided he didn't care to close the deal. He knew he'd be gossiped about by this bunch as soon as his back was turned. Better to be gossiped about for playing hard to get, as his father had accused him of just that morning, than for taking advantage of a perfectly pleasant young woman he had no interest in seeing again. He was home in bed alone before midnight.

* * *

Now in his early eighties, Grandpa Romanovsky no longer took any cases, but he still went to his office every day. Nick knew this was one of the secrets of the success of his grandparents' marriage. They spent as little time together as possible. Grandpa left no one in any doubt that he was still senior partner in the firm. He had come to America as a teenager, his parents fleeing the 1905 Revolution—the one that had been crushed by the Czarists. His forebears had been progressives, free thinkers, and anarchists, but these days he was as much an autocrat as the emperor they had failed to depose. When Nick stopped by the office on his last day in Chicago he found his grandfather in full "world domination" mode, yelling into the telephone as if additional volume would make him better understood and gesturing operatically to his senior clerk, Mikah Nazarian's brother, Alik, not to leave the room.

"Ah, Nikolai Sergeyevich," Grandpa smiled as soon as he had slammed down the receiver. "Good of you to stop by. Good of you to take the time out of your busy schedule."

People always said Grandpa Romanovsky was sarcastic even in his sleep. Grannie insisted that he would continue his sarcasm from beyond the grave. Nick had spent three decades now ignoring it. His siblings and cousins had all modified their patronymics into all-American sounding middle names, but Nick still proudly bore his in its original form. He suspected that this was the one thing about him his grandfather approved of.

"Good to see you, too, Grandpa."

"I'm sorry I can only give you a few moments of my time this morning."

Obviously this was more sarcasm. Regret did not feature in Grandpa's repertoire.

"But Alik here will show you the office we've got prepared for you. I'm hoping you'll be available to join us full time by the Tuesday after Labor Day. There are several cases I think you might be adequately prepared to handle. Minor ones, you understand."

"Actually, Grandpa. . ."

"Sorry," Grandpa said, grabbing the receiver on the first ring. "Sorry. Here's another call coming in. We're preparing an appeal to the Supreme Court."

"Washington?" Nick asked.

"Springfield," Grandpa frowned. "Alik, take him. Show him his office."

"Goodbye, Grandpa."

"Later, Nikolai Sergeyevich."

And that was that.

"I won't tell him you didn't show me the office if you won't tell him I sneaked out," Nick suggested.

"No problem, Nick," Alik smiled.

They parted at the elevator. Nick thought it hadn't gone badly at all.

* * *

Nick's sisters had invited him to their club for tennis. Katya was eight months pregnant and didn't play that day. She contributed to Irina's victory over Nick in straight sets by keeping him distracted with her trenchant commentary on all things Romanovsky/Krakowiak. This was her third baby. Her Cubano husband, Raf Allende, a filthy-mouthed surgical resident, planned on a big family. A former seminarian, he had been expelled for "acting on my heterosexual tendencies and impulses, dude." Nick liked him a lot, but in small doses. Irina's husband, Polish-Ukrainian Jerzy Radobenko, flew 727's for American. He was much more to Nick's taste.

The girls rolled their eyes at Nick's tales of their grandmothers' and aunties' matchmaking aspirations. But then Katya spoiled his mood by saying "but you know, Nick, all the current medical research indicates that married men live longer than single ones," while Irina nodded emphatically.

Traitors.

* * *

That just left one stop.

Nanna and Pops Krakowiak had never legally divorced. "A divorce? What do I need with that?" Pops always asked by way of an explanation for their marital status. "A piece of paper is all it is. What does that prove? It's nothing but a waste of money. And what do you Romanovskys need with more of that?" The case was not as settled as this made it sound, however. "That woman is the love of my life," Pops would say with a couple of drinks in him. "The whole world knows that. Just like the whole world knows I can't stand the sight, smell, or sound of her." But his most characteristic lament was, "be careful what you wish for. Satan will invariably present it to you gift wrapped."

Instead of a legal document to indicate the Krakowiaks' new status, there had been a change of address. But even this was ambiguous in its implications. Pops had moved into a smaller apartment five floors up from the one Nanna continued to inhabit in their building on the lakefront. Nick didn't bother going inside that afternoon. He knew exactly where to look for Pops. Except in the most inclement weather Pops spent his days on a bench, "his" bench, contemplating the water of the lake. Each morning the maid, a good Polish woman—because to have employed any other brand of domestic would have been indecent—fed him breakfast before accompanying him and his paraphernalia down to the shore just long enough to get him settled. She returned at noon with his lunch and again in the evening to fetch him and his things inside for the night. A cold supper would already be waiting for him upstairs. Finally, after turning on lights and closing drapes, she would catch the bus to her good Polish neighborhood. This was Pops' routine six days a week because on the seventh day the good Polish woman rested, and nobody knew exactly what Pops did in her absence but scuttlebutt held that it involved women of a different profession altogether.

Nick sat down next to him on the bench.

"So, Niko," Pops said without any preliminaries, as if six days rather than six months had passed since their last conversation, "Walt Whitman was right about it, you know. 'What shall it profit a man if he shall gain the whole world and lose his own soul?'"

"I believe that's the New Testament, Pops."

"Verily I say unto you, Niko, unless ye read Whitman more perceptively, ye shall not enter into the sublime awareness that all he ever did was paraphrase scripture."

"Really."

"Abolutely."

"What about his—orientalia? 'Passage to India' and all that?"

"Eastern scripture, Christian scripture, Hebrew scripture. Wouldn't surprise me if there's some Book of Mormon in there, too. The old bastard ripped them all off. You have to admire a man like that who didn't discriminate. 'What shall it profit a man. . .?' That's what I told your mother's Cousin Michael."

"You did? When was that, Pops? Recently?"

"He was in high school. He was talking about going to Harvard and majoring in finance."

"Finance? Are we talking about the same Michael Krakòwiak?"

"Ah," Pops smiled. "You get my point, I see."

"I hear he's not doing so well lately."

"Family gossip," Pops scowled. "You should never pay attention. 'What shall it profit a man if he should gain the good opinion of his family and lose his own soul?' You see? It's one of those quotations that can be adapted to almost any situation. That's what Whitman comprehended. That's the sublime epiphany all his plagiarizing finally led him to. Never forget, Niko, the good opinion of your family isn't worth going after. If they can't love you exactly as you are, what the hell are they for?"

"I suppose."

"You'll see Michael soon. You can draw your own conclusions. And I hope to God you'll keep them to yourself."

"Oh?"

"That stupid old cow didn't tell you? He's moving out by you."

"He's leaving France?"

"The concert career is winding down. I guess he's no Van Cliburn. He's taken a teaching job at a university."

"In California?"

"In San Francisco. I'm sure he'll be looking you up."

"Well, I'm not that hard to find."

"Aren't you?" Pops asked, as if he knew something to the contrary. "'What shall it profit a man?'"

"You weren't at the big wedding."

"I don't go to weddings any more. They're a stupid waste of everybody's time. What's the point?"

"Well, Pops, surely when two people love each other. . ."

"Love?" Pops laughed. "What does that have to do with getting married? Getting married is all about the money, Niko. Don't forget that. I wasn't missed. I wrote those kids a check. It was for more than that stinking old bat spent on some piece of junk they don't want and won't ever use. Mikah will appreciate the money even if Joanna doesn't. He's a smart one, that Mikah. Not as smart as I used to think he was, but smart. Just not as smart as you. I had such hopes for that boy. Oh, well."

* * *

There was something about the Midwest, Nick thought as he boarded his plane. Fitzgerald had sensed it. There was an impulse abroad—Nick didn't know where it originated, but you couldn't doubt its existence. It was unmistakable as the skies, the broad plains, the dense forests, the sparkling lakes and rivers. An impulse to fetishize conformity. An impulse whose doppelganger was an indolent, unquestioning smugness, as if somehow everyone who lived here had lost the power of imagination. How easy it must be to conform if one couldn't conceive of alternatives. How easy it must be to be self-satisfied, how easy to sit in judgment.

He could no more come back to Chicago to live, Nick thought as he fastened his seat belt, than he could give up oxygen.

III

In Nick's absence, two incidents took place that alarmed him when he heard of them. The first involved one of the gang's most celebrated stewardess friends, who had been hospitalized with complications after terminating a pregnancy. Abortions were not unheard of among the men's many female acquaintances, though they were little talked about. The illegality of the procedure was universally decried as silly and old fashioned, not to mention as posing obstacles and inconveniences that made life more difficult and far more expensive than necessary. But that one of their own girls had almost lost her life as a result of a botched procedure was as much of a sensation as the group was generally willing to acknowledge much less tolerate. The men thought of recreational, as opposed to matrimonial, sex as their birthright, and here was something interfering with their free exercise of it. On his return from Chicago, Nick found his friends highly agitated. He had always known the young woman in question to be highly cooperative and particularly adventurous. He thought of her as one of his regulars, though "regular" was a dubious term to apply to someone who only showed up in San Francisco every other month. Still, he felt somewhat responsible for her predicament. Not that the child could possibly have been his. In this instance, he hadn't seen the young woman in at least six months. But he wished he had known of the pregnancy in time to steer her in the direction of a different doctor, a man he knew personally and who he was certain wouldn't have left her in such a condition.

He visited her in the hospital. He took roses and a basket of fruit. Her friends ooh'ed and ah'ed over these offerings, but the girl herself wasn't especially pleased to see him. He couldn't blame her. It seemed awfully unfair that she alone was suffering the consequences of what had been a collaborative effort. He left her his number and insisted that she call him if she needed his assistance but on his way back down in the elevator he knew he really hoped she wouldn't, and he thought less of himself for it. He resolved, at the very least, to be more careful in the future. There were things one could do to avoid putting a young woman in such a position, practical things, things that could still bring satisfaction, and he resolved to alter his repertoire accordingly. Still, the idea that sex had to be planned and plotted like that threatened to take at least some of the pleasure out of it.

The second incident was more serious by far. It really had the gang stirred up. One of the men, Denny Sterling, had misbehaved very badly. He had gotten drunk and groped another of the men, Michael Chamberlain, in the showers at their health club. He had actually gone so far as to try and kiss Michael on the mouth, as it turned out. A drunken grope could be explained away in all sorts of ways. Fraternities had a long and honorable tradition of grabassery and it was all considered a big joke, but an attempted kiss was another matter completely. It was as serious a scandal as Nick could remember the group experiencing. Michael himself hadn't said anything about the incident, but it turned out that there was a witness who did, Crosby Lowell, who was, unfortunately, one of the least discreet men in San Francisco. Michael was a scorchingly attractive individual, one of the few men in the city that Nick thought of as his equal in the looks department, so it wasn't completely impossible for him to understand the impulse involved in the incident. Indeed, some men were just so darned sexy that thinking about trying something seemed almost above censure. It was probably more common than anyone realized. But if one were inclined to attempt a thing like that, why do it in such a public place? That couldn't be described as anything but stupid. Under those circumstances some sort of disaster was pretty much inevitable, and it was this that Nick couldn't forgive. In Denny's own apartment, for instance, or in Michael's, an indiscretion could have been concealed effortlessly with no harm done. As it was, both men had been deeply embarrassed, and Nick made sure to go out of his way to be friendly to Michael the next time he saw him. Denny he didn't see again for a long time. By then, both their circumstances were substantially altered, and Denny had decided that he thought of the incident as an enormous joke.

* * *

Nick knew it was just a matter of time. He had seen the threat in Grandpa Romankovsky's eyes during that last encounter at his office, so he wasn't really surprised when he was passed over for a promotion in favor of Bob Maibaum. The firm had always been scrupulous in its avoidance of preferential treatment for family members of partners, but even that policy wasn't enough to account for Bob's good fortune. Nick saw his grandfather with his hands on the levers. Of course, the San Francisco office was supposed to be more or less independent under the guidance of Joe Poliakoff, but Nick knew that Grandpa's "suggestions" carried plenty of weight. This was a warning shot, nothing less: "get yourself back to Chicago where we can keep an eye on you—or else."

Chess was, of course, one of the primary national obsessions of Russians, and Nick already had his next several moves planned. He made a few phone calls as soon as Bob Maibaum's promotion was announced, and during lunch he skipped his usual visit to the secretarial pool and left the building briefly. When he returned, he typed his two weeks' notice and on his way out at the end of the day left it on Joe Poliakoff's desk.

* * *

That evening at his gym he overheard a conversation which further propelled him toward his future.

"I don't know who he thinks he's impressing."

Nick recognized Kyle Pettigrew's nasal twang.

"Really. It's grotesque, is all," Ted Bowen agreed.

"I'm all in favor of a man staying fit. That's just good sense. A healthy mind in a healthy body. But he's muscle bound. There's no other way to put it."

"And the way he is with women. Like a shark. Nobody else has a chance with him around. And once he's had those girls they're ruined for everyone else."

"He's a pig, is all. Somebody really ought to do something."

So Nick did, though he didn't suppose it would please them. He cleaned out his locker. It was time to join a new gym.

* * *

In neither of these instances was he running away. He knew that's how it might look. But he was clear in his own mind that he was running toward something. What it was he wasn't certain. But that didn't trouble him. Why would he let it?

There was an immediate reaction to his resignation. The phone rang off the hook that first evening. Grandpa Romanovsky blustered, Grannie screeched bilingually, Mom sobbed. He heard from Mikhail and Piotr, as well as several cousins. Romanovsky, Krakowiak, Nowitzki—they even enlisted Max Tetzlaff, husband of one of Grannie's cousins and up until then the blackest of sheep. Most ominously, Dad didn't call at all. Either he had a stroke when he heard the news or he was too angry to discuss the situation. Once the first wave of calls subsided—around midnight, Chicago time—Nick unplugged the phone and left it that way for the rest of the week.

* * *

Nick's new job in the prosecutor's office meant, among other things, a pay cut of over fifty per cent. Sacrifices would have to be made. He immediately found himself declining invitations based on the necessity to economize but found he really didn't miss going out as much as he might have expected. It was astonishing how much he had been spending on entertaining himself and others, not to mention the wardrobe all that socializing required. This retrenchment quickly eroded his reputation as a bon vivant, but really, what a thing to be known for.

His new work focused him in a way he might have anticipated but somehow hadn't. No longer did wrestling with stultifying estates and contracts leave him crosseyed with boredom by mid morning. Now it was questions of guilt and innocence. Previously, the crimes of his clients, generally having to do with taxation, were victimless and the penalties subject to endless negotiation.

Now people, living, breathing human beings, had been harmed. Punishments were necessary. Perpetrators had to be made examples of. Nick felt like a backslidden vegetarian with a plateful of bloody sirloin. It was strange and little disorienting to be as alive at work as he was accustomed to being at the gym or in bed with someone pretty.

In keeping with his economy drive Nick moved to a new apartment, a much smaller one that had just become available in the same building. The second "bedroom" was hardly large enough to contain an actual bed. It was much better to think of it as an annex to his closet. The new apartment was on a higher floor than Nick's previous one and it faced the bay, so he paid less money for better views. What could he do but congratulate himself on the switch? The new place was so small most of his furniture didn't fit. Since it had all been rented he sent it back. More savings! He bought a mattress and laid it directly on the floor. That and his color television were all he had at first. He resolved not to buy anything else until he knew from doing without that he had to have it.

In the past, Nick's apartment had been far more than a place to sleep and hang his clothing. Above all it was a stage set. While Act I typically took place in a restaurant or bar, Acts II and III played in his living room and bedroom respectively. He could hardly depend on his new, bare but cramped, surroundings to serve a similar purpose as an aid to seduction. Young women couldn't be expected to respond with enthusiasm to such a spartan setting. But this didn't really worry him. He was in a kind of sexual transition. The elaborate rituals associated with the chase had come to bore him. They required time and patience he now begrudged them. They entailed expenses he refused to continue to incur. What he cared about was not the hunt but the kill.

It was analogous, really, to a newly developed attitude about meals. He had recently begun buying groceries and preparing meals at home as another way of saving money. But he experienced a satisfaction in this far beyond mere economics. It was such an efficient use of his time and energy. No more deciding where to go for dinner, no more poring over menus, dealing with waiters, waiting impatiently while cooks performed the mysterious sorcery of their craft. Instead, he simply marched into his kitchen—it wasn't more than half a dozen paces from wherever he might happen to be in the apartment at the time— whipped something up and ate it. He wanted a sex life that was equally expeditious and elemental. Worrying about the cleanliness of his ashtrays, the comprehensiveness of his beverage offerings, and the state of his towels and linens seemed wasteful and trivial. There had to be a simpler, more direct approach to the act itself, which, he had concluded, was all that mattered to him. He wasn't looking for a girlfriend. He was intent only on physical satisfaction—both given and received. And the act could take place anywhere. Young women—at least the ones he encountered, available, willing, and attractive—invariably had accommodations of some sort. If you went home with them the condition of the hand towels was their responsibility. Often they had roommates, and some of these came in surprisingly handy. And since you weren't playing host you had greater control of the schedule. You could leave when you were finished. You didn't have to lie around waiting for someone else to decide that it was time to go. Some girls took forever to come to the realization that they hadn't been invited to breakfast.

These newly focused impulses coalesced into a mantra: "eat in—fuck out."

* * *

Nick's new gym was the Y. It was cheap and convenient to his office. Those things made it the best possible choice under the circumstances, but it did seem like a comedown when he first considered it. When he actually started going there, however, he was pleasantly surprised. It didn't feel like a consolation prize at all. The gym at the Y was as well equipped as any he'd ever seen, and the clientele, though not of the class of people he was used to, actually made a pleasant change. There were serious bodybuilders there. More of them than he had ever encountered at his old gym or the fashionable establishments he had gone to back home in Chicago. He'd ended up almost by accident at a gym where the distractions were few and he'd make more progress than ever.

* * *

One day when Nick stopped in after work, about a week after he started going to the Y, a young man he hadn't seen there before was working out. An astonishing young man. He was as handsome as any man Nick could remember having seen. At the same time, he was about as built a specimen as Nick could remember ever having encountered. Handsome men were everywhere in San Francisco, and there was a man this built in just about every gym, but until that moment Nick had believed he held the monopoly on the combo package. He stood and gaped until he realized he was gaping. Then he forced himself to go into the locker room and change for his workout.

It wasn't until he got home that evening that he allowed himself to think about this astonishing phenomenon. Then, with Brahms on the stereo and a fire in the fireplace—because June truly was one of the coldest months of the year in San Francisco—he went over it in detail. The guy had left him speechless. He was several inches shorter than Nick. Five-ten, perhaps. Certainly no shorter than that. But his shoulders seemed nearly as broad as Nick's. Partially, Nick knew, this was an illusion due to his shorter stature and different proportions. He had been a nearly perfect equilateral triangle, with those broad shoulders tapering down dramatically to a waist almost too small to credit. Nick had a V-taper too, but his, due to his height, was more gradual. The impression, though certainly imposing, was totally different. And the guy's musculature was both more dense and more defined and separated than Nick's. Really, the young man had achieved a substantially more advanced level of physical development than Nick could boast. He was going to have to work much harder to match it. And now that he had seen it, he had to match it. Not doing so simply wasn't an option. In addition, Nick was going to have to start shaving his body. He had always found the idea a little off putting, but seeing that guy's perfectly smooth skin and the way that smoothness made the quality of his development so much more apparent—well, Nick would just have to get used to it. Once again, there was no option.

Looks he could do nothing about. They were subjective, anyway. Nick could easily discern his own inferiority in the physique department, but who was to say which of them was the better looking? The young man's face was handsome in a different way than Nick's was. His cheekbones weren't as prominent, his features not as dramatically sculpted. He was more All-American than Nick, less exotic. It had been hard to tell much about his hair, matted with sweat like that. It was certainly short—far too short to be fashionable. It looked a shade or two darker than Nick's Slavic blond, but it was still blond. It also looked like it was of a somewhat finer texture. Perhaps sometime Nick would see him before he started his workout and these questions would be answered.

There would be a next time. There had to be.

* * *

In just a few weeks his eating in and fucking out left Nick pleasantly satiated and with a surprising amount of spare time. He could have devoted it to reading good literature, but he sensed he lacked the required attention span for *War and Peace*, while *Crime and Punishment* was too much like working overtime at the office and *Anna Karenina* implied the kind of sex life, replete with drama and potential tragedy, he was in the process of putting behind him. He could have taken up playing the guitar or painting with watercolors, but these activities struck him as unacceptably ephemeral. While he pondered the question, nature, with its abhorrence of vacuums, answered it for him.

* * *

Observing the young blond man working out every day, Nick had to face facts. He might be one of the handsomest men in the city and he might have built a physique few could match, but there was a great deal he had left undone. He was thirty years old, and though he was certain he hadn't yet reached his physical peak he now realized that unless he changed his approach he might never realize his full potential. His impressive build was the result of years of hard work at the gym, but the young man's example demonstrated clearly that simple hard work wasn't sufficient. The young man's workouts were carefully thought out. They were strategic. He worked out hard, but that was only the tip of the iceberg. He knew what he was doing in a way that Nick didn't. Nick had always felt too self-conscious to walk up to a newsstand and buy a magazine with a picture of a nearly naked muscleman on the cover, but the new situation meant he could no longer afford to shut himself off from such an important source of information. The man on the cover wasn't important at all compared to what was inside. Overnight, Nick became an avid reader of physique magazines. Soon, he had totally revamped his workouts. His diet, to which he'd hardly paid attention in the past, required radical alterations. He learned about supplements and began taking them. He pored over photos of men performing the mandatory poses required of contestants in bodybuilding competitions and spent hours practicing them, watching himself in a full length mirror he installed in the small bedroom. For the first time in his life, he actually had a quest that entailed something other than orgasms. Paradoxically, his orgasms benefited from his new regimen, both in frequency and intensity.

* * *

There was a spartan air about the young man, a rigorousness to everything he did. Nick sensed something military in his manner. With hair that short he might even be on active duty. His exercise outfit was the simplest. Jockstrap, sweatpants, and a white athletic shirt. The clothing he wore to and from the gym was as unvarying as a uniform. Jeans, white crewneck, motorcycle boots. Except in the worst weather that was all, though Nick occasionally saw him with a black leather motorcycle jacket slung over one shoulder.

Nothing exemplified his persona more unmistakably than his smooth textured blond hair, which he wore neatly trimmed in the manner of a decade earlier, parted on the side and gleaming with pomade. Nick's crowd decried this look as hopelessly outmoded. They had observed it with rigor when it was still fashionable but quickly moved on as tastes changed. Indeed, the current social context viewed the style as emblematic of fascist tendencies. But Nick thought it suited the young man perfectly. Copying it exactly wasn't an option. Nick didn't believe the cut would suit the shape of his head, and the idea of oiling his hair to keep it in place didn't appeal to him. He had never liked the sensations involved. But the young man's appearance convinced him to give up the unisex shag he and his buddies had begun sporting in some form or other in favor of something shorter, less sensitive to the vagaries of the local climate, and more masculine looking. He simplified his wardrobe as well, moving to more conservative colors, fabrics, and tailoring. He sent bag after bag of flashy shirts and theatrical neckties to charity shops.

* * *

All his focus on his body changed his relationship to it in unexpected ways. For example, learning to shave his armpits forced him to pay attention to them as he never had before. It would never again be as simple as dousing them with deodorant and forgetting about them until his next shower. Shaving his chest made his nipples almost obscenely apparent. Avoiding injury to them as he shaved brought them vividly into his consciousness whereas before he'd hardly spared them a thought. And his newly achieved hairlessness brought his skin into focus. It was much more than a container. Nor was it merely a barrier that kept him in and everything else out. It was a surface that represented where he stopped and the world began, the point where he and everything else encountered each other.

His experiences with women had taught him that, properly manipulated, every square inch of the female body could be an erogenous zone. Now he began to suspect that the same might be true of his own body as well.

IV

Labor Day weekend came and went, and with it Grandpa Romanovsky's deadline. Nick was more surprised than relieved when no substantial repercussions manifested themselves. His mother called weekly, Grannie and Nanna wrote letters. So did his aunties, Krakowiak, Nowitzki, *et al.* They kept him filled in on family news and neighborhood gossip but they asked no questions and made no pleas. He received a letter from the Romanovsky family's account-ing firm and left it unopened for several days, anticipating that they had writ-ten to inform him of changes in the provisions of Grandpa's will. But when he finally opened it, it was nothing but an account statement. His trust fund, on which he wasn't drawing though he had become eligible to on his most recent birthday, was growing nicely.

For the present, it seemed, they were letting him get away with his life.

* * *

Once Nick dispensed with the cumbersome rituals of dating, things re-ally heated up. He no longer spent hours in bars or at cocktail parties looking for women to have sex with. He spent the time he had previously devoted to the chase actually engaged in the act. Almost before he knew it, he insinuated himself into a subculture he had hardly been aware existed. There were women out there who were looking for no-strings-attached sex as single-mindedly as he was. They weren't necessarily the most beautiful women or the most charm-ing. But once he discovered them he never regretted the fact that his partner for the evening didn't read French poetry in the original or play the violin or paint watercolors, or wasn't ten pounds lighter.

Every sortie was successful. His batting average had always been strato-spheric, but the level of satisfaction he experienced had varied dizzyingly. This now became highly consistent. These new women were skilled beyond any-thing in his experience. They frequently surprised him, and he wasn't easily surprised. They were experienced, they were adventurous, and they made no demands at all outside the bedroom. He was astonished that they were such a secret. Why weren't men lined up for miles? When he wasn't thinking of his sex life as a smorgasbord, he was thinking of it as a kaleidoscope.

* * *

One Friday night he got himself attached to a likely looking group. Nick had been with one of the girls, a redhead who worked for Air France, more than once and knew that a good time was assured. There were four or five other girls, a tall, blond man a few years older than Nick who seemed to be a pilot, and a young man who was the Latin lover type from the neck up and a hulking mon-ster below that. Though he was several inches shorter than Nick, he was easily as broad in the shoulders. Connoisseur of gym rats that he was, Nick couldn't help wondering what this creature looked like in less clothing. They left the bar and piled into two taxis bound for who knew where. On the way, the redhead told Nick that the younger man was a baggage handler from the airport. Nick always found it poignant when he learned that some demigod or other from the gym lived an extremely mundane existence. It seemed horribly unsuitable for such a specimen as the young man sitting between two stewardesses in the cab ahead to have to make a living in a manner that seemed barely one level above servitude. Shouldn't someone so young, handsome, and built be able to parlay those qualities into more than that?

They pulled up in front of the Fairmount, which was a promising sign. Nick had had sex in some truly putrid places lately. It was apparently the price you paid for the kind of sex life he was enjoying. The pilot, it turned out, had an entire suite. One of the girls informed the group that his job with Lufthansa was only a hobby. He was actually some sort of minor aristocrat who quickly became bored if he remained in Europe, or even on the ground, for too long at a time. Room service arrived quickly bringing sufficient beverages to fill a Jacuzzi. After a quick round, they all got down to business.

In Nick's experience orgies usually failed to live up to their advance billing. But just this once everybody seemed truly committed to the bacchanalian ideal. Before long Nick was being worked over quite expertly by two of the girls. This in itself wasn't especially unusual. Over the previous months he had made kind of a specialty of being picked up by pairs. What was unusual was that unlike the typical scenario where one of the girls instigated the scene and the other was just along for the ride or there on a dare, these two were equally committed to the action. They kept him distracted to a gratifying degree for an unusual length of time. When they had finished with him he was truly in need of a breather.

And that's when it happened. Pleasantly satiated though far from finished for the night, he looked in just the right direction at just the right time, and there it was—an astonishing vision. The pilot was deep fucking one of the women, really giving her the business, while at the same time sucking the cock of the baggage handler, who stood with his biceps flexed in a classical body-building pose. This was something Nick had never witnessed before, the cock of one man in the mouth of another. He was aware of the practice, of course. He understood that there were men who made a specialty of it. There was nothing especially outré about the combination of cock and mouth. His own cock had been in countless mouths, albeit never a male one. That idea was, of course, inadmissible. But the exoticism of the current scene, the unassailably masculine blond pilot sucking the cock of that astonishingly built baggage handler, enthusiastically sucking on it—there was no question about it, his expert technique was apparent: he'd done it before—almost made, Nick thought, a kind of sense.

Nothing else the pilot did the rest of the night called his essential masculinity into question. He made love to several more of the girls. He was unquestionably a sexual athlete. Nick had witnessed enough mediocre performances in the past months to know a superior one when he witnessed it. The baggage handler didn't fuck anyone. His whole repertoire, it seemed, consisted of striking one or another bodybuilding pose and then allowing someone or other to worship him orally.

* * *

After getting over his initial shock—not to mention finishing the night's business—Nick realized that there was a great deal to consider in what he had witnessed. He couldn't imagine what benefit there had been for the pilot in that episode, but from the baggage handler's perspective the attraction was blindingly obvious. Though it had never occurred to Nick previously, being sexually worshipped by another man seemed as though it might be the supreme affirmation of one's masculinity. It couldn't be just any man, certainly, but to be worshipped in that manner by a man whose own masculinity was absolutely irreproachable: in a strange way this seemed to eclipse any similar affirmation that could be offered by a female. After all, females worshipped masculinity as naturally as they breathed, but also, it had to be said, rather indiscriminately. It was a biological imperative over which they had limited control and which proved nothing at all about the object of worship. But for a strong, handsome man to be so moved by you as to approach you in that way—well, that was really saying something about you. To be desired that much, so much that a by an act of conscious will a real man would risk actually being seen, risk seeing himself for that matter, as less than a man; admit to himself with his own body the inadequacy of his manhood compared to yours: it was hard to imagine anything more affirming than that. Theoretically, at least.

The more Nick considered it, the easier it became to imagine himself in the baggage handler's position. The more he thought about it the less it seemed like a hypothesis. It glimmered in his imagination as a concrete possibility. Almost, to be honest about it, an aspiration. But merely possessing motivation for an act, as any prosecutor or writer of mystery novels could tell you, was neither here nor there. There had to be method as well. There had to be opportunity. And it was at that point that Nick's imagination bogged down. He could imagine the act, but he couldn't imagine placing himself in a situation that would make the act possible.

* * *

"Thanks for agreeing to see me, Nick."

"Thanks for not calling me at the office," Nick said. "I'd have had to turn you down."

Brad's grin said that he might be dumb but he wasn't that dumb. They had agreed to meet at this little hole in the wall in North Beach. It wasn't likely that anyone either of them knew would show up, but in that unlikely event nothing about their presence should raise eyebrows.

"Arch nearly had a stroke when I told him I'd called you," Brad said.

"Quite right," Nick said. Arch Masters had defended Brad in his recent case, which Nick prosecuted. Ordinarily, prosecutors didn't take cases involving people they were acquainted with, but this was a low level prosecution. By the time Nick and Arch worked out the agreement, the offense in question had become a misdemeanor. Since it was a first offense, what Nick did was common practice if not totally by the book. There wasn't a single eyebrow in the prosecutor's office that would rise so much as a millimeter at it. It was a real break for Brad. Nobody would give a conviction for disturbing the peace a moment's notice. But honestly, Nick would have done the same for anybody under the circumstances. It wasn't usual at all, however, to sit down for a post mortem, or even coffee like this, with the man you'd helped convict of a crime, no matter how insignificant.

"He was almost as upset," Brad continued, "as when he first heard that I was acquainted with the prosecuting attorney. You should have heard him then, Nick. 'This will either be really, really good or really, really bad. Depends on how much of a hardass your guy turns out to be—what he thinks he has to prove downtown. And with him relatively new in the prosecutor's office, he may think he has a lot to prove. . .' But it all worked out, didn't it?"

Nick shrugged.

"So thanks," Brad said. "Coffee's on me. And how can there be any harm in the two of us talking about it now? The case is over. I pled guilty. I paid my fine."

"No harm," Nick agreed, in a tone he hoped also conveyed the sentiment, *but no point, either* clearly but in the least offensive way possible. You had to respect Brad for his guts. Not everybody would have been willing to face someone like Nick with that in their history.

"We're off the record, right?"

Nick nodded.

"I talked with Arch about this at the time," Brad said, "but he refused to pursue it. He said it wouldn't get us anywhere. It would just be my word against that of the cop, and with a charge like that nobody would believe me. It would only piss you off and make it less likely we could negotiate a deal."

"Piss me off? Why?"

"I don't know," Brad said. "But Arch was—well, you know Arch."

Nick did know Arch, but not that well. He was part of Nick's set—or what had been Nick's set when he was still a member—but only peripherally. Defense attorneys weren't highly thought of in that company. Until someone got arrested. They were a necessary evil, like enemas.

"Go on," Nick said.

"I've done some reading up on it," Brad said. "Since the case. Turns out, the police have rules."

"Rules?"

"Procedures," Brad said. "What they can do and what they can't do in the course of performing their duties, right?"

"Sure."

"So that undercover cop who arrested me wasn't playing by the rules."

"How so?"

Brad had been arrested in Golden Gate Park for soliciting a sex act from an undercover cop. In the course of working on the case, Nick had read the police report several times, but since they hadn't gone to trial he'd had no occasion to examine Brad's statement. He'd taken the officer's story at face value. Neither Brad nor Arch contradicted it. They simply wanted to settle the matter as quickly and quietly as possible.

"For one thing, he initiated the conversation," Brad said. "I didn't so much as say hi. He spoke first, and he immediately made an offer."

"That's a no-no," Nick agreed. This was assuming that Brad was telling the truth. But there wasn't really any point in trying to establish that. The case was closed.

"It's not just that," Brad continued. "That cop behaved provocatively. They're not allowed to behave provocatively. That constitutes entrapment."

"Right," Nick nodded. "But 'provocative'—what does that mean? I bet if we looked in the police manual there wouldn't be a clear definition of the term. The determination of whether or not the officer's behavior constituted a provocation would be left up to the judge in the case."

"That's what Arch said," Brad admitted.

"So?"

"He had his shirt off, Nick," Brad said. "He had his pants open and his cock out. He was leaning back against a tree and he was playing with his nipples with one hand and stroking himself with the other. Now if you saw a man acting like that and then he said, 'hey bud, you want to suck on this big one?'—not you, of course, Nick, I didn't mean *you*. . ."

"It's O.K.," Nick grinned. "I get it. And I get your point. If that's really what happened, then yes, he provoked you. Of course getting a judge to take your word for what happened wouldn't have been easy."

"Oh, I'm not saying I'm innocent," Brad said. "Not at all. I'm happy with the way you and Arch handled things. I was in the park looking for sex. I did try to touch him."

"So what's the point of all this?"

"Vindication," Brad said.

"You're not asking to re-open the case," Nick protested.

"Personal vindication," Brad said. "That's all."

"I'm not sure how I can help you there."

"You already have," Brad said, "you've listened to me. You've agreed that, at least in principle, I was entrapped."

"Hypothetically only."

"Granted."

"Tell me one thing."

"Please, Nick, you don't want me to explain what possesses a man to kneel down in the dirt and ruin his dress slacks. . ."

"No," Nick laughed, "not that. But that police officer—would you recognize him if you saw him again?"

"Would I?" Brad blushed. "I guess so. He was stunning. You probably don't want to hear that, but yeah, he was spectacular."

"Spectacular how?" Nick asked. Brad was a handsome guy, a personable guy. Surely, even with his, um, specialized requirements, he didn't have to pick up strangers in the park. There had to be easier, safer ways to satisfy his urges than that. So what had there been about this man?

"Oh," Brad said, blushing even more furiously, "you don't want a detailed description."

"Maybe I do."

"All right," Brad said, looking dubious. "He was handsome. Kind of boy next door grows up to be a Hollywood superstar handsome. Like that."

"O.K.," Nick said. "But that doesn't give me much to go on."

"You want more than that? You can't want more than that."

Nick nodded.

"You do want more than that. O.K., so he was built. Really built. You must know, Nick, how people used to talk about you behind your back."

"So he was 'musclebound'?"

"It's a stupid word," Brad said. "But yes, that's how most people would describe him. Not as tall as you. No more than medium height, really, which makes shoulders like that seem really broad and massive."

"Yes."

"And one of those amazingly tiny waists."

"What else?" Nick asked. "Coloring? Tattoos? Hair?"

"Gosh, yes," Brad said, "his hair. He was wearing it the way we all used to back in the early sixties. Before the Beatles. You remember. Neat, trimmed, parted on the side. And greased down."

"Uh huh," Nick nodded. "Color?"

"Blond," Brad said. "Not blond like you. A shade or two darker. But true blond. Hard to tell for exactly with that stuff in it."

* * *

There couldn't be two of them. It had to be the same man, the guy Nick saw working out at the Y every day. The crucial detail was the hair. Handsome, built. That description left open a near infinity of possibilities. But that hair. Nick had practically smelled the pomade the guy used on his hair as Brad was describing it. How many times over the past few weeks had Nick luxuriated in the reverie? Imagining himself looking down at the top of that neatly trimmed, perfectly combed, fragrantly oiled hair; looking down at those broad, heroically muscled shoulders, looking down as the young man hungrily took Nick in his mouth.

* * *

What the young police officer had done to Brad was unthinkable. Not that Nick was a fan of Brad's. He'd never had any use for Brad, so it wasn't feelings of friendship that made the incident so offensive. And even if Nick hadn't been a prosecutor he would have come down on the side of the relevant statutes, so it wasn't some anarchic impulse that fueled his censure. Sex acts in public? Even between consenting adults? Nick had had plenty of sex in the great outdoors. He understood the attraction of it just fine. He even had a name for it in his *lexiconus sexualis*: The Seductions of Eden.

But in an urban park? With children riding bicycles just yards away? With Chinese grandmothers pushing strollers down paths just the other side of that bank of shrubbery? No, the proximity of unwilling witnesses, the potential disruption to the social order—that's why Nick sided with the law. Those who wished to give themselves up to the sylvan ideal, to be carried away *al fresco*, had a responsibility to choose locations remote enough that privacy was assured. That's why certain laws existed.

But that was a peripheral issue. What was truly repulsive about Brad's case was how that police officer had perverted himself. He had used his masculinity as a lure, not to lead another person to an act of physical worship or the experience of pleasure, or even to the exchange of money or gifts, which would have been questionable but perhaps inconsequential under the right circumstances, but to harm, to potential ruin. It was evil in a way that few other acts of evil could match. It was as bad as rape. It was the strong preying on the weak. It was the power of manly sex turned into a tool of oppression and destruction, and was thus antithetical to everything Nick believed about physical relations.

But the next time Nick saw him at the gym, the young man's physical perfection was so transcendent as to seem sufficient excuse for almost any transgression. Nick could only gaze and ponder this phenomenon in silent astonishment. Vainly he looked for a sign, anything that might hint at the inner depravity that must exist beneath the godlike surface.

How many times had he been on the point of striking up a conversation with the young man? How many times at the end of his workout had Nick been tempted to use the shower head immediately next to his? How much time had he devoted to contemplating the slow, gradual progression by which they were to become acquainted, then familiar, and eventually close enough for Nick's continuing fantasy to enter the domain of reality and flesh?

If Brad was to be believed, at some point along the way the young man would have shown his true colors. And when that happened, Nick couldn't have depended on the good offices of a friendly fellow prosecutor. In his case no deal would have been possible.

If Brad was to be believed. Knowing what he knew, Nick was breathless at the risk he'd have been taking. He would never have been willing to take the chance that Brad was lying. He hadn't known Brad's story before, of course, and his ignorance had made everything seem possible. Now, though the fantasy persisted, it seemed more elusive than ever. He felt like the dying Arthur heartbroken that he had never found the Holy Grail.

* * *

Nick's curiosity sent him back to re-read the police report. He wasn't searching for signs of its truth or falsehood. That remained impossible to determine. All he wanted was a name to call the young man—not to speak to him, but to apply to him in his own mind—and he got it.

Jeffrey Trent.

V

The day Jeffrey Trent didn't show up at the gym, Nick told himself he wasn't alarmed. Trent had been regular as sunrise since the very first time Nick encountered him almost exactly six months earlier. To his chagrin, Nick remembered the exact date. But anything could have happened to keep Trent away that day: an illness, a change of shift, vacation time—there were a thousand possible explanations. By the fourth day, however, Nick could hardly contain his—he didn't even know what it was. Annoyance? Anxiety? That he was concerned at all made him anxious. It shouldn't matter. He shouldn't care.

Finally he hit on an explanation that he could just about live with. He didn't care what might have happened to Jeffrey Trent the human being, but never to lay eyes again on the aesthetic and physical spectacle that went by the name Jeffrey Trent was too much to accept. To have perfection like that pass out of his life without warning—he wouldn't tolerate it.

He could have asked any of the gym regulars what they knew but was reluctant to betray his interest. There was an easier solution. Several weeks earlier he had begun following Trent as he left the gym. Say, once a week on average. Certainly no more often than that. At least he didn't think it had been. Trent always led him to the same address, an apartment building at the edge of the Tenderloin. Nick had no way of knowing if that was actually where Trent lived, but he did know that each time Trent let himself into the front door of the building with a key, which seemed to settle the question.

* * *

"I'm interested in speaking with one of your tenants," Nick told the land-lady, a Mrs. Wilkins. "His name is Jeffrey Trent."

"I'm sorry, but I don't have a tenant by that name, Lieutenant."

"I'm not a policeman, Mrs. Wilkins," Nick said. "I told you. I work in the prosecutor's office."

"Yes, Lieutenant, you said that," she nodded.

"You're sure you don't have a tenant named Jeffrey Trent?"

"Oh, absolutely. I know all my young men. Like my nephews they are. Not a Jeffrey among them. Or a Trent."

"Perhaps he's a friend of one of your tenants," Nick suggested. "A very good friend. I know he comes here often."

"This Mr. Trent," Mrs. Wilkins said, looking faintly alarmed, "is he sup-posed to have done something wrong?"

"No," Nick said. "I believe I mentioned to you that he might turn out to be a witness in a case we're preparing for trial. That's all."

"Well, I don't know him, I'm afraid."

"You're quite certain? A short-haired blond man in his early to mid twen-ties? Looks like he spends a great deal of time lifting weights?"

"Oh," Mrs. Wilkins said, "I know the man you mean. But his name's not Jeffrey Trent. That's Mr. Bentley. Tristan Bentley."

"Tristan Bentley?"

"Moved in just about six months ago. Third floor rear. Yes, Mr. Bentley. Such a handsome young man. Just about gives me the vapors every time I set eyes on him. So neat and clean cut. You don't encounter young men like that very often nowadays. And that's certainly a pity. I think he must have been in the military. Always on time with his rent. Pays in cash, you know. I never have to worry if his check will clear, like with some of my young men. A very quiet, very respectable gentleman. Simply a model tenant, Lieutenant. Wish I had a house full of Tristan Bentleys, I do."

Nick listened to her with mounting excitement. Everything she said seemed to match up perfectly with the young man at the gym. At the same time, the way Mrs. Wilkins described her tenant didn't mesh with Jeffrey Trent as Nick had come to imagine him. Brad Davenport's story had sent him off in a wrong direction. Or maybe it hadn't. Maybe this addled landlady had only a dim idea of who her tenant actually was. The rent payments made in cash particularly troubled Nick now that he thought about it.

"I must have been given a wrong name, Mrs. Wilkins," Nick said. "I can't imagine how a mistake like this could have happened. But the young man you're describing must be the one I'm trying to locate. You said third floor rear, didn't you?"

"That I did. But I'm afraid you won't find him there."

"He's gone out?" Nick asked. "Perhaps you have some idea when he might be expected to return."

Mrs. Wilkins struck him as the kind of busybody who'd know all about the comings and goings of her tenants. Particularly ones she found so "interesting".

"Not gone, out, Lieutenant," Mrs. Wilkins said. "Moved out. In the middle of the night a few days ago. Left me a nice note. And an extra month's rent for my trouble."

"Did he leave a forwarding address?"

"No. Said he'd take care of that through the post office."

"That's all?"

"I've told you everything I know about him," Mrs. Chalmers nodded, "and right sorry I am that I can't help you. I always try to be of help to law enforcement, you know."

* * *

There were no Tristan Bentleys in the DMV records. Nick tried all possible spelling variations just to be sure. He drew a blank in voter registration rolls as well. Those absences might point to a fake identity. Which wouldn't be unknown for an undercover police officer working a case. But since the simplest explanation for any phenomenon was usually the right one, it was more likely to indicate a new arrival to the city. San Francisco was full of those. And Mrs. Wilkins' establishment was exactly the kind of place where you'd be likely to find such an individual. It was also the kind of place where you might set up shop if you were living some sort of double life, either as part of an undercover police operation or on a private basis. The man's sudden disappearance could easily fit multiple possible explanations. There were several Jeffrey Trents in the records Nick had consulted, but none of them at that address in the Tender-loin. If Nick wanted to pursue things further he'd have to go through official channels, and he had no reasonable pretext for that.

For all he knew, there might be a Tristan Bentley and a Jeffrey Trent both. Two different people, Brad's cop and the guy from Nick's gym. From Brad's physical description of his cop, it had seemed obvious that the man at Nick's gym was the same guy. He hadn't seriously entertained the other possibility. But now Nick couldn't be certain of anything.

* * *

On his way home from the office one evening a few days after the inter-view with Mrs. Wilkins, he stopped on a street corner to ponder the future of his quest. Perhaps there was an angle that hadn't occurred to him. Perhaps he hadn't reached a dead end but only believed he had. He was going to have to think very carefully about how to proceed. Every minute of delay meant that the trail was getting colder, but he didn't see what he could do about that. He wasn't even certain what was at stake. He wondered if he had become obsessed without realizing it.

He looked around. He was standing in front of a bar. An unfamiliar one. He barely even knew what block he was on. He stepped inside and im-mediately felt better. Inside, all bars were alike. Noise and smell. Cigarette smoke and a babble of conversation. A few stewardess types, a few business-men reluctant to go home to their wives and dinners. A surly looking, middle aged bartender flanked by a young, slick looking guy who Nick suspected worked there only to pick up women. The last thing it looked like was the anteroom to his future.

He spied a familiar face. Michael Chamberlain. He couldn't remember if he had seen Michael since that incident back in the early summer when that idiot Denny—no, Denny wasn't an idiot any more than Nick was. Denny was just clumsy. And thank God for it. It seemed to Nick that Michael had dropped out of sight afterwards, though to be accurate about it Nick had. Perhaps they both had. Perhaps Michael would rather Nick didn't speak to him.

* * *

"One more for the road?" Michael smiled,

Really, Nick thought, Michael was extraordinarily good looking. Denny was a clumsy idiot, but you couldn't fault his taste.

"I have a better idea," Nick said.

Michael's left eyebrow went up, just a millimeter.

"My apartment's not far from here," Nick said. "Great views, and I make a mean cup of coffee."

* * *

It was ridiculously easy, he thought half an hour later as he eased himself into a part of the male anatomy he had never before visited. Michael shuddered but gave no hint of resistance. Nick wondered how Michael squared all of this with the existence of the heiress fiancée he'd been talking so avidly about earlier. But really it was none of Nick's business. He had no interest in any business right then except the task at hand. Transcendently beautiful Michael squirmed and bucked and whimpered but not in a way that indicated he wanted Nick to exit. Rather the contrary, actually. Nick felt his inhibitions begin to melt. He knew from extensive experience that you couldn't hurt a stewardess by entering her this way. How could you hurt a hundred eighty-five pound athlete? Once Nick decided he was ready for the experience, the mechanics of it turned out to be ridiculously easy. But what struck him, really, was how totally natural it felt. How ideal and perfect. The friction, the titillation, the quickening pulse, the roaring in the ears, the irresistible forward momemtum, yes, all that. But beyond it all, something more—in the silence at the end a strange sense of completion and arrival.

Nick hadn't expected Michael to kiss him when the two of them returned to his apartment. He hadn't planned to kiss Michael back. He hadn't expected Michael to begin unbuttoning his shirt, to reach inside and explore his chest with avid fingers. He hadn't planned to stroke Michael's silken hair and later sniff it. None of this had been in his mind when he left home that morning, when he left the office in the late afternoon, when he left the gym after his workout, or when he glimpsed that familiar face in the shadows of that unfamiliar bar entered on the most random of whims. He simply let everything happen. But it could never have happened if in some way it hadn't been meant to happen. If he hadn't been ready for it to happen. Michael had initiated everything. Michael was obviously experienced at this sort of thing. But Michael wouldn't have dared initiate anything if he hadn't somehow sensed an opportunity. And that opportunity? Where had it originated?

That, intended or not, was what Tristan Bentley was responsible for. It was the path Tristan Bentley had led Nick down.

After a brief rest period, they went at it again. Nick had to be certain what he had just experienced was no fluke. He was pretty certain he already knew the answer to that question, but verifying it in this way seemed absolutely necessary.

* * *

Tristan Bentley might be anywhere, Nick mused in the shower afterward, as a depleted Michael catnapped. Short of organizing a full scale manhunt, something Nick was obviously in no position to do, Tristan Bentley, if that was even his real name, might never be located. For a brief time it had seemed absolutely crucial to do so. Nick's future had appeared to depend on it in a way it had never depended on anything before. Now that the door had slammed definitively in his face, shouldn't it seem like a tragedy? But the last hour or so had made it impossible to think of it in that way. Perhaps Nick was merely satiated, but it was hard to believe it mattered in the way it had previously. Perhaps Tristan Bentley had already fulfilled the only purpose he would ever have in Nick's life. He pointed the way to an awareness of something Nick had never suspected about himself. Nick might well have achieved that same awareness in countless other ways, at no telling what stage or circumstance of life. Anyone else, some not yet encountered, unimagined individual, might have led him to the same epiphany,

But it had been Tristan Bentley and no one else. Tristan Bentley, who, Nick sensed, had been transformed from a young man at his gym into a symbol—no, an archetype. From that point on, Nick's allegiance would be to a new and different ideal. The epoch of the stewardess had ended and the epoch of the handsome bodybuilder had dawned: a handsome bodybuilder of a certain spartan orientation. Tristan Bentley might have vanished as surely as though he had never existed, but he had inhabited Nick's consciousness for a certain time: long enough. Meanwhile, that young man's avatars—and they must exist, and Nick would find them—surely could be encountered, perhaps more than one of them, in every gym in the city. Nick simply hadn't bothered to look. It had all been about Tristan Bentley the man. Now it didn't have to be any more. It was bigger than that.

The gift Nick received had been much more than just a conscious shift in the nature of his attractions. He saw that it had been nothing less than the opening of a door to a truly authentic life. Everyone understood that men of that type existed, but Nick had never thought it possible he might ever have anything in common with them, such a sorry, weak, trivial crew they seemed. It had never been, he finally understood, a question of what they did in bed, but of who they were. Even now he had no intention of joining their club. But to truly know himself, to inhabit a world where he knew where to find what genuinely moved him and how to savor it once he did—that was a prize worth giving up anything for. It entailed owing a debt he didn't know how he'd ever be able to repay even if the opportunity to do so presented itself.

One thing was certain. He wouldn't attend Michael Chamberlain's wedding without the promise of a certain consideration.

Cooper Luxemberg:
March, 1978

I

Chanel Rococo was never happier than when she was the center of attention. She wasn't just any drag queen. She thought of herself as a force of nature, albeit nature in its most capricious mood. A pagan goddess in other words, who could redeem or kill at a whim. Anarchy was her preferred element, outrage her métier. Which meant that she required an audience more or less perpetually, the more adoring the better. Her troupe of drag princesses, contessas, and duchesses was suitably reverent and deferential, at least to her face, but didn't constitute an audience, really, though many of her choicest *mots* and soliloquies were previewed before them in the house where they all squatted in Haight Ashbury. Parties were a more effective showcase for Chanel. Cooper had escorted her to plenty of them, from the Tenderloin to Pacific Heights and everywhere in between both geographically and socioculturally. But parties, though enjoyable, limited Chanel's scope to an extent that was often intolerable. At a party, insufficient attention might be paid. Or insufficient allegiance might be expressed. Worst of all, competition might be present. Scenes frequently ensued, with unpredictable and sometimes deplorable consequences. So yes, parties were great, but they didn't afford Chanel a broad enough canvas upon which to wield the brush of self-expression. Besides, regardless of what success she might achieve at a party, too much was never enough. Finally, however, she had clawed her way to the top of the pyramid, and this was her reward: emceeing "community events". On these occasions, she alone held the mike and thus the attention of the gathering. And the agenda was hers to control minute by minute. The chaos she truly reveled in was the sort that whirled dizzyingly about her—the ultimate and rightful vortex. Cooper got all this. He'd have been unusually stupid not to, given the number of times the whole thing had been explained to him. But he'd have gotten it anyway. He was a keen observer and smarter than nearly anybody took him for. In addition, Chanel didn't constitute much of an enigma, cryptic as she liked to consider herself.

Tonight's event was a benefit, though Cooper couldn't remember what for. Not that it mattered. There was always a worthy cause, either bona fide or conjured into necessity, requiring some madcap display or other and calling for Chanel's ministrations as diva and hostess. Cooper had been auctioned off as a "bachelor" more times than he could remember, for instance. Sometimes the resulting dates had been just that, polite dinners before theatre or opera. Sometimes they degenerated into scenes most charitably described as questionable. Sometimes he actually made new friends, though most of these friendships, it had to be said, were extremely transitory in nature. Tonight's benefit didn't entail the sale and/or purchase of bachelors and the ensuing scheduling of engagements, however. Somebody, although most certainly not Chanel, whose creativity pretty much began and ended with her own persona, had hit on the exquisite concept of oil wrestling, and when bare skin was the object, Cooper was in more demand than ever. Few men in the city were as impressive as he was when gleaming and nearly naked. And few men could muster his level of self possession when thus displayed. At an occasion such as this, he'd have been the main event even if Chanel hadn't regarded him as her own particular mascot and billed him accordingly.

* * *

Cooper didn't appreciate gratuitous nipple tweaking. If anybody was going to be granted the privilege of access to that part of his anatomy, he wanted the event to have greater significance than could be lent it by a drag queen bent on titillating a raucous crowd of drunks and assorted sensation hounds. But he refused to complain. Chanel would accuse him of having hang-ups, or worse. She was the one with the problem, though. She was so freaked out by close encounters with a certain brand of masculinity that her only defense was to demean it, no matter how much she might protest afterward that she was merely joking. Cooper clearly comprehended all this, though as a musclebound galoot he wasn't supposed to be capable of such subtle analysis. It was no skin off his nose, really, though he did hate seeing her get away with classless behavior. Still, tonight was for a good cause. Or good enough.

* * *

"And now for our final bout of the evening," Chanel crooned into the mike, "it's that perennial crowd favorite, Cooper. . ."

Applause and general rowdiness from the crowd as Cooper struck a classic front double biceps pose.

". . .versus new boy in town, Kent."

Kent was floppy haired, ridiculously cute, and built like the platonic ideal of a go-go boy. Cooper figured he outweighed Kent by sixty pounds, all of it lean muscle mass. It probably wouldn't be much of a contest, but that wasn't the point. There was apparently a never ending supply of guys like this one. Regardless of what it might say on their drivers' licenses, they invariably looked nineteen. They had perfect teeth. Their hair texture was terrific, though the styles they sported were often questionable. They had slim, wiry physiques, not from gym attendance but because nature had given them active metabolisms, in addition to which they were constantly in motion, often with lubricious intent. Those sleek bodies were hairless, either naturally or with assistance, because that was the accepted presentation for the type. And the type verged, actually, on being an archetype: one of the dominant ones in the gay community. Chanel knew her audiences, and the collision of musclehunk and uber-cute twinkie was a deeply revered local fetish.

This business of archetypes was courtesy of Ned Westerleigh, Cooper's business partner, who had been everywhere and seen everything at least once, and knew all there was to know about gay on this or any other continent. If Chanel was a high priestess, Ned was an oracle. Even if Chanel wasn't exactly as billed, Ned's eminence was impregnable. And Ned had to explain "archetype" to him, because Cooper either missed that day of college or wasn't paying attention. For all he knew or cared, an archetype was some obscure but complicated item of office equipment, but once Ned illuminated it he grasped the concept instinctively. In addition to being popular with the great gay public, the archetype Kent represented seemed personally significant to Chanel, who kept throwing examples of it at Cooper and then dishing the resulting impacts with the members of her coven, frequently in public and at the top of her lungs. At first Cooper thought of this as representing some new spectator sport aimed at the particular interests and preoccupations of drag queens as a class, though lately he wondered if a somewhat different hypothesis might be required to account for it.

Tonight's example was honey blond and honey skinned, with eyes too blue to be believed, larger than average nipples, and a provocative smirk. Cooper estimated his height at five feet nine and his I.Q. at no higher than the low nineties, though that might be an act. He was so exactly what the community currently labeled "cute" as to constitute a living, breathing definition of the term, and Cooper recognized that in his own way he was supposed to be considered an icon, just as Cooper was himself.

Chanel might have introduced him as Kent, but go-go boys all had breezy names like that, as if such monikers were as regulation as their g-strings. It was analogous to the calculated appellations of the drag queens who salivated over them or those of the porn stars of song and legend. Cooper had checked enough go-go boy I.D.s over the years to know that a good percentage of those Chads, Marcs, and Bobbys were actually Huberts, Freds, and Georges. This was how powerful drag queens were in gay: they had abolished Shakespeare's law about the scent of roses.

* * *

"Word on the street is that your cock is so big it has its own zip code."

"You can't believe everything you hear," Cooper growled. Kent was undisputably cute, but Cooper was certain he'd be cuter without the smirk.

"You say that," Kent answered, "but it's established fact that people call it 'The Hindenburg.'"

"We going to wrestle or just exchange pleasantries?" Cooper asked.

"I'll let you beat me if you'll promise to fuck me raw before sunrise," Kent muttered.

"Let me win?" Cooper growled. "This crowd is not going to cough up serious money for the charity *du jour* because some twinkie rolled onto his back for some muscle dude. They're here for a show and we're going to give them one. Besides, do you really think I'd have sex with a guy who'd just give up? If a sausage party is what you have in mind, you'd better show me you really want it by fighting like hell."

"In that case," Kent said, "I'll try not to leave any marks."

"Doesn't matter if you do."

"Tough guy, huh?"

"Try me."

* * *

"Nice car," Kent said.

"Thanks," Cooper grunted, unlocking the passenger side door.

"Really," Kent laughed, "like a penis on wheels."

"Think so?"

"Calling Dr. Freud."

"You getting in?" Cooper asked.

"We going somewhere?"

"Your place," Cooper said. "Where is it?"

"Why not yours?" Kent asked. "Too many wives and kids in residence?"

"Three vicious dogs," Cooper said, turning the key and listening as the Jaguar whoomped to life. "Rip you to shreds before you're halfway in the door. I won't be able to do a thing to stop them."

In truth, the Labradors were about as fierce as a bag of marshmallows.

"Nineteenth and Castro," Kent said.

Awfully close to home, but Cooper didn't have to tell Kent that.

* * *

How many of these squalid, cramped apartments had Cooper visited in the course of his dating life? At least Kent's place didn't smell. Cooper hated smells. And though the bed was unmade when they arrived, the sheets appeared to have been laundered within the past seventy-two hours. Cooper had been known to take one look at the sheets and walk out on a trick without a word, preferring to go back on the hunt to lying down in insufficiently hygienic bedding. There was always some guy out there ready to have sex with him, but the state of the linens was non-negotiable. In Kent's studio, conditions were acceptable, if only just.

Cooper preferred not to take guys to his place. It agitated the Labradors for one thing, and there was the more serious problem—perennial, unfortunately—of getting his tricks to leave afterwards. They lingered. They ignored his hints. More than once, he'd had to evict a guy forcibly. Worst of all, once they'd been to his place they often proved capable of finding their way back there. Sometimes when he wasn't present. Over and over he arrived home to find them camped out on his doorstep. That was unacceptable. He'd been forced to take steps. First by moving, then by instituting his rule.

People saw a guy like Cooper, huge, muscular, movie star handsome, and all too often they simply lay back and let him do whatever he wanted. Cooper knew how that worked. In general he was O.K. with such scenes. He always got himself off at least. And he could count on the fingers of one hand the times he had failed to give his partner satisfaction. But there was something about the passivity of guys like that which disturbed him, though it had to be granted that this reaction on his part was invariably a retrospective one. In the moment, his approach to the matter was purely existential.

But when he thought back on these encounters, they seemed to him like so many lost opportunities. No matter how strenuously he exerted himself, when his partner just lay there it placed limits on what could be achieved. And this offended Cooper's sense of what sex was for and what it could be. Each new encounter brought with it the potential for the hottest sex ever, and every time that potential remained unfulfilled Cooper thought of the experience as a failure regardless of how satiated he was as he headed home to his dogs. Why didn't more people see that sex was hottest when both partners put everything they had into it?

Kent certainly understood it. That's why Cooper was inclined to grant him a rematch. In general, Cooper didn't believe in rematches. He didn't believe in rewarding any sex that was less than ideal—and it almost invariably fell into that category. The other problem with rematches was less philosophical and more pragmatic. Rematches implied relationships, or at least the potential for them. And Cooper was strongly inclined to avoid such complications at any cost. But every now and then the universe threw someone into his path who was sufficiently committed to bedroom activities that it convinced him to bend his rules, though he never broke them.

That's how good Kent was.

II

Big Steve Fabiani had reinvented Sunday brunch. When it was the Bentley-Fabianis' turn to host, he rolled out platter after platter of high protein, low fat-and-sodium delicacies that had the gang clamoring for the recipes. Sunday brunch wasn't usually thought of as a bodybuilder-friendly meal, but it turned out that a little ingenuity, informed by the kitchen wizardry of Big Steve's Auntie Violetta, was all that was required to make it so. Thus, the real trick to the occasion was not navigating the buffet without risking the sharpness of your abdominals but making the guest list in the first place. The Bentley-Fabianis preferred intimate entertaining, and most of their brunches included no more than one or two meatheads in excess of the regulars. Today's new faces were Stan Rybrczyk, a powerlifter who'd been invited because T. was fascinated by the idea of a last name that had no a, e, i, o, or u in it, and Jordan Kelly, a mass monster from Boston who'd won the Massachusetts bodybuilding championships and dropped out of seminary the same week. As a bonus, he had one blue and one green eye.

Nick Romanovsky was currently auditioning him for the role of permanent sex slave.

* * *

"So how much money did you raise last night?" Scott Bailey asked.

"No idea," Cooper said. "I didn't stay around for the final tally."

"No," Stan Rybrczyk laughed, "you were too busy dragging that go-go boy off to your lair for rape and pillage."

"His lair, actually," Cooper said.

"Heard about it from Walt Kaminsky," Stan said. "He was there for your bout. Ran into him later in the back room at Pecs."

"What go-go boy?" Scott Bailey asked.

"Name of Kent," Stan said. "Walt said he's the cutest thing on two legs."

"He's cute, all right," Scott said, "if it's the Kent I'm thinking of. And dangerous. He invited my husband and me to breakfast recently."

"How is that dangerous?" Cooper asked.

"He issued the invitation at ten p.m.," Scott laughed. "It was part of a package tour."

* * *

"Cooper," Bella smiled. "I was hoping I might run into you here."

Not much of a surprise, really, since it was her gallery and she'd sent out printed invitations to this opening, which featured a brunch buffet and art you only knew was art because someone told you so. A hostess had to pull out all the stops when she scheduled an opening on Sunday. She was competing with Glide Memorial Church and God only knew what other local attractions.

"Great to see you," Cooper said, kissing her cheek.

"I've already sent you a card," she said. "You should get it soon. But I always love to thank people for their gifts in person when I get the chance."

"You're welcome," Cooper said.

"You really shouldn't have, you know," she insisted.

"I give all my clients housewarming gifts when their escrows close," Cooper said.

"Of course you do," she nodded, "but we both know you don't give all your clients such a special gift as that."

He did. But he didn't contradict her. She wanted to believe what she wanted to believe, and she wasn't the sort of young lady to be dissuaded. He might as well save his breath.

"And I insist," Bella continued, "on showing my gratitude by taking you to lunch. Shall we say Tuesday?"

"I'll have to check my calendar and get back to you," he said. He was pretty sure where she thought she was headed, and he was reluctant to encourage her. But the Steinbergs were a huge tribe, so he didn't want to shut her down cold. Bella had literally dozens of sisters, cousins, and friends from her current temple and her old Hebrew School likely to buy condos in the next few years. They'd all need representation.

Even given Bella's overheated attentions, the event was a successful one for Cooper. He was able to give his business card to several prospective clients, and after Big Steve's cooking the brunch buffet didn't pose much of a threat to his abdominals. He easily got away in time to go see Lance Garrison, who lived over on Russian Hill in a condo Ned Westerleigh had sold him before Cooper got into real estate.

"Ran into Stefano last week," Lance said. "He told me you're working out harder than ever."

Lance was the only guy Cooper knew who called Big Steve by his legal name. There were rumors of some history between the two men that predated the arrival of Tristan Bentley in San Francisco. As far as Cooper was concerned the rumors were lent credibility by the fact that Lance was exactly the type Big Steve would have gone for. An Olympic wrestler, Lance had already won a handful of bodybuilding trophies by the time Big Steve first encountered him. And he was almost supernaturally handsome, with wavy dark brown hair, gray eyes, and dimples.

"That placing at the Western America was kind of a breakthrough for me," Cooper said.

"It works that way sometimes," Lance nodded.

"You ever think of competing again?" Cooper asked. "No question you'd do great."

"I don't have the focus for it any more," Lance said. "I stay in good shape, but it's that final five per cent preparation that wins high placings. And these days I'm putting all that energy into photographing you guys instead of working on my own body."

"I get that," Cooper smiled.

"I meant to have you over sooner to see these photos I took of you at the show," Lance said.

"We're both busy guys," Cooper shrugged.

"Which one is your favorite?" Lance asked.

"You take such fantastic photos," Cooper said.

"No hedging," Lance laughed.

"This one," Cooper said.

"I knew you'd pick that one," Lance said. "I've got a framed print of it for you to take with you."

"How did you know it would be my favorite?" Cooper asked.

"It's my favorite, too," Lance said, "especially since I found out Friday that it's going to be the inside rear cover of *Muscle Training Monthly's* August issue."

"You're kidding."

"No," Lance said. "I'm not. I already deposited their check in my account. You're going national."

* * *

By the time Cooper met them at tea dance, Chanel and her acolytes were well lit up. Chanel preferred big, flashy cocktails festooned with paper umbrellas and assorted other embellishments, but Holly Montezuma and Marina del Rey were two-fisted drinkers. In keeping with their Latino roots, Holly favored tequila, while Marina restricted herself to Corona, which she ingested by the barrel. Her minimal body fat defied the laws of physics as Cooper understood them.

"I could have eaten you two with a spoon, darling," Chanel said. "And the crowd loved it. Nobody expected Kent to put up such a fight."

"*Tigrito,*" Marina said, faking the heaviest possible accent. The reality was she'd grown up in a household where despite their surname the family hardly spoke a word of Spanish that didn't refer to a menu item.

"*Muy delicioso,*" Holly Montezuma purred in confirmation.

"*Si. Exquisito.*"

"Can it, girls," Cooper growled. "Glad you enjoyed the show, of course."

"Just wait until you see the writeup in my column," Holly said. She was a featured contributor to *Gay by the Bay*, a periodical which featured "community news", bar gossip, and page after page of personal ads. To hear her talk about it, the rag would be winning its first Pulitzer any day now.

"Photos, too," Marina said. "Oswaldo was there last night, camera in hand."

"That wasn't all he had in his hand," Holly hooted.

"Yes," Marina said, "that chorizo of his truly is a whopper."

"And *muy sabroso*."

"Girl!"

"I'm surprised he's not with you this afternoon," Chanel said.

"Who?" Cooper asked. He wasn't about to make it easy for her. "Oswaldo?"

"Why, who else? Darling little Kent, of course. Don't be coy, big boy. I know you spent the night with him."

"Not the whole night," Cooper grunted.

"Tesoro," Marina del Rey panted, "the streets resound with whispers of the night of love you shared with him. The very pavements sing."

"As did the sheets," Holly said.

"Kent, huh?" Cooper said. "Didn't really catch his name."

"No?" Chanel raised an eyebrow. "I suppose circumstances dictated that certain social niceties had to be dispensed with."

"Oh, to have been a fly on the wall," Holly Montezuma moaned, fanning herself.

"So you really don't know who he is?" Marina asked.

"You mean he's actually somebody?" Cooper asked, "as opposed to a generic twinkie? Could have fooled me."

"He's no mere twinkie, my dear," Chanel declared.

"He's *Das Ubertwinkie*," Holly boomed in a German accented basso.

"Right," Cooper said, dubious.

"Oh, we assure you," Marina said. "He's a twinkie among twinkies. *Twinkissimo,* one has to say."

"Who he is," Chanel said, "or rather, who he's in the process of becoming, is the pre-eminent go-go boy of the impending season."

"Indeed," Marina sighed.

"The veritable *prima donna assoluta* of that universally worshipped species," Chanel continued, "and thus, a force to be reckoned with."

"As are you, *divo mio*," Marina said.

"Watch it, girl," Chanel snapped. "I don't know that *mio* is really the best possible choice of pronoun in that sentence. Though *our* Cooper is certainly is divine."

* * *

"I thought they'd never leave," Nick said sauntering over, a club soda in his massive paw.

"They're not so bad," Cooper shrugged.

"They're positively dire," Nick.

"It's just their shtick."

"One man's shtick is another man's poison," Nick laughed.

"Chalk it up to local color."

"Hear you were a big hit last night," Nick said. "Sorry I missed it."

"I'm sure you found a much better way to spend your Saturday evening," Cooper said. "Wouldn't have taken much effort."

"*Hedda Gabler* as a matter of fact," Nick said.

"Egad."

"With an all female cast," Nick laughed, "and then the back room at Bolt."

"From the sublime to the ridiculous," Cooper said.

"And vice versa."

* * *

"Hi, Cooper."

"Kent. I didn't expect to see you here. You said you were dancing at Rascals tonight."

"Gig got canceled," Kent said. "Unresolved dispute between labor and management."

"I see."

"Lucky for us, though."

"Oh?"

"I told you I wanted to see you again," Kent said, "and *voila*, I'm free tonight."

Which made that labor dispute seem a little too convenient.

"I'm not," Cooper said.

"Sure you are," Kent grinned.

"In fact," Cooper said, looking at his watch, "if I don't leave soon I'll be late."

"That's easy," Kent said. "Make a call. I'll even give you the dime if you haven't got one. Make an excuse. Fake a headache. Problem solved. It'll be worth your while, I promise. You know I mean it."

"Listen to me," Cooper said. "This is not how it's done. If you don't understand what I'm telling you, go find somebody to explain it. I can see half a dozen possibles in the room and the rush hasn't even started."

"Hard to get?" Kent asked. "Is that how you're going to play this?"

"That's your mistake," Cooper said. "I don't play anything. When I say I have plans, I have plans."

He didn't, but Kent didn't need to know that. Kent didn't need to know anything but his place.

The guy Cooper eventually went home with was in his early thirties. He drove a Ferrari and lived in a Craftsman in St. Francis Wood. There were unmistakable signs of a female presence in the house, but it wasn't good manners to let your host know you noticed a thing like that. Cooper knew all about this type. Despite their apparent hang-ups and contradictions, they could be surprisingly good sex. Maybe it was a reaction to the double life they led. Or maybe it was deprivation.

Lance Garrison

"There doesn't seem to be any doubt about it, Your Grace," Dr. Davidoff said in his strangely accented English. The duke didn't understand why it was that French speakers insisted on addressing him in English. He understood why they didn't speak to him in German. History prohibited it. But English? He wished they wouldn't bother. He spoke French far better than he did English. He'd studied both languages in school. The perverse lack of consistency that characterized English grammar offended his sense of order, and the language's pronunciation seemed not only inexcusably unpredictable but profoundly un-aesthetic. He was certain he lacked both the charm and the gravity in English that he would have in French. His wife had told him this more than once, and even if her judgment in the matter didn't reinforce his own it might as well be gospel. He adored her that much.

"We've tested your ejaculate three times now," Dr. Davidoff said. "The result is the same."

Outside the window of the small, elegantly furnished office, the skies were gray. Lake Geneva was a leaden sheet in the distance. That one of the loveliest cities in Europe could appear so drab seemed only fitting under the circumstances.

"I'd be happy to give you the names of some other specialists, if you'd like a second opinion," Dr. Davidoff said. "That can never hurt."

"I've already consulted two doctors," the duke said.

"May I ask who?"

"Morgenthau in Frankfurt and Tedesco in Milan," the duke said. "I'm sorry to say your finding concurs with theirs. I suppose I'm going to have to accept that I'm infertile."

"They're both very fine men," Dr. Davidoff said.

"That's what I was told," the duke nodded.

"I know this is very difficult for you, Your Grace," Dr. Davidoff said. "It isn't easy for any man to hear such news, but I understand that your family situation makes it particularly disappointing."

"Indeed."

* * *

"It is as we feared, Janko," the duke said as they belted themselves into their seats in the small cabin. "Exactly."

Higgins and Marconi already had the jet engines running. They were anxious to get into the air before the weather became any more threatening.

"I'm very sorry to hear that, Your Grace. It is a grave disappointment."

"Certainly," the duke said, "but nothing is to be gained by wallowing in it. One must face facts."

"Yes, Your Grace."

"And in facing facts, one must adapt oneself to them. Her Grace must bear my heirs. There is no alternative. We must simply find our way forward from here."

"Yes, Your Grace."

"I need you to do further research. We need another sort of doctor altogether."

"I've already taken the liberty of making inquiries, Your Grace."

"Good man."

"I've identified a suitable doctor in New York."

"Is he Jewish, Janko? You wouldn't waste my time by sending me to a doctor who isn't Jewish? Surely you know better."

"Of course not, Your Grace. I understand your requirements."

"I suppose a Jewish specialist in New York might have a very full calendar."

"I took the liberty of scheduling a consultation with him several months ago, Your Grace."

"You did, Janko?"

"I did, Your Grace. In the spirit of being prepared for any eventuality. And in the fervent hope, of course, that the consultation would prove unnecessary. It is easier to cancel such an appointment than to arrange one at short notice."

"Very good, Janko."

* * *

It was a long flight. They stopped to refuel in Glasgow, Rejkjavik, and Gander before flying on to New York. The duke fended off boredom by taking shifts at the controls of the jet. He quite enjoyed flying but hadn't really mastered takeoffs or landings. Higgins, an RAF veteran, and Marconi, a retired formula one driver, were worth every cent he paid them and then some. They had each mastered both takeoffs and landings. What he did for diversion, they did as professionals. They never got tired or distracted or bored. They were ready and willing at all hours, in all conditions. Not only did he trust his life with them, he trusted the lives of his wife and his mother with them as well. The most important lesson he had learned from his late father was to surround himself with men who could be relied on without reservation and pay them whatever was necessary to keep them from moving on to other employment.

The duke held out very little hope for this expedition. Still, he promised his mother he would leave no stone unturned, and he had never broken a promise to her. An heir had to be provided, and he would provide one. The title would not be allowed to go to those petit bourgeois cousins she so despised. Somehow it would be done. It was up to him. Konrad, his brother, couldn't be depended on at all. There was, indeed, no reason to believe he was capable of performing the task even if he'd been inclined to. There were plenty of homosexuals who could have. The duke understood that perfectly well. The history of Europe was full of men who had done what had to be done despite their proclivities. His brother simply wasn't one of them. His brother wasn't really good for much of anything, but he certainly was decorative. That was of very little practical use, yet their mother took inordinate joy in it. Thank God for Janko, stalwart Janko with his nerves of steel and resolve of iron. The Ledwinkas had been in the service of the duke's family for over two centuries, and during that time there wasn't anything a Ledwinka hadn't been willing to do when asked. But really, Janko, it had to be admitted, had gone above and beyond the call—and had performed that bizarre duty unflinchingly for nearly ten years now. Every time he called on Janko for something that required his absence from Konrad's household, the duke knew he was taking a grave risk. Konrad might get up to just about anything without Janko there to keep him in check. But sometimes it couldn't be helped.

* * *

"I've reviewed Her Grace's medical records," Dr. Rappaport said, "and I believe she's an excellent candidate for our services. The procedure itself couldn't be simpler. We screen our donors with the utmost care, and we provide you with profiles to select from. I've already taken the liberty of doing a pre-screening based on the parameters Mr. Ledwinka shared with us. Or, if you prefer, we could make a discreet search for someone you would find suitable. On a sort of one-time-only basis. That way you'd be guaranteed that there wouldn't be any half siblings as a result of our service."

"I appreciate your efforts," the duke said.

"I have to caution you, however, that it isn't possible to guarantee success. Our procedures are state of the art, but we can't perform miracles. We can't guarantee conception, we can't guarantee that there won't be a miscarriage or a stillbirth, we can't guarantee that any child born won't suffer from defects. Unfortunately, we run a distant second to mother nature in every aspect of the process."

"Thank you for your frankness, Dr. Rappaport," the duke said. "You have given me a great deal to consider. If Her Grace and I should decide to proceed in this direction, Mr. Ledwinka will be in touch with you concerning the arrangements."

* * *

"It won't do, Janko," the duke said, cutting into his very rare filet mignon. He had to hand it to the hotel. Their room service actually lived up to its name. American beef wasn't the equal of Argentine beef by any means, but occasionally you encountered an American kitchen that knew how to prepare the native product properly. "It won't do at all. It's all well and good to employ such procedures with livestock. I'm fully aware of that. We use those methods ourselves on the estates. We'd be foolish not to. Animal husbandry depends on it these days. It's far safer and more efficient than moving the animals themselves all over the place. But I won't have Her Grace treated like livestock. I won't have it. She's a fine girl. She understands her duty in this matter perfectly, and I know that should I ask her to she'd submit to the procedure without a murmur of complaint. But I can't be responsible for it. It's too clinical. And according to Dr. Rappaport, the success rate isn't that high. Imagine having Her Grace come all this way and go through that, and for nothing."

"It would be most unfortunate, Your Grace."

"Unfortunate? It would be tragic. And I would be responsible. How could any husband put his wife through that? It would be impossible to make such a request. No, it just won't do."

"As you say."

"I'm afraid we have no choice. We'll have to move on to plan C."

"So it would seem, Your Grace."

"I've given it a great deal of thought, as you may imagine."

"Indeed."

"I think, Janko, that we what we require is an American. We must do everything we can to avoid future complications, dynastic ones you understand, and from that standpoint an American seems ideal. There's that great, bloody ocean out there between us and them for one thing."

"Yes."

"And better than that, they don't understand Europeans or the aristocracy the slightest bit. They seem to lack even the most rudimentary knowledge of how our world works. I'm convinced that we can use that ignorance to our advantage. Best of all, Americans are the most mercenary people on the face of the earth. It seems that over here one can buy—or as the case may be, rent—anything."

"So I suppose that's our plan, Your Grace."

"I believe it has to be," the duke nodded. "If you have any notions to the contrary, you should speak up now."

"No, Your Grace," Janko said, "I believe you put the case most succinctly. I can't find a single detail to take exception to."

"Thank you, Janko. That certainly goes a long way toward instilling confidence. And if we handle things correctly, we can make it appear that nothing out of the ordinary has taken place. Her Grace comes to the States on an extended vacation, and I join her here from time to time—except I won't really, of course. But that's the story we'll put out. Eventually she returns rested, refreshed, and with child."

"It shouldn't be difficult to manage, Your Grace."

"Not at all," the duke said, "except that it can't be just any American. Obviously. And really, there's only one man I can trust for the job of finding exactly the right American."

"I understand, Your Grace."

"I know we didn't discuss this before leaving home."

"Nevertheless, Your Grace, I anticipated it."

"Is there any way you could see your way clear to performing this duty while, say, conducting my brother on an extended tour of this great country?"

"His Lordship is extremely easily entertained, Your Grace. It shouldn't present too much difficulty."

"Now, as to the parameters."

"Allow me, Your Grace."

"With pleasure."

"A family resemblance is desirable, of course, but only in general terms. We won't attempt to go overboard there. Coloring, size, proportions—all within a reasonable range. No one will expect your child to look like your twin. Appearance is really the least of our concerns, beyond a reasonable approximation."

"Quite," the duke said. "Please continue."

"We'll need an individual of proven academic achievements. American universities don't meet a very high standard from what I'm given to understand, but a degree from one of the better ones is probably an indication of the level of intelligence and diligence that Your Grace could take confidence in.

"An acceptable family background, as well. We won't look for an actual pedigree because that could lead us too close to home—it's a very young country, and anyone with a notable lineage will inevitably have connections on our side of the Atlantic that might prove problematic in the long run. We'll just look for a family tree that's reliably bourgeois over the last few generations.

"Finally, Your Grace, you and His Lordship, your brother, have been recognized for many years for your athletic accomplishments. Your father and uncles as well. I'm not talking about American sports. They're meaningless at best in terms of true athleticism. I'm thinking of looking at individuals associated with the kind of Olympic sports European gentlemen of your class might interest themselves in. Rowing, the decathlon, gymnastics, wrestling perhaps. Things of that sort. Winter sports don't seem as promising, except perhaps for speed skating and hockey. I'm not saying that the search should be limited to actual Olympians. That might make suitable discretion difficult. But athletes of the second tier, so to speak."

"Janko, I couldn't have put it better."

"Thank you, Your Grace."

"I feel I need to make an addition or two, however. First, as you say, this is a young country, and one in which a great variety of nations and cultures are represented among the population."

"Indeed, Your Grace."

"It may well turn out, Janko, that an individual will be found who satisfies all our parameters but is a Jew."

"Yes, Your Grace."

"You must not consider that a disqualifying factor, you understand?"

"I'm aware of Your Grace's great regard for the Jewish people, certainly. Thank you for clarifying that your regard reaches to such a level that you would accept them as members of your family, so to speak."

"Indeed."

"And the second thing, Your Grace?"

"To the extent possible, Janko, the whole experience needs to be as unobjectionable as possible for Her Grace. Find someone meeting our requirements who can be as pleasant as possible a temporary companion for her."

"I'll do my best, Your Grace."

"I have every confidence in you, Janko."

* * *

When Konrad had been forced to leave his third school in as many years, the duke's father despaired—to the extent that the cerebral hemorrhage he suffered resulted in his death. Dealing with the matter of his younger brother thus became the duke's first duty upon succeeding to the title. He was only twenty-five at the time and Konrad sixteen. There was no question of enrolling him in a fourth school. No reputable institution would have taken him at that point. The wealthy and aristocratic families of Europe didn't send their sons to exclusive schools in order for their private parts to be interfered with by perverted classmates. Not even a pervert with as venerable a family name as the one Konrad bore. Other families locked their homosexuals up in sanatoria or sent them off to former colonies in other hemispheres or married them to unsuspecting heiresses and held their breaths, but the new duke considered such solutions beneath the family's honor. What he lacked, however, was a clear alternative.

What he could count on was the support of his father's closest advisor, Ottmar Ledwinka, who suggested a novel solution. On the family's principal estate, located not far from but safely out of sight of the castle which served as the family seat, there was a small lodge. Ottmar suggested that the structure be renovated and outfitted as a sort of bachelor establishment. Konrad could reside there, supervised by a majordomo who would be a sort of cross between a drill instructor and chaperone. He even had a candidate in mind for the position—his second cousin, Janko, a young man recently relieved of his duties by an employer who was thought to be the French intelligence service. He was blameless, having played no more than an unwitting, ancillary, and ultimately inconclusive role in the scandal which had brought down some of the organization's top men. Nevertheless, he was now considered unemployable through no wrong doing on his part. Such was the way of the secret world. The duke would have been dubious had this suggestion come from anyone else, but Ottmar had proven his wisdom and loyalty time after time and thus must be taken seriously. And for that matter, while French intelligence might well be an oxymoron—indeed, almost certainly was—Ottmar's seal of approval was iron clad. As it later turned out, Janko's previous employers had not spoken French but the Queen's English, and he hadn't been relieved of his duties at all, simply placed on reserve. However, only a few men in the world knew this.

Tall, broad shouldered, golden haired, and with severe features reminiscent of a Prussian cavalry officer, Janko was, as Konrad gushed several years later, the answer to a horny schoolboy's most fervent prayer. It seemed to be asking far too much of a family retainer that he serve as a homosexual concubine, regardless of the terms being offered. But Ottmar insisted that nothing was beyond the capability or willingness of a Ledwinka in the service of such a noble and ancient family and that the duke need have no concerns of any sort. And in any case it quickly became apparent that if anyone was to play the concubine, it was Konrad himself. The duke couldn't imagine Janko as the kind of man who'd tolerate indignities of any sort to his person, yet Konrad described his satisfaction with the arrangement in unabashedly sexual terms. Thankfully, he did so only in private, but it could only mean one thing—Konrad tolerated the indignities himself. More than that, he apparently relished being used in certain ways that the duke preferred not to think about. He chose instead to reward Janko's loyalty with the title "Chief of Security" and adjust his remuneration upward. The young duke was a bona fide billionaire, and having a Chief of Security in his employment struck him as only reasonable. Certainly, having Konrad effectively disposed of made the duke feel secure in a way he hadn't anticipated, only dreamed of.

The arrangement quickly bore more conventional fruit as well. Janko instituted a strict timetable and put Konrad on a rigorous physical conditioning program. Janko instructed the cook in the preparation of simple, wholesome foods such as the local peasantry had subsisted on for centuries. Janko lived up not only to Ottmar's billing, but to his own spartan appearance. The duke held his breath, but Konrad staged no insurrection. He seemed perfectly contented. No one had ever seen him in such a state of serenity and focus. Janko got him into and through university with an actual degree. He got him onto the Olympic team—twice—as a discus thrower. Konrad didn't medal but he scored a respectable placing each time. He was still fundamentally lazy and disorganized, though his manners and his personal hygiene had improved almost beyond recognition, but he caused no further embarrassments to the family. Nobody could do a thing with him but Janko. But that was enough. Their mother declared that thanks to Janko she could die a happy woman if ever she was granted the wish of grandchildren.

Occasionally, the duke would find himself feeling guilty about the life Janko was giving up in order to be a sort of consort to Konrad. More than once he suggested that if Janko ever wished to incorporate a female companion for himself into the small household at the lodge, he would have no objection. Each time Janko thanked him for his consideration but said nothing further on the subject, and no female companion ever materialized. Indeed, Janko insisted that all the domestics employed at the lodge be male. Eventually the duke couldn't help drawing a certain conclusion.

* * *

When Konrad graduated from the university, he turned into a serious globetrotter. Every few weeks he was off to some exotic destination or other, accompanied of course by the ever faithful Janko. Konrad couldn't have told you with certainty how many of his journeys were his own idea and how many had been suggested by his mentor. Janko made sure to keep his charge just distracted and addled enough for this to be impossible. He was no longer on the active roster of the intelligence service of any nation, and his hands might be full keeping Konrad occupied, but he had never truly retired from the work. Free lancers were always in demand. Something always needed doing somewhere in the world whether it was taking photographs, serving as a courier, or following someone and reporting on their movements. The intelligence services had never had the resources necessary to cover these low level activities with their own staff, and the longer Europe went without war breaking out the more the parliaments of the continent cut their budgets. A travel addicted young aristocrat and his companion could go anywhere without attracting the wrong sort of attention. Janko couldn't have planned it any better.

Janko didn't do it for the money. The duke housed, clothed, and fed him in fine style. The nation provided for his medical care. The duke bought expensive automobiles every year or two for Konrad's use, which Janko generally ended up driving. The salary the duke paid Janko went almost entirely into accounts in Switzerland. Someday his circumstances could change. There was no way of predicting what might happen. Or when. But he was provided for, whatever transpired. Thus, extra income wasn't his motivation. His extracurricular activities didn't bring in enough to make a difference in that respect. What they did was keep him sharp, prepared for whatever that uncertain future might send his way. They allowed him to maintain his relationships with men who might be of assistance in an ever changing world. Most important, they kept him from feeling too much like the duke's servant and Konrad's plaything. You couldn't put a price on independence. Or even the illusion of it, he found.

The upshot of all this was that when Konrad announced that he was off on an extended American adventure, it occasioned no comment whatever in the household or the surrounding community. Janko had suggested that their absence might run to as long as two months, and that's what Konrad told anyone who would listen in the days before their departure.

* * *

Their second morning in New York, Janko left Konrad dead asleep in the hotel suite and made a visit to a brownstone on the Upper East Side. Despite its resolutely residential location and aspect, it was the headquarters of an organization in whose service he frequently exerted himself, and he received the heartiest of welcomes on his arrival. It was a private enterprise, a sort of clearing house for information, and had no permanent staff in the field. Everything done outside the four walls was done by freelancers such as Janko. He was known there as Dmitri Stepanik, and indeed, possessed a passport in that name. A brief consultation was all it took. He was assured that his request presented no insurmountable difficulties and that the investigative component of it could be performed with complete discretion.

He was back at the hotel before Konrad stirred.

Two months later, on their way back through New York, he stopped there just long enough to receive the stack of dossiers he had commissioned. One hundred of them exactly. He paid one hundred and fifty dollars apiece for them. This was substantially less than the retail price would have been. He qualified for an employee discount. He didn't look at them until Konrad and he were safely back home and then did so in private. He and the duke were in agreement that the less Konrad knew about their activities the better.

Many of the one hundred candidates he struck off the list immediately. Married men, engaged men, divorced men—such ties made the proposed transaction too problematic. He had not disqualified individuals with such domestic attachments from the original search because he didn't want to leave any telltale parameters that might tip off even trusted associates as to the nature of his efforts. He marked off other prospects for a variety of reasons. He made a special stack for discards that might be resurrected if it proved that he'd been too stringent in his screening. When he finally finished, he had an even two dozen files to share with the duke.

* * *

The yacht *Katryjn* rode at anchor in the inner harbor, overlooked by the casino and the palace. They had been to dinner there last night. Not a state affair, just a simple meal *en famille*. The palace was a rather poky residence by the duke's standards, but it had to be granted that the views were spectacular. Adriana and his mother had gone off shopping after lunch, and Janko had Konrad running wind sprints on the beach, shirtless, to the delight of a handful of paparazzi. The duke used the solitude to take some sun and survey the stack of dossiers Janko had presented him with that morning. He'd looked through them once already and had to hand it to his deputy. Any one of the young men—all two dozen of them—appeared ideally suited in every respect to their requirements. He had a couple of favorites already but had promised himself to go through the entire stack at least four times before finalizing his short list.

Each of the young men exceeded the brief in one respect. The duke hadn't specified handsomeness as a requirement, reasoning that pleasant looks would be enough. But the young men Janko had unearthed were all stunners. Every last one of them.

"Never send a man to do a homosexual's job," he muttered to himself.

* * *

"Look here, Janko," the duke said, "I've had a glance through these dossiers of yours."

"Yes, Your Grace?"

They sat side by side on the deck of the yacht surveying Monte Carlo by night. Konrad had escorted Adriana and the dowager duchess to the casino for the evening. Janko and the duke might join the others there later if His Grace decided he felt like facing all that noise and smoke.

"You've done a capital job. Truly capital."

"Thank you, Your Grace."

"On paper, at least, any of those young gentlemen would be suitable."

"I'm glad to hear it."

"I've prepared a short list. There are six of the young men I'd like you to investigate more thoroughly."

"As you wish."

"I suppose it will mean another trip to the States for you."

"I don't see any practical way of doing the job otherwise."

"I'd think that at this point in our enterprise you might find my brother's presence a distraction."

"I've already given some thought to that, Your Grace."

"You have?"

"There's an expedition leaving soon for the Himalayas," Janko said. "I'm acquainted with several of the organizers. They would be happy for Konrad to accompany them. It will be a good experience for him and it will give me an opportunity to continue work on our undertaking unobserved and without distractions. They'll be gone for three months at least."

"Good thinking, Janko. Three months should be long enough to conclude this phase of our project."

"Ample time, Your Grace."

"You'll have the plane and pilots at your disposal, of course."

"If Your Grace can spare them, it would be a great help."

* * *

The duke's short list exactly matched Janko's own, which was highly gratifying to both of them. Arrangements were quickly made for Konrad's departure on the Himlayan expedition. The pilots were briefed on Janko's needs. There was just one thing lacking. They had come to a point where Janko's English could take them no further. Assistance was required.

II

In the world where Ned Westerleigh and he sometimes collaborated, Janko was known as Til Krieger. He had a passport in that name. A very good passport. He had spent what seemed at the time like a ridiculous amount of money acquiring it, but it was worth the price. It hadn't raised the least suspicion at a single border crossing on any of the five continents he had visited using it. Yesterday afternoon, coming through immigration and customs in San Francisco, it had been as if his arrival was in response to a special invitation by the State Department. His taxi driver from the airport spoke even worse English than he did but at least didn't get him lost. The reception staff at his hotel was too slow to really be described as efficient, but all the particulars of his accommodations and billing arrangements were correct. And then there was the driver Ned sent to bring him to the office this morning. Every time he came to America, it was the same. Examined in absolute terms, people's etiquette and manner of performing their duties might leave something to be desired but they invariably made up for it with friendliness. The whole place simply had to be judged by its own set of criteria, he supposed.

A case in point was the receptionist who greeted him and ushered him to Ned's office. Ravishing, socially inept and probably not overly intelligent, but as happy to see him as if she'd been one of his sister's favorite classmates.

"I have Mr. Krieger here for you, Mr. Westerleigh," she announced at Ned's doorway.

"So I see, Giselle," Ned said. "Thank you so much. My dear boy. What a delight to have you here."

Janko had never observed Ned in his role of successful businessman. It was extremely illuminating.

"Ned, my old friend," he said, surveying the office, which he suspected would have had remarkable views if not for the fog.

"Interesting business, this," Ned said.

"Interesting for you," Janko said. "Crucial for my employers."

"Indeed," Ned nodded. "I'm confident that we can accomplish the task they've set for us."

"I'm of the same mind."

"You do realize, of course, that beyond a certain point, things are all in the lap of the gods."

"My employer is a very determined man," Janko said, "and I'm pledged to do all I can to assist him in this matter, as indeed I am in all matters. But he is no fool. He understands that there are no guarantees. Once we have done all we can, he's certain to be satisfied regardless of the result. It is, essentially, about living up to one's duties whether the war is won or lost."

* * *

"Such an ambitious itinerary as this would hardly be feasible," Ned said, belting himself into his seat the next morning, "if your employer weren't so generous with his aircraft."

"Well, Ned," Janko said, "as you see, he couldn't be more serious about this business."

* * *

"That was certainly instructive," Ned said, walking across the parking lot toward their rental car. It was a Buick, which Janko believed had something to do with the Opels the duke used as staff vehicles on his estates.

"Alas, yes," Janko said, regretting the hour and a half it would take them to get back to the airport.

"What a horrifyingly warped young man."

"I wouldn't have believed it," Janko said, "if I hadn't seen it with my own eyes. To think that such a person is permitted to walk around free."

"It's the way things are done here in the States," Ned said. "They have very strong sentiments about prior restraint. In Europe things are handled differently. Nevertheless, he won't be a free man for much longer, I shouldn't think."

"One can only hope he doesn't hurt too many people before the authorities realize he needs to be put away."

"If anything, it demonstrates the wisdom of your employer in insisting on this phase of the screening."

"Even if he hadn't," Janko said, "I would have. There's just so much one can learn about a person from reading even the best dossier."

"Exactly."

"I'm not certain," Janko said, "so perhaps I shouldn't mention it. But I received from my employer the strong impression that the young gentleman we've just so unequivocally disqualified was his first choice."

"Not surprising," Ned said, "when all you know of him is contained in the documentation."

"Indeed."

"I sense, however, that your own preference lies in a different direction."

"It does," Janko nodded.

"As does mine."

* * *

It was one of the remoter American cities. The landscape was bleak and the climate was shocking. The university campus itself was lush, but the city surrounding it seemed unrelievedly barren. Here in April it might well have been high summer in North Africa. Ned Westerleigh had the foresight to specify a rental car equipped with air conditioning, something it wouldn't have occurred to Janko to do. Such a thing was almost unheard of in European autos. And in those that were equipped with it the apparatus rarely functioned properly. Still, he wrote himself a memorandum on the subject in his private notebook. He might never find it of use, but one never knew. His private notebooks had reached volume number seven. He kept the earlier ones under lock and key, not due to anything incriminating they contained but simply because that way he always knew where they could be located should he need to refer to them.

Ned and he spent several days interviewing professors, coaches, teammates, and fellow students of their subject. Subsequent to this they deliberated at some length until Janko was quite certain that he was ready to recommend the young man to the duke should their interview prove satisfactory. They spent another two days sightseeing in the region because of the young man's absence from the area on a trip with the university wrestling team. This pause had previously been accounted for in Janko's planning of the itinerary. The pilots were ecstatic at the prospect of several days off in easy flying distance of Las Vegas. There were a great many antiquities in the vicinity of the university, as it happened, though Janko wouldn't have credited it. Ned claimed he found them fascinating.

Now, finally, they were ready to meet the young man face to face. Their cover story throughout these weeks had been that they were in the service of the United States Government, investigating the suitability of their young men for sensitive, and thus not clearly specified, employment. In the current instance, the fact that the young man's major was physics lent credibility to the possibility of his having applied for such work. In Illinois the week before, the young man in question had been a musician and writer of poetry as well as a gymnast, and their legend lacked, Janko feared, a certain credibility. Nevertheless, wherever they went, Janko was amazed at how prepared everyone they met was to believe the story despite Ned's accent and his own limited ability to converse in English, and what lengths everyone went to in extending the pair their utmost cooperation. As a people, Americans seemed to possess an enormous, not to say ridiculous, faith in their government both with regard to its rectitude and its technical competence. Europeans weren't nearly so credulous.

Of course, now that it was the young man at the top of their list they were about to interview, the cover story had to be dispensed with. They were beyond the point where such a misrepresentation could be useful, and it would be awkward to have to backtrack on it more or less immediately if the young man showed interest in their proposition. Some word of their presence on the campus seemed to have gotten back to him, because when the wrestling coach who was their primary contact ushered him into the small conference room, his first utterance subsequent to the introductions and departure of his coach was to the effect that he didn't know what they were doing there because he had no interest in doing government work of any kind.

"Of course not," Ned said. "That story was just for our convenience as we made our inquiries."

"What I'd like to know in that case," young Mr. Garrison said, "is why you gentlemen have been investigating me in the first place. I have no idea why you'd be interested in me unless it's because the country where my mother grew up is behind the Iron Curtain. But she's no communist and neither am I. And if you've investigated me at all you already know that I'm not involved in any kind of political activity. Coach says I need to listen to what you have to say, but I don't think you've been very honest with him. And if you don't have a good explanation for all this, I'm leaving. You can do whatever you want to."

Garrison wasn't angry, nor did he seem especially confrontational in his demeanor. What he was, Janko decided, was determined. He was reacting, in fact, exactly as Janko would himself under similar circumstances, and this disposed him even more strongly in the young man's favor. Even so, it was at this point that Janko found his anxiety rising to a level he could hardly remember ever having experienced. And that was saying a good deal, considering his history. But Garrison, handsome, impressively built, well spoken, and so perfectly groomed and carefully—if casually—dressed, struck him as being so ideal for the task that the idea of his turning his back on them and walking out of the room was intolerable. Thank God Ned was there. He'd see to it that things didn't go that way.

"We understand your skepticism perfectly," Ned said, "and we apologize for the subterfuge. There's nothing sinister involved. I can assure you of that. My associate and I are private citizens who undertake many different projects all over the world on behalf of clients who are also private citizens. In this instance, we're working on behalf of a married couple, Mr. and Mrs. Brown, who are childless. It's very important to them to have children of their own. Their personal circumstances make adoption unacceptable. Extensive medical testing has established beyond any doubt that it is Mr. Brown who is infertile, and hence, we have been instructed to locate a suitable young man. . ."

"Aren't there sperm banks for that?"

"There are indeed," Ned said. "The Browns considered that alternative."

"And?"

"They decided that in their circumstances the process was simply too impersonal."

"I see," Garrison said. "And getting a complete stranger involved in their private business? They don't consider that impersonal?"

"I suppose you might consider them somewhat eccentric," Ned said, "but I can assure you that they are the most respectable of couples."

At this point, Janko took a moment to congratulate himself for involving Ned in the matter. If anyone could allay the suspicions of this rather skeptical young American, who better than a polished British aristocrat?

"And I'd be remiss if I didn't also share with you that Mr. and Mrs. Brown have quite substantial resources to call upon. The child, should one actually be born, will want for nothing. I mean that quite literally."

"So how would this work exactly?" Mr. Garrison asked.

A question like that, Ned and Janko had agreed ahead of time, would be a good sign. The fact that the young man hadn't left the room already and was at least showing an interest in the practical aspects of his proposed role gave Janko, if not reason actually to hope, at least reason to resume breathing at a more normal rate.

"It's our understanding that you'll be graduating from the university in a few weeks," Ned said.

"That's right."

"Well, first we'd need you to submit to a series of standard medical examinations and tests," Ned explained. "If the results of those are satisfactory, we'd ask you to relocate to San Francisco for a period of time not to exceed six months. Mrs. Brown's physicians believe that either she'll be able to conceive within that amount of time or some other tactic will be called for. During the period when you'll be involved, your housing and all other expenses will be provided and you'll receive a stipend of twenty-five thousand dollars, with a further twenty-five thousand to be paid to you at the end of the six months or upon confirmation of Mrs.

Brown's pregnancy, whichever should occur first. After that, the agreement is concluded and you go on with your life. Except for one thing. On the birth of a healthy infant, you'll receive a final payment of fifty thousand dollars. And Mr. Brown's accountants have done their homework. You are to receive the payments in the form of gifts. For tax purposes, you understand. You won't be required to declare the funds as income at a later time. Those are net sums in other words."

"That's a hundred thousand dollars," Garrison said. "For having sex with some woman I don't know over a period of up to six months."

"In a nutshell," Ned nodded.

"That's crazy," Mr. Garrison said, "if you'll pardon the expression."

"We prefer to describe the situation as rather unusual," Ned said. "I assure you, Mr. and Mrs. Brown are anything but crazy, however."

Garrison shrugged.

"Just for your peace of mind as you consider your decision," Ned said, "although for reasons of security I'm not allowed to show you a photograph of Mrs. Brown, I can tell you that she is twenty-five years old and in perfect health. She is a brunette who is generally considered quite attractive and her weight is in proportion to her height. She actually did some professional modeling in the not too distant past. We're not trying to insert you into 'The Wife of Bath's Tale' or any situation of that sort."

III

Mr. Marconi accompanied Adriana through immigration and customs while Captain Higgins remained with the airplane, preparing it for an immediate return flight should she decide that was necessary. His Grace had been adamant on the point. Adriana must feel free to call the project off at any moment, and she must be accompanied at all times until she was relinquished to Mr. Westerleigh's care. Adriana appreciated her husband's concern but she had gotten herself successfully through immigration and customs without assistance on several continents in the past and didn't see the need for such precautions. She didn't protest, however. Or resist. She quite liked Mr. Marconi and had no intention of being troublesome. She had been to the United States many times but never to its west coast. San Francisco she knew only from songs and photographs. She planned to remedy that if she accomplished nothing else during her visit. At the exit to the customs hall, she saw waiting for her that nice Mr. Westerleigh who had visited them back home. Standing with him was a woman about his age, and Adriana thought at first that she must be Mrs. Westerleigh. But almost immediately she recalled that Janko had told her Mr. Westerleigh was an unmarried man. This, then, must be the companion he had proposed to engage for her while she was in the city. It seemed a thoughtful gesture, to have brought the woman with him to meet Adriana at the airport.

"Mr. Westerleigh," Adriana said. "How nice to see you again."

"The pleasure is mine, Your Grace. I trust that your journey was pleasant."

"I'm a nervous flier, I'm afraid. Even with our expert pilots."

"Well, you're on good old *terra firma* now, at least."

"Yes, thank the gods."

"Please allow me to present Miss Millicent Peabody, Your Grace."

"A pleasure to meet you, Your Grace."

"A pleasure to meet you, Miss Peabody," Adriana said. "Any friend of Mr. Westerleigh is a welcome acquaintance."

"Miss Peabody will be staying at the cottage with Your Grace."

"How nice."

"She's a qualified nurse," Mr. Westerleigh continued, "and she speaks fluent French, as well as fluent German."

"Ah, Mr. Westerleigh," Adriana sighed, feeling suddenly not nearly as brave as she'd believed herself, "*merci. Merci mille fois.* I've been so concerned about my English. Oh, dear Miss Peabody, I'm so pleased that it is you who will be staying with me."

"Don't you worry about a thing, my dear," Miss Peabody said. "Please pardon me, I mean Your Grace, of course."

"I think I rather like being called 'my dear', Miss Peabody," Adriana said. "After all, I'm just simple Mrs. Brown."

* * *

The cottage was enchanting, like something in a storybook. Adriana hardly felt that she was in America at all. The rooms were cozy and comfortably furnished. There was a sitting room with a fireplace and color television, and adjoining it was a small dining room. Upstairs there were two bedrooms, one for Miss Peabody and the larger one for her, outfitted like a chamber for a princess. Outside there was a veranda with breathtaking views of the city and the bay. There was an arbor overgrown with fragrant vines of a species she didn't recognize. Surely Miss Peabody would be able to identify it for her. There was a rose garden just like one of her aunties had cultivated during her retirement in the south of France. It was all so perfect that her anxiety at being so far away from home began to melt away. She marveled at Mr. Westerleigh's ability to anticipate her wishes. Of course, her dear Todor had a hand in the arrangements and the always magnificent Janko never disappointed, but more than anyone's she saw Mr. Westerleigh's work in all this.

"My dear," Miss Peabody said, "wouldn't you like me to fix you a nice cup of tea? And Mr. Westerleigh has laid in a supply of the biscuits we were told you're particularly fond of. Then perhaps you'd like a bath and a nap to help you recover from your journey."

"That all sounds heavenly," Adriana said.

* * *

Mr. Westerleigh had even placed a car and driver at her disposal. Not one of those huge, vulgar American things but a sober, comfortable Peugeot much like the one she drove at home when she didn't want to attract attention. Todor would have preferred to supply her with a Mercedes, but there was something about a Peugeot that Adriana found completely disarming. And Miss Peabody, in addition to her other skills, was an expert, if amateur, tour guide. She had a particular knack for knowing what kinds of things Adriana would be interested in seeing. And, better than that, for knowing just how long an expedition should be allowed to continue before they made a stop somewhere for a light lunch or afternoon tea. Adriana's first several days in the city felt more like a vacation than anything else.

Except, of course, that Todor wasn't with her. Or her mother. Or his mother. Or all three of them, for that matter, driving her crazy with their constant chatter and worrying her to death with their solicitude. She preferred this. And she certainly appreciated the anonymity. Whether or not anything materialized out of this—escapade, she supposed it could best be termed, the experience of seeing a strange city in this manner was something she must remember, must insist on next time someone encouraged her to plan a journey. Perhaps Miss Peabody could even be prevailed upon to accompany her. Dear Miss Peabody. So frightfully well informed, yet so ready to keep her mouth shut in order that Adriana could enjoy everything with a minimum of distraction. What a jewel the woman was. Truly a jewel. How different her mother's life would be with a companion like Miss Peabody instead of the rackety, know-it-all Frau Richter, her companion back home.

* * *

It wasn't a vacation, really. Despite the beauty of the city, the delightful-
ness of the climate, and the congeniality of Miss Peabody's company, Adriana
was never quite able to forget that. Not a word was ever said in her hearing about
the true purpose of her visit, but it remained always in the back of her mind.
Sometimes the awareness of her task crashed in on her, filling her with terrible
anxiety. Miss Peabody seemed to have a sixth sense about this and was inevitably close at hand at such moments. She dispensed hot cups of tea, soothing
bowls of the delicious fruit salad always waiting in the refrigerator—the woman
who prepared their meals was a great believer in fruit salads, apparently—and,
in extreme cases, those funny, tinfoil wrapped chocolates called kisses.

It was like being a girl again and back under the tender but businesslike
care of her governess. Still, Adriana was never quite able to forget that she was
here on a grown woman's mission.

* * *

Then, on the fourth afternoon of her stay, out of nowhere there he was.
Miss Peabody had just served Adriana's tea on the terrace, and he came sauntering across the garden like the hero of a romantic novel.

"Mrs. Brown? Good afternoon. My name is Derek."

As he spoke this name, Adriana saw a tiny flicker of what she later decided was bashful irony. Of course—"Derek" was no more his name than "Mrs.
Brown" was hers.

"How nice to meet you, Derek," she said, as if reading from a script.
Then she summoned Miss Peabody for another cup and saucer.

He stayed less than an hour. After he left she couldn't remember what
they'd spoken of except that their conversation never touched, even peripherally, on the business at hand.

* * *

As that evening wore on, she found herself more and more agitated. Even
the ministrations of dear Miss Peabody were unavailing. The whole thing was
impossible. Derek had been as handsome as any woman could have hoped for
in a companion. And that thick, lustrous hair—what woman wouldn't want to
run her fingers through it? But then, unfortunately, there was the rest of him.

Adriana had a younger brother and a couple of cousins who had gone in
for that sort of thing, spending days on end at the gymnasium grunting like
apes and heaving those heavy weights to and fro as they built their bodies into
caricatures. They went around flexing their ridiculous muscles and looking

grotesque. She had no practical objection to it, really. It gave them something to do. And God knew they all needed a diversion that soaked up their massive energies. But the idea of lying next to something like that, of feeling it pressed against her. . .

She couldn't do it. He seemed like a nice enough young man, and she fully understood the effort and expense dear Todor had gone to, but she just couldn't force herself. She didn't have the will power. She lay there in the darkness thinking of it and her skin seemed to crawl.

Then, just before dawn it came to her. The young man hadn't been selected as a lover for her. She'd known that from the first, and how silly she'd been to react as if he had. He represented, instead, what Todor wished their son to be like someday. Handsome, broad shouldered, stalwart. Equal, really, to any occasion or situation. That was Todor's wish—his vision for the future of his family. Contemplating this realization, Adriana felt her misgivings begin to subside.

Miss Peabody must have noticed that she had spent a restless night and relayed the information. Derek made no repeat visit that day, which Adriana spent reading on the terrace, having declined the offer of even the simplest outing.

* * *

By the next afternoon, however, she was prepared to greet Derek with genuine pleasure when once again he arrived unbidden at tea time. He really was extremely handsome—she hadn't imagined it. And he truly had lovely manners. At first she suspected that his story about having a European mother was just part of the cover that Janko and Mr. Westerleigh had provided for him. But observing his manners over tea, Adriana came to believe that that much of his story was genuine. As pleasant and eager to please as Americans were, they generally seemed flummoxed in the matter of truly refined manners. Either they were oblivious to the way in which things were supposed to be done or they knew too well what etiquette demanded and overdid their observance of it. But Derek struck just the right note. He was as natural as breathing, and Adriana felt certain that this was not something which he could have been taught over a period of days or even weeks. That mother of his—she was the real thing.

* * *

Each afternoon he came to tea. And each afternoon he left within the hour. He gave no indication that he had any expectations beyond that. He had apparently been instructed not to suggest further meetings, not to invite himself inside the cottage, even. He seemed perfectly satisfied to wait for her to take the lead in any and all things. She couldn't help admiring his delicacy and restraint.

Finally she was ready to move forward, and she suggested that they have dinner together. One dinner became two, became a week of dinners, and still he exhibited no impatience. No temperament of any kind, really, other than that sunny, easy going disposition and those unfailingly beautiful manners. Every time Adriana saw him, he seemed to have gotten better looking.

* * *

Adriana had always thought of her beloved Todor as the most considerate of lovers. He was always concerned not to hurt her or force her into acts which might distress her in any way. He was tender and loving, and she did adore lying in his arms and feeling how special she was to him. Her friends told all kinds of stories and alluded to many different experiences having to do with sex, but hardly anything of what they said made sense to her. It was as wildly speculative as after lights-out chatter in the dormitory of her old school. The reality was much simpler. It was about dear Todor and those feelings of closeness in the darkness, and if other aspects of it made her a little uncomfortable she ignored them because wives understood that there were things about their husbands— and particularly the way their husbands' bodies differed so completely from their own—that simply must be accommodated. Not merely to make their husbands happy, but for the noble womanly purpose of bringing children into the world. And so when she anticipated the moment that Derek and she were together like that, alone in the darkness, she supposed that it would be very much like it was with Todor. A little messy but not really very distressing, and over with quickly.

But it wasn't at all as she had imagined it. It was, instead, the way her friends had described it. And for the first time their stories made sense. She was astounded. Shocked almost beyond reason. It was not at anything Derek did, however, but at her own responses. She had never imagined such sensations. Her body, it turned out, was a repository of astonishing powers just waiting to be awakened. She felt a little guilty at first at the way Derek was able to unlock all her unsuspected secrets without even seeming to try. But she soon came to believe that this, as much as any pleasure she would eventually experience in motherhood, was what she was meant to receive in exhange for giving Todor what he felt he must have.

As for Derek, Adriana had no idea what recompense he was to receive. She assumed that money, presumably a substantial amount of it, was to change hands. But that was between him and her husband. Yet she sensed that this was not enough. She came to believe that she must express an appreciation separate from whatever agreement had been made between gentlemen, though she couldn't imagine what form it might take. It came to her one morning in her bath and it was as simple, really, as the sunny morning, the roses in the garden, the breezes off the bay. She must learn everything there was that the young man could teach her about her body.

* * *

When it happened, she knew it immediately. She cried out so that Derek paused and asked her if he had hurt her. By answer, she kissed him as if her life depended on it, and the moment passed. But not the memory of it.

When she woke the next morning, she was still certain. As certain as she had ever been of anything. It would be a couple of weeks before a doctor could confirm it, but her certainty never flagged.

IV

"Thank you for coming by," Ned Westerleigh said. "I hope you didn't have any trouble finding your way here."

"Your directions were very clear," Lance said.

"I'm glad. Can I offer you anything? Tea, coffee?"

"A glass of water, thanks."

"Coming right up."

As always, Lance was neat, freshly shaven, as crisply turned out as a military cadet on leave. He was casually dressed but nevertheless totally presentable. It was a joy to see. Young men were so slovenly these days that Ned despaired of them. But a specimen like this went a long way toward redeeming them all in his eyes. He understood the current impulse toward more anarchic manners of self presentation, but he was fairly certain he'd never be able to approve of it aesthetically.

"Just set the tray right there, Winthrop," Ned said, "and Mr. Garrison will take a glass of water, please."

Winthrop was exactly the sort of young man Ned despaired of, but his business partner, Sonny, wouldn't hear a word against him. For now. Ned had never expected to miss Giselle, which just went to show you.

"Thank you, Winthrop," Ned said, when Winthrop seemed inclined to linger.

"Very welcome I'm sure, sir."

"Close the door on your way out, won't you?"

"As you wish."

It was almost as if Sonny had instructed Winthrop to spy on this interview. Ned had made this appointment specifically for a day Sonny would be out of the office, and he didn't want Winthrop's curiosity or misplaced loyalty gumming up the works.

"First of all, Lance," Ned said, "you'll be happy to know that Mrs. Brown arrived home safely. And the family doctors have confirmed that she is indeed expecting a child. So I'm instructed to hand over to you this check in payment of the second installment, as per our agreement. If you'll just sign this receipt, please."

"Certainly."

Ned watched as the young man scanned the document and then signed it.

"In addition, they've asked me to communicate to you their sincere thanks. Mrs. Brown was particularly appreciative."

"My pleasure."

"Now, we'll need you to let us know how you can be contacted if and when it's time for the final installment to be disbursed. What are your plans? Do you mind sharing them with me?"

"Actually," Lance said, "I really like it here in San Francisco. I don't know what I was expecting before I got here. But it's kind of gotten under my skin. I think I'd like to stay on."

"What do you think you'll do here?"

"My first love is photography, Mr. Westerleigh."

"Please, my boy, call me Ned. With this business satisfactorily concluded, I believe we can dispense with formalities."

"Well, Ned, I'm thinking about using some of this money to set up my own studio."

"I see. Portraiture, I assume? Weddings? That sort of thing?"

"I suppose that's what it will be," Lance said, "to start with at least. My true interests lie in a somewhat different direction, but you have to make a living."

"Indeed. Well, you'll have to have an appropriate facility to operate a business like that."

"I've been looking already," Lance said, "but I haven't gotten very far with it. I don't really know the city well enough."

"Perhaps you'd let me be of help in that regard," Ned said. "As you will have noticed on your way in, in my day to day existence I'm in real estate. And as it happens, I know of a property that you might find ideal."

"Oh?"

"Yes. And the location is a very good one for the kind of clientele you'll want to cultivate."

"That's very kind of you, Ned," Lance said, "but I wouldn't want to put you out."

"Nonsense," Ned insisted.

* * *

When the Browns first inserted themselves into his life, Lance was scheduled to graduate in a few weeks. He had originally planned to continue his studies. He had no idea what practical use he would be able to make of a master's degree in physics, but he had applied and been accepted to a graduate program. It wasn't a ploy to stay out of the military. The days of student deferments were over. The extremely high number he had drawn in the draft lottery was all the insurance he needed on that score. It was, rather, a way of staying on at the university in order to remain in contact with his coaches and continue his preparation for the Munich Olympics.

Then those men showed up.

He had sensed something about to happen. A couple of his professors had looked at him strangely in the days leading up to the visit. The head coach had made some kind of remark, half under his breath, when they ran into each other one afternoon. Lance hadn't heard it clearly. He only perceived its cryptic nature instinctively. But something was up. Either that or he was getting paranoid. There was a lot of that around. It was practically an epidemic on campus. He supposed the local student radicals were behind it.

A few mornings later there was a note from the Athletic Director inviting Lance—though he read it as an order—to report to his office. When he arrived, exactly on time, the A.D.'s administrative assistant escorted him to a conference room, and there they were.

The Englishman was tall and distinguished looking. He gave the impression of being James Bond's uncle. The Slav—at least his accent sounded Slavic—was blond and severely handsome. He looked like an Olympic Decathlete a decade or so after winning his bronze medal. What the two men shared were a decided military air and expensive clothing that seemed to have been selected for a combination of nondescriptness and excellent fit.

* * *

It was a lot of money. The first installment alone would buy him a Ferrari. The second, a speedboat. He could go to Los Angeles, rent an apartment on the beach, and date starlets. But it wasn't things that he was really interested in. The money represented opportunity. He really hadn't thought beyond the Munich Olympics, but now he had to.

He was in no doubt about his ability to perform the task. It seemed ridiculously easy.

He graduated on schedule and left the very next morning on his motorcycle for San Francisco. He traveled in stages. A stop in Los Angeles, which disappointed him, though he couldn't have said why. A drive up the coast through spectacular landscapes that made him feel like he was in a movie. Then on to the city.

The Englishman, whose name was Ned, met him on his arrival. He had everything arranged.

* * *

It wouldn't be accurate to say that Lance fell in love with San Francisco. He'd never been in love. It wasn't a capacity he recognized in himself. Not for person, place, or thing. What he did was form impressions. Strong ones, actually, that this person or that thing or such and such a place met his requirements better than any other member of its category, and that made his decision for him. Hence his Triumph Trident. Hence his twin Leicas. Hence a long—but admittedly very thin—line of friends and former lovers. That's how it worked. Sometimes his selections resulted from extensive research. Sometimes the certainty just struck him. But it was always clear-headed knowledge, unadulterated by emotionalism, of what he had to have to move a single step further in his life. That was the insight he'd experienced his first week in the city, walking up and down its hills, studying its architecture, sniffing its air and listening to its vibrations, as he waited for Mrs. Brown to materialize.

Long before she did, his mind was made up.

* * *

He was not truly lacking in human impulses. He sincerely liked people and things. He liked them extravagantly in some cases. But it was always liking, never loving. What he experienced internally was never a lion rampaging across the veldt. It was a giant sheepdog instead, perfectly disciplined, trained to the leash, instantly obedient to any and all commands. And because his "likes" were so completely under his own control, he found he never had to have expecations of anyone. He could take them as they were or leave them, but in either case without emotional investment.

Paradoxically, this made him almost supernaturally empathetic. It was, he understood, the true secret of his success with Mrs. Brown. He could honestly say that he hadn't spent a moment in her company, not a single one, thinking about the money. Yet at the same time he hadn't thought much about the sex. At least not in terms of what pleasure he stood to experience from being in bed with a woman, a gorgeous woman it had to be admitted, only a few years older than himself. He focused simply on being present, and when the moment came, on giving her whatever it was she believed she wanted from him.

He hadn't fallen in love with her. He was never supposed to have fallen in love with her, but the degree to which there had never been any danger of it might well have astonished most observers, considering how beautiful, how refined, how charming she was. Presumably those astonished would have included her husband.

No, he hadn't fallen in love with Mrs. Brown, sublime as she was. He didn't suffer a single pang, after she left, at the idea of never seeing her again. And he didn't fall in love with the city, either. But by the time of Mrs. Brown's happy departure, he knew that he couldn't live anywhere else.

* * *

Ned Westerleigh was invaluable. Lance could have found an apartment, selected a location for his business, gotten himself set up generally, without help. There would have been no excuse for a man with as much money as Lance had in the bank not to launch himself successfully. But going it alone would have been inefficient and slow. He would certainly have made mistakes. Ned's assistance made it all happen quickly and smoothly. And Ned's referrals got him his first jobs. Weddings. Portraits of the graduating class at St. Dunstan's, an exclusive school for boys north of the city. Photos of houses Ned had listed for sale in some of the most expensive neighborhoods in the region. It was more than Lance would have expected of anyone, but

Ned acted like none of the arrangements he made on Lance's behalf was a big deal. It was as if Lance had acquired a fairy godfather. It was as if Ned read his mind and understood his exact requirements before he could voice them. Best of all, Ned knew a man who knew a man who lived in San Bruno and had been assistant coach of the Czech Olympic wrestling team until defecting just after the Tokyo games. Thus, Ned was even able to arrange for Lance to continue his training for the Olympic trials more or less uninterrupted. That had been the clincher.

When Lance thought about it carefully, he decided that in going it alone he would have missed out on a friendship he sensed he would appreciate deeply as the city became truly his home. That friendship was probably destined to mean more to him than any of the practical matters Ned actually handled on his behalf.

* * *

The one thing Lance did on his own was find a gym. He was certain Ned would have a suggestion to make in that regard, because it seemed that there was nothing about the city Ned wasn't conversant with, but Lance didn't ask. His search was painstaking and comprehensive. He ended up joining an out of the way, rather down at the heel establishment an inconvenient distance from his apartment. It wasn't his first choice according to any criterion but one. He had nothing against homosexuals—truly, nothing. And it wasn't as if he was looking for a gym that was completely free of them. That, he had realized early in his search, would have been all but impossible in San Francisco. He wanted to be left alone, that was all. At all of the gyms he preferred in other respects to the one he actually joined, homosexuals were too present, too friendly, too welcoming. He didn't want to have to explain himself. Speaking respectfully but forthrightly was insufficiently discouraging to a small but persistent minority of them, it seemed, and he refused to be placed in a position of having to be forceful, or worse, obnoxious, in expressing his wish that they ignore him. He knew that what he was asking of them was contrary to their instincts. He accepted that. He didn't assign blame. He was flattered by the attention they paid him because of his looks and his physique. Exactly as he would have been, he told himself, if the attention had come from women instead. He didn't find it offensive in the least. What it was was distracting. That was what he couldn't tolerate. If and when he decided he wanted anything from men like that, he knew where to find them. And that went for women as well. His focus was on starting his business and on training for the Munich Olympics. Those two things. Only those two. The city itself inspired him. That was all he needed.

* * *

He knew some people would call him a hypocrite for choosing his gym on such a basis after happily accepting all that assistance from Ned Westerleigh, but he saw no inconsistency in it. Ned was homosexual, sure. But Ned was the kind of homosexual who gave them all a good name. Every time Lance had mentioned wanting to return some favor or other Ned was doing him, Ned made a specific suggestion as to how it might be done. And not a single one of his suggestions involved a sexual component. Ned understood, no, he exemplified, the reality that between men such as them a *quid pro quo* of a totally businesslike nature actually could exist. It was probably the characteristic Lance appreciated most in his benefactor.

Lance recalled this one night a month or so after opening his studio. He'd been contracted to do wedding photos by a prominent family, the Molinaris, and he was packing up at the end of the night after finishing with candid shots at the reception, when he was approached by a man who was, he could tell instantly, Ned's polar opposite. He introduced himself as Sonny Dallas and engaged Lance in a conversation consisting almost entirely on his side of double entendres and other suggestive talk. He was creepy and his eyes were downright rapacious. This was the sort of individual Lance wanted to avoid at all costs. It wasn't his first encounter with such a man, nor his second or even third. He wasn't angered by the approach, merely dismayed. He turned Mr. Dallas down as charmingly and inoffensively as he was able.

* * *

"Ned, old man."

"Good morrow, Sonny."

Ned knew Sonny liked it when he spoke in a rough approximation of Shakespearean English. Usually he couldn't be bothered to indulge that fetish, but just occasionally, like this morning, he was in a mood to play along.

"Good weekend?"

"Not bad," Ned said. Now that he looked carefully, he didn't much like the glint in Sonny's eyes. He'd seen that glint before, lots of times, and it always meant trouble—or at least the prospect of it. "You?"

"Met the most remarkable young man Saturday night," Sonny said. "Just really amazing, you know? He was taking the photographs at Andrea

Molinari's wedding. Name of Lance Garrison. I asked Cleo Molinari about him, and do you know what she told me? Silly question. Of course you know what she told me. She told me you recommended him. You've known about that spectacular young man for goodness knows how long, yet you said nothing about him to your nearest and dearest. I can't tell you how disappointed in you I am."

V

The young man was more handsome than Stefano had realized seeing him on stage. The facial features had more refinement than was apparent from that distance, and the hair was of a thicker, more luxuriant texture. The juxtaposition of that head with that physique represented an ideal that Stefano found especially compelling. Add in his youth, and the result was formidable.

"Congratulations," he said. The young man had just won the Mr. San Francisco Bodybuilding Championships.

"Thanks," the young man answered, his eyes slightly glassy.

Well of course. He had to be exhausted. And starving.

"Seriously," Stefano smiled. "Really tough group of competitors. Impressive win."

"I didn't expect to come in first," the young man said, "not really. I was just hoping to make the top five."

Stefano heard it—that whiff of the east coast. Not New York. But not as far north as Boston. Connecticut, he decided, but far enough away to be out of the commuter belt.

"A couple of them were bigger than you, certainly," Stefano said, "but nobody else had the proportions and refinement."

"Size isn't everything," the young man said.

"Such an important lesson, yet so few men ever learn it. I'm Stefano, by the way," he said, offering his hand.

"Lance."

"Pleasure," Stefano said. "Well, I shouldn't keep you. I'm sure you have people to meet."

"Actually," Lance said. "I'm here on my own."

"Really."

That didn't seem possible. These young bodybuilders generally traveled with at least a buddy or two. And often, Stefano knew, a girlfriend. Girlfriends seemed as indispensable to young bodybuilders as Stefano's service revolver was when he went on duty. And for much the same reasons.

"Well, in that case," Stefano said. "I'd be honored if you'd let me treat you to a celebratory dinner. You must be starving. I've competed myself. I know how it feels after a contest."

"That's very kind," Lance said, "but I couldn't."

"Why not?" Stefano asked.

The reason was obvious. That insane tango between men who didn't know each other. If either of them had been female there wouldn't have been any problem. At least not at that point in the evening.

"Come on," Stefano said. "I insist."

They went to a place Stefano knew in North Beach. He was right. Lance was starving. Stefano recalled all too well the feeling of almost total depletion which followed competing in a bodybuilding show. You dieted ruthlessly for the last several weeks prior to the event so as to achieve your optimum condition and then the exertion of the competition itself nearly put you flat on your back. Still, Lance didn't gorge. He ate slowly, apparently savoring each bite. He ate neatly, almost as if he was at his own mother's table.

* * *

"You really should give my gym a try," Stefano said, as Lance tossed his gym bag into the back of his Volkswagen van. "Great guys there. Serious bodybuilders. No posers. And all the best equipment."

"I'll think about it," Lance said, smiling. "Thanks for dinner."

"My pleasure," Stefano said. "You've got my number."

"Yeah," Lance said. "About that."

"What?"

"I don't. . ." Lance said. The silence grew awkward. "It's just, oh hell, you know what I'm talking about. Not saying I think you're like that, you understand. Just putting my cards on the table. Always a few of those guys at bodybuilding contests. I get it. It's a free country. They've got a right to go wherever they want, and God knows they're an appreciative audience. Enthusiastic as hell, actually."

"Didn't mean this as a pickup," Stefano said, although he halfway had.

"And I don't mean I thought you did," Lance said, "I just don't go that way. So there's no misunderstanding."

"Sure," Stefano said.

"But thanks again. Really."

* * *

So that was that. Stefano wasn't supposed to be looking, but Bentley was taking his own good time. It had been months since he'd showed up on Auntie Violetta's doorstep. He should have arrived in San Francisco if he was coming. Each week when she called, Auntie Violetta told Stefano to be patient just a little longer. So he was. But meanwhile that business was hypothetical and he was under no obligations, either to her or to Bentley. And that Lance. Lance was the choicest thing he'd laid eyes on since coming to San Francisco. Still, Lance said he wasn't in the market for what Stefano would be offering if Stefano actually offered, and if he wasn't, he wasn't. Stefano wasn't the type that went around thinking every hot guy in the world could be had, that they were all secretly gay and just needed a good firm shove to get them through the closet door. Stefano believed it was beneath him to argue the point with guys like that. And besides, there were plenty of available ones, even if they weren't exactly what you wanted. He could have them, maintain his dignity, and avoid misunderstandings. So that's what he did.

And Lance said he wasn't, so he wasn't.

Maybe when Stefano ran into him at the California championships next spring, things would be different. And maybe they wouldn't.

Maybe by then Bentley would have shown up and it wouldn't matter anyway. But that Lance. God damn.

* * *

Stefano put Lance out of his mind, or at least tried to, and went back to thinking exclusively about Bentley.

Every now and then some young man would show up at his gym who reminded him of one or the other of them enough that he couldn't help taking an interest. Sometimes they were the type he could take home with him for a night or two, but of course statistics dictated that usually they weren't. But while there was always the evil science of statistics to consider, it was balanced perennially in his hopes by the sublime reality of fate, which, he believed, would hardly have exerted itself so strenuously as it had to bring him to the present time and location only to abandon him to perpetual solitude and dreams unfulfilled. He chose to believe that the universe he inhabited didn't work that way. If a desire existed its fulfillment must also exist, at least potentially. So he remained committed to that potential. He prepared himself daily for it to materialize.

Time passed slowly, but it passed.

* * *

One minute Stefano was shaking parmesan onto his pasta and the next minute he looked up and Lance was sitting across the booth from him. It had been a couple of months since their first meeting. Lance hadn't used the number Stefano had given him and Stefano hadn't tried to find him, which, as a police officer, he was pretty sure he could have done if he'd wanted to. Fellow cops did it all the time even though they were not supposed to. Stefano had been to at least one wedding that resulted from "non-regulation" activities of that type.

"They told me at your gym that you come here sometimes on Friday nights."

"They told you that, did they?" Stefano grinned. Not provocatively, he hoped. "Well, it looks like they were right. Here I am. I'd tell you to have a seat but you already did."

"Yeah."

"What do you want?" Stefano said, "I'll call the waiter over."

"Already ate," Lance said. "Thanks anyway."

"You sure?"

"I'm sure."

"You training for the Cal State?" Stefano asked. "Look pretty hard under that shirt."

He hoped it didn't sound provocative. He hadn't really meant it that way. Or only about half.

"Working on a couple of things," Lance said, "but I don't think I'll be doing the Californias for another season."

"Things?" Stefano grunted. "Like what?"

"Olympic trials in the spring," Lance said. "I wrestled in college."

"Really? Any good at it?"

"Ranked number five nationally in my class."

"So it's not just a pipe dream," Stefano said. "Well, good luck to you. I don't know the first thing about wrestling. At least not the kind of wrestling you guys do."

That got a grin out of Lance. Just a tiny one.

"You said a couple of things," Stefano said. "Wrestling's just one thing."

"I hate to seem like the kind of guy who just shows up out of nowhere and asks for a favor," Lance said.

"But you need one," Stefano said. "You sure you aren't hungry?"

"I told you. I already ate."

"That better be the truth."

"You want to hear the menu?" Lance said. "Two grilled chicken breasts with no skin, fresh spinach with lemon juice on it, and two baked potatoes, completely bare. Healthier than what you're eating."

"It's my cheat day," Stefano said.

"No kidding."

"What's the favor?"

"Maybe you remember I told you I have my own photography business."

"Sure."

"I want to branch out."

"Branch out how?"

"I want to do physique photography," Lance said. "Legitimate stuff only, not talking about pornography."

"O.K."

"Thing is, other than looking at a few guys' work I don't know anything about it. And I was thinking. The best way to learn anything is just to do it, right?"

"Right."

"Which means I need a model. Somebody who'll be patient with me while I make the mistakes and learn the ropes. Somebody who'll be discreet. Somebody I can trust."

"Uh huh."

"Somebody I can stand taking several thousand pictures of over the next few months. Somebody whose body can teach me everything I need to know about taking pictures of men."

"What makes you think I'm the guy?"

"Been to your gym several times, actually," Lance said. "Checked you out."

"I know. I saw you there."

"You didn't say anything."

"You didn't look like you wanted to be spoken to."

"I didn't," Lance said, "and you got that. That's the other reason I'm here right now."

* * *

It wasn't at all what Stefano had been expecting. For starters, Lance's place was on a really good stretch of Union Street. Boutiques and bistros. A few antique shops. Expensive cars parked at the curb. And when he went inside there was nothing seedy about the studio. It was clean and pleasantly decorated. Lance had said he wanted to be legit, and the place screamed it.

"Can I help you, sir?" The receptionist looked like Barbie's roommate— what was her name? "I'm afraid we're about to close."

"I have an appointment with Lance," Stefano said, setting down his gym bag.

"Oh," the girl said. "You must be Mr. Fabiani."

So she knew about him, and, presumably, Lance's plans. She must be the girlfriend. That would explain everything—or almost.

"Yes," Stefano said. "That's me."

"I'll tell him you're here."

* * *

Every Thursday after that Stefano went to Lance's studio when he got off shift. Lance and he pored over the previous week's proof sheets, critiqued them thoroughly, talked about poses, lighting, backdrops, developing, and every other conceivable detail of the process. Then they shot some more. They shot in black and white. They shot in color. Stefano posed in posing trunks, g-strings, and eventually the nude. Lance might not swing his way, but he obviously understood that the kind of work he was trying to learn to do sometimes involved nudity and wasn't fazed by it. Stefano quickly recognized he had judged Lance correctly. The kid was serious. He was as serious as Stefano had ever seen anybody about anything. If nothing else, the project had to be costing him the earth in film and supplies.

Stefano couldn't help but be impressed with his commitment.

* * *

Week after week. Pose after pose. Shot after shot. Lance's eyes. Stefano's muscles. Lance's hands. Stefano's bare skin.

The lights. The camera. The intent look on Lance's face. The intensity in Lance's eyes.

And later, huddled together over the proof sheets. Voices barely audible. Foreheads almost touching.

It wasn't just the technical stuff Lance was working to master. Lance was working toward a new and comprehensive understanding of the male body. Feeling Lance's hands on him as he adjusted the extension of an arm here, the angle of the head there, Stefano realized that in his whole life nobody had known, really known, his body the way Lance was coming to. As they ranged over Stefano's body Lance's hands gave it life in a way it had never been alive before. In a strange way it was far more profound than if they'd actually had sex. The connection Stefano sensed between them was almost enough to explain how some men could be celibate for life, or in relationships with women, though Stefano knew he'd never be satisfied with that and suspected that Lance wouldn't either even though he might not have realized it yet.

* * *

"What do you think?" Lance asked, as they looked at the latest batch of proofs.

"I think you've got it down," Stefano marveled. For the life of him, he couldn't think of one detail to criticize. Lance was a genius, no doubt about it.

"No," Lance said, "no I don't. There's something I'm still missing."

Stefano gazed at the photos for a moment and then closed his eyes.

"I have an idea," he said. "It's going to sound crazy."

"I know what it is," Lance nodded. "I pose. And you take the shots. We set them up together so that all you have to do is get me into the positions properly and then click the shutter. You're absolutely right. I'll never really get it unless I experience it from the other side of the lens. Some guys can, of course. But that's not how I comprehend things."

"Didn't know you were a mind reader," Stefano said.

"I'm not," Lance said. "It's not surprising that we came up with the same idea at the same time as closely as we've been working together on this."

"Just about gave me the willies," Stefano said.

* * *

So they went through the whole process again exactly like the first time, except this time it was Stefano's hands on Lance's bare skin—never a flinch, not once. His hands on Lance's body transformed them. They sensed, they knew, they understood. Stefano's hands had never had that kind of wisdom before and if Bentley ever showed up, watch out. His eyes, squinting as he placed Lance into just the right position in front of the camera, became new eyes. It was an experience like no other in his life. Coming to know the male body in its totality without resort to sex. Before this, he would have told you such a thing was impossible. He still believed it was for almost everyone. But for his buddy Lance it wasn't. Nor was it, eventually, for Stefano himself. It was a new reality. It was a different reality. It was a reality that called into question his previous understanding of what constituted reality. And in pursuit of it, he had become a stronger, truer, finer man than he had suspected it was possible to be. That's what Lance was giving him, and, quite frankly, why he found Lance so fascinating yet at the same time frightening.

* * *

And still Bentley was a no-show.

* * *

Then they took a break. Lance went off for a preliminary round of the Olympic trials. Stefano drove him to the airport, where they exchanged the manliest of hugs. Truly, a hug with old style passion but without a hint of implication. The Gods of Olympus hugged that way. Stefano was sure of it. Watching Lance walk into the terminal, Stefano had only been that terrified once before in his life, on that medevac flight out of 'Nam, thinking of Bentley by himself in the boonies.

He pored over the newspapers every morning for results of the trials. He was distracted at work. He'd never been one for indulging in "what if?" but found himself pondering the horrible possibility that Lance would fail in his quest.

The proofs they huddled over together the night after Lance's triumphant return told the tale. Stefano could see, and Lance was finally prepared to admit, that he truly had it.

"Friday night," he told Stefano. "Cancel all your dates. I'm taking you out to dinner to celebrate."

* * *

Stefano hadn't been to Lance's apartment before, and just like with the studio it wasn't at all what he was expecting. In his experience, guys Lance's age didn't have that kind of taste even if they had the money. It made him curious, but buddies didn't ask questions like that. Buddies waited until explanations were given or silently did without. That was how it worked.

"Great restaurant," Stefano said, "you shouldn't have spent that kind of money, but thanks."

"Don't talk crazy," Lance smiled. "You know what you've done for me? You've helped me make my dream come true. It's the greatest thing anyone has ever done for me, and I'm not sure any other person in the world could have. How can you put a price on that?"

"Making me a little nervous here," Stefano chuckled, "all this philosophical talk."

"Seriously, Stefano," Lance said. "Dinner was just dinner. I still owe you. Don't think I don't understand that."

Suddenly Stefano recognized the look in Lance's eyes. And had Lance been standing quite that close to him a moment ago?

"I mean it," Lance said. "Anything you want from me. Anything at all."

"Huh?"

"Yes, including that. Just say the word. As long as you understand that it's a one time deal."

"Lance, no," Stefano said. "We worked through all that a long time ago."

"Did we?"

"Didn't we?" Stefano asked. "I thought so."

"You've been a perfect gentleman through this whole thing," Lance said, "but you're a man. The real thing. You want what you want. You can't help it. I know how that works. And God knows you deserve it."

"You said anything."

"I know what you guys do, Stefano," Lance said. "It's O.K."

"All right," Stefano said.

He leaned in. He kissed Lance slow and deep and real. Lance didn't kiss back, not quite, but he didn't resist. There was no question in Stefano's mind that Lance was ready to go through with it. He could feel it in the relaxed alertness of the muscles inside the thin fabric of the shirt and in the slow, steady heartbeat underneath that. He could have this. Every bit. He could even see them still being friends afterward. That's how solid Lance had proven himself to be.

"Nice," Stefano said. "Very, very nice."

Lance began unbuttoning his shirt.

Stefano reached up and stopped his hand.

"No, buddy," he said, "that's all. Paid in full."

VI

"Five doctors, Janko," the duke said. "Five different doctors have examined my son. All of them are Jewish, so you can be certain they know what they're talking about. There can't be any question about it."

"Indeed, Your Grace."

"At or above the ninety-eighth percentile in each and every measurement they track. Size, strength, neurological development."

"Surely Your Grace didn't need the testimony of medical professionals to know that His Lordship is an exceptional baby."

"Of course not," the duke smiled, "but what are medical professionals for if not to confirm one's own observations?"

"Well put, Your Grace."

"And Her Grace couldn't be happier. She's glowing. Surely you've noticed. Motherhood fulfills her. She's a new woman."

"It is most gratifying, Your Grace," Janko said, "to see the two of you so happy. And Her Grace, the dowager duchess, as well."

"Exactly," the duke said. "Her above all. My father's legacy, what? I can't express my gratitude lavishly enough, my friend. Of all the things you have done for our family over the years, this is the greatest."

"I'm deeply moved, Your Grace. It is a wonderful thing, to feel one has been of service."

"Yes, well, Janko, about that. I'm afraid that you've fallen into the worst of all possible traps."

"Your Grace?"

"Great successes imply even greater possibilities, as it were."

"I see," Janko said.

"Is there any possibility, do you think?"

"One can only ask," Janko said.

"You'll want to give your friend a call. You'd have to go to America soon anyway to supervise the payment of the final installment. But if at the same time you were to find a way of raising the possibility that the agreement might be renewed, it would truly make the journey worth while."

"I'm sure Mr. Westerleigh and I will find a way of approaching the subject with the young man."

"I'll alert Captain Higgins to prepare for the flight to America."

"Actually, Your Grace," Janko said, "the flight will be much shorter than that."

"Oh?"

"We'll be going to Munich."

"Oh?"

"Don't you recall my telling you that the young man had earned a place on the United States Olympic Team?"

"So you did, Janko, so you did. In my excitement over His Lordship I forgot all about it."

* * *

As luck would have it, Ned Westerleigh was already in London for the wedding of a distant relative to another distant relative, both the bride and groom coming from titled families. And with even greater good fortune, his schedule and affairs permitted a side trip. The routing to Munich by way of London took surprisingly little additional time.

"My dear Mr. Krieger," Ned said, boarding the plane where Janko was waiting in the passenger cabin, "what a pleasure it is to see you again."

"The pleasure is mine, Ned."

"I have to say I'm not in the least surprised at this turn of events."

"Nor I, Ned. Nor I."

* * *

Security around the Olympic Village was tight in the aftermath of the terrible attack on the Israeli athletes, but Ned proved his incalculable worth yet again. A couple of telephone calls that morning was all it required to gain them access. They moved through the checkpoints with no delay whatever.

Ned had arranged through a representative of the U.S. Olympic Committee to meet with Lance in a private office. If he was surprised to see them, he gave no indication of it.

"First of all," Ned said, "congratulations on your placing. Competition in that weight class was remarkable."

"I would have liked a medal to take home with me, of course," Lance smiled.

"In that respect," Ned said, "it's probably better that you placed fifth than fourth."

"You got that right," Lance laughed. "Seen much of the Games?"

"Mr. Krieger and I just arrived in Munich this morning."

"Right."

"We don't want to keep you," Ned said, "so why don't we get right down to the reason for our meeting?"

"Fine," Lance nodded.

"First of all, there's the matter of the remaining installment. I have here a check for fifty thousand dollars and an additional check for twenty-five thousand dollars which the Browns would like you to accept as a kind of bonus. That's how pleased they are with the way things have turned out. The child, as Mr. Krieger here can tell you, is hale and hearty. He is the baby's godfather, as a matter of fact."

"He's a fine boy," Janko nodded.

"I'm glad," Lance smiled. "Glad they're pleased, glad the baby is well. And I won't pretend I'm not pleased that you've brought the money. But Ned, seriously, I have nowhere to keep those checks here in the village. I would have to sign them in at the security desk, which would probably be safe enough, but they'd ask all kinds of questions—you understand?"

Ned and Janko had discussed this during the flight from London. They decided it was a kind of a test to see if Lance was truly as level headed as they both recalled. Before his departure, Janko had insisted on obtaining the duke's permission to abort the next phase of the mission should either of them think it necessary, but now Lance had renewed their faith in him.

"Perhaps you'd allow me to hold them for safekeeping," Ned suggested, "until you return to the States."

"Would you mind doing that for me?"

"Not at all, my boy. Happy to be of service. As always."

"You're one in a million, Ned," Lance said. "You know that, don't you, Mr. Krieger? Our Ned is one in a million?"

"I assure you, Mr. Garrison," Janko said, "no one knows his value better than I do."

"Good," Lance said. "Now about the other thing. You did say 'first of all', didn't you Ned?"

"Indeed I did," Ned smiled. "As I told you, the Browns couldn't be happier with the new addition to their family. So much so that they've asked Mr. Krieger and me to approach you about the possibility of renewing the arrangement."

"You mean they want another child?"

"Yes," Janko said. "That is the case. They would very much like another child. And, if you are agreeable to it, they'd like the second to be as closely related to the first as possible."

"Same arrangements as before," Ned said, "but a slightly different fee structure."

"How different?" Lance asked.

"A total of two hundred thousand dollars, paid out in installments divided as previously. Same arrangements with regard to taxation, as well."

"That's an awful lot of money."

"As you say," Janko nodded. "The Browns think of it as an investment in their family's future."

"As it could be in your own," Ned suggested.

"I get that."

"Perhaps you need time to think about this," Ned suggested.

"The Browns understand that your circumstances may have changed," Janko said. "Their request may entail more and different complications for you than last time. If you feel you need to say no, don't hesitate."

"It's fine," Lance said. "I'll be happy to help out."

* * *

"It's a lot of money for a man his age," Janko said as they drove back to Munich airport.

"Undoubtedly," Ned agreed.

"I hope he won't come to harm under its influence."

"It's always a concern," Ned said.

"There are such distressing stories," Janko said. "The Lord Konrad, for instance."

"Ah, but you have him well in hand, don't you? That's certainly what one is given to understand."

"I do my best," Janko said, "but I shudder to think what might have happened to him."

"As you say. And for every Lord Konrad, with a wise and stalwart protector such as yourself, there are dozens of others."

"So many," Janko agreed.

"Try not to worry too much about it," Ned said. "My associates and I keep a close eye on young Mr.Garrison. So far he hasn't put a foot wrong. And do you know what? I don't believe he's going to. He has successfully started his own business with the money he's received so far. And I'm going to try and interest him in investing in real estate with his new windfall."

"Excellent plan, Ned," Janko said. "Something that will offer him security for the long term."

"Exactly," Ned said. "Now tell me, my friend, just between the two of us."

"Yes?"

"Where do you see this going? Over the long term, you understand."

"His Grace has always regretted that his family was so small when he and Lord Konrad were young. I know he feels that it is better for children to grow up among many brothers and sisters."

VII

Returning to the city was like being reunited with an old friend. At the first few glimpses of the skyline through the airplane windows, Adriana didn't feel like a stranger at all. Her few weeks spent here over a year ago, short as they had been, seemed enormously significant, more so than she realized as she had first held the baby to her breast. It was as if the months since then had been the vacation and here was her real life. Dear Ned Westerleigh met her at the airport, Millicent Peabody at his side. He had employed the very same driver and the same Peugeot. The only difference she could see was that the cottage had received a fresh coat of paint.

* * *

But she was seeing it all with different eyes. On her return home the year before, she had made a casual remark about the extreme fancifulness of Miss Peabody's stories. This earned her the coldest of looks from Janko, something she had never before experienced. It shocked her. But before she could protest or ask how she had given offense, he said "*Please understand, Your Grace, that our friend, Mr. Westerleigh, would never consider engaging a person of questionable character as your companion while you are in San Francisco. I have made thorough investigations myself, and the lady you mention is no Baroness Munchausen. All those experiences she speaks of, though you find them so unbelievable, are nevertheless true in their essentials. I have not heard her stories myself. It may well be that she embroiders them somewhat with regard to insignificant detail, as people almost invariably do, but she is a remarkable woman who has done remarkable things. With all respect, of course, Your Grace.*"

It was a lesson to her. Not least because of her almost mystical faith in Janko himself. And so the very first morning she was back, sitting at the small table in the kitchen while Miss Peabody prepared that unusual porridge the Americans called "oatmeal" and which Adriana found surprisingly soothing for breakfast, she reminded herself that she must listen more carefully to the stories this time. A woman who had flown aircraft across the Atlantic during the Second World War, driven military ambulances during the Korean conflict, climbed nearly to the top of Mount Everest, and worked as an operating theatre nurse in Africa and as a member of a medical support team on an Antarctic expedition must have a great deal to teach anyone willing to listen carefully.

The fact that such a woman even existed was phenomenal enough. The fact that she seemed so ready to treat Adriana with the utmost deference and care was almost incomprehensible. It brought home to her how seriously everyone involved took each aspect of the enterprise, and it made her regret how silly she must have seemed to them during their previous encounters. She must try harder to demonstrate her worthiness.

* * *

"How's the baby?" Derek asked.

She had been sitting on the terrace surveying that ravishing view, and he simply materialized.

Another difference, or rather two more. He had had his hair cut. The new style was shorter, almost military looking. It was far less romantic, yet it suited him perfectly. And she found as she greeted him that she didn't feel shy in his presence at all, though on the journey westward she had believed she was certain to and wondered how long it would take her to break through her reserve. She also realized for the first time how much her infant son resembled his father. Looking at Derek was uncannily what looking at Franek would be like in another quarter century. Really, she should have a picture of Derek to keep with her. She was reluctant to ask Ned Westerleigh to supply one because she assumed that the request would be reported onward and she didn't want to distress Todor. Miss Peabody would, she assumed, be happy both to help and to keep the secret. But until Adriana could make the request without feeling somehow disloyal to her husband, she supposed she'd simply have to depend on her eyes as imperfect cameras.

"The boy is well," Adriana said, unable to speak her child's name. "No, not well—fabulous. Angelic. Enchanting. Getting ready to walk."

"Isn't he a little young for that?"

"He is an extremely advanced child," Adriana laughed. "My husband has had the facts of his case verified by some of the finest pediatricians in the world. They all concur. He is some sort of prodigy. Time will tell us exactly what sort."

"It must be horrible for you to be separated from him."

It must be horrible for you never to have seen him, she thought.

"He has an army of nurses watching over him. And his devoted father. And a doting uncle. And two Grandmamas. They hardly give him a moment's peace. I doubt he'll notice I'm gone."

"Of course he will," Derek insisted. "And you must miss him very much."

* * *

This time there was no prolonged courtship. By the third evening Adriana was practically begging Derek to come into her bed. She begged inaudibly, to be sure, and so it was the next night before he actually joined here there. Over the past months she had come to wonder if her memories of him had been accurate. She had returned to her home certain that her experiences in his arms would transform the way in which she responded to her husband. Surely the tepid nature of their relations in the past must have been her fault. But no such miracle occurred. If anything, Todor seemed even more tentative with her than he had been before. Of course there had been her pregnancy at first. And then, after the birth of the child, a certain awkwardness as her body returned to a semblance of its former self. But it was almost as if Todor found touching her somewhat distasteful now that she had borne another man's child—that in spite of his fine intentions and his basic goodness as a person he found it impossible to break out of the traditional male ways of thinking of women as their possessions. How ironic for Todor. And how tragic. He had made himself a cuckold for the highest of purposes. He had done it willingly. It had, to be completely honest, happened at his own instigation and would never have happened otherwise, but he was still as undone by it as if he'd been both unwilling and unwitting until the child's arrival had forced him into consciousness of it. Not even the perfect child that had resulted was enough to assuage the damage to his ego, apparently.

Yet here she was, once again at his insistence, once again in Derek's arms, which over the intervening months had grown even more astonishing in their size and strength.

* * *

"My dear Adriana," Millicent Peabody said as they enjoyed their morning coffee a week or so after her arrival, "there's a piano recital at the conservatory on Tuesday night that I should very much like to attend."

"Why certainly, Miss Peabody."

"If you feel you can spare me, of course."

"Nonsense," Adriana said. "I adore piano music, you know. I studied the instrument myself in school, though I'm sorry to say I wasn't a gifted student. I'd love to come with you. If you won't mind the company, of course."

"Why, my dear, don't be ridiculous. It would be wonderful having you attend the performance with me."

"Who is the artist? Anyone famous?"

"No, I don't believe you'd consider him famous," Miss Peabody said. "I'd be very surprised if you've heard of him at all, in fact. He's a professor at the conservatory. But I've heard him perform, and he plays divinely. I believe you'll find him quite as fine as many of your European artists. Oh, silly me, he is European. A Frenchman, in fact. Professor Schein."

"Professor Schein? Jean-Pierre Schein?"

"Yes, that's his name. You've heard of him?"

"Jean-Pierre's sister, Adele, and I were at school together. We were very close friends, actually. Oh Miss Peabody, this is so exciting. I had no idea he was living here in San Francisco."

"I believe he joined the faculty of the conservatory fairly recently, as a matter of fact. But he's made quite a sensation with his playing."

* * *

Derek went with them to the recital as well. Adriana was surprised by his interest in it at first. But when she considered it further she didn't see why she should have been. When he wasn't with her he wasn't Derek. He was someone else. And if that someone else enjoyed classical music, so be it. It was an all-Liszt program concluding with the *Dante Sonata,* one of Adriana's particular favorites. She remembered Jean-Pierre playing it in the family's music room on the occasion of his grandmother's eightieth birthday. The grandmother's name, Adriana recalled, was Beatrice, just like Dante's beloved, and they were all enchanted by the reference that evening. As the applause died away at the end of the performance, she realized that these few moments had been her first waking ones since Franek's birth that she hadn't been thinking of him.

"I must go backstage and speak to Jean-Pierre," she said, as the lights in the recital hall came up.

"Of course, my dear," Miss Peabody assented.

Derek piloted them through the crowded aisles to the backstage entrance and on to the green room, clearing the way forward with his broad shoulders and manly assurance. Jean-Pierre was thronged with fans. No surprise. The years since Adriana had seen him last had been extremely gentle to him. He still looked for all practical purposes like a conservatory student himself rather than a revered professor. She waited her turn, exhilarated by the atmosphere of the crowded room.

"*Mon dieu*," he shouted, catching sight of her over the shoulder of the matron haranguing him. "Adriana? Is that you?"

The matron turned to stare down this distraction, but Adriana was incapable of being deterred.

"Jean-Pierre," she said, moving toward him. "How wonderful to see you. How divinely you played."

Then, realizing the threat, she turned to the woman before Jean-Pierre could speak again.

"I'm Adriana Brown," she said, extending her hand. "I'm so sorry to interrupt your conversation, but you see my excitement got the better of me. Jean-Pierre's dear sister, Adele, is my close friend."

* * *

"What a charming cottage," Jean-Pierre said as Adriana ushered him onto the terrace, where luncheon had been set. "Trust you always to place yourself in the most felicitous of surroundings. You always had a knack for that, my girl, even before Todor began courting you."

"And you always talked nonsense," she laughed. "Sweet nonsense, but nonsense. I'm surprised it hasn't gotten you into trouble."

"How do you know it hasn't?"

"From your playing, my dear. From your playing."

"Fair enough. You must tell me all about your baby. Is he here with you?"

"Alas, no. Todor sent me on this rest cure because he believes that the stress of motherhood has quite undone me."

"Todor," Jean-Pierre smiled. "Always one for the grand gesture. Always the romantic."

"That's Todor all right," Adriana said. "I sometimes think he was born into the wrong century."

"You're not the only one to make that observation," Jean-Pierre said.

"I know. I stole it from my brother-in-law."

"The black sheep," Jean-Pierre nodded. "The supernaturally handsome Konrad. But my dear, what about that divine creature who was with you last night at the recital?"

"Miss Peabody?" Adriana laughed. "She'll be so flattered to hear that she's been described as a divine creature."

"No, you goose," Jean-Pierre said. "The other one. I suppose he's your bodyguard. Todor would have insisted on your having a bodyguard, and your own tastes would have specified a bodyguard like that—a veritable Count Vronsky."

"I hope not that," Adriana said, "but Derek can tell you all about himself. Here he is now."

* * *

"Aren't you curious about him at all?" Jean-Pierre asked, watching Derek's backside as he went into the house for more refreshments.

"No," Adriana laughed. She hoped Jean-Pierre couldn't tell she was lying. "Why? Should I be?"

"I certainly am."

"He's my bodyguard," she said. "How much does one ever know about such people? Their lives are closed to us, far more than ours can ever be to them."

"But Adriana," Jean-Pierre said, "he's so completely exquisite. He's a mythological creature, practically. He almost belongs in a museum."

"Ah," she said. "You misunderstand yourself, my dear."

"What do you mean?"

"You don't want to know about him."

"Of course I do."

"No you don't. When you go to the Louvre, you don't say to yourself, 'I wish to know all about the woman in that painting.' The idea is ridiculous."

* * *

"You seem much more relaxed this year, my dear," Miss Peabody said.

"It was all so unfamiliar before."

"Of course."

"And, dear Miss Peabody, if you could only see my baby you'd understand why I'm so happy to have returned. Now that we have him, just the promise of bringing another such child into the world makes everything about this seem so much easier. Last year it was all a hypothesis. Mix the chemicals, you know, and see what sort of explosion results. Now I feel I know what to expect and that makes it possible to be much calmer. Even though I'm away from my husband and baby."

"You explain it so charmingly. It's a joy to see you this happy."

* * *

It took surprisingly little time. She didn't even admit it to herself when it happened. She ignored all the signs for the better part of two weeks because she didn't want to think of going back home so soon. She knew it was wrong of her to feel this way, but every night when Derek stole from her bed she found herself praying for just one more time with him. She couldn't believe that she'd once found his body ungainly and grotesque. Really, he seemed to define masculine perfection.

Finally it was Miss Peabody who looked at her one morning over breakfast and insisted on calling the doctor.

* * *

"My dear Adriana," Jean-Pierre said. "I shall miss you terribly."

"You will come stay with us at the *schloss* the next time you are in Europe," she said. "I insist on it. Todor will have the Bechstein tuned, and you will play for us. Baby Franek must learn to love great music without delay."

"I look forward to it."

"And?"

"What?"

"There's something you're not telling me."

"Nothing," Jean-Pierre shook his head. "It's silly."

"It's not silly, dear Jean-Pierre," Adriana said. "It's about Derek, isn't it?"

"Am I that transparent?"

"I can't answer for him," she said, with her heart sinking. But letting Jean-Pierre down easily required only a small lie. "I have no idea, really, what to tell you on that score."

"Oh, I know, of course, that he'd hardly be interested in me in that way. But I'm really quite infatuated. There's no getting around it."

"Dear Jean-Pierre," Adriana said.

* * *

It was heartbreaking, really, she mused as she packed the last of her jewelry. Poor Jean-Pierre. So handsome, so charming, so talented, and so completely at sea when it came to matters of the heart. Or of certain other sections of the anatomy, for that matter.

And how ironic, for her to be the one pondering how that last might best be taken care of.

* * *

"Darling Derek," she said.

"Dear Mrs. Brown," he smiled.

"Once again, Mr. Brown and I cannot thank you enough."

"You're very welcome."

"I suppose," she said, reaching into her purse for the small envelope, "that it would seem ungracious of me to ask for one additional small favor."

"Don't be silly."

"My friend, Jean-Pierre," she said, "is having such a difficult time adapting to life here in the United States. He confessed to me that he's often very lonely. If you'd be so kind—just look in on him from time to time. Go to lunch with him, for instance, or a movie. If you wouldn't find it too objectionable."

"He's a nice guy," Derek said, accepting the envelope, "I'll be happy to look out for him."

VIII

"Lance," Stefano said. "This is Tristan."

Standing next to Stefano was a young man almost exactly Lance's age and almost precisely Lance's build. With his blond hair and blue eyes he seemed too beautiful to be human. The expression on Stefano's face told the tale. Lance was happy to see that Stefano had finally found the one. Lance hadn't been the one himself, but he never begrudged Stefano his quest. Seeing this young man he could only take it as a compliment that Stefano had been so interested in him. Looked at purely as a physical manifestation, Tristan was amazing.

"Tristan," Lance said. "Nice to meet you."

"Nice to meet you, Lance."

"I don't know how to say this, exactly," Stefano said.

"You don't have to," Lance said. "It's obvious. Tristan needs to be immortalized on film."

Stefano smiled.

"It'll be my pleasure," Lance said.

"Not too much, I hope," Tristan said, looking a little nervous.

"Quiet, you," Stefano growled.

"I've seen the two of you around town," Lance said. "I'd have had to hunt you down if you hadn't brought him to me."

* * *

"Ned," Lance said. "I have to hand it to you."

"I knew you'd like the place, my boy," Ned said. "And it truly is time you stopped being a renter."

"Like it? I like French films, Italian cars, and German opera. This—this I don't like, this is something I have to have."

"Shall we write an offer, then?"

"For full asking price."

* * *

"Nick, if you don't mind," Lance said.

But by that time Nick already had his shirt off and was unzipping his jeans.

"Thank you, Stefano," Lance murmured into the camera. The photos of Tristan had been sublime. The photos of Stefano and Tristan together were a revelation. Stefano had suggested that project to begin with—scenes from mythology. But they'd quickly moved on from there as more and more abstract visions evolved. Lance knew he'd barely scratched the surface of his creativity. He knew he was nowhere near the peak of his skills.

And now Stefano had sent him Nick.

IX

Janko stepped through the door into the small, luxuriously decorated waiting room. The young woman at the reception desk was tall, blond, buxom, and virginal in a way that seemed improbable, given her looks. Janko recognized this as an American type.

"Can I help you?" she asked.

"My name is Krieger. I'm here to see Mr. Garrison."

"Mr. Krieger," she said, scanning her book.

"I'm sorry," he said. "I don't have an appointment."

"Actually, you do," she said. "A Mr. Westerleigh called it in. Is he with you?"

"I'm meeting him here."

"I'll just go tell Lance you've arrived."

* * *

"You again," Lance said.

But he was smiling, and the smile was genuine. Janko was a master at deciphering smiles.

"Mr. Garrison," he said.

"Good to see you, Mr. Krieger."

"Mr. Westerleigh is not here?"

"He called," Lance said. "He's been detained. He said to give you his compliments and tell you that he believes we can conduct this business on our own. Feel free to call him if you'd like to verify that. I can step outside."

"There's no need," Janko said.

"Mr. and Mrs. Brown, I suppose?"

"You don't appear surprised."

"Seems like they're the kind of people you're never free of," Lance said.

"Yes," Janko nodded. "Now, as to the terms. . ."

"Unless there's some substantial change, I don't see why we need to discuss terms. Just keep Ned informed of the times and dates. He'll let me know."

"If you're certain."

"I'd much rather go get some lunch than talk about Mr. and Mrs. Brown. You're my guest, of course."

"Thank you," Janko said. He couldn't remember the last time he'd been taken to lunch by an attractive young man who wasn't Konrad. Indeed, if Konrad knew of this, or that Lance Garrison existed for that matter, he'd torch the entire estate.

X

Millicent Peabody couldn't believe her good fortune. Dear, dear Adriana had invited her to the christening. Again. Those lovely twins this time. Now the Browns had four sons in all. She still thought of them as the Browns, though by now she knew better. Three times she had been Adriana's companion during her visits to San Francisco and a fourth visit was apparently in prospect. It would be so lovely to move back into the cottage for a few weeks. She knew she shouldn't, but she couldn't help thinking of Adriana as the daughter she had never had. It was almost as if those dear babies were her own grandsons. And an invitation to the christening was really more than enough thanks. But this time, instead of Pan American, she'd be flying to Europe aboard Adriana's own jet. Yes, Adriana was sending the plane for them—Millicent, and dear Ned

Westerleigh, and that gorgeous Professor Schein. What fun it was going to be. Even first class on Pan American was like riding on a glorified bus. Not that Millicent would have dreamed of turning up her nose at it. But still, it wasn't flying. And Millicent knew about flying. That she did. Nobody could take it away from her even after all these years. But that sleek little jet of Adriana and dear Todor's. That was an airplane. That was flying.

* * *

"My dear Miss Peabody."

"Mr. Westerleigh. How lovely to see you."

"Please allow me to assist you up the stairs into the aircraft."

"Thank you, Ned, dear. This is so exciting I'm quite lightheaded."

"Just leave your bag there on the tarmac. The attendant will make sure it's properly stowed."

Professor Schein arrived just moments before they were scheduled to take off. Such a lovely man, Professor Schein, Millicent thought. So handsome. So charming. Such lovely, lovely manners. Millicent found him quite disarming. He always seemed to look a little sad around the eyes. Artistic temperament, she supposed.

* * *

"Miss Peabody?"

"Yes, Mr. Marconi?"

"Captain Higgins' compliments, madame. Now that we are at cruising altitude, he invites you to join him on the flight deck."

"Oh my," Millicent sighed. "Really?"

"You're quite the legend, Millicent dear," Ned said.

"This is so exciting. But won't it make things horribly crowded up front?"

"You are to take my seat, Miss Peabody," Marconi said. "I intend to have a nice long rest back here since you'll be able to spell Captain Higgins at the controls should he require assistance."

* * *

"Dear Miss Peabody," the duke said. "How wonderful it is to have you once again under our roof."

"Thank you, Your Grace. The pleasure is all mine."

"I understand you are to be thanked for your assistance in piloting the aircraft."

"Oh, Your Grace," she said, "I hardly flew it at all."

"Why, Captain Higgins assures me you took a shift at the controls."

"The craft was on automatic pilot the entire time," she laughed. "Certainly the good captain must have told you that."

"Standard operating procedure, Miss Peabody, standard operating procedure. Ah, here is Adriana now."

* * *

Adriana was ravishing, the duke at his most courtly. The babies were, as he had been assured, divine creatures. It was their older brothers that Jean-Pierre found almost unbearably disquieting. They looked so uncannily like their real father back in San Francisco. Their real father, yes. Jean-Pierre eventually figured the arrangement out, though it had never been hinted at in his presence. Adriana hadn't meant any harm, he supposed. He would never blame her, however things eventually turned out. It had seemed like a dream come true at first. But then one woke up. Lance was still there, faithful as clockwork. But the dream? Well, it wasn't dead. He could hardly have expected it to die, even after his realization. He didn't love that way. But it could never again be the dream it had been. Not at the rate of one night a week, no more no less, no matter how expertly, no, he had to be fair about it, thrillingly, Lance attended to his needs. This, he supposed, was what they meant when they referred to a certain kind of enslavement. He seemed always to have been destined for it.

"Be careful what you wish for," he muttered, pushing his namesake, young Jan-Petr, on the swing.

"Tell me, Jean-Pierre, how is our friend?" Adriana asked, watching Franek with his soccer ball.

"He doesn't change," Jean-Pierre said.

"Thank God for that."

"Yes," Jean-Pierre said. "Thank God."

* * *

No matter how expertly plans were executed there were always loose ends. Ned knew this from decades of experience. So far their execution of every detail related to this matter had been flawless. Yet he supposed those pesky creatures were at least partially responsible for the half dozen gray strands he had sighted in Janko's luxuriant hair. That they were well earned was, he hoped Janko would understand, sufficient compensation for their appearance.

"*Also gut?* my dear Mr. Krieger? *Tout va bien?*"

"One finds, my old friend," Janko smiled, "that one's accomplishments are only as good as one's next assigned task."

"Truer words," Ned smiled. "Truer words."

"All is in readiness?"

"Ship shape and Bristol fashion down our end," Ned said in his broadest Royal Navy twang.

"Thanks, Ned," Janko said. "Thanks a million."

* * *

The great cathedral was festooned as if for the highest of holy days. Janko looked down at the child in his arms.

"Do you renounce Satan and all his works?" the archbishop asked.

Oh, Your Excellency, if it were only that simple, Janko thought. Once again he was standing, as he had with the older brothers, as godfather to a child whose conception he had been very nearly as responsible for as anyone on the face of the planet. This ceremony, he knew, was merely a ratification of the role he was to continue playing in all their lives.

"I renounce Satan and all his works," he said.

The archbishop turned to ask the same question of Professor Schein, who was to be the other child's godfather.

"As I understand them," Janko muttered to himself.

* * *

"A most satisfactory conclusion to this chapter," the duke said. "Most satisfactory indeed. The celebrations were a great success. Thanks to you. Once again, Janko, our family finds itself ever deeper in your debt."

"You are far too kind, Your Grace."

"Not at all, Janko, not at all."

"The young Lord Sten was particularly well behaved during the ceremony."

"What child would dare misbehave in your arms?" the duke laughed.

"At that age, how would he know?"

"They know, my friend, they know."

"I'll have to take Your Grace's word for it."

"Yes, do. Now, the preparations for Her Grace's next visit to San Francisco: they are well in hand?"

"Yes, Your Grace."

"Capital. Capital," the duke said. "One thing does bother me."

"Yes, Your Grace?"

"Your associate, Mr. Westerleigh."

"Yes?"

"I find myself somewhat uneasy on that account. Have Her Grace and I done enough to express our appreciation to him, do you think?"

"Your Graces have hosted him to each of the christenings," Janko said.

"Yes, Janko, I know that. But. . ."

"But nothing, Your Grace. Any additional expression on your part might be perceived as indelicate. Perhaps even insulting."

"Insulting, Janko? That seems rather strong."

"You know the English, Your Grace. Their ways are not our ways."

"Well said," the duke laughed. "God is an Englishman, after all."

"And not one of them more certain of the fact than dear Ned," Janko said.

* * *

Every night, except when she and the duke were away from the castle, Adriana tucked the boys in. Tonight, even with hundreds of guests celebrating in the great hall, she would make no exception. She quietly made her way to the children's floor. The nurses and cook had everything in order for the boys' bedtime snack, and she sat on a tiny chair at their small table and shared it with them.

They were transcendently beautiful. They were funny and charming. They changed with every new morning. It was unfashionable nowadays to think of motherhood as the crowning achievement of a woman's life, but it was difficult for her to imagine what else she might do that would rival it.

Still, she was a person individual from her children. Their welfare might be her primary concern—her *raison d'etre*, as it were—but there were other satisfactions she longed for beyond witnessing their emergence as the magnificent sons Todor had envisioned. And unfortunately, more and more those personal satisfactions seemed to lie outside the walls of the castle, far away on the shores of a remote sea, on steep hillsides teeming with strangers who didn't speak her language.

She was no longer certain that her beloved Todor saw her as anything but the mother of his boys. Her saner mind told her that the other one had no reason to see her as anything at all except a rich woman with eccentric ideas about life. But her heart insisted that somewhere there must be someone capable of knowing her as she was. She had no intention, of course, of trying to seek such a person out. But her certainty as to his existence was a thing she held and nurtured as her supreme consolation as she prepared once again to do as she was bidden.

* * *

The celebration that night had left Konrad somewhat overstimulated, which required rather more than the usual effort from Janko in calming him. He had to admit that he found pleasure enough it it himself. Indeed, on a night like tonight, he felt completely satiated. Konrad was a demanding lover but also a remarkably generous one. To the point of profligacy, it had to be acknowledged. Still, there was no way of escaping the fact that for Janko the act itself held, in one aspect at least, the status of a duty. That was Janko's life. Living always on someone else's calendar and in response to someone else's needs. Almost to the extent of forgetting that his own needs even existed, or indeed, that he was human enough to have any. Doing always what he had committed to, not, like other men, what he had chosen.

He was well compensated for what others described as his steadfast, unwavering faithfulness. He had no complaints on that score. And beyond that, he recognized that he was truly appreciated in a manner that transcended all possible tangible rewards. But still, his life was not his own. It never had been. And at this point it was difficult to see how it ever could be. The duke had paid him generously over the years of his service, and with the help of Ned Westerleigh he had invested wisely. He could walk away from all of it—all of them—tomorrow, never work another day in his life, yet want for nothing. But even if he desired that, and he truly didn't, doing so would be no solution, really, to his predicament. The years he had devoted to his duty couldn't be recovered any more than the life of a creature sacrificed on an altar could be restored to it. More than that, the young man he had been at the beginning of this path no longer existed. That young man could never be resurrected.

He had no idea what the young man in San Francisco thought of his own situation though he often tried to imagine what his feelings might be. They had never spoken of such matters and never would. It would probably be impossible for either of them even to begin such a conversation. But if there was anyone in the world who might, just might, comprehend Janko, it would, he sensed, be that young American.

* * *

Michael was waiting for him at the airport. Jean-Pierre had returned by commercial flight. Affairs, he told Adriana, required him to return earlier than he had anticipated. That necessitated the purchase of a ticket on Pan Am. What a word——affairs. Love. He should have said love. They might all have considered him crazy, but it would at least have been honest.

Michael Krakowiak, his oldest friend. Grinning as he waited outside customs. That grin said, among other things, "I told you so". Fair enough. It had been a mistake to go to the christening. Just as it would have been a mistake to stay away. In a predicament such as Jean-Pierre's you truly were damned if you did and damned if you didn't. And nobody knew that better than Michael. Though Michael might be far from Jean-Pierre's favorite person, he was unquestionably Jean-Pierre's dearest friend. They should have been lovers, unsuited to each other as they were. That's how love worked, apparently. Yes, no question about it. They should have been lovers. It might have been soul destroying much of the time, but it would have been a kind of salvation for them both.

"How was it?" Michael said, lounging behind the wheel like an actor in a porn video.

"Everything you'd imagine," Jean-Pierre said.

"Both for better and worse, I'm guessing."

"Why do you always insist on reading between my lines?"

"Because the real you is never to be found anywhere else," Michael said.

"*Touche.*"

"*Gesundheit.*"

"Did you see him while I was gone?"

"Him?" Michael asked. "You mean Lance? He has a name, you know."

"Lance."

"Yes, I saw him."

"Did you sleep with him?" Jean-Pierre asked.

"Of course."

"Even after the talk we had?"

"You had the talk," Michael said, steering the Mercedes through traffic like a kamikaze pilot. "I listened. We came to no agreement that I can remember. You expressed a preference and I chose not to argue at the time. That's all that happened."

"But. . ."

"But nothing, J.P. It's not up to you. You have no claim on him. Even if I let you call me off it won't make him yours any more than he's ever been."

"But. . ."

"Stop," Michael said. "It would be a show of loyalty on my part. I under-stand that. But it won't solve anything. Despite what you think, it might make the situation worse rather than better."

"How in the world could it do that?" Jean-Pierre asked.

"Why does he sleep with you?"

"Let's not go into that again. It's humiliating enough."

"All right," Michael said, "if you won't say it, I will. He sleeps with you because he's paid a stipend."

"And I suppose you're going to say he sleeps with you because he actually wants to. Because you're handsome and you go to the gym five times a week and I don't even know where one is."

"Not at all," Michael said. "I'm not stupid enough to believe that. The reason he sleeps with me is to keep you at bay, my darling one."

"Absurd."

"No," Michael insisted. "It really is as simple as that. I could call him up tomorrow and tell him I never want to see him again and it won't help you out a bit. He'll just find someone else, someone younger and hotter than me, you can bet on it. And he'll make sure you know about it. Not because he's cruel, because he isn't.

It's the only way he has of setting limits on what goes on between the two of you."

"I repeat," Jean-Pierre said, "you're being absurd."

"Listen to me. It is never going to be the way you want it to be. Not be-cause you're wrong to want it, but because he's the wrong man for you to want it with. He is not to be possessed. Not by you. Not by anyone. Haven't you figured that out about him by now? We know he can be rented, though that's truly a terrible way to put it, but that's his limit. Sleeping with me is his way of making it possible to go on sleeping with you. Period. Besides, you idiot. What he really likes are women. You can't win against that. No man like us can, despite what the queens insist."

"Michael."

"I know, darling. I do know. I love you more than you understand. More than you think I'm capable of. I know you're miserable over this. If I were your fairy godmother I'd fix it for you. But there's only one solution."

"Yes, you taking yourself out of the picture."

"No," Michael said. "You'll never be happy if you don't learn that the only way you can have any part of him is to share him."

Cooper Luxemberg:
April, 1978

"Sorry," Cooper said. "I can't go."

"Of course you can," Chanel smiled. Lately she seemed to be channeling the Cheshire Cat. It was as if whenever she smiled the rest of her head disappeared. If only her larynx would. She was too calculating for the phenomenon to be an accident, leaving Cooper to wonder why she thought it was good presentation. Not that Chanel was known for having good ideas generally. Her judgment was almost unerringly faulty even by drag queen standards. Her closest adherents were starting to wake up to the fact.

"No," Cooper said. "I really can't. That's the first night of Passover and I'm invited to a Seder."

"Listen to me, you big lug," Chanel insisted, emphasizing her consonant sounds (*hyooo pick luck*) like a *film noir* actress overacting during a climactic scene, "Passover comes around every year or so, at the very least. But this extravaganza, well, it's only going to be one of the most stupendous, amazing—or at least it will with *Miss Chanel Rococo* headlining. And I absolutely must have you at my side. You, Cooper. No substitute accepted. I simply refuse, darling one, to take no for an answer."

* * *

"You are planning to wear your tux, of course," Chanel said when Cooper ran into her outside Harry Gordini's piano bar a few nights later. "Your best tux, that is. Not that second stringer you tried to pass off on me at *La Traviata* last month."

"A tux? Am I going somewhere that fancy?"

"On the twenty-second, silly. You can't have forgotten."

"The twenty-second? Oh, that. Nobody wears a tux to a Seder. It's not that kind of gathering. I mean, I suppose you could if you wanted to, but I've never heard of anyone. . ."

"But you're not going to a Seder, darling," Chanel said. "We settled it weeks ago."

"I think you've got it backward," Cooper told her. "Seder, yes; tux, no."

* * *

Apparently she still didn't believe him, because as he left for the Steinbergs' that evening he heard her fuming into his answering machine. Where the hell was he? Didn't he realize he was late picking her up? He didn't bother taking the call to explain.

Estelle and Sol Steinberg, Bella's parents, were the kind of people Cooper's parents had for friends back in New York. Affluent, gregarious, hospitable. You felt at home the minute you walked through the front door of their house, which, though they referred to it as a cottage really deserved to be described as a mansion. Cooper had an interesting history with that particular stretch of Pacific Heights, and not exclusively as a realtor. He wondered how much the Steinbergs knew about their neighbors at the end of the block.

Like Cooper's parents' friends, though not like his parents themselves, the Steinbergs were ridiculously indulgent of their children. Bella's older brother, Brent, played polo on their dime and the middle brother, Barry, lived on his own yacht out in Tiburon. For her graduation from Berkeley, they'd bought Bella an apartment on Nob Hill that set them back six figures and Sol never batted an eye at the cost. Though as expected he'd driven a very hard bargain.

There was something about being in a roomful of Jews, Cooper thought, even Jews who were more or less strangers. People he had never met nevertheless got him in a way nobody else did. Jaded as he pretended to be—even to himself most of the time—Cooper found a charm in the solicitude of these fellow tribesmen that was highly seductive. The men slapped him on the back and offered him drinks. He might well have been their nephew. The women interrogated him about his family, his studies at the university—degree almost finished, thanks—his budding real estate career, his girlfriends—most of all his girlfriends, because as a handsome, successful young Jew with no visible defects he had to have at least one of them and if he didn't it was imperative that steps be taken more or less immediately. And these matrons knew exactly what steps: "Cooper, darling, I'd like you meet my daughter (or niece, second cousin, friends' daughter, second cousin's niece *ad infinitum*) Ruthie, Alannah, Rachel, Nancy, Yael. You'll come to dinner(or theatre or the opera). . ."

The feeling was, when he considered it, analogous to what he experienced in a roomful of gay men or bodybuilders. And, as he supposed was to be expected, he felt it most intensely in the company of his own gang of gay bodybuilders. "At home" was the most accurate way to label it, yet those words were ridiculously inadequate. Clichés trivialized even the most profound emotions, and there was nothing Cooper hated more than having anything about himself trivialized. Or merely threatened with it. What he felt in the Steinberg's home that evening was the kind of contentedness his Labradors exhibited on a cold night when he built a fire in the fireplace and distributed extra rations of Milk Bone. Introduce him to a gay Jewish bodybuilder, even a merely presentable one, and Cooper would probably propose to him on the spot out of a sort of reflex. And regret having done it more or less immediately. And then spend the next decade or so, because his fellow tribesmen were as tenacious as he was, trying to wriggle his way back out of the commitment.

There were no gay Jewish bodybuilders, presentable or not, *chez* Steinberg that evening. The closest thing to that species was one of Bella's cousins, Judah Isaacs, who was probably gay and unquestionably Jewish, inexcusably cute though apparently never having been inside a gym in his life, and seemed destined in a few more years to gyrate his way into the pantheon of "historically significant" go-go boys currently presided over by Kent Norberg. Even at this point, he'd stop traffic on Castro Street without effort. Nevertheless, Cooper took only an academic interest in Judah, who was extremely young—he got to ask the four questions during Seder—and who, if indeed he was as much like Kent as Cooper suspected him of being, would be more trouble than he was worth once the Jewish component was factored in. Still, Cooper marked him down in his mental list of young men to keep an eye on. It was a long list, yet, paradoxically, a selective one.

Cooper had never been to a Seder that didn't eventually turn into an endurance test regardless of how good the company and cooking might be, and that night was no exception. As the event dragged on, his discomfort was compounded by the way Bella kept looking at him. In recent weeks, she had made no secret of her interest in him. It was her motivation for inviting him to the Seder in the first place. Cooper got that, even though he had done nothing to encourage her. In fact, he'd gone as far as he could to fend her off without actually being unpleasant about it. And he'd been as honest as it was possible to be. That should have taken care of it right here. If Bella wasn't going to take his sexuality seriously enough to accept that it disqualified him as husband material, he wished she at least wouldn't be so blatant in her misguided attempts to seduce him away from it.

"Cooper, dear," Estelle Steinberg said as he was leaving, "thanks so much for coming tonight. It was lovely to have you with us. And please send holiday greetings to your family."

"My pleasure," Cooper said. "I really enjoyed meeting everyone."

"I'm sure we'll be seeing you again soon."

Her eyes were gleaming in a way that a Jewish mother's could only under very specific circumstances. In other words, Bella was lying to her. That meant Cooper had miscalculated. He was going to have to make an adjustment. He might have to cut her off completely. It wouldn't be a good decision from a business perspective, but he was willing to face the consequences.

II

Ashby opened the door. He had a paint smudge on his nose and a brush in his right hand.

"I saw the lights on and thought I'd stop by," Cooper said.

"Look at you," Ashby said, motioning him inside. "Not your usual Saturday night drag."

"You're one to talk," Cooper laughed. "Painting at eleven p.m. The sellers had the whole house done to your specifications before escrow closed, and look what I find. It's enough to make a realtor cry."

"I know," Ashby said. "I really didn't want you discovering that less than an hour after you handed me the keys I was having buyer's remorse. But the more I thought about it, the paint we chose for the master bedroom just didn't work. I mean, can you really imagine anyone having sex in a room that color?"

"It's not about me," Cooper said. "But you're right."

"Seriously, though," Ashby said, "what's with that suit?"

"First night of Passover," Cooper said.

"Oh, right. Whose Seder?"

"The Steinbergs."

"As in Bella?"

"As in Bella," Cooper nodded.

"You want to watch it with that one," Ashby said. "She's a very determined young woman."

"It's not like that," Cooper said.

"Yes it is," Ashby insisted. "You just won't admit it to yourself."

"My parents know some cousins of theirs in New York. It's a family thing. That's all."

"Sure," Ashby said. "Did I tell you I'm looking for a co-investor in a bridge that a nice gentleman offered me a cut-rate price on in the dead of night last week? The moon was full, the foghorns of Alcatraz were hooting, and he walked right up to me on the Embarcadero."

"Very funny."

"That's me," Ashby said.

"I met someone there tonight who knows you," Cooper said.

"Really?"

"One of Bella's uncles. Dr. Paul Isaacs. He teaches at the medical school. If I didn't know better, I'd think he has a major crush on you. 'Ah, yes, Dr. Sainte-Claire. One of the finest young men it's ever been my privilege to teach.'"

"He's a great guy," Ashby said. "One of the best."

"Well, he's a big fan of yours."

"It's nice to be remembered," Ashby said. "You wouldn't believe the letter of recommendation he wrote when I got ready to apply for my residency."

"I probably would, actually," Cooper said. Ashby was one of those guys who never felt deserving, as opposed to the majority who thought they deserved far more than they did. "Listen, I'm going to go home and change and come back and help you paint."

"No, you're not," Ashby said. "I've just about got it wrapped up. And I'm leaving for the airport in twenty minutes anyway. Got to pick up my husband from the Frankfurt run."

"Those 747's have astonishing range, don't they?" Cooper marveled.

"He says they're a dream to fly, too," Ashby nodded.

* * *

So Cooper walked the Labradors and then changed clothes and went out instead. The bar was festive that night. The bartenders were shirtless and sported rabbit ears. The go-go boys had dyed their g-strings the pastel colors you'd see at an Easter Egg hunt. The braying banter of drag queens filled the room like—well, like the foghorns of Alcatraz, to borrow Ashby's simile. Not Chanel's crew, who were otherwise engaged—these were several gangs of her rivals. Standing off in a corner was an acquaintance of Cooper's, Gregory Yates. Tall, elegantly slim, and sad faced, Greg was a babe in the woods and helpless at getting dates. Unless Cooper intervened, he generally went home alone.

Greg had been Cooper's English T.A. for freshman comp his first year at State. They'd had a half assed little affair. Several times Greg claimed to have fallen in love with him. Instead of cutting him off completely, Cooper rode it out and managed not to get married. At the end of the semester, Greg had fallen back out of love and gave Cooper a B minus in the class. Cooper thought this spoke eloquently about both Greg's good taste and his essential integrity. He had finished his Ph.D. a year or so previous and then scandalized the western world by taking a job teaching in a public high school instead of trying for a university position, explaining that it was the only way he was assured of staying in San Francisco instead of being exiled to the boonies. Later, Cooper researched the salary scales of high school teachers relative to junior level university faculty in the Humanities and came away more convinced than ever that Greg was a genius.

"I can't decide which of them I like best," Greg said, staring at two go-go boys dancing on a platform on the other side of the room.

"I'll make it easy for you," Cooper said. "The light haired one is named Kent. The dark haired one is Ugo. I know he looks kind of tough, but he's actually a sweetheart. Art major at State. Paints abstract expressionist soft core porn."

"Huh?"

"Maybe he'll show you his work," Cooper said. "And he's an absolute dream in bed. Kent, on the other hand, skins guys like you alive."

"Yikes."

"They should be getting off shift soon," Cooper said, looking at his watch. "Wait right here. I'll fix it up."

He didn't mind helping Greg out. Greg was always appreciative and invariably treated his dates like princes. Cooper only wished he'd figure out how to hang on to one of them permanently. He was the kind of guy who needed to be married.

* * *

"I prepare a mean breakfast," Kent said, sitting up in bed, "but you never stay the night so you'll never know about it."

"The dogs wait up for me," Cooper said.

"I bet they don't," Kent pouted. "I'm not sure they even exist."

And if you keep complaining, Cooper thought, *you'll never get invited to my place, so you'll never meet them.*

Ashby Sainte-Claire

I

Ashby wasn't surprised when Principal Chaminade invented a technicality to disqualify him from being named valedictorian or salutatorian. He had spent his entire conscious life being the town's black sheep, and this was merely one more chapter in that long, miserable saga. It would take more than straight A's in high school and a perfect score on the SAT to escape that status. It would take a sign from God, hovering in the acrid murk above the refinery, to fundamentally alter the townspeople's view of him. He had no intention of devoting any more of his life to watching and waiting for such a manifestation. He'd willingly accept being third in his graduating glass. It was true that Sarah Jane LaPeyrouse had earned a slew of her A's working as an office aide and an equal number singing in choir and still more for cheerleading. Just as it was true that Joey Thibodeaux had earned lots of his in gym classes and working as audio visual tech in the library. Ashby had earned more college prep credits than the two of them combined. The injustice of Principal Chaminade's maneuver was obvious. But Ashby didn't care. Honest to God. Because by the morning of graduation day he had a fair sized stack (four dozen in all) of letters of acceptance from colleges and universities located at substantial distances from his hell hole of a home town to take comfort in. And more to the point, he had eight offers of full ride scholarships to choose from. Every last one of them from a school out of state. In Ashby's situation a letter of acceptance was more or less meaningless, but a full ride scholarship was an iron clad promise of escape.

And for as long as Ashby could remember, his sole goal in life had been to escape. It started with his surroundings. He wanted to escape the humidity, the steaming summers and sodden winters, the ubiquitous molds and fungi that thrived in the ubiquitous damp, the bugs and assorted other wildlife that constituted the local food chain, the oppressive green flatness of the landscape, the spongy ground that never completely dried out and firmed up under foot. Worse than that, he wanted to escape the interminable reek from the refinery where his grandfather had worked until the accident; where, indeed, most of the menfolk of the town spent their working lives. It operated twenty-four hours a day, seven days a week, the shift changes unvarying as the seasons and the smell never abating.

But it wasn't just the place he wanted to flee. More than anything it was the people. First and foremost was his family. There was his grandfather, foul mouthed, seldom shaven, and evil smelling, who for as long as Ashby could remember had worked double shifts as often as the company would allow it for the stated purpose of avoiding contact with "that drunk old bitch and her bastard grandson". The first day Ashby could recall escaping a beating from the old man was the day he never came home from work—the day of his accident. The old man took several weeks to die from his burns, and every day of his suffering Grannie made Ashby stand outside the window of his hospital room from where he could listen to Gramps curse everyone in the universe, most notably God, the company, Grannie, Ashby's jailbird whore of a mother, his never to be named father, and Ashby himself. The old man's death was no liberation for any of them, Grannie, whose drinking was her prison, Ashby himself, or Ashby's mother, whom he scarcely remembered, rotting away month after month in prison until she died in a knife fight over contraband liquor.

It wasn't just Ashby's family he longed to escape, however. It was everyone in the town, really. The schoolmates who beat him up regularly, the girls who sneered because of his thrift shop wardrobe, the teachers who pursed their lips and averted their gazes when Ashby was assigned to their classrooms, and the succession of preachers at First Baptist Church who ignored Grannie's drinking and general slovenliness and referred to her as a long suffering saint of God because she never missed services. Rounding out Ashby's list was the surprising number of local men who feared they might be his father but wanted nothing to do with the son of a convicted murderer they'd rather forget they ever knew and the other men who thanked their lucky stars for their narrow escapes. There had never been and apparently never would be a solitary resident of the town of any age, color, or description who could be bothered to treat Ashby with the least consideration, and he dreamed of a time when they would all be in his past.

How did you escape a tiny Louisiana refinery town? If you were poor and nobody thought of you as anything but an annoyance or an embarrassment or an affront to public order? In the best of circumstances it wasn't an easy place to put behind you. Young men generally left only to join the service—

there was a steady stream of condolence letters from the Pentagon—or to serve prison terms. Young women left town with their boyfriends or husbands only to return, if they returned at all, single mothers. Occasionally you'd hear that one or another of them was working in a New Orleans whorehouse. Rarely, if ever, were there success stories. Sissie Manigault, for instance, had been "discovered" in New Orleans and was now starring in television commercials for a statewide chain of tire stories. The Roubideaux twins had parlayed their natural pugnacity and hulking physiques into notoriety as a tag team on the southern pro wrestling circuit. And that was about it. Ashby couldn't see how those examples provided him any roadmap.

But the books he read in the public library on the days when Grannie was drunk enough not to notice him sneaking out of the house offered not just inspiration but pointers of a practical nature. Other people seemed to achieve success through a combination of hard work, persistence, self reliance, thrift, and purity of heart. Ashby had no first hand knowledge of those qualities, but there seemed to be no harm in trying to develop them. The hardest part was talking himself into his first part-time job, doing yard work for Miss Elyse Rochefort down the block. Everything Miss Elyse had ever heard about Ashby and his family made her dubious, but God bless her, she gave him a chance. He did everything he could think of to provide her satisfaction. And it must have worked because from then on everyone he applied to for odd jobs said to him"I've heard about you from Miss Elyse," and he was hired on at least a trial basis. Eventually the jobs came looking for him but that didn't denote anyone's real approval.

Ashby could easily have spent his earnings on comic books, ice cream, moon pies, and R.C. Cola. But the people in the books that inspired him were made of sterner stuff. Inspired by them, he instituted a new regime. He budgeted for a hair cut every three weeks without fail, nearly new clothing from the thrift shop run by the ladies of St. Theobald's church, and, because even when it wasn't broken Grannie's washing machine left everything with a nasty odor, twice weekly trips to the laundromat. The little money he had left he squirreled away for "his future", though this was a nebulous goal at best. Not to mention remote. Meantime, Grannie was a greedy old drunk and he had to exercise every bit of ingenuity he possessed to evade expropriations.

He had no clear notion of how his efforts might serve to help him escape but at least he went about town looking and smelling less disreputable. People didn't actually start treating him well but gradually they seemed to view him with somewhat less disdain. That was worth a great deal but didn't really solve anything. He was still that illegitimate little Sainte-Claire boy, about whose paternity his mother had told so many different, extremely colorful but totally unlikely stories that even someone far more impressive than he might aspire to become could hardly hope to live them down. He always would be that boy. Unless he could get away.

Before Ashby knew it, he was in fifth grade. Then sixth. Before he knew it he was getting decent grades, then good grades, then straight A's. And when you're neat, obedient, and diligent, you get labeled a "good student" almost before you know it. Adults paid attention—a different kind of attention than he was used to. He didn't become respectable exactly. But close enough to it to escape the worst of their censure. Eventually he found he stopped worrying so much about planning his escape because it seemed that other people were starting to plan it for him. By the end of 10th grade he had been informed that his future included *college*, where he would prepare for a *profession* and most likely meet the girl who would become his wife and the mother of his children. It all sounded like someone else's biography. But he quickly realized that that there wasn't a college or university closer than New Orleans, and that most of them were farther away even than that. He couldn't imagine where the money would come from to make all this possible, but when you're neat, respectful, and diligent and you have straight A's stretching back all the way to seventh grade and you get a perfect score on your PSAT, things that seemed like insurmountable obstacles start to take on a different look.

As far away as possible, but not in a cold climate. A real city, not a small town. Near a body of water that didn't stink. That was his checklist. He didn't give a damn how good the football team was or even if there was one. Or about how many of the grads got into Harvard Law or were recruited by the State Department or any of the dozens of different factors he knew he was supposed to consider before making his selection. He visited no campuses, attended no presentations, contacted no recruiters. There was a campus out there with beautiful buildings, people who had no idea about him or his lineage, and no smell of either refinery or swamp. It would find him.

II

If Michelangelo had lived and worked in Southern California, the guy Ashby discovered when he arrived at his newly assigned dorm room would have been the model for *David*. Broad shouldered, small hipped, flat bellied, bulging intimidatingly in the chest and arms—Ashby was familiar with the term "mesomorph" from his reading. Here was the living, breathing definition. The guy's marble smooth skin was deeply tanned and a thick mop of silky blond hair just brushed his shoulders. He was wearing nothing but a pair of ridiculously short cutoffs which were threadbare almost to the point of uselessness and faded to the palest blue. He was standing on a chair screwing something to the wall opposite the bunk bed.

Ashby had arrived in the city several days earlier. He checked into a youth hostel and began exploring his new home. From the sweeping, unexpected curve of the bridge under construction in the bay to the pristine beaches, the rows of houses climbing the tree lined hills, the expansive parks, the cerulean skies—everywhere he looked he saw evidence that he had indeed arrived in paradise. And here was exactly the sort of Adam you would expect to find inhabiting this particular Eden. Ashby stood in the doorway and stared.

The guy finished his task, gave the contraption he had attached to the wall a tug, nodded, and stepped off the chair. Only then did he seem to register Ashby's presence.

"Bicycle hooks," he explained. "Have to make the most efficient use of the space in here."

Ashby noticed a second set of hooks a few feet farther down the same wall. He had seen the bicycles themselves leaning against the wall out in the corridor. Peugeot 10-speeds of a type he had often coveted, a red one in full racing trim, the second, more sedately outfitted, in electric blue.

"You must be the roomie," Apollo said, fixing Ashby with eyes almost as pale as the denim of those ridiculous shorts. "I'm Nate. Nate Duckworth."

"Ashby Sainte-Claire."

They shook hands.

"I've got one more set of hooks," Nate said, "if you've got a bike."

"No," Ashby stammered. "No bike."

"Really?"

"No."

"No problem. We'll adjust the seat and pedals on the blue one. You can use it."

"I don't ride," Ashby admitted, chagrined.

"Really?"

"No."

"Not at all?"

Ashby shrugged.

"Don't?" Nate asked, raising an eyebrow, "or can't?"

Ashby felt like he'd been stripped naked.

"Well," Nate mused, "there's no time to lose. We're going to have you riding like a champ by sundown."

* * *

"So what's your major?" Nate asked, grinning at him across the first pizza Ashby had ever tasted—his reward for successfully, and he suspected uncomplainingly, taking his first bicycle ride.

"Pre-med," he said. "English, actually. The AMA likes doctors to be renaissance men."

Nate chewed his pizza and looked thoughtful.

"What about you?" Ashby asked.

"Undeclared," he said. "I've got no idea, really. I'll probably go into Grandpa Rousseau's yacht brokerage eventually. You don't need a degree for that. College just seemed like more fun than a full time job at this point in my life. I can't believe you've never had pizza before. Are you sure you're really an American?"

"No," Ashby said just as seriously as he could.

It took a moment for Nate to realize he was joking.

"Girlfriend back home?"

"No." Making this admission gave Ashby an uncomfortable feeling in the pit of his stomach.

"You're better off," Nate assured him. "Mine got into Columbia. I won't get to see her until Christmas."

* * *

Ashby had never had a friend before and had no idea how to go about it. But Nate was the oldest of seven sons in a household where the father, an airline pilot, was away most of the time. He was used to being a combination of scout master and drill sergeant, monitoring the hygiene of his charges, enforcing the house rules, and generally laying down the law. Ashby didn't have to do anything but play follow the leader. Learning to ride a bicycle was only one item on a very long list of skills no one had ever bothered to teach him. He was nothing if not a dedicated pupil, and Nate's upbringing and temperament made him an

ideal coach, patient, articulate, and just firm enough to override any resistance
whether philosophical or practical. He never made Ashby nervous and he never
made him feel stupid. Each new skill Ashby mastered further cemented the
bond between them.

* * *

Everything about Nate fascinated Ashby. He had never before had the opportunity to observe another person, particularly one his own age, this closely.
It was almost like discovering a new species. Nate was simultaneously profoundly alien and comfortingly familiar.

Ashby had come to the university with what he thought of as very little in
the way of clothing. But even by that standard Nate's wardrobe seemed remarkably limited. There was a couple of pairs of jeans and a navy blue sweatshirt
bearing the logo of his high school, but those garments were reserved for only
the most inclement weather. There were half a dozen or so t-shirts, only one
of them with sleeves still attached, and a similar number of tank tops. A good
supply of cutoffs, a pair of flipflops, and a pair of sneakers which had lost their
laces at some point were pretty much the rest of it. No underwear, either, just a
couple of jockstraps Nate wore under the skimpiest pairs of cutoffs. Nate's collection of grooming items was equally limited. A toothbrush and toothpaste, an
electric razor he never used, a bottle of lemon scented shampoo, Ivory soap, and
a small flask of cologne he spritzed in the direction of his armpits in lieu of deodorant. No such thing as a brush or comb. His hair was of such a smooth texture that it never tangled despite its length and always fell naturally into place.

This minimalism was far outweighed by the elaborateness of his other
accoutrements, however. The two bicycles were just the start of it. Three
surfboards—of varying lengths and other characteristics too esoteric for Ashby
to appreciate—stood on end leaning into the corner of the room just beyond
the head of the bunkbed. Nate's kayak hung from bungee cords hooked to the
ceiling. Two drawers of his dresser contained two complete sets of snorkeling
gear. Three wetsuits occupied his closet. He surfed daily and hated wearing
the same wetsuit twice in a row. There were half a dozen Frisbees, assorted
tennis rackets, and multiple balls for both soccer and volleyball. There was the
requisite turntable, tuner, and set of speakers, accompanied by four wooden
produce crates full of record albums. Under the lower bunk, two guitar cases
nestled out of harm's way. Nate played both six and twelve string varieties, and
Ashby might find him at any time of the day or night strumming away. Oc-

casionally he would let loose with some elaborately figured classical lick, just enough to demonstrate a fairly remarkable facility, but typically he restricted his repertoire to the simple chord progressions of the current Top-40 hits. He could sing pleasantly enough in a husky but tuneful baritone, but he indulged himself in this only rarely.

It had to be said that playing the guitar was the least energetic thing he did. Except when asleep he was a kind of perpetual motion device, leaping, trotting, running in place, propping himself against the wall to perform his specialty, handstand pushups, in sets of fifteen, chinning himself on the bar he had installed in their doorway, clambering onto and back off his top bunk, and constantly fidgeting.

He was funny and charismatic, a complete social animal. Being in his company entailed lots of physical contact. Several times a day Ashby would see—and hear—him in the process of putting some classmate into a headlock or other wrestling hold. He especially liked to hold Ashby down and tickle him until he nearly hyperventilated. Indeed, on one occasion, Ashby showed distinct signs of actually passing out. True to form, Nate had a paper bag ready for Ashby to breathe into. He sat Ashby up, crouched next to him on the floor, and stroked his back with infinite tenderness until it was clear the crisis was over.

As popular as Nate was with them, the men of the dormitory instinctively feared him as a formidable threat to their relationships with women. This seemed perfectly reasonable given his looks and charisma. How many girls Ashby saw melt under Nate's gaze, grow giddy in his presence. But Nate never actually gave cause for worry. He seemed totally devoted to his absent girlfriend, Joanie, talking about her constantly and often staring pensively at her framed photo sitting in its place of honor atop the chest of drawers. Ultimately, he was far too much of a gentleman to poach. He treated all the girls who dropped in and out of the building exactly the way he treated all the men—minus, of course, the wrestling holds.

It was never entirely clear to Ashby how Nate found time to attend classes.

In another time or place he would have been the quintessential frat boy. But that year, on that campus, fraternities were so unfashionable as to be almost universally considered a joke, and one in extremely questionable taste. As Nate was heard to observe more than once that fall, "those guys aren't greeks, they're geeks." Ashby believed that he was the only one among Nate's adherents who truly appreciated the irony of Nate's disdain.

III

The Wednesday before Thanksgiving was sunny, clear, and warm. It might well have been August. Nate put the top down on the Volkswagen and Ashby helped stow their things in the back seat. He was reluctant to miss his chem. lab, but Nate was in a hurry to get on the road.

The Volkswagen roared like a chorus of enraged lawn mowers as Nate steered it into northbound traffic on the freeway. Ashby had only the faintest conception of California geography. He knew that the university was in La Jolla, which wasn't its own place, really, but part of San Diego. He knew that Mexico was immediately to the south and that in the opposite direction, up the coast, you found Los Angeles, San Francisco, and eventually Canada. "Orange County" and "Newport Beach" conveyed nothing to him. If he hadn't already known of them as Nate's home territory, he might have thought of them as located in France or Australia.

The noise of the engine, the tires on the pavement, and the wind blasting past them made listening to music impossible. Conversation as well. The invitation to spend the holiday with Nate's family had come as a kind of last minute surprise—only because Nate mistakenly believed he had issued it weeks earlier. Ashby had been suppressing his curiosity about Nate's home and people. Now he was about to learn about them by direct observation. He'd much rather have read about them in a book but wouldn't have dreamed of trying to decline the invitation. Nate's persistence would have won the day sooner or later, leaving all the energy Ashby had put into resistance wasted.

The neighborhood where the Duckworths lived was a region of broad, velvet smooth, deep green lawns. The houses were low slung, rambling structures of stone, glass, and wood. Ashby knew they were called "ranches", though there was nothing either rustic or agrarian about their appearance. He couldn't begin to imagine any of them actually situated in the country, surrounded by cattle and with windmills looming in the background.

Halfway up the block Nate slowed the car and steered into a driveway already occupied by a dark blue Mercedes with a black convertible top. Nate pulled up behind it and switched off the engine. The ensuing silence lasted only seconds before two golden retrievers, barking frantically, erupted from the front door of the house, followed by what looked like a life sized Barbie doll.

"Mom," Nate said, "this is Ashby."

"Call me Eleanor," she said, shaking Ashby's hand. "It's so very nice to meet you. You must make yourself completely at home. I insist on it."

In stiletto heels and with her hair piled elaborately atop her head, she was noticeably taller than Nate. She didn't look old enough to be his mother. She didn't look remotely like a housewife.

"Your things will be fine in the car," she said. "Come on inside and have something to eat."

On the kitchen counter sat a platter of sandwiches covered with plastic wrap.

"There's ham and cheese on brown bread and tuna salad on white. And you'd better eat up because the minute Ollie and Peter come in from school it'll disappear. If I don't feed them as soon as they get home they make unspeakable messes in here feeding themselves. Cleaning up after them makes me late getting dinner ready."

She turned to Nate.

"I've already made up the bed in the Captain's office."

"Ash doesn't think he has anything nice enough to wear to Grannie's tomorrow," Nate told her. "He wanted to stop and buy something, but I told him we're fully equipped around here."

"Turn around," she said.

Ashby did.

"Peter for the pants," she said. "Quinn for a shirt and sweater."

"What I was thinking," Nate agreed.

"Best get something picked out as soon as you've both eaten," she said. "Once that bunch gets home, it's Katie bar the door."

* * *

"Why are you all alphabetical?" Ashby asked as Nate rummaged in his brother's closet.

"It's a family thing," Nate said, emerging with a pair of trousers on a hanger. "The Captain's first name is Matthew, and his younger brothers are Nicholas and Owen. Grandpa Duckworth is named Llewellyn and his brothers are James and Keith. It goes all the way back to great-great something or other Anthony."

"That's amazing."

"Is it?"

"I think so."

"Not seriously."

"Really," Ashby insisted. "Think of the organization it took. Think of the commitment."

"It only required two things," Nate said. "Lack of imagination and famili- arity with the Roman alphabet."

* * *

One wall of the Captain's office was taken up by a trophy case, which was crammed full of gleaming hardware.

"What's all this?"

"He's a bodybuilder," Nate said, hanging Ashby's borrowed garments in the closet. "He won all those in contests. Mostly state and local, but he came in third at the Mr. America a few times."

There were framed photos on the wall. The man in them, amazingly built, was unmistakably related to Nate. Except for his fantastically inflated musculature and the radically dissimilar haircut, he could have been Nate's twin.

* * *

"Will we be seeing anything of the Captain this weekend?" Nate asked, reaching for another piece of fried chicken.

"You know what flight schedules are like at Thanksgiving," Eleanor said.

Ashby thought he detected a slight note of defensiveness in her voice, as if she feared that Nate considered the Captain's absence her fault.

"Hey," Nate said. "Not trying to start anything. Just requesting some information. He's our father, after all. Nice to see him every now and then."

"The last I spoke to him," Eleanor said, "he thought he might make it home for a few hours tomorrow afternoon. He didn't promise. You know any- thing can happen. But he's definitely got a redeye out of LAX tomorrow night."

"He'll have to report for duty too early to make it to Thanksgiving dinner at Grannie's," Ollie speculated.

"Probably," Eleanor agreed.

"Very convenient," Nate said, "leaving us to fight her off on our own."

"Now, Nate," Eleanor protested.

"He's right, Mom," Peter said. "No getting around that."

"Yes," Eleanor nodded. "But he doesn't have to say it."

So this was what he'd been missing all these years, Ashby thought. Was this the innocent grousing of a generally happy family or something more sinister? Having no frame of reference, he found it intensely interesting. And they were all so fabulous looking. Even the littlest boys, Sammie and Ted, looked like they belonged in cereal advertisements.

"You know he loves you boys," Eleanor said. "He hates being away from us so much of the time."

"That's why he does it for a living," Quinn said.

* * *

Ashby had a hard time getting to sleep, looked down on by those photographs of the Captain on the wall. Even in the darkness, it felt like being stared at by Hercules. He had just about gotten used to living in close proximity with a specimen like Nate, though that had been far from easy. It seemed silly to be so unnerved by these disembodied images. Surely, should the actual man materialize, his powers were bound to include mind reading and Ashby's days as Nate's roommate would be numbered. What demigod would tolerate such an association on the part of his son?

* * *

"The Captain's here," Nate yelled over the roar of the engine. He switched off the ignition and they coasted up the driveway and into place behind a silver Porsche Targa.

After his more or less sleepless night, Ashby was dreading meeting the Captain. Just occupying his study for a few nights seemed presumptuous.

"He'll be in the pool," Nate said, sliding his surfboard over the side of the car from where it was nesting in the back seat. "We'll go out back and say hi. Just let me stow this."

Ashby went inside the house.

"Ash, dear," Eleanor greeted him. "Would you help me carry these things out back?"

She handed him a platter of sandwiches.

"If I don't feed the tribe they'll decimate Grannie's *hors d'oeuvres* the minute we get in the door and I'll never hear the end of it."

"'Lead on, MacDuff'," Ashby said. He had figured out that Eleanor liked it when he quoted Shakespeare as long as he chose lines obvious enough not to stump her.

"'Caesar shall go forth'," she giggled.

He followed her out the back door into the yard. Ollie and Peter were a few minutes behind them leaving the beach and hadn't arrived yet. The younger boys, Quinn through Ted, were in the pool presided over by the Captain, whose photos hardly did him justice. His golden hair was plastered to his head and his deeply bronzed skin gleamed with tanning oil. He was larger and more powerful looking than it seemed possible for a human being to be. Really, he was more a force of nature than a man. Ashby felt the ground move beneath his feet. He couldn't help staring.

* * *

Ashby's borrowed clothing couldn't have fit him better if he'd bought the outfit himself. He almost approved of the image he saw in the mirror.

"Time to go, everyone," Eleanor yelled from somewhere down the hall. "Now remember, Sammie and Ted ride with me. The rest of you divide up however you want to in the VW's. And no, Peter, you are not driving tonight. Captain's orders. Don't give Ollie a hard time about it."

In the driveway, the Duckworth menfolk clustered around the Porsche. Peter was helping the Captain latch the removable roof panel in place prior to takeoff. It seemed highly unlikely that a man of the Captain's magnitude could actually fit behind the wheel of the sleek little car, but those Germans were better engineers than Ashby had given them credit for. And apparently the Captain had gotten plenty of practice mounting and dismounting. Just before turning the key in the ignition, he extended an enormous paw out the window and gave a thumbs up sign.

"Pleasure to meet you Ash," he grinned. "Make sure you keep that good for nothing son of mine in check."

"Aye, aye," Ashby said, hoping to strike the right note of jaunty camaraderie.

"In the cars now," Eleanor called. "Grannie hates it when we're late."

* * *

"Don't be too upset with Nate," Eleanor said, sliding pancakes onto a plate. "There's butter, syrup, and juice already on the table."

"Thanks," Ashby said.

"Did you hear, me, Ash?"

"What are we talking about?"

"Those stories Nate told Grannie Helena about you last night. Please don't be too angry with him."

Ashby wasn't angry. He was humiliated. He hadn't planned to say anything about it because addressing it with anyone would only compound the feeling. He stared at the steaming pancakes and felt his appetite evaporating. He
wished he was anywhere else.

"My mother is an extremely difficult and unpleasant woman," Eleanor
said, moving toward him. "She disapproves of everybody and everything. And
she doesn't disapprove silently. She doesn't talk about people behind their
backs. Whatever she has to say she says to their faces, no matter how awful
it is. Nobody's ever been able to stop her. What we've all learned to do over
the years is cut her off at the pass. And yes, that generally means lying to her.
That's what Nate was doing. It's not a reflection on you at all. Honestly it's
not. Nate's Joanie is the sweetest girl in the world. She comes from a wonderful family. Her father manages a supermarket and her mother is a nurse. Now,
you'd think that would be good enough to satisfy anyone, wouldn't you? That
her parents love her and work very hard to give her and her brother and sister a
good home? But Nate knew—we all knew—what Grannie would have to say
about it if he told her the truth about Joanie's family. And he wouldn't subject
Joanie to that. No decent person would.

"And you should have heard the whoppers I told about the Captain back
before we were married. You'd have thought he was a real live prince instead
of just a kid from the other side of town. Now, the Captain doesn't approve of
all this. He thinks we're wrong to cater to Grannie's obsessions. He says if we
all challenged her prejudices every time she expressed them, she'd soon get the
message. And I suppose he's right, in a way. But I always say it's about nobody's
feelings getting hurt.

"The saving grace of it is she's such an old drunk she never remembers
what she's been told from one day to the next. But she always remembers
whether she approved of you or not. The next time you meet her she'll say, 'oh,
yes, Nathan's handsome young friend with the beautiful manners,' and she'll
kiss you on the cheek and offer you a canape, and I'm sorry, but if you ask me
there's no harm done."

"Well, to be completely honest. . ."

"Eat your pancakes, dear, before they get cold."

"I do come from about as disreputable a background as you could imagine."

"You don't have to tell me," she said, sitting down across from him with a
cup of coffee. She looked extremely interested in what he might be about to say.

"For starters," he plunged on, compelled somehow to lay it all out for her, "I'm illegitimate. I'm not sure who my father was, and apparently nobody else is, either. At any rate, nobody's talking. And my mother went to prison for killing her boyfriend and his wife before I could even talk. She died there in a riot between opposing gangs that erupted over a bottle of contraband whiskey."

"You're not making this up," Eleanor said quietly.

"No." Ashby looked her dead in the eye. "My Grandpa went to work drunk every day. And one morning he accidentally blew himself up along with half the refinery. And Grannie is just about the meanest drunk in the Western Hemisphere. If I hadn't figured out how to clean myself up, I'd be on that same road myself."

"Nate knows all this?"

"No. He knows there's something, but he doesn't know what. He's never asked, and I've never had the guts to tell him about it."

"He's always been that way," Eleanor said. "He shows remarkably little curiosity about his friends. It's how he expresses his anger with Grannie and her horrible snobbishness. By being the opposite. You see that, don't you?"

"Perfectly," Ashby told her.

IV

New Year's Day, Ashby was able to move back into their dorm room. The university had arranged special housing for students who for various reasons, most having to do with geography, had nowhere to go over the Christmas break, and he moved in right after his last exam. He had been invited to spend the break with the Duckworths but was quite sure Nate needed tome away from him. Besides, three weeks seemed like too long to accept anyone's hospitality. He had agreed to three days instead, and three days under their roof was more than enough. When he left, they were all still friends. The Captain had been absent for all but a few hours on Christmas Eve. Back on campus, Ashby shared a room with a Rumanian piano student who repeatedly begged him to give his heart to Jesus. Ashby fended this off by pretending that the boy's accent defeated him.

He was stowing the last of his underwear back in its drawer and basking in his relief at being on his own territory again when the buzzer rang. A single buzz was supposed to indicate that the call was for Nate, but the guys on the front desk invariably made mistakes so he hurried down the hall to the telephone.

"Hello."

"Ash? It's Matt Duckworth. Happy New Year."

"Thanks, Captain. Happy New Year to you. Nate isn't here."

"I know. They weren't back from the beach yet when I pulled out of Newport. Listen, I've got some time before I have to head up to LAX. How about joining me for dinner?"

"Well. . ."

"No excuses about studying. It's a holiday. And you have to eat."

"All right."

"I'll pick you up in front of the dorm in twenty minutes."

Back in the room, Ashby brushed his teeth, slipped into the khakis and sweater Eleanor had given him for Christmas, and combed his hair. He wanted desperately to look like the kind of son or nephew the Captain would be seen in a restaurant with.

* * *

The Porsche snarled up out of the darkness and Ashby got inside.

"Ash. Great to see you."

"Thanks for inviting me."

"No. Thank you. You'd think after all these years eating by myself wouldn't bother me, but I've never gotten used to it. I hope you're hungry."

"I'm pretty much always hungry," Ashby said.

"Good man."

* * *

The restaurant was nice but not too nice. Ashby was perfectly turned out for the surroundings. At a couple of other tables he saw guys his age in jeans and t-shirts. They looked as out of place as chimpanzees at the opera and their mothers were obviously annoyed by it. Ashby was glad he'd gone to the trouble. Across the table from him, the Captain was resplendent. His hair was shiny and his teeth could have starred in a toothpaste commercial. He seemed more enormous every time Ashby encountered him.

"I'm not drinking tonight because of the flight later," the Captain said, "but if you'd like wine for dinner, go ahead."

"I never drink."

"No?"

"Doesn't agree with my stomach." Ashby had learned that this excuse was pretty much unassailable in any circumstances, though his real objection had to do with the alcoholics in his family tree.

"Can't have that," the Captain smiled. "The food here is too good to waste. I'd really like to order the Chateaubriand for two. I love Chateaubriand, but restaurants never prepare it for a single diner. If that's O.K. with you?"

"Sounds great," Ashby said. He had a vague idea Chateaubriand had something to do with beef, so that was all right. He was generally nervous about seafood, crawfish being about the extent of his familiarity with it and far from his favorite.

It was a pleasant dinner. They mostly talked about Ashby's classes and his plans to go to medical school after graduation. The Captain seemed genuinely interested. Ashby supposed that as the father of an extensive tribe of boys, such conversations were second nature to him. He found it intriguing that both of Nate's parents showed much more interest in him than Nate did himself. Perhaps this was simply adult good manners, but in the back of his mind Ashby was always a little afraid that it indicated some suspicion of him on their part.

As far as he was concerned, any suspicion they might have was entirely justified. He just hoped they weren't mind readers. The minute they figured him out, he'd probably be drawn and quartered.

The Chateaubriand lived up to its billing, and though the Captain refused dessert he insisted that Ashby order some cheesecake. Apparently the restaurant was famous for its cheesecake.

"Listen, if you don't mind," the Captain said. "I'd like to stop by my hotel to pick up my bags on the way to your dorm. Then I won't have to double back before I can get on the road north."

"Sure."

* * *

The Captain's room was as neat as if the chambermaids had just been there. This was the fleeting impression Ashby got before it happened. He was standing at the window looking out at the beach while the Captain was in the bathroom. He could hear the tap running. Then it shut off, and he turned, and there the Captain was, looking at him. A little strangely, he thought. He couldn't be certain of it at that distance, and the light in the room was dim.

"Come here, Ash."

It didn't occur to Ashby to ask why or to say no or simply not to move. They were across the room from each other and then they weren't. That was all. The Captain smoothed Ashby's hair with a massive hand, and just that touch made Ashby woozy in a way that was completely unfamiliar and yet totally disarming.

He wouldn't have been at all surprised if someone had told him that the Captain was a good kisser. It seemed obvious he'd be as expert at that as he was at everything else. But finding it out in such an existential manner during the next several moments was the most astounding experience of Ashby's life to that point. This astonishment was followed by a series of others. The fragrant, satiny firmness of the Captain's smoothly shaven, ostentatiously swelling chest against his face. The amazing magnitude of the shoulders and arms. The totally unexpected permission Ashby had apparently been granted to touch whatever and wherever. The remarkable delicacy of the Captain's touch at certain instants, and the almost terrifying force of it at others. And finally, the completely indescribable, almost paralyzing sensation that Ashby couldn't have imagined wishing to escape.

* * *

"Oh God, Ash," the Captain murmured afterward, his head resting on Ashby's chest. "Oh God, oh God. Ever since Nate brought you home at Thanksgiving I haven't been able to get you out of my mind. I've never felt this way about anyone. Never in my whole life. You're just, I don't know, some kind of miracle."

This was not the way Ashby had ever imagined being spoken to. And it was those words, more than any of the physical sensations he had just experienced, that finally made it impossible for him to control himself.

"Jesus, don't cry," the Captain said. "I didn't mean to hurt you."

"You didn't," Ashby sobbed. "I'm all right."

"Really? You're not just saying that? Because if I hurt you, I'm so very sorry."

"It's fine."

"I thought you wanted it."

"I did," Ashby said. "I just never imagined. . ."

He stroked the Captain's disarranged hair, hoping by this gesture to demonstrate his good faith. He felt somehow that he'd like to go on stroking that amazing golden hair for the rest of his life.

"Ash? Was this your first time with a man?"

"First time with anybody."

They did it again, this time in the shower. And Ashby managed to be more than just a stunned bystander. His avidity surprised him. Afterward, dressed again, he watched as the Captain shaved, spritzed his underarms with cologne just like Nate did—though the cologne was a different one—and oiled and combed his hair. It was like being in church, Ashby mused. Or, more accurately, like being in church should be but never had been.

* * *

The Porsche idled turbulently at the curb in front of the dorm. Ashby knew better, but it sounded as if the car was impatient.

"Ash, listen to me," the Captain said, grasping his hand. "I've fallen in love with you. Do you understand?"

"I'm not sure," Ashby said, unwilling to lie about it.

"Fair enough," the Captain said. "I'll just have to make you understand."

"All right."

Ashby climbed out of the car. The engine raced. He heard the Captain shift into gear. Behind him, as he turned toward the entrance to the dorm, the car roared off into the darkness. In the window of their room he could see a light burning that he knew he had turned off before leaving earlier.

Nate must be back.

V

The next day, Ashby couldn't believe it had really happened. In daylight, the impossibility of the encounter was unmistakable. It wasn't real. None of it. It violated every known principle of the cosmos and several yet to be discovered ones. Or maybe dinner had been real but nothing else. The curse of the Sainte-Claires had entered some new phase and Ashby was losing his mind. Meanwhile, the Captain was far away in a shining airplane, unaware of Ashby's existence, oblivious to the riotous fantasies his rampant masculinity had unleashed in an unstable and impressionable psyche.

But though Ashby couldn't believe what had transpired, he couldn't disbelieve it, either, try as he might. It was as if the experience had left some weird stigmata upon him, invisible to the naked eye but unmistakable, like an amputee's phantom limb.

Until the Captain's arms closed around him and the Captain's lips pressed themselves against his, Ashby had believed he was in love with Nate. Since the moment he had entered that dorm room for the first time and seen Nate screwing bicycle hooks to the wall he had known it. All his life Ashby had been waiting for that moment and that vision and there it was, as if it had been placed there by fate for him to encounter. Ever since, there had scarcely been a waking moment when he wasn't conscious of his worship of Nate. Glory in it or deplore it as he might depending on his mood, adoration of his roommate had more or less immediately become the focus of his existence. Everything else he did was just filling in time, going through the motions, living a life with no other purpose. Seeing the light on in their dorm room as the Porsche snarled away into the darkness forced those familiar feelings back into his consciousness. He was a man washed up on a beach after being tossed around helpless in the surf for a certain vertiginous period. Now he was back on dry land, heart still beating yet still only partially in command of his faculties. It had been a close call, an epic encounter with unknown and unknowable forces, but it was over. Whatever it was, he had survived it. He was forgetting it with each breath he drew. He repeated his accustomed mantra on his way upstairs, feeling that it was his road back to sanity. Entering the room he encountered his beloved propped against the wall doing handstand pushups, golden hair brushing the floor on each down stroke, bare chest glinting with sweat in spite of the chill entering the room through the open windows. That was real, not some bizarre hallucination. That was beautiful. No question about it. That was worth devoting himself to.

But as Ashby entered the room and tried not to stare, a new reality hurled itself at him. And the next morning, determined as he was to ignore it, it was no less apparent. Nate's resemblance to the Captain was obvious. Looking at his roommate called all too clearly to mind what Ashby was struggling to convince himself hadn't taken place. The lines and shapes were recognizably the same, the contours uncannily familiar. That recognition was what he couldn't account for absent an acknowlegement of what had taken place, which now seemed less a bizarre catastrophe than a revelation. Yes, the lines and shapes, the color, the texture, the configuration of certain elements. Even to a casual observer Nate and the Captain couldn't have been mistaken for anything but close relations. It wasn't just comfortably above the neck that all this was true. And Ashby's new knowledge forced him to confront what had changed. His worship of the son had been fatally disrupted by his encounter with the father. He'd never be able to look at Nate the same way again. Nate was still beautiful, but the Captain was transcendent. Nate was strong and stalwart, but the Captain seemed downright immortal.

Because it hadn't really happened, because it couldn't possibly have happened since there was no way of explaining how and why such a thing might occur, Ashby's devotion to Nate should have persisted undiminished. That passionate but chaste adoration should have burned on unaltered in his heart like the purest flame. But despite Ashby's frantic determination to will things back into how they had previously been, his own body betrayed him. It seemed to have been inhabited by a stranger while he wasn't looking. While he was lost in his hallucination. Involuntarily, he recalled those all too vivid sensations with which he had previously been unfamiliar. Sensations which had been nothing but hypotheses until the Captain took him in arms that caressed yet permitted no resistance. Sensations the memories of which transformed themselves over the next few days into cravings. More than once he found himself on the point of reaching out to stroke Nate's silken chest as he stared out the window observing the weather and weighing whether he should attend class or go surfing. More than once Ashby only prevented himself from sniffing Nate's hair as he bent over his algebra homework by the strongest, most rigorous of self control. More than once those dark nipples taunted him. They would taste the same as those other, remembered ones. They had to. But maybe not.

Something had happened to him to coax his temptation from the realm of the imagined to the reality of the moment. His restraint saved him each time, though barely. That restraint was not, he understood more clearly each day, based in morality or fear of the consequences or innate delicacy of feeling but in the certainty that, since Nate wasn't his father, the result of such an act would be more than anything else a simple disappointment. The skin was not as smooth. The muscles, though impressive enough to be seductive, didn't bulge as astonishingly. The hair was not as shiny or as perfectly groomed. Nate was unfinished, Ashby realized. Everything about him lacked calculation.

Ashby had believed he was in love with Nate. And though he continued to try to be in love with Nate, though he ached still to be in love with Nate, who was familiar, whose habits he knew and behavior he could predict, who was mortal like himself, this now seemed impossible. It could never be possible again, apparently, after what he still insisted to himself hadn't actually happened because how could such an occurrence be explained? Contrary to his expectation, his hope, the memories didn't fade. His astonishment didn't abate. With each passing day, the experience loomed grander and more compelling in his consciousness. He felt it transforming itself into an obsession. And even in his sleep he didn't escape it. The dreams came every night, over and over. He woke from them sweaty and sticky, terrified of what Nate might have heard or only sensed from the upper bunk. Real or not, those brief moments wrestling with the god had ruined him for anything less. Even if he never experienced anything similar again, he was lost and it would take more than a boy like Nate to save him.

VI

"It's going to be so great," Nate said, tossing bathing suits into a duffel. "Acapulco is amazing. The water. The sand. The sunsets. The girls. And you won't believe the seafood. Did I tell you Grannie Helena's vacation house is right on the beach?"

"Yes," Ashby said. "Yes, you did."

Ashby had never been to a foreign country. California, with all its unaccustomed and spellbinding wonders, didn't count.

"You're sure I don't need a passport?" he asked.

"For the thousandth time," Nate said, "driver's license is all you have to have. The Mexicans don't care. They'll let anybody in. It's just about getting back into the States."

When they got to Casa Duckworth, as it had been dubbed during the weeks of planning for spring break, they transferred their bags to the trunk of Eleanor's Mercedes. She'd be driving them and the oldest two of Nate's younger brothers to LAX for their flight.

* * *

In the departure lounge, Nate's brothers could hardly contain themselves.

"I'm going to have shrimp for every meal," Ollie announced. "Even breakfast. I'm going to make the Captain fix me shrimp omelets."

"He's famous for his shrimp omelets," Eleanor told Ashby. "They truly are out of this world. But if you don't like shrimp, don't pretend you do. He'll make you anything you want for breakfast. He really should have been a restauranteur."

"And I'm going to go cliff diving," Peter said.

"Easy, pardner," Nate cautioned. "I think you have to have a license for that."

"Really?" Peter asked, crestfallen. "Is that right, Ash? Or is Nate making it up? He's such a spoilsport."

"There's probably some kind of rule," Ashby said. "And anyway, I'm not sure the Captain would think it's a good idea."

"That old daredevil?" Ollie laughed. "He's gone cliff diving himself. Hundreds of times."

"You're joking," Ashby said, astonished.

"The cliffs at Acapulco are much higher," Nate said. "The Captain's never been off anything more than seventy feet or so. And I believe the water at Acapulco is much shallower. You really have to know what you're doing. People have been killed."

"You will not go cliff diving," Eleanor said. "None of you. The Captain and I already discussed it."

"Boo," Peter complained.

"Make them behave, Ashby," Eleanor said, kissing him on the cheek as the others headed for the gate. "At least promise me you'll try."

"I'll do my best."

"And have a wonderful time, dear."

Ashby had never flown before. He didn't know what he'd been expecting but he was surprised that it was so reminiscent of riding on a bus.

* * *

The Captain was waiting at the airport when they got to Acapulco. They piled their bags into the back of his rented VW van.

"Shotgun," Peter yelled.

"Son, Ashby is our guest this week," the Captain said. "He rides shotgun."

"Oh, all right."

"Good to see you young man," the Captain said, turning to shake Ashby's hand. "Doing all right, I hope?"

"Thanks for inviting me," Ashby said.

* * *

This was Ashby's chance to observe the Captain as a man and not just somebody he had had sex with half a dozen times. That's who he kept trying to convince himself the Captain was, though he knew better. He had heard, of course, all about what a perfect husband and father the Captain was but couldn't help being suspicious. His own experiences inevitably seemed to call all that into question. Still, he couldn't help being impressed at the way the boys respected the man. They fell over themselves trying to be the fastest to follow his simplest instructions. Even Nate, strong willed, self possessed, independent Nate, fell right into line. When the Captain gave an order, and give orders he constantly did, they all hopped to. The orders themselves, Ashby couldn't help noticing, were reasonable in the extreme and expressed in the calmest, most non-coercive tones. There was nothing particularly militaristic in play. But there was no question who called the shots. The Captain's entire style rested not on brute authority but clearly, as Ashby's high school government teacher would have put it, on the consent of the governed, which in this case seemed enthusiastically given. It was a triumph of charisma, the same charisma, matured, refined, and intensified, that he'd always so admired in Nate.

God help Ashby.

But the Captain was much more, it turned out, than the layer down of laws, however benign. He was the ultimate scout leader. As adept in the kitchen as Ashby assumed he must be at the controls of his jetliners, as organized and hygienically minded as a nurse in a military field hospital, as imaginative as a kindergarten teacher at keeping his charges entertained; if ever a man was qualified to be a father, the Captain was. Extravagantly so.

For Ashby, who had never experienced or even witnessed anything like normal parent-child interactions, it was spellbinding. How different his life would have been with such a man in charge of it during those terrifying years when he'd had to make his own way without the least understanding of what was required.

* * *

"Complexion like yours, you'll burn to a crisp," the Captain said as everybody was getting ready for the beach the first morning. "Better let me put some of this on you."

"Should you do that?" Ashby said as the Captain tugged the t-shirt over his head. "The boys might see."

"Relax. I've been putting suntan oil on the boys all their lives. They won't think a thing about it."

"If you say so," Ashby said. The feeling of those strong, confident hands on him made him lightheaded.

"This is a good thing, Ash," the Captain said. "Chance to really get to know each other."

"We won't have a minute to ourselves."

"Does it matter?"

"Of course it does," Ashby said.

"Really?" the Captain asked. "No relationship is just about sex."

"That's not what I meant."

"I know. But try to go with the flow. You'll see. We'll have a great time."

* * *

Watching the Captain with his boys was like being on the set of one of those old gladiator movies. Their oiled bodies gleamed in the sunshine and their hoarse laughter echoed up the beach. The Captain was the legendary warrior and they were his band of men, all strong and fearless and beautiful. They rampaged up and down the sand and frolicked in the surf. They were perfect in every possible way. They were, it appeared, the fabled happy ending made flesh. Except it wasn't make believe. They weren't actors. They weren't even the mythological heroes who had inspired the actors. It was real, and all the more compelling for that. Ashby couldn't for the life of him see where he fitted into such a picture.

There were excursions to the marketplaces, long afternoons on the beach, and cookouts on the terrace in the early evenings. They went every day to watch the cliff divers. They rode tour boats and donkeys—even a helicopter. The Captain knew how to keep them busy. The Captain knew how to tire them out. By evening, Ollie and Peter could barely keep their eyes open and dozed in front of the television, missing programs they couldn't understand anyway. By evening, Nate had had his fill of company and went for long walks. The Captain and Ashby sat side by side on the terrace, looking out at the dark water. Talking or silent, it didn't matter.

The week passed like one night's dream. It was over before Ashby knew it, and, to his regret, long before he was ready. Their last night in Acapulco they went to a famous restaurant and gorged themselves on seafood. Afterward, Nate and his brothers insisted on seeing a movie.

"You know it won't be in English," the Captain said.

"That'll make it even funnier," Ollie said.

"All right," the Captain said, "but I'm taking Ashby back to the house and putting him to bed. He hasn't complained about it, but I can tell he's got a touch of sunstroke. He'll be miserable on the plane tomorrow if he doesn't get some rest."

It was a masterful performance.

* * *

Afterward, the Captain was in the mood to talk.

"Don't worry," he said, cradling Ashby from behind. "It'll be hours before the boys come in. You know they'll be in no hurry to head back after the movie gets out."

"You're not worried about them? Out there on their own? Mexico isn't Southern California."

"Do you think I should be?"

"No," Ashby said after a moment's consideration. "They're good guys. And very smart. You and Eleanor have done an amazing job."

"Thanks."

"I mean it," Ashby said, a catch in his voice. "They have no idea how lucky they are."

"That's how you know you've done a good job as a parent," the Captain said, stroking Ashby's hair. "When they seem to take everything you've done for them for granted but at the same time you can tell they're going to be the same way with their own kids."

"I don't guess I ever thought of that way."

"I've been watching you this week, Ash."

Here it came. Ashby had known from the minute the trip was proposed that it would probably mean the end of things.

"You're feeling guilty," the Captain said.

"Of course I am."

"That wasn't the idea of this trip. To make you feel guilty."

"I can't help it. How else am I supposed to feel? Seeing my boyfriend or whatever it is you are with your sons. Thinking all the time that if they found out about us it would ruin everything. "

"When Eleanor and I got married we made an agreement," the Captain said. "Either of us ever wanted out we wouldn't fight about it. We'd shake hands and go our separate ways. Well, that's what's happening."

"Oh, God," Ashby said. "I never wanted things to turn out that way. She's a wonderful person. She's always been so nice to me, and here I've gone and. . ."

"Easy there, pardner. It's not what you're thinking. Thing is, Eleanor's fallen in love."

"What?" Ashby was astonished. "You mean with somebody else?"

"Old flame," the Captain said. "Guy she should have married in the first place, I guess. His wife died a while back. He's ready to move on. And Eleanor's decided to move on with him. It'll be fine. He'll make her happier than I've been able to, and he's crazy about the boys."

"But what about you?"

"I'll still be in the picture, of course," the Captain said. "See them whenever I want. Very little will change."

"You're still talking about them," Ashby chuckled. "What about you? What about Matt Duckworth?"

"Me?" the Captain smiled wistfully. "That all depends, Ash."

"I don't understand."

"I think you do," the Captain said. "I'm asking you to. . .well, I mean, this thing between us isn't going away. You know that as much as I do. It's. . .it's once in a lifetime, isn't it? I'm crazier about you every time I see you. And this week has made me sure of it. I want us to be more than just guys who fuck whenever we get the chance to sneak off somewhere. I know you want that, too. That's what it all depends on. That's what I told Eleanor."

"You told Eleanor about us?"

"She says it's a dream come true. Each of us gets the man of our dreams."

"I can't believe it."

"So what do you say?"

VII

"Ash, dear, it's so kind of you to meet me for lunch," Eleanor cooed once they were seated and their drink orders had been taken.

Acapulco had been over a month ago.

"No, Eleanor, you're the one who's being kind, inviting me like this."

"But Ash, I know how busy you college students are this time of year. I can hardly get Nate to stay on the phone long enough to tell me he doesn't have time to talk."

"A free lunch is something no busy college student wouldn't make time for," Ash said. "And you of all people should know what a freeloader I am."

"You're the sweetest young man in the world, I'm sure," Eleanor said. "You must know we all think the world of you."

Ashby didn't see how that could possibly have been true even if the circumstances were radically different. Just then the waiter arrived to explain the intricacies of the menu to them. He made it seem as complicated as it could be, as if they were journalists being conducted on a tour of some amazing new industrial plant which only three or four of the best minds on the planet could be expected to grasp the intricacies of. They disappointed the young man with their orders, a chef salad for Eleanor and a bacon avocado cheeseburger for Ashby.

"Ash, dear," Eleanor said, looking somewhat pensively at the waiter's retreating backside. "You and I have something to discuss."

"Yes," he said. He'd been dreading this part since her call.

"I know you know that the Captain and I are getting a divorce. We haven't told the boys yet, but of course you're in on it."

"I am," he admitted.

"Now you must listen very carefully to what I have to say. You're not to hold yourself one bit responsible for this. . .situation we find ourselves in. Not one bit, do you understand?"

"I don't see how you can say that," Ashby stammered. Having no experience at playing the other woman, he really wasn't sure how to proceed.

"Well, dear, because it's true, that's how. Matthew and I have been drifting along in this certain direction for quite some time now. Even before he told me about himself—and you, of course—I had come to the conclusion that both of us would be much happier with other people. It's like an answer to prayer, really, that we've each found someone at pretty much the same time."

Ashby only hoped she was being truthful with him about her feelings. It all seemed too good to be true, and in his experience too good to be true inevitably was what it said it was.

"He's quite torn. If it were up to me, he'd just sit the boys down and come out of the closet to them and have it done. That is what you say, isn't it? Come out of the closet?"

"I think usually it's just 'come out'," Ashby said, "when you're talking about telling people about yourself."

"Ah. Well then, if it were up to me, that's what he would do. But he's concerned, you see, that some of the younger ones—well, it might confuse them a little. At the phase they're in. He's afraid they might begin to wonder about their own feelings. I say he's too cautious. The boys are going to be whatever they're going to be. Just like you and he are. But he's really very worried about it. You need to understand this, dear. It has nothing at all to do with him being ashamed of himself or of you. Please promise me you won't let yourself think that it does."

"I'll try not to," Ashby said.

"Good boy. Ah, here comes our food. The kitchen certainly must be on the ball today."

The waiter served their plates with what Ashby thought was a quite unnecessary flourish. His fries looked a little underdone. He preferred them all but burnt but he dreaded the sort of negotiation with the waiter which would be required to remedy this. Guys as attractive as that were still pretty much impossible for him to cope with. In any case, he probably shouldn't be eating as many fries as he did in a typical week.

"This looks delightful," Eleanor observed, attacking her chef salad with her accustomed gusto. She had a remarkable appetite for such a slender woman. Her friends must absolutely despise her.

"I don't suppose," Eleanor said, sipping her iced tea, "Nate has ever told you how the Captain and I got married in the first place."

"No," Ashby said. "No he hasn't. But there's something—I don't know how to put it exactly—something about it that makes him uncomfortable."

"Well of course he's uncomfortable," Eleanor laughed. "He was born just five months after the wedding."

Ashby tried not to gape.

"Darling Ash, if you could see the look on your face."

"Sorry."

"You youngsters think you invented sex, is the problem. Well, you didn't, all right? How on earth do you all think you got here in the first place? It's so silly of you. But my friends and I were the same way. Anyhow, the story is this. I had graduated from college and was about to start my master's program, and my roomie from the sorority house, Giselle Van Dyke, well she and I made a bet about the Captain. Although he wasn't the Captain at the time, just Matthew Duckworth, her parents' pool boy. Anyway, our bet was to see which one of us could sleep with him first. Just innocent, girlish fun, right?"

"Innocent girlish fun?"

"A joke, Ash. We were what was known at the time as 'fast girls'. Nowadays I suppose we'd just be called sluts. Anyway, I won the bet. What neither of us knew was that he was only sixteen at the time. He was extremely mature for his age. Physically at least. Very much like Nate is now, if you see what I mean.

But there's no getting around it. We were contributing to the delinquency of a minor. The other thing we didn't know was how extremely fertile he would turn out to be. I was pregnant more or less immediately. Which was a big surprise to me, let me tell you, because I'd been sleeping with my boyfriend, Hobart McKinney, for just ages, no precautions of any kind, mind you, and never so much as a false alarm. Mummy and Daddy insisted I get married. Mummy expected me to tell Hobart the baby was his. But I couldn't bring myself to do it. First of all, it would have made Mummy happy, and that's never a good thing. I refuse to do it except when absolutely necessary, although sometimes when I'm not careful it happens accidentally. But the real reason was I didn't want to lie to Hobie about it. I had never lied to him before, and it didn't seem right to lie to him about a thing like that. I mean, I'd certainly left things out when I told him about my day, you know? All girls do that. But I'd never made anything up. And I'd never actually denied anything that he asked me about directly. So I thought of myself as reasonably honest with him. And what a good thing it turned out to be that I didn't lie to him that time. Because Nate looks nothing like him. People would have figured it out more or less immediately. Newport Beach wasn't that big a place in those days. Everybody knew who Matthew was. And anyway, it turned out later on that Hobie couldn't have children at all. Something about a severe case of mumps he had in tenth grade. So there I would have been, caught red handed. Because he always said he wanted a big family, and when there were no more babies after Nate he'd have gone to the doctor just like he did when he and Giselle didn't have any—yes, the same Giselle. She married him on the rebound from me.

"Anyway, Giselle passed away a couple of years ago, which was very, very sad, and since that time Hobie and I have become quite close again. And he's really devoted to the boys. Then when the Captain fell in love with you—well, it's just like a fairy tale ending, don't you think?"

"Perhaps not exactly."

* * *

"So you will remember, won't you?" Eleanor said, turning the key in the ignition. "Not a word to Nate?"

"Who's Nate?"

"Exactly."

"Don't worry."

"I know it's a terrible position we're putting you in, dear," she said, frowning into the rear view mirror. "Of course you must be used to that by now."

"I don't think you can ever get used to keeping secrets from people you really care about," Ashby said.

"I'm sure that's true," she agreed. "Still, it won't be for long. I can promise you that. Just as soon as the Captain can get his schedule under control so that we can all be together for a family meeting. It shouldn't be more than a week or two. You can keep it under your hat for that long, can't you?"

"Of course."

"Oh, Ash," she said, shifting the car into gear, "you have no idea how happy it makes me to think of you and the Captain together. He's a new man these days. Just absolutely a new man. You're a miracle worker. That's all there is to it. You and I really need to sit down with Joanie and give her some pointers about dealing with Nate. I'm sure she'd find our advice valuable. I think that boy keeps her tied up and crosseyed most of the time. That's a terrible position for a young woman to find herself in."

* * *

"She's being so nice about the whole thing," Ashby said, nearly in tears. "I can't believe how nice she's being."

"What did I tell you?" the Captain grunted, nuzzling the back of his neck. "I know."

"You could have saved yourself a whole lot of worry if you had just taken my word for it," the Captain said. "Still, it's good that the two of you had a chance to sit down together and talk it out."

"She talked," Ashby said. "I listened."

"Yes," the Captain said. "That's how it works with Eleanor."

* * *

"Look who I found in the lobby," Ashby said.

"What the hell, Ollie?" Nate said, sitting up in his bunk. "Why didn't you come on up?"

"He was afraid you'd still be asleep."

"I was."

"See, Ash," Ollie said. "I told you."

"So, what is this? Run away from home to join the circus?" Nate yawned.

"Cut the sarcasm," Ollie said. "We've got a crisis on our hands."

"Not an air disaster, I hope," Nate said, pulling back the sheets and beginning his dismount from the top bunk. This daily maneuver occurred in the nude, and Ashby invariably turned his back—subtly as he could. But Nate's remark had him so paralyzed that he just stood there and watched things flop around. It wasn't as much like the Captain's as he would have expected given all their other physical similarities. For one thing, Nate was circumcised.

"You know the Captain refuses to participate in plane crashes," Ollie said.

At this information Ashby felt his heart start beating again.

"What is it, then?"

"I really should head to the library," Ashby suggested.

"No, Ash," Ollie said. "You're practically a member of the family. And God knows you're smarter than this lunkhead."

"If you're sure," Ashby said, and was ignored.

"So?"

"We think Mom is cheating on the Captain."

At this information Ashby felt his heart stop once again.

"Cheating on the Captain?" Nate mused. "That makes no sense at all. Though I suppose anything is possible. But who is it that thinks so?"

"Well, with you down here doing nothing but surfing and chasing tail, Quinn has had to step in as brains of the operation."

"Makes sense," Nate said. "Better him than you or Peter."

"Recently he came to Peter and me with his suspicions. We decided to investigate."

"And?"

"We're pretty certain of it at this point. You know how many eyes and ears we've had on the job."

"I hope you left the little ones out of it," Nate cautioned.

"As much as we've been able to."

"What the hell, Ollie?" Nate demanded, finally starting to pull on a pair of gym shorts, "could you possibly mean by that?"

"We told Sammie and Ted to keep their eyes and ears open," Ollie explained. "We just didn't tell them what for."

"And how did that work out?"

"They were a wealth of information," Ollie said.

"Jesus."

"None of which they understood the significance of."

"Thank God," Nate said, finding the gym shorts unsatisfactory and pulling them back off again. "You know, I don't think I'm up to this on an empty stomach."

* * *

"You drive," Nate said, handing Ashby the keys. "Ollie, ride shotgun."

"Right," Ollie said. "How are the driving lessons going, anyway?"

"You'll see, won't you?" Nate grinned.

Ashby got the engine started and managed to back the car out of the space without stalling.

"Where to?" he asked.

Where to was one of their usual weekend joints, a greasy spoon right on the beach that served enormous omelets accompanied by mountainous heaps of home fries, or, in Ashby's case, a steaming bowl of grits. On hearing of his choice of university, Miss LaMontaigne, his high school guidance counselor, solemnly told him that no one in California had ever heard of grits. Imagining the expression on her face should he ever bother to correct her always made him smile.

"Aren't you afraid you're being missed?" Nate asked. "I know there are a lot of us, but Mom's always been pretty good at keeping track."

"I spent the night at Joey Baum's house is my cover story," Ollie explained. "I even let his mom tuck me in."

"Gross."

"And if Mom should happen to call, which she won't because she thinks Sheila Baum is icky, the story will be that we've already hit the beach."

"So supposing you pack of wolf pups are correct and Mom is cheating on the Captain," Nate said through a mouthful of toast, "exactly who is she cheating on the Captain with?"

"Uncle Hobart," Ollie said.

"Uncle Hobart? What happened to Mr. McKinney?"

"We've all been instructed to address him as Uncle Hobart," Ollie said. "Captain's orders. Goes for you, too, probably."

"Uncle Hobart," Nate mused. "I can't believe it."

"The Uncle Hobart part or the other part?" Ollie asked.

"Both, I guess."

* * *

"Now remember, young Oliver," Nate said, "you guys keep your mouths shut about this for now."

"Aye, aye, lieutenant," Ollie grinned. "Look at him Ash. See how he hates being called that?"

"Then why do it?" Ashby asked, ever on the alert for the esoterica of fraternal conflict.

"Because he hates being called 'young Oliver'," Nate said, once again lounging in the back seat.

"Is it really that simple?" Ashby asked.

"There's nothing simple about it," Ollie said. "There never is where brothers are involved. I'll relay your instructions to Quinn, and he'll decide whether we'll follow them or make it up as we go along."

"Great," Nate said. "And while you're at it, have Robbie go over the quadratic formula with you."

"Asshole."

"I really have to get to the library," Ashby said, steering the car into a parking space in front of the dorm.

* * *

"Hello."

"Eleanor, it's Ashby."

"Ash, dear, how are you?"

"I've been better."

"What's wrong? Has something happened to Nate?"

"You and the Captain need to sit down with your sons as soon as possible."

"Really? Why?"

"The boys are onto you and Hobart. Ollie's just been here talking to Nate about it."

VIII

"Where are we going?"

"You'll see. It's not much farther."

The Porsche knifed through the sunshine. With Nate back home in Orange County for the summer, Ashby's relationship with the Captain had changed. They saw each other more often and there was hardly any sneaking around. After getting used to this degree of freedom, Ashby was dreading the fall semester. That was making a big assumption, however. Every time they parted, Ashby still felt like the Captain was exiting his life forever.

"Why don't you put on that Mahler tape?"

The Captain was devoted to Mahler. This both surprised and fascinated Ashby. He slipped the cassette into the player. They were spending the whole day together. This was a first for them. Acapulco didn't count because the boys had been there. Ashby had already added today to the mental list of firsts he was keeping. There had been several this weekend, and it was only Saturday morning. The first time he had watched the Captain shave his chest, the first time they had performed that sex act in that position, and in a few more miles it would be the first time they had crossed a county line together. Last night was only the third time they had been together for a whole night. Being spooned by the Captain—as mind blowing as their sex was, the memory of being held all night long by that giant was the thing most likely to drive Ashby to suicide in the event the Captain ever moved on. The first time it happened Ashby was overwhelmed by the sensation. It had seemed to fill some deep, primal need he didn't know he suffered from until the moment those enormous arms closed around him. The intensity of the emotion was such that he feared he was losing his mind, as if those arms were the only force anchoring him to reality. It was the most profoundly disturbing and at the same time comforting experience of his life to that point. That included their first time together. That night, Ashby recalled, he had experienced a kind of paralyzed terror. This, he thought, was what happened when the handsome prince rode up. He didn't reach down and swing you into the saddle with him, he dismounted, ripped off your clothing, threw you down, and shoved a certain part of his anatomy into a place you had never imagined that part of anyone's anatomy would ever go. For his own part, Ashby's astonishment at all that happened had been eclipsed by his astonishment at his absolute unwillingness to resist it. He didn't scream with pain, didn't shout for the Captain to stop, didn't do anything but lie there hoping inexplicably that whatever was going on would never stop. Since then it had stopped, but only intermittently. It was as if when they weren't having sex they were just getting over having sex or getting ready to have sex, no matter how extended the intermission turned out to be.

The morning after the Captain first held him all night long, Ashby sensed that he was somehow transformed. Contrary to his expectations, that feeling that he had become a new, somehow better, person persisted.

* * *

The sign on the building said "Joseph Schnittker Volkswagen/Porsche Repair and Service."

"Is something wrong with the car?" Ashby asked, as the Captain pulled into a parking space.

"They sell used Volkses here," the Captain said, reaching across him to pull an envelope out of the glove compartment.

"Oh?"

"You're going to buy one. Here's the money."

Ashby peered inside the envelope at the stack of hundreds.

"I can't take this."

"Ash, I'm tired of picking you up and dropping you off at the dorm. It takes up time that could be better spent. And it's a constant risk. All Nate has to do is look out the window at the wrong moment. This isn't for you; it's for both of us. Besides, I spent way more than that on new bikes and surfboards for the boys last Christmas. And Robbie's orthodonture alone. . ."

"All right," Ashby said. "I get it. But how am I supposed to explain this much money to Nate? You know I'm a terrible liar. Talk about risky."

"He's mentioned several times how thrifty you are, how careful you are with your cash. You must have saved it out of your scholarship money."

"Nate might buy that," Ashby conceded, "I guess. But what about this place? Do you know anything about them?"

"I haven't done any business with them myself. But I have good friends who have. You're not going to get ripped off."

"All right. Now just who are you supposed to be when we go in there? My uncle?"

"It's none of their business whether I'm your uncle or the man in the moon. You're buying a car, Ash, not running for the senate."

* * *

"We've got some very nice cars for sale," the shop owner said. "Have a look. I'll be out in a couple of minutes."

They stepped out of the office into the back lot. Two rows of VW's faced each other across freshly seal-coated asphalt. The little cars almost looked like they were grinning, Ashby thought.

"How about this one?" the Captain said, standing beside a red convertible.

"Nate knows I'd never buy something like that," Ashby shook his head. "There's no way he'd believe it was in my budget. A plain one, I think. Maybe with a sunroof."

* * *

"So, youngster," the shop owner said, "you ready to go inside and start the paperwork on this one?"

"Hang on a minute, Ash," the Captain said. "Before you do anything, I think you should have a look at this Karmann-Ghia."

"That's a very nice little car," Joe said. "A couple years older than the Beetle you just drove, but it's got very low miles. We just put a new set of Michelins on it. Old ones weren't worn out, just dry rotted. Sat in the garage mostly."

* * *

"Very nice doing business with you," Joe said, holding out the keys.

"I'll take those," the Captain said. "Ash, you drive the Porsche. I want to check out this Ghia."

"The Porsche?" Ashby protested. "It has five gears."

"Use second through fifth," the Captain said. "They're in the pattern you're used to. Don't worry, it's just like a grown up VW. You can't hurt it."

Ashby got behind the wheel of the sleek silver car. It took a minute to get the seat and mirrors adjusted. Foot on the clutch, dab on the accelerator pedal, and the engine started on the first crank. Shifting into second as the Captain had suggested, he realized that it was indeed just like a grown up Beetle.

The blue Ghia was already pulling out onto the street. Ashby followed.

* * *

"That Ghia's a great little machine," the Captain said that evening, cutting into a steak so rare Ashby halfway expected it to go "moo". "I really like the color. I'm very proud of you."

"What for?" Ashby asked, squeezing lemon juice onto his fish, "spending your money?"

"Our money, Ash," the Captain said. "Everything I have is yours."

IX

"Who is Blaine Fanshawe?" Nate asked, handing Ashby the note.

"It's a very long story," Ashby said. He'd have given anything never to hear that name again.

"And where the hell is he calling from that he has an area code like that?"

"He's an old friend of the family, I guess you'd say," Ashby answered.

"Oh."

"Right," Ashby nodded. "This can't be good news."

* * *

"They think she must have been smoking in bed," Ashby said. "It's as good a guess as any for why the house burned down."

"God, Ash, that's awful."

"I can't tell you how many times I went into her bedroom and put out her cigarette after she'd fallen asleep. Once a week at least. It's a miracle she didn't burn herself to death any sooner. And me with her, come to that."

"What a horrible way to die."

"She wouldn't have felt a thing," Ashby said. "She'd have been dead drunk that time of night. Smoke inhalation probably got her before the flames did."

"I'm calling the Captain," Nate said.

"Why?" Ashby asked. Did Nate know something? Could he tell somehow that all Ashby could think of was how much he wanted those arms comforting him? He'd been so careful. He assumed the Captain had, too.

"He'll make arrangements with the airline to get us there."

"What are you talking about?"

"I'm going to the funeral with you," Nate said.

"Who says I'm going? Midterms are next week."

"Of course you're going. It's your grandmother. Your last living relative. And you don't think I'm going to let you go by yourself. Don't worry about a thing. The Captain knows how to handle stuff like this."

* * *

When they landed in New Orleans, the Captain was waiting at the gate. He hugged Nate before greeting Ashby with the manliest of handshakes. That was the price of their secrecy, and though he understood and accepted it, it broke Ashby's heart. The Captain had already rented a car and Nate got into the front seat with him as a matter of course. Having to pretend was going to be the worst part of the whole thing, Ashby thought.

Staring at the immaculately groomed back of the Captain's head was like visiting a famous monument. You contemplated something impassive and magnificent, something that couldn't help but make you feel smaller than life. Still, as inaccessible as he might be at the moment, the faint scent of the Captain's hair oil was strangely comforting.

The Captain had reserved two rooms at the hotel. They weren't nearly as nice as the hotel rooms Ashby had shared with the Captain over the past months, but that was no surprise. Standards were different around here. It was humiliating, being observed in his native habitat. Back in California, the stories he told about his previous life had, he thought, a quality of quaint eccentricity rather than squalor. Why had he agreed to this trip?

The change of time zones knocked Nate for a loop. The next morning his snoring filled the motel room as Ashby finished dressing and prepared to leave. The Captain met him at the car.

"We've got time for breakfast before we go to the mortuary," the Captain said.

"I'm really not hungry," Ashby said, "but don't let me stop you."

'You're going to have breakfast, young man," the Captain said, in a tone Ashby knew he had been employing with the boys for nearly two decades.

"Aye, aye."

* * *

When Mama died the Goodhugh Mortuary retrieved her body from the prison for burial. When it was Grandpa's turn, the Goodhughs were on the job again. But those times Ashby hadn't been allowed anywhere near the building. Grannie said it wasn't a decent place for a child. He recalled Marcel Goodhugh as a tall, stoop–shouldered man in a dark suit, and his recollection didn't lie. The office smelled of something Ashby thought was supposed to remind people of lilies.

"Let me say how sorry we all are for your loss, Ashby."

"Thank you."

"We received some preliminary instructions from Mr. Blaine Fanshawe, who said he was calling on your behalf. I hope it was all right for us to arrange things in accordance with his requests."

"Perfectly," Ashby said. On the telephone, Blaine Fanshawe had suggested helping out in that way. At the time Ashby wasn't planning to come and didn't see what it could hurt to let someone else be in charge. He still didn't. There was, Fanshawe had told him, a modest burial benefit provided by Grandpa's company pension and another smaller one from Social Security. He promised to do his best to keep the whole thing within that budget. Ashby listened carefully as Mr. Goodhugh went over the plans.

"Of course, if you'd rather have something more elaborate than a simple graveyard service, the chapel here is available tomorrow afternoon. And I'm sure I could arrange for the use of the sanctuary at First Baptist, for that matter."

"That won't be necessary," Ashby said.

* * *

"You handled yourself really well in there, sweetheart," the Captain said once they were back in the car.

"It didn't feel like it," Ashby said.

"It never does in the moment," the Captain said, backing out of the parking space.

They turned right out of the parking lot. Main Street looked even smaller and shabbier than it had just a few minutes ago.

"Turn left here," Ashby said.

In two blocks they were there. Burned to the ground was no exaggeration in this instance. And days after the fire the stench was still surprisingly strong. It was hard to see how anything could be salvaged, even if Ashby had been in the mood to try.

"I'm so sorry," the Captain said.

"I'm not," Ashby said. "This is exactly how I want to remember it."

* * *

The graveyard was practically in the shadows of the refinery towers. The afternoon was clammy and the air as rancid as Ashby recalled. Pastor Winslow had rounded up a gaggle of church ladies for the occasion. They dabbed at their eyes with hankies and made all the customary noises and gestures. They hugged Ashby tearfully but seemed as embarrassed as he was. Well, why not? Grannie had no secrets. Her life had been an open book—the kind no reputable library would have on its shelves.

The church ladies' curiosity about Nate and the Captain caused Ashby no special anxieties. Even if it did, what would be the point? Now more than ever he had no reason to return to those parts. With what was left of Grannie safe in that spongy soil he was finally free.

* * *

When Ashby heard the key in the door he thought Nate must have left something behind. But the next moment, there was the Captain.

"I saw Nate leave to go jogging."

Of course he would have made sure to get an extra room key. Almost faster than he could think of it, Ashby was across the room and in the Captain's arms. The dam burst. All the emotions he had been bottling up for days erupted. The sudden outburst astonished him. He felt, as he had so often over the past months, like the Captain's arms were the only place where he was safe.

"It's been killing me," the Captain said huskily, "not being able to hold you."

"I'm O.K.," Ashby said, finally regaining control of himself.

"You're being very brave."

"Right."

"A real trooper."

"I wasn't expecting to feel like this," Ashby said.

"What do you mean?"

"She was a mean old drunk. When Grandpa wasn't beating me, she was. I always promised myself I'd dance on her grave."

"Feelings aren't simple," the Captain said. "You never know how you're going to react when the time comes."

* * *

"So who is this guy you're supposed to go see tomorrow?" Nate asked.

"Blaine Fanshawe," Ash said, as casually as he could.

"That's him," Nate nodded. "Who is he? What does he have to do with all this?"

"Some attorney," Ash said. "I expect it's about Grannie's estate. Not that there is one."

He could tell the Captain knew he was hiding something. He didn't want to say any more. He needed Nate and the Captain both to go into the meeting without any preconceptions. Somebody had to be objective, and Ashby knew it wouldn't be him.

"Somehow I had the idea he was a distant relative," Nate said.

"Not that I know of."

* * *

Blaine Fanshawe's offices were across the street from city hall. Ashby had tried to eat breakfast but once more his appetite failed him. The Captain was trying his best, but Ashby knew his patience was wearing thin.

Ashby approached the reception counter. The woman behind it had piled up church lady hair of a color that had probably never been seen in nature.

"Good morning," he said. "I'm Ashby Sainte-Claire. I have an appointment with Mr. Fanshawe."

"Why, Ashby, dear, don't you recognize me? I'm Nelda Roubidoux. I taught your Sunday School class when you were five years old."

"I'm sorry, Miss Nelda," Ashby said. He'd been stupid to come here. He should just have left Blaine Fanshawe twisting in the wind. He remembered this woman just fine. He'd been hoping to avoid admitting it. She was one of the worst gossips in the whole parish. He'd never forget overhearing Grannie's end of their long conversations on the telephone. "Of course I remember you. I'm just not at my best this morning."

"Certainly not, child," she crooned. "Under these horrible circumstances. Please accept my deepest condolences. We're all so deeply sorry. Miss Melanie was a local institution you know."

"Yes'm," Ashby said.

"And I see you have some friends with you."

"My roommate, Nathan Duckworth," Ashby said. "And his father, Captain Duckworth."

"It's a pleasure to meet you both," she said, turning her charm in their direction like a laser beam. "And what an answer to prayer, what a mercy from the Lord Jesus Himself, that young Ashby has men like you standing beside him in his hour of need. I'll just buzz Mr. Fanshawe and let him know you're here, Ashby dear."

* * *

"Now, Ashby," Blaine Fanshawe said once the weather report was over, "first of all, let me say how sorry I was to miss the ceremony. I had a business engagement that took me into New Orleans and I was unavoidably delayed in returning. I don't know how I'll be able to forgive myself."

"Please," Ashby said. "Don't worry about it."

"Ah, but I do, young man, I do," Fanshawe said. "I know that we're not kin, of course, but I've always taken an interest in your family."

"You've been very kind."

"Your mama and I were in school together from first grade right on through to high school graduation, you know. I wish you could have seen her in that cheerleader's uniform."

"Grannie had a snapshot or two," Ashby ventured. "And her high school yearbook. She'd get them out and look at them from time to time."

"I expect she did. Now speaking of Miss Melanie, well, it's heartbreaking, of course."

"Yes."

"But the good Lord works in mysterious ways."

"I've heard."

"Now, Ashby, you know that the house was rented from the company. And Miss Melanie had nothing but your grandfather's Social Security and his company pension to live on."

"Yes."

"Really, she had nothing of her own, you understand, but her personal goods. And I'm afraid there's nothing left of that."

"Yes," Ashby said. "We drove past the old place."

"Burned right down to the ground," Fanshawe nodded slowly. "Nothing but ashes. So I'm sorry, boy, to be the one to have to tell you that there's nothing for you. Nothing at all she could pass on. Even her checking account was overdrawn, and she owed money at the pharmacy and the Piggly Wiggly both. I'm afraid I have no idea what to tell you about your school costs and such things."

"Everything's being covered by my scholarships," Ashby said. "Even my textbooks and incidentals are paid for. I wasn't receiving anything from Grannie in the way of help. So really, this shouldn't have any effect on my situation at all."

"Really," Fanshawe said. "Well, that's certainly a blessing, isn't it? When all else fails we can always depend on the Lord to meet our needs. But, you know, young man, you must remember that you can call on me at any time. Please promise me that you will if there's ever anything I can do to be of assistance to you. It's the least I could offer to honor your Mama's memory."

* * *

The Captain had barely started the car before Nate spoke.

"Ash, you always told me you had no idea who your father is."

"I don't."

"But it's obvious. Why, you look exactly like him."

"Do you think so? I never saw the resemblance."

"You're joking," Nate said. "I mean. . ."

"Take it easy, son," the Captain said.

"But Dad, that Mr. Fanshawe and Ash look at least as much like father and son as you and I do. Maybe more. The resemblance is unmistakable. Don't say you didn't notice it."

"I noticed it," the Captain admitted.

"So?"

"I think what Ashby would say, if you'd let him get a word in edgewise, is that it's not as simple as biology."

"Thanks," Ashby said. "That about sums it up."

"You're going to have to come up with a better explanation than that," Nate insisted.

"I spent my whole life hearing the rumors," Ashby said, "but that's all they ever were. Rumors. Nobody would ever say for certain, but at the same time some people seemed to take it for granted, though others didn't. And there were rumors about other men, too. It's a common physical type around here. The only thing I was ever sure of was that I looked a lot more like him than any of his lawful children. Everybody saw that. People who didn't know any better would come up to Mama and me in public and say, 'are you the little Fanshawe boy?' Mama thought it was funny, but it embarrassed the hell out of me. Blaine Fanshawe didn't want anything to do with us. He never lifted a hand to help us out. And we could have used it, believe me. But how could he? The Fanshawes are one of the most respected families in this part of the state, and we were barely even white trash. And he already had a wife and kids to take care of. Mama just laughed about it, but I know it drove Grannie crazy. She'd made up her mind he was the one. She thought he owed us something. Of course if he'd ever tried to help out, she and Grandpa would just have drunk up whatever he gave us. Finally I got tired of hearing about it and tired of thinking about how my life might have been different. I just decided that a man who doesn't want to be your daddy isn't your daddy. Simple as that."

"But didn't you hear him back there?" Nate asked. "He offered to help you. I was watching him. He was that close to pulling out his checkbook."

"Only after I made it quite clear that I don't need any help. That's what that whole scene was about, really. He's been sweating bullets ever since Grannie died, worrying about what she might have told me and that I might come back here and make demands on him. He knew that as long as she was alive she'd keep the lid on me. But now all bets are off. He's got a wife and two ex-wives and ten kids that are legally his. He's got his reputation to think about, too. Everybody knows he'd like to go into politics. He never did because he couldn't be sure what story somebody might worm out of Grannie. Now that threat is out of the way. It's not just having a bastard son. It's way worse than that. It's having a bastard son by a woman who killed her boyfriend and his wife and went to prison for it. That kind of story would kill any chance of a political career he might have."

"And you're just going to let him off the hook," Nate said, disgusted. "A man who'd turn his back on his own son."

"Yes," Ashby said. "Yes, I am."

"Unbelievable."

"But you know what, Nate?"

"What."

"Kind of guy he is," Ashby said, "he'll never be able to be completely certain that I'm not coming after him. He doesn't know what it's like to trust anyone that way. And God knows, I'm my mother's son and capable of anything."

"You see, son," the Captain said, chuckling, "your pal Ashby is better at taking care of himself than you give him credit for."

* * *

It was almost time to board, and Nate went off in search of the men's room. The Captain would stay behind. His flight for New York wasn't for another hour. He'd be picking up a redeye to Paris.

"You know I love you," he said softly. "I love you and I intend to spend the rest of my life with you."

"I know," Ashby said. "It's the only thing that's gotten me through this."

X

"This is nice, just the two of us," Eleanor said, cutting green tinted cookie dough into Christmas tree shapes. Nate and Joanie had taken Sammie and Ted out for some last minute Christmas shopping, and the other boys were at the beach. "I can't believe Nate hasn't gotten around to teaching you how to surf."

"I promised the Captain I wouldn't let Nate teach me," Ashby said, "but I do think it's strange. The man flies airliners for a living, which seems to me should indicate he's fearless."

"He hasn't been on a board since that shark attacked his best friend, Chuckie Kimball," Eleanor said.

"He never told me."

"He doesn't like to talk about it. He was there when it happened. Chuckie bled to death before the Captain could get him to shore."

"Still," Ashby said, "he let the boys learn to surf."

"I really had to put my foot down," Eleanor smiled. "It was touch and go."

"How many of these things do we have to make?" Ashby asked, cutting out another row of pale blue stars.

"Several thousand, I believe," Eleanor shrugged. "It's going to be a very big party. Everyone will be there."

"Even Grannie Helena?"

"You know, she's a new woman ever since her doctor put her on that multi-vitamin."

"What multi-vitamin?"

"It's called valium."

"You didn't."

"Something had to be done," Eleanor shrugged. "Either she was going to kill someone or someone was going to kill her. Isn't that in your Hippocratic Oath? First do no harm? Don't tell me. I know that's not what it means. Still. All for the best. You know, I can't believe my Nate is engaged. They're both so young."

"So says the woman who married a seventeen year old."

"The Captain was seventeen going on thirty."

"I can imagine."

"Anyway, everything is different nowadays. It's gotten so that grownups have to actually be adults. It's hard to imagine Nate pulling that off. So tell me, are you all moved into your new place?"

"Just about. I mean, everything's out of the dorm but it's all just kind of in a heap in the living room."

"You'll have time before classes start back up. The Captain says the place is very cute."

"I bet he didn't use the word 'cute'."

"You're right," Eleanor giggled. "He said it's tiny but has a commanding view of the ocean."

"That sounds more like him."

"I envision a perfect little love nest."

"It is," Ashby said. "Or will be eventually. It's also very expensive."

"He wants to do it, dear. You shouldn't feel awkward about accepting money from him."

"No, Eleanor," Ashby said. "I mean really ridiculously expensive."

"He can afford it. The boys and I don't need a cent from him, you know. Dear Hobie left me a very wealthy woman. It's obscene for a woman to have as much money as I do after being married for such a short time. Really, I should be writing alimony checks to the Captain. Maybe I'll start."

"It just makes me nervous. Nate knows I can't afford a place like that."

"It's that slimy secret father of yours, isn't it? That Mr. Fanshawe."

"Is that it?"

"Well it has to be, doesn't it? It just makes sense. And it's only fair for him to help out. That's what I told Nate."

"You shouldn't have."

"Why ever not? He knows you're keeping secrets from him, Ash. Let me do the explaining."

"Oh."

"Seriously," she said. "I know how to do it."

"Oh."

"These are ready for the oven," she said. "And look how many stars you've gotten cut. I'm going to turn you into a baker yet."

* * *

The first time Ashby met Joanie he was certain that Ollie and Peter were playing a practical joke on him. Nate had dropped him at the Duckworth's house and gone on some errand or other that he promised Eleanor he'd do and then promptly forgot and had to retrace his steps or face her disappointment. And when Ashby walked in there Joanie was, sitting at the kitchen table with Ollie and Peter, playing hearts. Ollie introduced them, and Ashby nearly accused him of trying to pull one over on him. The problem was this girl didn't live up to her advance billing. She didn't even come close to it. She was pretty, but not that pretty. She was nice enough, but not what Ashby would ever have called charming. She might be smart, but she couldn't play cards to save her life. Even Ashby could tell that, and he was still learning the game himself.

Simply put, she wasn't any of the things he had been told she was, except personable. She absolutely wasn't spectacular, and he couldn't for the life of him imagine her as the love of Nate's life. At the time, of course, he was still at the stage where he was toying with the idea of himself as the love of Nate's life. And there was no question at all that whether that ever came to pass or not, Nate was truly a spectacular example of whatever it was he was. Ridiculously good looking, built like a Greek god, or at least a Greek god-in-waiting, charismatic as the day was long. It seemed to go without saying that the love of his life should be as incredible as he was. Anyone could see that. And this girl—she just wasn't.

Since that afternoon, nothing had happened to alter Ashby's initial impression of her. Even now that he no longer entertained any romantic notions at all about Nate, the unsuitability of the match disquieted him. What could Nate possibly see in this young woman? What was there about her that quickened his pulse? It was baffling, that's all. Since that afternoon, however, Ashby had had the experience of witnessing Eleanor in love with a spectacularly unspectacular individual herself, and he began to wonder if Nate's attachment to Joanie might be evidence of an inherited trait. Dear departed Hobart was about the most nondescript individual Ashby could remember ever encountering. And he wasn't the only one who thought so. Even now the Duckworth boys, Nate included, continued to shake their heads over their mother's unlikely passion. Perhaps Eleanor's instinct for misalliances had passed on to a new generation.

Of course, mulling this theory never got Ashby anywhere. He had met Ollie's and Peter's respective girlfriends, and they were absolute knockouts. Those young women were everything Joanie was not and then some. Given the generation's difference, Ashby could all too easily imagine them as Eleanor and her friend, Giselle Van Dyke, gorgeous, rambunctious, hot-blooded young ladies capable of bringing almost any man to heel. For that matter, Ashby never had any difficulty imagining Eleanor and the Captain as a match. And the Captain was, face it, a mythological hero reborn. Any way Ashby looked at it, Nate and Joanie seemed anomalous.

This line of thinking led in a very treacherous direction, however. Because of all the mismatched couples around the place, Ashby sensed that the Captain and he represented the most egregious example.

* * *

As always, it was difficult for Ashby to sleep in the Captain's study. This remained a constant even as the reasons for it changed. It was only to be expected, of course, that Ashby would miss the Captain worse here than anywhere else. And certainly, the burden of concealment seemed heavier under this roof, surrounded by the man's sons. There was, too, the influence of the season itself, which made everything seem more poignant. Ashby, who had been resolute in his agnosticism with regard to the holidays all through boyhood, now was entranced by the least detail of the observances, but the obligatory jollity of it all made him feel even bluer than the circumstances themselves would have warranted.

* * *

Ashby settled himself into his seat and leafed through the in-flight magazine. He had never flown first class before. He felt inexcusably pretentious. If the Captain hadn't gotten him the seat for free he'd have insisted on going standby just on principle. The Captain was already in the cockpit. He wasn't on duty. That's just where his free seat was located, apparently.

Just before they pulled back from the gate, Ashby's seatmate appeared. He was a tall, distinguished looking man. He was expensively dressed, and Ashby would have been extremely surprised if someone had told him that was the man's real hair color. He would probably have laughed out loud. The man was wearing too much jewelry and way too much cologne.

"Sonny Dallas," he smiled, offering Ashby his perfectly manicured hand.

"Ashby Sainte-Claire."

"I knew a Sainte-Claire at Choate. Actually, two of them. Cousins."

"No relation," Ashby said. "None of my family ever went to school there."

"Because you do rather resemble one of them, as I remember."

The stewardess arrived to take their drink orders, and by the time that business had been transacted, the plane was taxiing.

"So, Ashby, do you live in San Francisco?"

"Just visiting."

"Not your first time, surely?"

"Yes."

"And traveling alone. What a shame. Still, I suppose you'll find someone to show you the sights. San Franciscans are very friendly that way."

"Actually, I'm meeting my fiancé."

"Your fiance? How nice," Sonny Dallas said in a tone that indicated he didn't think it was nice at all.

* * *

"How was Christmas with Eleanor and the boys?" the Captain asked from the bathroom.

"You were missed," Ashby said.

"Best for all concerned."

"You know, I didn't think so when you first told me you wouldn't be there. But you were right."

"I'll be seeing Ollie through Robbie in Acapulco the middle of the month."

"They're so excited about the trip. It was practically all they could talk about the whole time I was there."

"You sure you won't come along?"

"They need time alone with you. And vice versa."

"I love you, you know."

"I know. Incidentally, when did you start shaving right there?"

"Like it?"

"I'm not sure."

"Well, you'd better get used to it," the Captain growled, "because I'm thinking very seriously about holding you down and shaving yours, too."

"Wow," Ashby said. "I'm tingling at the thought."

"Good."

"Is that what couples do on their honeymoons? Shave each other's privates?"

"I couldn't tell you. My experience of honeymoons is limited. This is only the second one I've been on."

"And last, I hope," Ashby said.

"That goes without saying."

"I have to say I can't imagine Nate and Joanie doing anything like that on their honeymoon."

"No?"

"No."

"You know," the Captain said, "I can't imagine those two getting up to much of anything."

"Really."

"That son of mine. I just don't know about him. He seems—what do the Freudians say? Sexually repressed?"

"Nate? Sexually repressed? You're joking."

"No."

"Well, why would you say that?"

"You lived with him for three semesters. How many girls did he bring back to the dorm with him?"

"None," Ashby said, "but that was because of Joanie."

"Nope," the Captain said. "Joanie's just an excuse. Nineteen years old and looking like that. Built like that. He's got to have girls throwing themselves at him constantly."

"He does," Ashby admitted.

"And nothing at all going on. There's no two ways about it. He's got some kind of thing about sex."

"Well, if he did," Ashby said. "Eleanor would say it has something to do with the circumstances of his birth."

"That's right," the Captain nodded. "She would explain it that way. But it would just be another excuse. Now, the other boys, Ollie and Peter, for instance, they've already got quite a track record from what I hear. Even young Quinn has stories to tell. You can see it in his eyes. Stories of an unconventional nature would be my bet in his case. But that Nate. Something's not right there."

"You know," Ashby said. "I'm not sure I'm comfortable speculating about the sex lives of your sons."

"Thank God for that," the Captain said, climbing back into bed with him.

"Perhaps you could think of something to help take my mind off of it."

* * *

"Now that Hobart is no longer with us," Ashby said over breakfast in bed the next morning, "Nate believes you and Eleanor are planning to get back together."

"He doesn't."

"He does. That's what he thinks the Acapulco trip is about. You're going to sit Ollie through Robbie down and talk it over with them."

"I wonder what could have given him that idea."

"Wishful thinking, I expect."

"He'd better not say anything like that to his brothers."

"He won't."

"You're sure of that?"

"Eleanor told him she'd kill him if he does. Slowly and painfully was how she described it."

"He spoke to Eleanor about it?"

"She brought it up, actually. She reads minds, you know. At least, she reads his."

"Yes, she always did," the Captain admitted. "What about the others? Have they said anything like that?"

"Not that I know of."

"I should talk to her."

"I think she's got it handled," Ashby said.

"Still."

* * *

"So," the Captain said, scrubbing Ashby's back for him. "How did you and Sonny Dallas get along last night?"

"You know Sonny Dallas?"

"I know *of* Sonny Dallas," the Captain said. "I have friends here who know him. They don't like him much."

"You have friends here?"

"Half of my flights either originate or terminate here. You know that. There's a gym I use when I'm on layovers. It's guys from there. They can't wait to meet you, by the way."

"I see."

"Hey, there's no reason to be jealous."

"I'll know whether that's true or not when I meet them," Ashby said. "Won't I?"

"Ash?"

"Just joking, silly."

"Good."

"But now, did you have Sonny Dallas seated next to me on purpose?"

"No," the Captain said. "I saw his name on the manifest, is all. The stewardess told me where he was sitting. So what happened? Did he put a move on you?"

"Yes."

"And?"

"I told him the truth."

"What truth would that be?"

"That I am the sex slave of a notorious S/M dungeon master. And that if he wanted me he'd have to be prepared to complete an extensive and highly detailed application form and pay a large cash deposit, as well as submitting to a physical examination by a designated physician."

"Oh, that truth," the Captain laughed. "I see."

"He didn't take it well."

"I saw him hand you his business card at baggage claim."

"I hope you also saw me throw it away just outside baggage claim," Ashby said.

"Better than that."

"Oh?"

"I saw him watching you throw it away. He looked just like Rumplestiltskin stamping his feet. My friend Ned is going to love this story. They're business partners. And perennial rivals in romance."

"Sounds like the perfect friendship," Ashby said.

XI

"She's lost her mind," Nate complained. He had taken to showing up unannounced at Ashby's apartment ever since renting a place in Mission Beach with Joanie, who started law school in San Diego after graduating from Columbia in three years. Ashby had assumed these developments all meant he wouldn't be seeing very much of Nate, but so far it wasn't working out that way.

"Who has?" Ashby asked. He knew who Nate was talking about but couldn't tip his hand. He had promised Eleanor and he had promised the Captain. As far as Nate was concerned, how was Ashby supposed to know about it? "Joanie?"

"Mom."

"Eleanor? What makes you say that?"

"It's not bad enough that she dumped the Captain for Hobart McKinney," Nate said, "but this is the last straw."

Of course he would see it that way. Nate wouldn't rest until his parents were safely reunited.

"I still have no idea what you're talking about," Ashby said. He had to keep the fiction going. Nate wasn't supposed to know that he'd been the last to know.

"She says she's getting married again. Some guy she's known for about fifteen minutes."

"You're kidding."

"Hobart's been dead for what? Six months?"

It wasn't fair. Ashby got that. He understood Nate's perplexity. The Captain, divorced from the mother of his sons. Nate's brothers, now being raised in what people referred to as a "broken home", though to be fair about it they spent at least as much time with the Captain as they had before and seemed happy as ever. Nate himself, hurt and confused by what had happened, losing more and more confidence in his parents by the day. And Eleanor, reunited after half a lifetime with the man she'd always been in love with. At least she thought she was in love with him until they were actually married. And then widowed so suddenly after such a short time. It seemed as if Ashby was the only one of the whole bunch who was getting what he wanted out of life. And he could hardly enjoy it for worrying about the rest of them. It would have been like a soap opera except it was real life.

He'd been thrilled for Eleanor when she called to tell him she'd met the man of her dreams. Thrilled but a little worried. It was awfully soon, for one thing. And when things seemed too good to be true they generally were. He thought he knew Eleanor well enough to believe that she knew what she was doing. But his own upbringing led him to question just about anything anybody did.

Her call had been as much a warning as anything. Nate, already moody, was likely to become even worse. Ashby needed to be prepared for turbulence.

He didn't have to work very hard at appearing surprised by the news. Nate had never been especially observant when it came to Ashby's emotional states, and now he was more preoccupied than ever. Still, Ashby was as careful as he could be not to give anything away. The only thing that could make the situation worse would be if Nate figured out that Ashby had heard Eleanor's news before he did. That would be a disaster. It would require more explaining than he was prepared for. And he hated the idea of letting Eleanor and the Captain down.

* * *

"It's not going to be anything fancy," the Captain said. "Just a quick trip to Vegas. The two of them. It's how she wants it."

"Are you O.K. with that?"

"There's only one person in the world I trust as much as her," the Captain said. "That's you. Even if I didn't, she gets to call the shots. It's her life, after all."

"Not many ex-husbands would be that understanding," Ashby said.

"It's not a competition."

"Obviously not."

"The younger boys have met him," the Captain said. "He made a very big hit with them."

"How does that make you feel?"

"Terrific," the Captain said.

"I know," Ashby smiled. "You're not in competition with anybody. Not even the man who's going to be raising your sons. But honestly."

"Honestly, Ash, I'm not afraid that he's going to replace me, if that's what you're worrying about. See, I know Eleanor. I mean, really know her. There was no way she was going to spend the rest of her life alone after she lost Hobart. She's barely in her forties. And she could easily pass for ten years younger than that. If it's going to happen anyway, it's far better for the new guy to be somebody the boys like than somebody they hate."

"That makes sense," Ashby said.

"Besides," the Captain said. "After being married to me and being married to Hobart, who was an absolute prince of a husband despite any deficiencies he might have had as a man, do you really think she'd marry just any guy off the street?"

"No."

"It'll be fine. You'll see."

"I hope so."

"Oh, and one other thing," the Captain said.

"What's that?"

"That stuff I said about 'just the two of them' at the wedding?"

"You mean that's just what she's telling Nate? She's taking the other boys? He's bound to find out."

"No. Their grandmother's housekeeper will be staying with them for the weekend."

"What, then?"

"I'll be there," the Captain grinned. "I'm giving her away."

* * *

That's what Ashby had already known when Nate showed up looking like a kid who'd lost his puppy.

"So who's the guy?"

"Some Newport Beach surf bum," Nate mumbled.

"Seriously?"

"Sells Ferraris and Maseratis for a living when he's not out on his board or lifting weights at the gym," Nate sneered. "Not that that's a bad job. Probably makes pretty good money. But you can just imagine what a slimy character he has to be."

"I don't know," Ashby said. "Didn't your grandfather make his pile selling yachts?"

"That's hardly the same thing," Nate bridled.

"And aren't you kind of a surf bum yourself?"

Ashby could go that far.

"Jesus, Ash."

"Sorry."

"No," Nate said. "You're right. I am a surf bum pretty much. That's not really what bothers me about him. And it's not that he's a bodybuilder, 'cause of course the Captain is, too. It's one of the reasons Ollie and Peter are so worked up over him. He's taking them to the gym and showing them how to lift."

"Then what is it you hate so much about the guy?" Ashby asked. "I'm not saying you're wrong to feel the way you do, just that you haven't explained it to me yet."

"He's twenty-five years old, Ash," Nate said. "Hardly older than us. And Mom's practically middle aged. He's twenty-five years old and Mom has fifteen million dollars in the bank that Hobart McKinney left her. What does that sound like to you?"

"Eleanor's too smart to fall for a gold digger."

"Not so sure," Nate said.

It wasn't Ashby's job to talk Nate around. Eleanor and the Captain had both insisted on that. But he cared about Nate a lot and hated to see him so unhappy. It wasn't like there was anything he could do about it. But that wasn't much comfort day in and day out with Nate moping around like someone had died. And Ashby could hardly get him to go home. That would present a problem if the Captain showed up unexpectedly.

* * *

"Is he there?"

"Hi, Joanie," Ashby said, holding the phone away from his ear. Joanie always yelled on the phone. "He's not with you?"

"His surfboards are all here," she said, "and both bikes."

"Kayak? Snorkeling gear? Guitars?"

"All present and accounted for," Joanie said.

"But no Nate, huh? He must have chem. lab this afternoon."

Chem. lab was their designation for Nate's unexplained absences, which were becoming more frequent by the week. So far, Joanie was accepting the situation with good humor. God only knew how long that would last.

"I guess you heard the news," she said.

"About Eleanor? Nate stopped by yesterday."

"He's really upset."

"Not upset," Ashby corrected her. "More like pissed."

"God, yes," she said. "He's like a little kid who's not getting something he thinks he deserves."

"You're right," Ashby said, "but it's worse than that, even. He identifies so strongly with his father that anytime something bad happens he perceives it as a preview of his own life. Not that Eleanor remarrying is bad. But Nate only sees it as one more thing keeping his parents from getting back together. That's the only outcome he can accept."

"That's it exactly," Joanie said. "Sometimes it almost scares me how well you understand him. All the Duckworths, really. It's like you're their therapist. Or priest."

"More like one of their dogs," Ashby said.

"Oh, you," Joanie laughed. "So, are the three of us still on for the movies on Sunday?"

"If you're sure you really want a fifth wheel," Ashby said.

"Jeez," Joanie said. "You want to be a doctor and you can't even count."

*　*　*

"Nate's loss," Joanie said, fastening her seat belt. "Great movie. She's my favorite actress."

"This week," Ashby said, shifting into reverse.

"That's right," Joanie laughed. "Make fun of me."

"Well, you do have an awful lot of favorite actresses."

"Your problem is you're a cynic, Ash."

"I thought you were in law school, not studying to be a shrink."

"Speaking of medical school," Joanie said, "you haven't called Nanette."

Nanette was Joanie's cousin who attended San Diego State and, like Ashby, was a pre-med student.

"I don't remember mentioning med school," Ashby said.

"You two could be studying for the MCAT together. All she talks about these days is the MCAT."

"The MCAT is crucial," Ashby said. "No question."

"So why not team up?" Joanie asked. "Only makes sense."

So far he had been able to elude Joanie's attempt to set him up with Nanette. And with Lisa, her friend from high school who'd just gotten a job in Coronado teaching kindergarten. And with Terri, her pal from Columbia who was trying to break into broadcasting here in San Diego. And with Ruthie, who was studying oceanography at Scripps, Elaine, who was the assistant manager of a ladies' clothing shop at one of the malls, and Christine, who did paintings of local landmarks and sold them to tourists in Balboa Park.

He knew his excuses and evasions were wearing thin. He knew, too, that Nate was even more impatient with him than Joanie.

"These moods of Nate's," she said as he pulled up in front of the apartment building where she and Nate lived. "Sometimes I wonder if we're making a mistake getting married at the end of the semester."

"I have no idea what to tell you about that," Ashby said, "except if you're that concerned about it, you really should talk to Nate."

* * *

"Ash, darling," Eleanor's voice over the telephone was so clear that she could almost have been in the room next door.

"Eleanor."

"How's everything?"

"He called earlier," Ash said. "'Surf's up. Sorry, can't meet you for lunch. You and Joanie should go without me.' First time in weeks."

"That's wonderful," Eleanor said. "Didn't I tell you he'd come around?"

"I wouldn't go that far."

"I'm his mother. I know."

"How was the honeymoon?"

"Short but sweet," Eleanor laughed.

"It's too bad you two couldn't have gone away for longer."

"There'll be plenty of time for that later on," she said. "Really, it was just like my honeymoon with the Captain. That one lasted about as long as a good sneeze. Long honeymoons are highly overrated. My extended honeymoon with Hobart is probably what killed him."

"Eleanor."

"I mean it. The poor man was never the same after we got home. His decline began on the French Riviera. I was there. I saw it. At least he was happy."

"Well, I want my honeymoon to last forever," Ashby said.

"Darling, I thought that's exactly what's going on, the way the Captain talks about it."

"I suppose."

"Speaking of the Captain, Ash, he was a real dear about the wedding. Make him tell you about it."

"All right."

"And you're both invited to a little get together we're throwing next month. I can't wait for you to meet Stormy. The Captain has all the details.

He'll fill you in. I already checked the date with Joanie. I know you and Nate don't have midterms or anything like that going on."

"I'll be there," Ashby said. "I can't guarantee Nate will agree to show. He's still not crazy about the whole thing."

"That's not your problem, dear."

XII

"What the hell are you doing?"

"Packing," Ashby said, though frantically stuffing his clothing into his bag hardly deserved that description. His hands were shaking. He felt like he was about faint. Or throw up. He hoped he would throw up before he fainted, because throwing up after you had fainted could, he knew, be fatal.

"I see that," the Captain said. "Why?"

"I've got to get out of here. I've fucked everything up. I ruin everything I touch. I've wrecked your family."

"Stop," the Captain said.

Ashby went on stuffing things into his bag.

"I said, stop."

Ashby stopped, but only because he was shaking too badly to continue and his vision was too blurred to see anything else to put into the bag anyway. He felt the huge arms close around him like they always did, and much as he wanted to resist, to wriggle free, to run and keep running and never stop running, he couldn't. The Captain was too strong. The Captain held him and stroked his hair and murmured in his ear. He couldn't really understand anything that the Captain was saying, but that never mattered.

Someone began pounding on the door.

"Oh, God," Ashby sobbed.

"It's all right," the Captain insisted.

"No."

"Ash, open up."

Ollie.

"Ash, we know you're in there. Both of you. We've been watching the door, and unless you two went out the window and repelled down from the sixth floor, you're still in there."

"We have to let him in," the Captain said.

"No."

"I'm opening the door. Don't do anything stupid."

"No," Ashby said. He didn't know if he meant "no" the Captain shouldn't open the door or "no" he wouldn't do anything stupid or just some incomprehensible, reflexive "no". He heard the door open.

"Ollie," the Captain said.

"Finally. I was about to send Peter to call the paramedics."

"And Peter. And Quinn."

Ashby wiped his eyes and watched them file into the hotel room.

"You two," Ollie said. Exasperation was his natural state, but he was well over his usual setting, like that time the accelerator on the Captain's Porsche stuck wide open. "You two."

"We have to talk," Peter said.

"Is there really anything to say?" the Captain asked.

Ashby thought he sounded exhausted, as well he should.

"It's all right," Ashby said. "The whole thing's over. I'm leaving. You can all get back to your lives."

"Don't talk nonsense, Ash," Ollie said, sounding exactly like his father.

"I already told him that," the Captain said.

"We're going to talk," Peter said, "and the two of you are going to listen. And nobody's going anywhere until we're finished."

* * *

"It's that simple, Captain, sir," Ollie said. "If we let Nate start making the rules about who's part of this family and who isn't, what's going to happen to Quinn when Nate finds about about him?"

"He's right," Peter said. "You and Ash have to stand up for yourselves, because it's not just about you. It's about all of us."

"I can't believe you've known about us all this time," Ashby said.

"Well, you can thank Quinn for that," Peter said.

"Quinn," the Captain said.

"Yes, sir."

"Don't just stand there, son, come here."

Ashby had never seen the Captain cry before. He had hoped he never would. Watching the Captain hug his son—his gay son, they now knew—the reaction seemed entirely appropriate.

"All right," Ollie said, "that's all settled. Peter, you stay here with Ash and the Captain. Quinn, you come with me. We'd better go find Mom and Stormy."

But before he and Quinn could get themselves out the door, someone knocked. "God. What now?" Ashby heard someone mutter, and realized it was him.

"Gentlemen," Stormy said, peering in at them from the corridor. "Eleanor has called a family meeting."

* * *

Stormy Davis was Eleanor's new husband—with the accent on new. He wasn't more than a few years older than Ashby and Nate. He and Eleanor had met a few weeks after Hobart's death at a birthday party for her friend, Martha Shipman. Stormy wasn't a guest that evening. He and a couple of buddies were the entertainment, dancing and stripping down to g-strings. Under normal circumstances, this wouldn't seem to be the best possible way for a middle aged woman to meet the man of her dreams, but knowing Eleanor's history as he did, Ashby saw that it made a kind of sense. *"It was a terrible mistake"*, she had said to him about her marriage to Hobart. *"I knew it immediately. I didn't let on, and only a few weeks later there he was in the kitchen floor, dead of a stroke. I'm so glad I never told him how I really felt. He died a happy man."*

Stormy was exactly Ashby's height. He competed in bodybuilding contests at two hundred pounds, sixty more than Ashby weighed, but still well short of the Captain's magnitude. He had dimples, what Ashby thought of as a confrontational chin, and perhaps the sexiest head of hair on the planet. The Captain had once said that the federal government needed to add Stormy to their schedule of controlled substances, but his grin as he made the observation convinced Ashby that he was not jealous or disapproving. It apparently indicated that he had identified the younger man as a kindred spirit. The boys—all except Nate, the perennial skeptic—adored him. He was already training Ollie and Peter at the gym where he worked out.

"Try not to look so much like Anne Boleyn being led to the scaffold," he muttered, draping an arm across Ashby's shoulders. "It's all going to be fine."

"No, it's not."

"Sure it is. Just watch. Eleanor will put it all back together."

* * *

"I don't want them here," Nate complained as Ashby and Stormy entered Eleanor's hotel room a little behind the others.

"Who, dear?" Eleanor asked.

"Your husband," Nate said. "And you know who."

"Say his name, son," the Captain said.

For a long moment it looked like the Captain might lose this battle of wills, and Ashby truly dreaded what might follow.

"Ashby," Nate said, barely audible.

"There," Eleanor smiled. "That wasn't so bad. Now I know it's your big day, and I know you've had a shock, and I know you're convinced it's ruined everything, but there's no reason you can't be polite. Your father and I raised you to treat people with respect whether you think they deserve it or not. And you're still our son, so the rules haven't expired. I'll sic Grannie Helena on you if you won't be nice."

"I'd like to say something," Stormy said.

"Go ahead," Eleanor said, looking, Ashby thought, a little uneasy.

"Nathan, I'm here because Eleanor is the woman I love. I know it's been hard for you to accept that, and that's all right. You have a right to feel however you want to about that. But I will always support her, and I believe my place is at her side."

He wasn't actually at her side, of course. He was across the room from her. But everyone got the message. And everyone appreciated his calling Nate "Nathan", because everyone was pretty annoyed with Nate, it appeared.

"But there's another reason I belong here right now. Nobody knows about this but Eleanor, not that I'm ashamed of it or anything, but I was raised by my mother and her girlfriend. They've been together over twenty years, since Dad left Mom and me for that stripper. And if this meeting is going to include any discussion about a certain subject, well that stuff matters to me. What people say about it matters to me. So I'm here to support Ashby and the Captain, too. I just want everyone clear on that."

He gave Ashby's hand a squeeze.

"Thanks, Stormy," the Captain said.

"Yes, darling," Eleanor smiled. Ashby saw her eyes brimming from across the room. It was a remarkable performance.

"Now, Nate, dear," Eleanor said, "it truly is unfortunate that you found out about your father and Ashby the way you did, and today of all days. I'm sure everyone feels bad about that. But family is family. You can't pick and choose. Either we're all your family or none of us is. So you just think about that for a minute before you make up your mind whether you really want to throw Ashby out. Good heavens, it's just a wedding."

* * *

When Ashby first met Nate he thought he was the handsomest boy in the world. He had, for all practical purposes, fallen in love at first sight. If the miracle of his life hadn't happened the way it did and when it did Ashby's heart would undoubtedly have been broken, and he knew that no matter what passed between Nate and him after this he would always remember that and honor those feelings. So it wasn't that hard sitting in the sanctuary, gazing at Nate up front, to forget all those terrible things he had said that morning, to stare at that beautiful boy who had befriended him and whose untold kindesses had included introducing him to the man of his dreams.

He could forget it for those brief moments, but he knew he couldn't forget it permanently. It had been too hurtful, and the things Nate said had included terrible things about the Captain. He had seen the Captain's face as he heard Nate's words and though he knew the Captain wouldn't admit it, they had wounded him deeply. He'd give anything for the Captain never to have heard Nate say those things. Anything under the sun. But it was too late for that. You can't unsay things ones they've been said. That's what Ashby wasn't sure he'd ever be able to forgive.

* * *

"Put on your sweatshirt. Let's go for a walk."

"It's nearly midnight."

"Need to stretch my legs," the Captain said.

Ashby had tried many times to imagine what it must be like to be an airline pilot. The excitement, the strange places, the potential danger. Mostly, he imagined having to sit at the controls of the aircraft for hours on end. Just sit. He'd have lost his mind if he'd had to do it. When the Captain said he needed to stretch his legs, Ashby always took it seriously.

It was a foggy night. The lights of the hotel were swallowed up immediately. As they walked up the beach, the Pacific was no more than the sound of waves exhausting themselves on the sand.

"Eleanor and I honeymooned here," the Captain said. "Seems like a million years ago. Like it happened to someone else."

"She's a remarkable woman."

"And you are a remarkable man, Ash."

The Captain's compliments always made Ashby uncomfortable.

"This thing with Nate has nothing to do with you. You're not responsible. You didn't make me gay. I seduced you. We're together now because we're in love and we want to be. That's all. We don't need anybody's approval."

"I feel like I do," Ashby said.

"I understand that. But you're a tough guy even though you don't think you are. Remember what you did back home when people got you down? You pretended what they thought of you didn't matter. And eventually it didn't."

* * *

"I'm sorry," Ashby said, shifting away from the Captain. "I don't feel like being touched right now. I feel filthy and horrible."

"When you let the things Nate said come between us, Ash, you're letting him destroy a little bit of what we are together."

"I know you're right," Ash said. "I can't help it."

"There's really only one way to put all that out of your mind. If you go to sleep feeling like this, you'll just wake up the same way. If you sleep at all, that is."

Ashby couldn't speak.

"Please," the Captain said, taking hold of him in the darkness. "Let me help you feel better."

XIII

"Osgood," Ashby said, staring at the Polaroid.

"Eleanor says it was the maiden name of one of Joanie's great-grandmothers."

"I guess—what? You'd end up calling a kid named Osgood Ozzy?"

"Probably," the Captain said. He was grinning from ear to ear. "Nate thinks he hates me, but then he names his kid Osgood."

"Somehow I sense Eleanor's influence."

"Thank God he still listens to her."

"But how much?"

"Still, Ash, it's something."

"It's so unfair," Ashby said. "They live less than two miles from us. But you have to hear about it from Eleanor. She's the one sending you pictures of your first grandchild."

"Don't worry. I'm going to have lots of grandchildren."

"Nate would let you see him if you didn't insist on taking me along."

"That's not an option," the Captain said. "You know that."

"Of course it's an option."

"It wouldn't be fair to you. That's why I don't consider it an option. I'm not about to go back on our agreement."

"But that makes me feel like I'm being unfair to you," Ashby said.

"You're not the one being unfair to me. And I'd much rather be in the position of having Nate be unfair to me than of being unfair to you myself. So how it is is how it's going to be. For now."

"He looks like you," Ashby said.

"Eleanor says that, too. Just one more thing for Nate to deal with."

"Osgood."

"By the way," the Captain said. "I spoke to Ned Westerleigh today. He's going to start looking for a place in San Francisco for us. I told him it had to be in a safe neighborhood near the medical school."

"You're sure you want us to buy a place?"

"Renting is just paying your landlord's mortgage for him. You might as well pay your own."

"No wonder one of your best friends is a realtor."

"Listen, Ash, this move is going to be great for me, too. So much of our transatlantic schedule is routed out of San Francisco now that we're getting more 747's in the fleet. The airline is really happy I'm asking for the transfer. And with Quinn starting at Berkeley this fall it's perfect."

"Should we get a place big enough so that he can live with us?"

"Absolutely not," the Captain said. "He needs to live his own life. And so do we."

Cooper Luxemberg:
June, 1978

It was the warmest afternoon of the summer so far, and the back patio at Rascals was packed with bare, sweaty skin.

"The float is going to be spectacular," Chanel said. "Nobody's ever seen anything like it. Jaws will drop all over the West Coast."

"The Hanging Gardens of Babylon will hide its head in shame," Marina del Rey said. Cooper believed he detected a note of sarcasm in her voice.

"I believe that's extinct," he said. "If not mythical."

"Surely not," Marina said.

"Who the fuck is Shirley, and why are we talking about her?" Chanel rasped.

"God," Holly Montezuma moaned, "look at the tits on that one."

"His name is Sean," Marina del Rey said. "He used to be a Mountie."

"He can mount me any time," Holly sighed.

"Cooper," Chanel snapped, "you're not listening."

Actually he was. He liked giving the impression he wasn't, however. People were less guarded when they suspected he wasn't paying attention.

"Sorry," he said, watching Kent and Ugo gyrate atop a black-painted packing crate.

"I was describing the float we're creating for the pride parade," Chanel explained.

"Float?" Cooper asked, to maintain the impression of obliviousness.

"It's just a couple of weeks away," Marina asserted, as if there were some disagreement as to the date.

"Jesus," Holly Montezuma muttered. "Why aren't we here for tea dance every Sunday afternoon? These are the hottest guys on the planet."

"Because you're usually not on this planet, darling," Marina said.

"Yes, Cooper," Chanel said, tapping the toe of her size sixteen stiletto heels, "float. It's going to be the equal of anything you'd see in the Tournament of Roses Parade. But it will have that certain San Francisco *je ne sais quoi*.. I've already enlisted Bo and Sean. They're going to ride at the front. They'll be wearing black leather jockstraps, military style caps, and aviator sunglasses, and they'll be performing bodybuilding poses."

Though the standings continually fluctuated, Bo and Sean always managed to place on Cooper's list of the ten hottest men in San Francisco. Bo was a younger, slightly prettier (as opposed to rugged), smaller (more Jared Bartok sized, say six three and two-fifty) version of Big Steve Fabiani. Sean was an object lesson in how big and ripped a guy of average height could appear without actually exceeding two hundred pounds. They were among the few men of their type in the city, aesthetically pleasing but huge, who didn't attend the same church—er—gym as Big Steve and his crew. Bo had been banned for life there for entertaining paying clients in the steamroom, and Sean was *persona non grata* too, originally by association but increasingly based on his own "achievements". Despite indications of monumental character flaws, or perhaps because of them, the two perfectly embodied Big Steve's Third Law of Sexual Dynamics: anything a really hot man does is hot by definition.

"Sean?" Holly Montezuma asked. "You mean that Sean over there?"

"Yes, dear," Marina del Rey said, "that's the one."

"On our float?" Holly demanded.

"The very same," Marina nodded.

"Why wasn't I told?"

"You just were," Marina said.

"I'd better go have a talk with him right now," Holly said, "about his costume."

"You just want to know what the stuff he uses in his hair smells like," Marina said, "but while you're over there why don't you dust his nipples for fingerprints?"

"You know those two will stand you up," Cooper said.

"They won't," Chanel insisted. "Surely."

"They will," Cooper said.

"They wouldn't think of it."

"Half of the gay men in North America will be in San Francisco that weekend, their wallets stuffed so full they can't sit down," Cooper said. "Bo and Sean are bound to come up with a better gig than riding on your float. One that actually pays."

"Like to put money on it, big boy?" Holly growled in her best trucker imitation.

"Are you still here?" Chanel asked.

"Sean scares me a little," Holly said. "I think it's those nipple piercings."

"Never make a bet with a Jew," Marina told her. "Only a sucker would consider it. Jews always have all the angles covered."

"Is that right, Cooper?" Holly asked.

"Marina's the expert," he said.

"Well," Chanel said, "those two gorgeous musclehunks will absolutely show up. Barring some inconceivable catastrophe, of course. And I know we can depend on you, darling Cooper. I've got something very special planned for you."

* * *

Next, Gregory Yates appeared, looking, as always, a little bewildered. Black haired and with truly exquisite blue eyes, he was unquestionably huband material. Yet year in and year out, and despite Cooper's efforts, he remained unattached. He didn't lack motivation, just self-confidence. Some guys would have found it chemically, but Greg was either too smart or too obtuse to go that route. Unlike most of the Ph.D.'s Cooper knew, he had a sense of humor.

"Ben's not with you this afternoon?" Cooper asked, though he had already heard the story from the other member of the cast.

"Moved on to greener pastures," Greg said, grinning a lopsided grin Cooper knew meant he was trying to show that he viewed the situation ironically. Or at least give the impression that he did.

"What shade of green, exactly?"

"Banknote green," Greg said. "Older gentleman named Sonny Dallas. I believe you know him."

Cooper's ex. The real estate mogul. Ben would live to regret it. But Greg wasn't supposed to wait for that to happen. In fact, Greg was supposed to get laid. Preferably before nine p.m., Sunday being a school night.

"Come with me," Cooper said, "there's a guy I want you to meet."

"You don't have to do this, you know," Greg said. "I mean, I appreciate it, but. . ."

"But nothing," Cooper said. "Great shirt, by the way. It goes with your eyes."

* * *

"God, would you look at that one," Nick said. "Exquisite. Sorry to piss in your kool-aid, Cooper, but he's even better looking than that go-go boy of yours."

Cooper recognized the young man in question.

"Kent's not my go-go boy," he said. "He's more of a public utility."

"He thinks he's yours," Nick said.

"That's his problem."

"He'll make it your problem, if you're not careful."

"Nobody's more careful about that kind of thing than I am," Cooper insisted.

"Well," Nick said, "all I know is I'd bag that one in a heartbeat, but he can't be a day over nineteen."

"Subtract two years from that," Cooper said.

"You're joking."

"'Fraid not. That's Bella Steinberg's cousin, Judah Isaacs. He just finished eleventh grade."

"Do you know every underage hottie in the metropolitan area?"

"Just the Jewish ones," Cooper laughed.

"I'm obviously in the wrong line of work," Nick said.

"I don't think dirty scoutmaster is an actual career," Cooper said. "More like a hobby. You'd have to fit it into your already grueling schedule. And how much rape and pillage can one man commit?"

"Supplier of fake I.D. is more what I was thinking of," Nick said. "It's apparently extremely lucrative."

"I really ought to escort that one home," Cooper said.

* * *

"I wasn't expecting to run into you here," Judah said.

"No kidding," Cooper said, grasping him by the elbow.

"I mean, aren't you dating Cousin Bella?"

"Is that her story?"

"Engaged is her story," Judah said, "but since nobody's seen a ring yet, folks are skeptical. If you hang out here, that would explain it."

"If your tribe believes Bella's stories they're not very bright," Cooper said. "I really ought to try and sell them something. Oh, that's right: half of them are already clients of mine. Let's step outside, why don't we?"

"I just got here," Judah said.

"And you're leaving while you're still in one piece," Cooper said.

"I don't think so," Judah laughed.

"I've got your father's business card in my wallet," Cooper said. "He's just a phone call away."

"You wouldn't."

"Try me."

"Does Bella know you're a closet case?"

"No," Cooper said. "Bella knows me as the gay man she's desperate to reform, so blackmail won't work. I've got nothing to hide from anybody. You, on the other hand, should be at home doing your trigonometry homework."

"School's out," Judah said. "I don't have any homework at the moment. What I do have is this research project. Cataloging the local fauna."

"Nevertheless," Cooper said. "One phone call. Your parents will have you on a kibbutz so fast it'll make your head swim."

"I hear there are some really hot guys in the IDF."

"Stop arguing and move your ass," Cooper growled.

"You drag me out of here, I'll just go down the block," Judah said. "I really like Bolt better anyway. The guys are hotter."

"The guys are sleazier," Cooper said.

"You say potato, I say potahto."

"Come on. I'm driving you home," Cooper said. "Once you're in the front door, you won't be my responsibility any more."

* * *

"That scary drag queen of yours wants me to ride on some float she's organizing for the pride parade," Kent said, unzipping his 501's.

"She's not my drag queen," Cooper said, lying naked on Kent's waterbed. Kent liked to strip him down before getting undressed himself.

"Earth to Cooper Luxemberg," Kent giggled.

"Scary, I'll grant you," Cooper said.

"And definitely yours," Kent said. "The way she talks about you when you're not around, you're her lapdog. And that can only mean one thing."

"What's that?"

"She's your lapdog, of course."

II

"Got time to speak with a prospective client, boss?"

"What the hell happened to you, Pip?" Cooper asked. Pip's weekend activities kept getting more and more dubious.

"Ran into a doorknob," Pip giggled. "What's it look like?"

"You really have to stop dating guys who hit you."

"Guys who hit you are the only ones worth dating," Pip grinned.

"You really don't think that."

"Oh, I really do," Pip said. "At least in this particular case."

"Then you're an idiot," Cooper said. "Go find Elizabeth and see if she can touch up that eye with some foundation or you'll have to go home. We can't have you in the office looking like you've been in a bar brawl."

"Spoilsport."

"I mean it, Pip."

"So the client, boss? You want to have a look at him at least. He's a stunner. If you don't bag him, I will."

"Does he look like the type who can throw a punch?"

"Among other things," Pip said. "I'd guess footballs are more in his line, however."

"Send him in."

* * *

Buzz Montgomery was undoubtedly a stunner. With his fair skinned Eagle Scout features, gym-pumped frame flattered by a polo shirt that matched his clear blue eyes, and thick, smooth textured light brown hair, he could easily be mistaken for Tristan Bentley's brother, though it was true that Tristan's hair was a couple of shades lighter and Tristan was somewhat more densely muscled.

"So Mr. Montgomery," Cooper said, "tell me what kind of property you're interested in."

"Call me Buzz, please."

"Buzz. And I'm Cooper."

"Well, Cooper, I'm in the process of moving here from out of state and I'm looking for a place to live. I haven't decided for certain whether to buy right away or rent at first while I get my feet on the ground."

"Would this be a family home?"

"I'm single."

"I see. And is this move work related?"

"Not specifically. I mean, I'll be looking for a job. But I'm moving here for personal reasons. I have some money. If I found the right property at the right price—one that I could pay cash for and still have something left over while I look for work—I thought that might be simpler than having to move twice."

"Certainly," Cooper nodded. Buzz was handsome, well spoken, perfectly groomed, and totally opaque. Cooper was always impatient with this part of the process—sizing up the client. It made all the difference in the world whether Buzz would be looking for a wife or a boyfriend once he settled into his new place. Even in San Francisco statistics favored the former, but Cooper's instincts went in the other direction. Not to mention current market dynamics. San Francisco was filling up with gay men, whereas the straight population was pretty stable. The gays were coming from everywhere. Straights and gays looked for different kinds of properties in radically different neighborhoods whether they realized it or not. Perhaps Ned was right and they should hang a rainbow flag in the front window to get this part over with. "What would you be prepared to spend at this point?"

Buzz named his figure.

"In a decent location," Cooper said, "that gets you a two bedroom condominium unit with one bathroom, or perhaps one plus a powder room, and a single deeded parking space. That may not sound important, but take my word for it. In this city it really is."

"My hotel is charging for parking," Buzz nodded. "A property like that would be all I need."

"Any particular neighborhoods that you're interested in?"

"I don't know the city well enough to say. But I'd like something close in."

"Because for that money you could get a substantially larger property in the suburbs."

"No thanks," Buzz grinned. "The whole point of this move is so I won't be living in the sticks any more."

His teeth, Cooper noticed, were as perfect as the rest of him.

"All right," Cooper said. "Well, you're in luck. There's lots of inventory available right now. I've got half a dozen things in mind right off the bat."

"When can we look at them?"

"There's no time like the present," Cooper said.

"Great."

* * *

"So what do you think?" Cooper asked.

"This is the best unit you've shown me so far," Buzz smiled. "I love everything about it. The fireplace especially. But I noticed the sign next door. Is that one of your listings as well?"

Cooper had left this unit until last in hopes of interesting Buzz in that one. Real Estate 101: always set up the opportunity to bump the client to a higher price point. The worst that can happen is the client won't go for it.

"That listing is not for a single unit. It's the entire building. The idea is for the buyer to live in one unit and rent out the other two. For instance, we've been talking about a cash sale on a single unit. But if you used the amount you're talking about spending as a down payment on a property like the one next door, the rental income would easily cover your mortgage payment. That's a great investment."

"I see," Buzz said, looking thoughtful. "Or if I paid the entire amount in cash, I'd have the rental income to live on while I look for work."

"That's another way to think about it," Cooper agreed.

"Could we look at it?"

"I can't show you the basement apartment," Cooper said. "It's occupied and the tenant sleeps in the daytime because of her work schedule. But you can see the main and top floor units. The top floor unit is particularly nice because the attic of the building has been converted into a loft space that makes a very pleasant den. And there's a fireplace in the living room at least as nice as this one."

* * *

"Ned," Cooper said, "what are you doing answering phones?"

"Miss Pip was indisposed," Ned said. "I had to send her home."

"I warned him," Cooper said.

"Permanently, I hope you understand," Ned said. "I'm not putting up with any more from that one."

"It's your call," Cooper said. "This is Buzz Montgomery."

"Ned Westerleigh. Extremely happy to meet you."

"Pleased to meet you, Ned."

"Has our man Cooper been showing you properties?"

"He has," Buzz smiled.

"We're just on our way upstairs to write an offer on the Winchester property."

"Indeed? The Winchester property?"

"That's right, Ned."

"You have discriminating tastes, sir."

"Thanks," Buzz smiled. "I'm very excited about it. The rental income will be a big help while I look for a job."

"What line of work are you in, Buzz?"

"I'm a high school English teacher," Buzz said. "At least I was back home. I understand that positions are extremely difficult to find here."

"You know," Ned said, "I have some contacts who might be of help."

Ned was thinking, Cooper knew, of his beloved St. Dunstan's, a West Coast clone of Winchester, the school Ned and generations of his male relations had attended before going on to Oxford. When Ned came across a possible acquisition for what he referred to as his menagerie, he didn't waste any time. By sundown, for instance, he would have arranged for Buzz to meet Big Steve Fabiani, who would subsequently swing into full matchmaking mode. Buzz was exactly the type of specimen Big Steve was continually campaigning to marry Cooper off to. This, Cooper knew, was at or near the top of Big Steve's current list of unfinished projects. But Cooper wasn't concerned. Nothing along those lines could possibly happen until after the close of escrow. Meantime, he supposed, Nick Romanovsky, Big Steve's other high priority bachelor, would have first shot. Or actually, the first dozen or so shots.

"That would be terrific," Buzz said. "Thanks."

"On the other hand," Ned continued, "if you're interested in a change of career, we have an opening here at the agency."

"Ned, you can't expect a man with Buzz's experience and qualifications to answer our phones," Cooper protested.

"That wasn't my intention," Ned said, "but something tells me he'd make a fine office manager."

"Office manager?" Cooper asked.

"I can't do this any more, Cooper. I've got to get back into selling before I lose my mind."

"I'm sorry," Buzz said, "but I don't know the first thing about managing offices. Or about real estate."

"My dear boy, you'd take to it like a duck to water. I mean, if you can wrangle a classroom full of high school students you're certainly up to anything you'd have to face around here. And as to salary, I'm sure we could match what you'd make in teaching."

"Ned," Cooper said, "we really ought to get that offer written."

"Indeed," Ned nodded, "but promise me, Buzz, that you'll think about it."

"All right."

"Now as to the Winchester property," Ned continued, "let's take, say, five percent off the asking price."

"What?" Buzz looked baffled.

"You sure, Ned?" Cooper asked.

"Oh, what the hell. Make it eight percent," Ned said. "Final offer."

"It's Ned's property," Cooper explained to Buzz. "You're buying it from him."

"Welcome to San Francisco, Buzz."

* * *

When Cooper got home from work that afternoon there were more post-cards from Bella. She was in Europe on a buying tour for her gallery. She sent him a postcard from somewhere different every day. Like the previous ones, these two declared her undying love for him and her determination to one day bear his children.

He'd been as direct with her as it was possible to be. She just didn't listen.

Buzz Montgomery

I

He lies awake listening to the distant roar of traffic on the interstate north of town. The sound comes to him through the moonlit half darkness of the sultry night, a night like far too many he can remember as well as he can remember his own name. It is uninterrupted, unchallenged by any competing sound, undistorted by breezes because there are none tonight though he and everyone else in the town would welcome them. Some of the traffic is heading east, toward Albuquerque. Some of it is heading west, toward Las Vegas and eventually the coast. He can't remember a time when the sound of the traffic wasn't there, and he's been sleeping in this room, under this window, for most of his life.

He imagines someone else, one of his neighbors perhaps, waking up momentarily and hearing the sound and thinking that it is nothing of consequence— just another sound. Like the sound of the trains that pass through the town several times daily, some eastbound, some westbound. Trains that gave the town its reason for existence a long time ago but never stop here any more, just as most of the traffic on the interstate doesn't stop. Like the sounds of cats rummaging in carelessly lidded garbage cans, coyotes howling in the foothills, dogs barking at them from backyards all over town, the crunch of shoes on gravel, the whisper of barely moving air in the limp, heat enervated foliage of every tree for miles around, a thousand sounds that might be heard instead of this sound through an open window on a night in late summer. He imagines that neighbor listening for a moment to identify whatever it is that woke him/her and then rolling over and going back to sleep. Nothing to take note of. Nothing to lose sleep over.

Somewhere else, the sound he hears through his open window might be the surf pounding on a rocky shore. Somewhere else it might be the wind sighing through tall pines. Somewhere else it might be palm fronds rattling softly. Somewhere else it might be the muted, eclectic hum of a great city. Somewhere else there might be no sound at all coming in through the open window.

But it is nowhere else. It is here. It is always here and nowhere else, and that is and has always been the problem. This inescapable truth is the reason he hates the sound of the traffic on the interstate north of town. That sound is always there to remind him, in the last, dreamy moments before he sleeps and in the first foggy moments he is awake and at various and random other moments of each and every day that he is indeed here. Still here. Nowhere else.

Much as he hates that sound and as much sleep as he has lost over the years lying awake as it taunts him, it is too hot tonight to close the window. And the bright moonlight streaming in like liquid silver through threadbare curtains hanging limp and motionless in the stillness and powerless to muffle the sound only makes the night seem hotter. Even if he did get up and close the window and shut the sound out that light would keep him awake, and he would lie there and imagine he could still hear the sound, and it wouldn't matter that he didn't really because he would know it's still out there and he's still here, not somewhere else—anywhere else. And that never stops being the problem.

He listens for other sounds, too. Not outdoor sounds. Sounds inside the house. He listens for them automatically, involuntarily, unconsciously, like a small animal in the forest listens for predators without having to think about it or curtail any of its other activities. He listens out of exactly that kind of instinct. But there are no other sounds in the house. At least not the particular ones he listens for so intently. Of course there aren't. There can't be any more. But the seven weeks since her death have not been long enough to break his habit of lying awake to hear them. Those sounds will never again issue from that upstairs room. They will never again rouse him from his shallow sleep and summon him to her bedside. That part of his life is finally over. He has closed up her room. He has disposed of almost everything that was left. Her clothes went to the Red Cross, though he has no idea what good they'll be, how anyone could possibly find them useful. Her hospital bed he donated to a rest home. Most of the rest of the furniture went to an outrageously effeminate antique dealer who drove all the way up from Phoenix in a pink Cadillac convertible with huge, ornately chromed tail fins. The car and the antique dealer himself, perfectly preserved, seemed like they belonged in a museum. He saved only what was absolutely necessary to go on living in the house. In addition to the furniture, the dealer took her china, her silver, her wedding crystal. He was surprised at the figure the dealer quoted him for the lot of it. It was much more than he had expected, but it still wasn't a lot. He suspected at the time and still half believes that the price the dealer offered was inflated by about thirty percent because of his looks, which had obviously aroused certain hopes in the dealer. He believes the price might have gone higher still if he had given the dealer any indication he was aware of the interest and welcomed it. Even the slightest hint might have sufficed. But he didn't give it because he isn't available, and not because he thought the dealer unattractive, because he has slept with men he didn't find attractive on more than one occasion and it wasn't the end of the world. But he never did it in this house. And it has been a very long time since he even did it in this town.

The dealer's money was enough to pay off the credit card charges it took to bury her in a fashion she would have deplored as wasteful, though by any other standards than hers the funeral was modest. He remembers looking at the check and realizing that those debts would be paid off. He still winces with guilt when he recalls his relief at the realization and at the way that relief persists, as though he begrudges her that casket, those flowers, that headstone any more than he begrudges her anything else. Nothing that happened to either of them was ever her choice any more than it was his.

Still, the funeral had cost money he didn't have at the time. It was a debt he would have been years paying off on his salary. And so it's one less thing to worry about, if he could only quit feeling guilty. But he might just as well attempt walking on water or self-levitation.

His father's library is gone now, too. He couldn't dispose of that with his mother still in the house. She wouldn't have heard of such a thing. Now the boxes that hadn't once been opened in all those years since his father's death are stored in the new rector's basement. He suspects that the new rector only accepted the gift of those books as an act of charity. The previous rector, who came to town after his father's death, wouldn't have taken them. Not even as an act of charity. Perhaps not even at gunpoint. His mother and he had both understood that and never offered them.

He rolls over and tells himself for at least the dozenth time since crawling into bed that he must sleep. Nothing matters more than this, regardless of how much he might think it does. But the traffic roars on in the distance, in the moonlit near-twilight. *It is not really loud enough to keep anyone awake,* he silently tells himself, *only me, only because I have let it come to mean so much. Too much.*

But knowing that, knowing that the sound he hears of traffic on the highway, some of it going east toward Albuquerque and some of it west toward Las

Vegas and on to the coast, is after all only a sound and that everything else is in his head, doesn't help. It doesn't change anything. Because that traffic is always out there going somewhere else, and he is always here.

II

After lying awake for twenty minutes waiting for the alarm to go off, he pushes down the plunger and gets up. In a few weeks he'll be sleeping until the alarm rings instead of lying awake anticipating it, but he is always like this at the end of summer vacation. He showers, shaves, deodorizes, dries his hair, dresses—too slowly, frustrated at having lost the rhythm of eight years of mornings like this one and at the same time knowing it will come back to him almost before he is aware of it, just as he's depending on lots of others things becoming second nature again.

He fixes breakfast. A banana. A nectarine. A glass of unsweetened grapefruit juice. A protein shake. He considers packing a lunch but decides against it. His colleagues will want to go out to lunch today. Next Monday, when the students are there and he will have only forty minutes to eat and go to the bathroom and check his mailbox for messages and his only alternative will be grisly cafeteria food, he will pack a lunch.

While he eats he wonders where the summer went. Silly question. Weeks at the hospital waiting for the inevitable, unable to do anything for her except sit at her bedside and hold her hand and listen to her halting, barely audible retellings of stories he already knew by heart. Stories of the three of them—him, his father, and her. Unable to do anything but listen and hope that somehow that could be enough. Unable to recall her as anything other than a sick, tired, frail woman old enough to have been his grandmother and not his mother at all. After those weeks the funeral and finally the aftermath. That's where the summer went. And now it almost seems like it was one long, hot late afternoon, with the merciless sun hanging low over the desert and silhouetting the Joshua trees and mesquite against a sky already turning to indigo.

He wonders about his colleagues. Except for two women who attend his church, he has seen none of them since May, though there were many cards and phone calls the week of the funeral. There were floral tributes from the English Department, the Faculty Benevolence Committee, and the teachers' association. Now that he is on his own and no longer solely responsible for an invalid mother, he knows that the single women on the staff will observe him even more keenly. He'd rather not deal with the scrutiny, though he knows that the annoyance, real as it may come to be, will only be temporary.

At the very least it's going to be a relief getting paychecks again. He can't remember being this broke since he was in college. Even with Medicare and the supplementary coverage she had seen advertised on television, the expense of her last illness and the funeral arrangements completely exhausted his savings. All he's got left is the house, which he has kept up the mortgage payments on since his father's death. Her Social Security widow's benefits had been a pittance. They barely covered the cost of her prescriptions, much less food and shelter. Still, he managed to take care of her and that's really all that mattered at the time. The mortgage will be paid off in a few more months. Then he will own the house free and clear. Not that he cares about that. Not that he wants to keep it, to live in it a minute longer than he has to. He'll put it on the market as soon as he dares. Now is too early. Principal Thompson will make this year a living hell if he suspects Buzz is planning to leave.

The house won't bring very much. Nobody wants to buy a house here. Everybody with any sense moves away. Nobody wants a house this old, either. It is such an ugly barn. He can't think why his parents bought it when there were new houses being built in town at the time, smaller, modern houses better suited to a family like theirs—not to mention the needs of an invalid. In Phoenix, this house would be considered quaint and—at least in the right neighborhood—would be worth three times what he expects it will bring. What he'll get for it might just be enough for a down payment on a small condo down there.

* * *

Every August when he drives into the faculty parking lot for the first time since May, it is like nothing has changed. Like it's been one long, hot weekend since he last pulled into his regular parking space. At this rate, he might as well be in purgatory.

Which would perhaps be preferable to what he's facing. He knows he's going to do basically what he did last year and the year before that. If he's not careful he'll wake up some morning an indeterminate number of years from now and find himself still here, still doing the same things, so numbed by his life that he won't even think to wonder why.

The sense of time standing still persists as he locks the car and goes up the sidewalk toward the main entrance of the school. He is early in spite of himself. Back in unremembered childhood he absorbed the lesson that punctuality is next to godliness. Though the doors are unlocked the whole place is empty, more like a mausoleum than a high school. The dense silence is only broken by the whisper of swamp coolers working somewhere far away and a faint buzzing from the fluorescent light fixtures.

He has a recurring dream about coming back to school at the beginning of the year. In the dream, he arrives early on the first day. He finds the building unlocked but empty. He goes into the faculty mailroom and pulls a thick stack out of his box. Memos, calendars, handbooks, gradebook inserts, welcome back greetings from the district superintendent, and most of all forms. Forms for ordering supplies, forms for requesting repairs to his classroom, forms for ordering the duplication of printed materials, forms requesting the use of audio visual equipment, forms to request personal leave, forms to request professional release time, forms to request a sabbatical, forms to request a salary adjustment based on continuing education, forms to request assistance from the teachers' association or the human resources department, forms to report an accident in the classroom, forms to refer students for discipline issues, to refer them for counseling assistance, to refer them to the school psychologist, to send them to detention or the nurse. Paperwork *ad nauseum*. He carries this haul back down the corridor to the main staircase. He climbs to the third floor of the building then walks along another corridor to his classroom, which overlooks the faculty parking lot. He sits down at his desk and starts to go through the stack of paperwork, methodically filling in blanks. He works on this all morning. The building is silent and still seems empty. From time to time he gets up from his desk and goes over and looks out the classroom windows at the parking lot below, and each time, except for his Volkswagen, it is empty. He continues to do paperwork, and time passes. The building remains silent. He is still sitting at his desk completing paperwork and less than halfway through the stack two days later when the bell rings to begin the first day of classes. He gets up from his desk, preparing to welcome his students as they enter the classroom, but no one arrives.

He is thinking about this dream as he pulls a thick stack of papers out of his box in the faculty mailroom and walks down the silent, empty corridor toward the main staircase.

* * *

"I can't tell you how sorry I was not to be here for Miss Amanda's funeral," Julia says. They have just returned from lunch. She crosses the classroom, pulls up a chair, and sits facing him across the already cluttered top of his desk. He knew that already. He would have known it even if she hadn't sent a card and called three times, twice long distance and once when she got back to town from her trip. But it is nice to hear it anyway. More than that, it is good to hear her voice, to be in the same room with her, alone.

"I would have come back."

"I know," he nods. He told her not to. She and Dr. Sundine—he calls her by her first name but can't bring himself to call her husband Paul—sent flowers instead. Three dozen yellow roses. His mother's favorite. Julia remembered that. Julia remembers everything. That makes her a good friend, though sometimes he wishes she remembered ninety-four per cent instead.

"How were the children?"

"Fine," she says. Every inch the southern gentlewoman in spite of her decades living in exile, she is uncomfortable bragging, reluctant to appear too proud of her handsome son, her distinguished husband, her charming daughters and their husbands, her ever expanding flock of grandchildren, her beautiful home, her own accomplishments and good works. "Fine" is all he'll get out of her on any of those subjects. This reticence of hers, along with her aristocratic bearing and accent, has always reminded him of his mother, though Julia is tall, statuesque—the picture of health, really—and two decades younger.

* * *

He stands at the lectern watching them enter the classroom. It is the last period of the day. This is his fifth group of students. They look the same as the ones in all the other classes he has met for the first time today. Yet there are subtle differences. Just enough to keep him aware of the passing of the class periods. Counting this bunch he's seen close to two hundred kids in all. Class counts are huge this semester. There was attrition from the department faculty last spring. Two retirements and one maternity leave. And due to cuts in state funding, only two of the three openings were filled. Julia, who is English Department chair, has been lobbying for an additional hire since June when preregistration figures came in at nearly forty students per section. So far the administration hasn't blinked. Hence the parade he has witnessed today. One hundred ninety-seven seventeen, eighteen, and nineteen year olds.

Practically the entire senior class. The only twelfth graders in the whole school he doesn't teach are a couple of dozen special ed. kids and a similar number of ESL students.

This particular group are college bound students—the cream of the school, though he despises that description. His first period class is the same. The rest of his students will go to work, go to technical school, go into the military, or go onto the welfare rolls after graduation. These kids are the ones the whole town is looking to. They are expected to be the success stories. He will have to remind himself of this all year long, and he will occasionally lie awake at night shuddering at the thought that they are the leaders of tomorrow.

Although he has never had any of them as students before, he knows many of them. The athletes, the politicians, the artists and performers, the celebrities. Anna-Yolanda Vazquez, president of the senior class and already campaigning for the state senate, parks herself in the front row to his left. He presumes she has chosen that particular seat just off of center because she's done her homework and knows he's a lefty and will focus in her direction the largest proportion of the time. Two rows back and on the extreme right, Brian Diaz Cota slumps in a desk that seems likely to collapse under his bulk any second. He won state championships in the shot put, discus, and javelin last season as a junior and broke a handful of records. He and his parents have been entertaining college recruiters all summer. Mandy and Mindy Smith, blond, bowheaded identical twins who run the cheerleading squad with an iron hand sit in the absolute middle of the room, popping bubble bum in unison and looking like they're on the point of erupting into uncontrollable giggles the minute he opens his mouth. And in the back row, far left corner, lounges Trevor Weitzmann, lion's mane of sun streaked hair belying his position as starting quarterback of the varsity squad. He wonders why the coach doesn't make Trevor cut it. He recalls the tight bun Trevor pulled it into last year when he won the state wrestling championship in his weight class.

As for the other seniors, they look like last year's seniors and the seniors the year before that. They sound like them, too. Hairstyles and fashions in clothing change, certainly, but so gradually that he has to think back several more years before he can recall a group of students who looked sufficiently different from these for it to be noticeable. These appear and sound so familiar, in fact, that he could almost swear they actually are the kids who graduated last year and the year before that. Of course, when he looks closely at the room instead of just scanning it, the familiar faces are absent. Still, strangers though they are, he knows exactly what will happen to these kids this year.

Five of the one hundred and three girls in his classes will become pregnant between now and next May. Three of the ninety-four boys will go to jail at one time or other. At least one of the girls will be raped, and there will be several close calls. At least half a dozen of the students will get in trouble for fighting. This includes members of both genders, because girls these days are shockingly violence prone. Somebody will nearly be thrown out of school for plagiarizing a term paper in government class. Several students will suffer through their parents' divorces. And then there's the part he dreads the most. It will be an unusual year indeed if all his students survive until the last day of school. There is typically one traffic fatality per year, suicides are rare but far from unheard of, and as remote as the town is, the kids still manage to know all about and acquire enough of the latest drugs to overdose on them.

Less serious incidents will also take place. Several of the boys will finally experience their long awaited growth spurts. The girls will become almost daily more sophisticated in their clothing, hairstyles, and makeup. Minor scuffles will break out among the boys over the burning question of whether Chevys, Fords, or Mopars rule. At least two of the boys, though it could well turn out to be more—and perhaps even a girl, the way the athletic program is changing these days—will suffer sports injuries serious enough to put them in casts. At least four couples will become engaged, though they all seem far too young to him to be making that kind of plans. All of the students, even those with no hope of or serious interest in attending it, will spend weeks and weeks in the spring term so preoccupied with the annual prom date sweepstakes that they'll be nearly incapable of useful thought, much less doing their homework or scoring well on tests.

The tardy bell rings. All the desks are full. He looks at them and they look back. He has never gotten used to the feeling of their eyes on him. It is the profoundest sense of nakedness imaginable.

III

He spends a ridiculously long time staring into his closet trying to decide what to wear to Annie's dinner party, though he has no idea why. It hardly matters how he looks. It wouldn't occur to him to go in a t-shirt, of course, even if it weren't October and likely to get down to freezing by midnight. Just like it wouldn't occur to him to go unshaven or with his hair uncombed or with holes in his trousers or wearing socks that don't match. But beyond that, beyond the well defined limits of middle class, small town propriety, it doesn't make a bit of difference what he looks like. That's the one thing he is certain of. And in spite of it he still gazes helplessly into the closet wondering why he can't decide what to wear.

He has known Mayor and Mrs. Weekes—Josh and Annie—all his life. He has been in their home more times and under more different circumstances than he can count. Julia Sundine he has seen every day at work for over eight years. Dr. Sundine, her husband, knows more about him than anyone else in the world now that his mother is gone. Judge and Mrs. Weitzmann were married by his father. No other clergyman in the county would agree to perform a ceremony for a Jewish man and a Chinese-American woman who had both been married previously. That's how they originally came to attend St. Michael's. He remembers their wedding in his parents' living room, twenty-five years ago last July Fourth. That leaves the new rector of St. Michael's, Bill Roberts, and his wife Nancy. They're newlyweds, and he'd be surprised if they spared him a single glance tonight.

* * *

Josh and Annie live outside of town. To get to their place he drives down a narrow country road whose cracked, faded blacktop—its worn surface invisible in the darkness—he knows like the back of his hand. He turns into the gravel drive leading up to the house just as the moon, huge and orange, begins to edge over a ridge somewhere out on the old Hardison place, whose gate he'd reach in another couple of miles if he stayed on the county road. If he went even farther, through the foothills and into the mountains, he'd eventually come to the small state park and campground where the pavement ends, though a dirt track, almost impassible except for vehicles with four wheel drive, goes nearly to the top of one of the peaks.

He steers the car carefully along the drive. He can already see the lights that Josh keeps burning all night, every night, whether or not company is expected. He pulls into the circular drive behind Julia's white Mercedes 220, Grace Weitzmann's green Volvo station wagon, and an aging Saab he assumes must belong to Bill Roberts.

He gets out of the car. He takes a deep breath and reminds himself that it doesn't matter how he looks, and more importantly, it doesn't matter how he feels. He heads for the front door. He has never gotten over the terror—there's no other word for it: sheer, blinding, piss and shit in your pants terror—that he feels for a brief moment every time he walks up to this door even after all this tome. He feels like the perpetrator returning to the scene of his crime. And there's no statute of limitations covering his particular offense. He feels the familiar grip about his abdomen, like a belt being cinched far too tight. He feels his heart begin to pound, feels himself fighting for breath as he rings the doorbell and squints into the light from a wrought iron fixture that probably shouldn't have more than a thirty watt bulb in it. Poor old Josh. As if all the bright lights in the world could make a difference, could even begin to dispel the darkness the three of them inhabit.

"Buzz! Buzz, Buzz, Buzzie!" Josh greets him with his perennial yelp of thrilled surprise as if his arrival is totally unexpected and a supreme pleasure. "Come in, boy, come in."

"Hi, Josh," he says, thinking that his voice always sounds small and wimpy in comparison with Josh's cowboy rumble. At least the worst moment is past. Once more the skies have not fallen. Raging seas have not swallowed him up. The ground has not opened under his feet. He starts to relax. The various symptoms of anxiety begin to subside, each at its own rate. Once more the unthinkable hasn't occurred, though, as always, he has seen that fleeting "why?" in Josh's eyes, still unuttered, never an accusation but merely a request for clarification—if it's not too much trouble.

Josh slaps him across the shoulders. Josh is a tall, big boned man. He weighs comfortably over two hundred fifty pounds, and though it's all pretty soft and flabby these days, there's enough of him to possess tremendous inertia. He tries not to wince at the impact. This manly exertion is the only way Josh can stand to touch him and the only way he can bear to be touched by Josh. He looks closely at Josh in the light of the foyer. In spite of the graying hair and the face of a man who smokes and drinks and above all worries too much and has maintained these habits for a long, long time, Josh doesn't look his age. It's a miracle of genetics. That's the only possible explanation.

"Annie can't wait to see you."

And indeed, before he's three steps into the room feeling like a dingy bobbing in the wake of an ocean liner, she's there to greet him. He kisses her on the cheek and accepts the glass of club soda she offers him. She takes his other hand and squeezes it and speaks one word only. His real name. Now that his mother is dead, Annie is the only person in the world who calls him Burton. He smiles at her. She blinks back tears and grins ruefully.

He looks around the room. The rector and his wife say good evening. Julia waves and smiles. Dr. Sundine gives him a brisk, businesslike nod, as if he has good test results to report. He can't recall ever seeing Dr. Sundine truly off duty. Judge Weitzmann nods and Mrs. Weitzmann smiles and says she's happy to see him. The Weitzmanns are standing beside the grand piano, and he looks away from them quickly. Too quickly, probably. But at all costs he has to avoid looking directly at the framed photo of a young man with curly black hair and sky blue eyes and the devil's own grin: a photo that is an accusation.

* * *

Halfway through dinner he figures out exactly what Annie's up to, placing him next to Nancy Roberts at the table. Annie's always up to something, and never more so than when that something concerns Buzz. The Robertses have recently moved to Hualapai from Louisville, and as he converses with Nancy he feels Annie watching him. She is undoubtedly hoping that the couple has some single friend, a teacher like himself perhaps, or a young attorney. The county attorney's office always has openings going unfilled for lack of applicants. He knows Annie too well, perhaps even better than he knew his own mother. He can practically read her mind. What's going on in there right now? Plans for a wedding. That young woman she's expecting the Robertses to introduce him to—Annie's already measuring her for the gown. It cuts him like a knife. It's even worse than the fleeting "why?" in Josh's eyes. Every time he sits at Annie's table, there's one moment when he regrets being present so profoundly he almost feels suicidal.

* * *

He sits listening as Bill Roberts plays Debussy on the grand piano. It is almost more than he can take. He can barely sit still, barely breathe, barely keep himself from screaming. He exchanges a quick glance with Annie, whose eyes glisten with unshed tears. She feels it, too. And Josh isn't even in the room. He left just as Bill sat down to play. If Bill would only hurry up and finish the Debussy. Then the three of them can relax. The Chopin and Ravel were bad enough. But the Debussy really is too much.

The silver framed photo had to be moved to the mantle so that the lid of the piano could be raised. He can't remember the last time the photo was moved off the piano. But even though he senses to the millimeter where it is now he doesn't trust himself to look at it, and he tries not to look at Bill Roberts at the keyboard, either.

He wishes he had left the room when Josh did. They'd be shooting pool this minute, Josh chomping away on a cigar and delivering a running commentary on everything under the sun. He'd be basking in the gruff, dependable warmth of that solid presence, the blanketlike security of Josh's refusal ever to ask questions. They might accidentally hear a few notes drifting down the hall now and then but they'd be doing what he knows Josh is doing even as he thinks of it. Pretending it's music on the stereo. He couldn't have done that to Annie, left her there to face it alone with a room full of guests and dessert waiting to be served.

He can't look at the picture though he longs to. Sometimes when he's alone in this room he dares to do it. He gazes through the polished glass at that face that once meant everything to him and now means only loss, fear, betrayal, guilt. Regardless of how he's feeling right now, with the music washing over him like a tsunami, he won't plead a migraine and rush home as soon as the music is over. He'll stay for dessert and he'll force himself to smile and congratulate Bill Roberts on his playing. It is exceptionally good. Better than Tim's? He can't answer that question objectively, even if he could remember what Tim made those pieces sound like all those years ago. What use is comparing them anyway? What competition can the dead be to the living?

Listening is agony. Not that it's Bill's fault. He couldn't have known when he stood admiring the Steinway and asked Annie if she'd mind him trying it out what he was about to do to the three of them. How could he? No, it's not Bill's fault. Just like it's not Annie's fault that she couldn't find a gracious way to say no to such a reasonable request. Who could?

Nothing is Annie's fault, though he knows she's still blaming herself after all this time. It wasn't Josh's fault, either. If it was anybody's fault, if anybody could have prevented it, he knows who he blames. He's lived with his guilt since the day it happened. It never gets better and he no longer believes it ever will. Most of the time he sleepwalks through life pretending he's forgotten everything. He figures that Josh and Annie do more or less the same.

But sometimes, like tonight, something happens that forces them all to remember it. And when he remembers it, he always thinks about all the ways it might have turned out differently.

Bill eventually finishes playing and everyone applauds. Annie insists that he play more, and it would take someone who knows her far better than Bill does to see that she doesn't really mean it, that she's desperately playing the gracious host. He fears for a moment that her apparent sincerity is doing its work. But almost before he's registered that thought, Bill begs off, saying he's tired himself out. And besides, he doesn't know any more repertoire from memory. Annie, bless her, doesn't mention the stacks of musical scores in the credenza behind them. Bill rises from the piano bench and Buzz breathes a sigh of relief. Maybe he'll be all right now. Or as close to it as he ever gets.

* * *

"Trevor just loves your class, Buzz," Grace Weitzmann gushes, a forkful of german chocolate cake poised between them like an exclamation point. "He talks about you all the time. Mr. Montgomery this and Mr. Montgomery that. He's never been this excited about school, has he, dear?"

"It makes a nice change," Judge Weitzmann smiles. "I thought Julia was going to end up killing him last year. Of course she'd have had to beat me to the punch."

"It's not that he's a bad boy," Grace protests. "He's just too smart for his own good."

"And we've spoiled him rotten."

"Now, Martin."

"It's true, Grace," he insists. "You know it as well as I do. There's no getting around it. You've got to promise us, Buzz, if he gets out of line in any way, just lower the boom. You don't even have to call us first. We're not that kind of parents. So just give him hell. We've got to knock some of that crap out of him before he leaves for college."

"Will do," he says, unable to imagine what they're going on about. He wishes he had about two hundred more students like Trevor. It would make his job a whole lot simpler.

Well, on second thought, not quite exactly like Trevor.

* * *

"Annie didn't tell me you'd be here tonight," Bill Roberts says.

"I rarely miss a free meal," he says, gulping decaf.

"Josh says you're practically a member of the family," Nancy smiles.

"I've known them all my life," he says, realizing too late how such a seemingly innocuous statement leaves him open to all kinds of questions about them, and worse yet, about himself. "They were always very kind to my parents."

Bill nods, and Nancy's smile doesn't waver.

"You know," Bill says, "this is my third parish. I have to say I've never seen anything like the way people still cherish the memory of your father's time here. Usually you hear at least some kind of minority report about your predecessors. But not in Father Montgomery's case."

He knows this to be true. People in town, even people who were never members of St. Michael's, do revere his father. He's always chalked it up as much to their intense dislike of his father's successor, Father Patterson, as to his father's own qualities.

"We wish we'd see you at services more often," Nancy chirps.

"Nancy, please." Bill looks embarrassed.

* * *

He drives home through bright moonlight. Halfway into town he pulls off the road. It's freezing under a bright moon. He doesn't know how long he will have to wait, but suddenly he wants to hear them. He shuts off the headlights and the engine and gets out of the car. His breath hangs like a cloud in front of his face in the still air. He waits. He stands there getting chilled to the bone and no traffic passes on the road. Finally they start. Off in the hills somewhere on the old Hardison place. Tentatively at first, just one or two voices. Soon, though, it's the whole pack in full cry. He listens to them out in the dark hills, descendents of the coyotes he remembers listening to as a boy. They sound like they've always sounded. They sound exactly like they used to sound through the open windows of Tim's bedroom on a chilly autumn night like this.

IV

This year Veteran's Day falls on Friday, and school is out. It's also his parents' anniversary, and he goes to leave flowers on their graves. The cemetery is as bleak as he's ever seen it. Dead leaves rattle across brown grass. Dead leaves lie in heaps against headstones. His flannel shirt is not enough to turn away the chill. He should have worn a sweatshirt over it. The roses will blow away or their blooms will be shattered unless he finds exactly the right spot for them where his parents' simple gravestones provide shelter.

There is a third space here, just next to theirs, which also belongs to the family. His mother insisted he buy it, apparently assuming that he would someday want to lie next to them. He didn't argue when she suggested this. He simply did it. But something inside him screamed "no" the minute he heard her request and still screams that same silent "no" every time he thinks about it.

He can sell the space just like he can sell the house—cheap, if and when he can find a buyer. That may well be never. But he will not be buried here. Once he leaves the town he will never come back to it. Never. Not even to put flowers on his parents' graves. He's long since paid off any debt he owed them. Or maybe he will return. Yes. Just once. To place flowers, but not on his parents' grave.

He hears a car speeding down the county road that runs past the cemetery gates. He looks up. It's a dark blue Porsche 914. The only one of its type in the county. The top is off, and Trevor Weitzmann's hair streams out behind him in the wind. He stands and watches until the car is out of sight. Then he turns from the road and tries to forget that he saw it at all or that he knows who was behind the wheel.

There is another grave here. He only visits it rarely and he has never dared to place flowers on it. He saunters down the path toward it, hoping it looks unintentional. Even after this long he couldn't face it if people were to suspect. And not just for his own sake. There are other people's feelings to consider and a memory to be protected and preserved. But it is still a betrayal. He knows that and he hates himself for it, for his weakness both now and in the past. It is no good telling himself that he is a victim just as surely now as he was then. He expects more of himself. But what else could he have done? A seventeen year old with an overworked father and an invalid mother?

At the grave he gazes at the headstone, rereading Tim's name and the dates, faintly shocked at how much time has passed. He can remember it like it was yesterday. He wipes a single tear off his cheek. Better not stay too long.

But it's too late to worry about being seen here. He feels eyes on him.

"Buzz?"

It's Bill Roberts, the new rector. He feels silly labeling Bill that way, but he recalls how the parishioners all referred to his father's successor as the "new rector" until the day he retired last spring.

"Hi."

"I wanted to get the lay of the land," Bill laughs. "I'm officiating my first graveyard service here on Monday and I hadn't laid eyes on the place."

"Well, this is it," he says. "Not much to look at, I'm afraid. The Catholic one is a mile down the road. They did a nicer job than we Protestants. We're the minority around here."

"It's actually very nice," Bill says.

"Think so? Well, I'd say that makes you the right man for the job."

"I wish more of your fellow citizens thought that."

"They'll warm up to you," he says. "It just takes time."

"I hope it won't be too long."

"Speaking of time. . ."

"I'm through here, too," Bill says, and they fall into step down the path to the gate. "Just got time to make it back into town for an altar guild meeting. That Annie Weekes is a pistol."

"That's one way of putting it," he says, surprised to hear himself laugh. "Just make sure you don't cross her."

"I think I already figured that out," Bill grunts.

* * *

What a waste of a three day weekend, he thinks, finishing his workout and heading for his second shower of the day. He really should have gone to Phoenix. He would have except he's already exceeded his travel budget for the season. Regular weekends are bad enough. Grading papers, catching up on his laundry, and doing the grocery shopping aren't enough to keep him occupied. No matter how busy he stays he's never able to turn off his brain. A three day weekend is fifty per cent worse because he has that much more time on his hands.

He's sure he's the only one at the whole school dreading Christmas vacation.

* * *

After nightfall the temperature plummets. It'll be in the high thirties before kickoff, so he dresses warmly and heads for school. It's the final game of the season and, if he has anything to do with it, the final game of his tenure at the school. With his record he could have gotten himself appointed head football coach at any time during the last eight years with just one visit to John Waggener's office. Everyone in town regards the reason he didn't as just one more installment of the price he paid for his mother's care, but it had nothing to do with that, really. He'd rather have stuck a sharp stick in his eye than set foot back in that locker room. Of all the forbidden territories in the town, that locker room is the worst. A place of sheer terror. All these years later the memories are still enough to push him to what he thinks of as the edge of sanity. The idea of sitting in that office hearing himself addressed as "coach"—he never could have stood it.

The field itself, the "stadium", though that ramshackle collection of bleachers hardly merits the designation, is a relatively safe place. Nothing bad ever actually happened to him there. There, it was only the constant threat. On that turf, under those lights, he must have seemed invulnerable. That's what boys that age make it look like. Only he and one or two others knew any better until it was too late. That's all he can think of every time he watches a game. Those young gods are far more fragile than his fellow citizens understand. They may be big, strong, loud. But what's inside them, which is the only thing that counts, is brittle and frail and may already have been crushed. Who knows? He kept his secret and there's no telling which member of this year's squad is as haunted as he was back in those days. No, there's no telling, but there is one certainty. At least one of those superb young animals has a secret he's willing to die to protect. Sure as the sun will rise in the east, one of them does.

* * *

It's an auspicious occasion despite his misgivings. The home team is going into tonight's contest undefeated. They're league champions, already assured of a trip to regionals. They stand a good chance of getting to the state championships. The school has always fielded successful football teams, but this is the best record in all the years since he was a senior himself. He was starting quarterback that season. He was the golden boy. The final home game had been, as far as the town was concerned, his apotheosis. That and the game for the state championship, which they won by one measly point—a missed conversion by their opponents. There were other athletic accomplishments later in the year, ones he's more proud of in retrospect, but the town's first love was football. It still is. He couldn't have stayed away tonight even if he truly wanted to. His absence would have been unthinkable. So he'll show up and give everyone what they think they want from him. And at the end of the game he hopes he'll be able finally to shed the mantle, hand off the invisible crown to a worthy successor. More worthy actually, if there's any justice in the world. Just a couple of hours longer carrying that particular weight on his shoulders.

* * *

As he steers into the parking space, the headlights' glare catches a deer standing in the tall grass at the edge of the lot. He always parks at the farthest corner, near the exit to the county road. Most of the fans will use the main exit, the one leading most directly back toward the middle of town. But his route by way of the county road, longer but far less traveled, will get him home faster.

By then he'll be half frozen and in a hurry. Snow has come early this year to the high meadows in the mountains outside of town. The deer are already having to forage in the foothills close in. This deer, a magnificent, many antlered buck, doesn't move as he brakes to a halt. That's how tame they are around here. It only runs back into the mesquite thicket fifty yards away when he slams the car door.

He treks toward the stadium across the uneven surface of the unpaved, unlighted lot, which is really no more than a cleared field. The band is already marching toward the stadium. The drums thump and the brasses blare fancily. His breath hangs in the air in front of him. He pulls the scarf tighter around his neck. He imagines the blue lips and watery eyes of the bare legged cheerleaders as they brazenly pretend not to be conscious of the cold. If the wind rises, some poor girl is going to end up with pneumonia.

* * *

The hero of the night is Trevor Weitzmann. He passes for five touchdowns and runs for two others. The opposing team is annihilated. In the process, Trevor eclipses all remaining records in the school's history. Walking to his car with the tumult of celebration still raging in the stadium, he thinks of this as his liberation. And what a country this is: it doesn't matter that Trevor's father is a Jew and his mother is Chinese and Trevor will probably graduate as salutatorian, all of which should disqualify him from glory in a town like this. All that matters is that he won the big game.

V

On a Monday morning three weeks before Christmas he wakes and looks out his bedroom window to see the ground outside covered with snow. There is, of course, not a lot of it. Probably not more than three inches, but it is enough to transform the vista. Where last night there was cropped brown grass, there is now a smooth carpet of white. Where there was a trio of bare ash trees there is now something that looks far less bleak. And there is the sound of water dripping off the roof. Overhead there are unfamiliar, low hanging gray clouds.

Just on schedule, two minutes after he's awakened, the music on the clock radio gives way to local news headlines. He knows in less than thirty seconds that this snowfall has not been judged sufficiently heavy by the district superintendent for school to be closed. He's not surprised. He knows from long experience that those clouds have left them about an inch and a half short of a day off.

Unlike everyone else, however, he'd just as soon be at work today. He needs to be busy, to have things to think about. He knows he'll hear plenty of bellyaching from his students and colleagues, but he will be more than happy to be there doing his job like always. He crawls out of bed into what feels like arctic cold. On his way toward the bathroom he glances at the clothes he laid out last night. They'll be warm enough. No need to dig out anything else.

He's been dreading this day for weeks, but now that it's actually here he knows he'll be all right. Perhaps it has something to do with the snow. Anyplace else it wouldn't be a remarkable coincidence to have snow twice on the same calendar date. But it is around here. Even with so many years intervening. There have been times when the town has gone five years running without so much as a flake, and he can't remember a single year when there have been more than a handful of storms like this. Josh Weekes once told him that the yearly average works out to two and some fraction.

In the bathroom he looks out the window at the snow outside and remembers the story his mother always told him about that day, a dark day exactly three weeks before Christmas, with new fallen snow outside the window of her hospital room. How she looked out the window at that unaccustomed phenomenon and held her newborn son close. Her first child, a baby she never expected to bear. How she looked down at that tiny infant and prayed that the God who had brought the miracle about would somehow give her the strength never to let him feel the cold she knew was outside that window.

* * *

At school there's a snowman standing in front of the main entrance. There is a spectacular snowball fight in progress in the student parking lot. The screams are bloodcurdling. They come through the air with a knife edge of cold. If he didn't know better he would think someone was actually being tortured or killed. He can see several dozen students involved, and the yearbook photographers—two of his students—are there with cameras, apparently immune from the carnage as if everyone else has agreed that the event must be memorialized on film. His feet swish along the slushy sidewalk and his breath hangs in front of him like a fluffy white plume.

Inside the building the furnaces have been working overtime. It's stuffy and hot and he'd almost rather be back outside. The halls are unusually quiet. Only a few students too nerdy to be included in various festivities outside mope silently, fiddling with their combination locks or standing expectantly outside unopened classrooms. The Christmas decorations that were hung last week suddenly don't seem so out of place. He slips quickly into and back out of the faculty mailroom and heads up the corridor to the main staircase.

Lots of his students will be tardy this morning. Others won't show up at all. The rest will be in no mood to work. It's going to be a trying day. He takes the stairs two at a time. Halfway between the second and third floors he hears heavy footsteps behind him and catching up.

"Mr. M."

He turns.

"Hi, Trevor."

Trevor Weitzmann smiles incandescently at him from two steps below. This morning his mane of hair, pale skin, and huge, soulful eyes make him look like some pre-Raphaelite version of a renaissance Italian prince.

"I've got that extra credit book report you said I could write," Trevor says in his deep, raspy baritone.

"Great."

"Only you shouldn't lie to your students."

"What?"

"You told us Forster wrote five novels. He wrote six."

"Oh."

"It was very naughty of you to misinform us like that," Trevor laughs. "Leaving the most interesting one off the reading list. Anyway, I hope you like this."

He hands over the typewritten sheets.

* * *

Two hours later, as he's grading quizzes from last week, Julia comes into the classroom. He can tell immediately that something's on her mind.

"Hello, Buzz."

"Julia."

"Happy birthday."

"Thanks for the card."

"You're welcome. You're certainly looking chipper today. Those personal leave days you took on Thursday and Friday must really have agreed with you."

"Yes," he nods.

"How was Phoenix? Warmer there than here, I hope. You didn't have any trouble driving back last night?"

"I got back just before the storm moved in."

"And you enjoyed yourself?"

He nods. She won't ask what he did there. Others will. At lunch later in the faculty cafeteria. And he'll lie, making up whatever story seems most likely to satisfy them. But Julia never asks what he does on his weekends in Phoenix, so he never has to decide whether or not to lie to her.

"Good," she says. "This place. . ."

They nod in unison.

"I had an interesting talk with Annie Weekes at church yesterday," she says. "Or perhaps I should say she had an interesting talk with me."

"Oh?"

"It hasn't escaped her notice that you're spending a lot of time in Phoenix lately."

"I didn't suppose it had."

"She knows practically to the minute how much time you've spent down there this past few months, and as far as she's concerned it can only mean one thing. Her very words: 'It can only mean one thing, Julia'."

"And what's that?"

"You're seeing someone down there. Obviously. Annie has convinced herself that it's serious. In fact, she's expecting an engagement to be announced soon. Perhaps during the holidays."

He shouldn't be surprised. More than anything he's dismayed by the news. He'd been hoping it would take longer than this.

"I'm not the only one she's spoken to about it," Julia says.

This is important information. It means more care has to be taken. It means more awkward questions have to be anticipated. When Annie Weekes talks, people around town listen. And when Annie talks about something, it's automatically O.K. for everyone else to talk about it. He knows he's been the subject of local gossip since before he was born, but up until now there was always an easily comprehended context for everything he did and, more importantly, didn't do. Now there's nothing for him to hide behind.

"I see."

"She's very excited about it," Julia says. "You can imagine. It's almost as if you're her own son, after all."

He nods. He knows what this means. Annie is mentally planning the wedding.

"Does she think she knows who I'm seeing?"

This is more than idle curiosity. Annie has lots of friends in Phoenix, and there might actually be someone there who knows someone who thinks she's seen him with some woman or other. It's important to know just what Annie thinks she knows.

"She doesn't know for certain. She thinks it must be someone you knew in college."

"Makes sense, I guess."

"She wondered if I'd heard anything about it. I told her I hadn't," Julia grins. "I also told her it isn't any of my business."

He chuckles.

"Exactly. Annie doesn't like it when I say things like that. I can't think why it bothers her. I've never once told her that it's none of her business, just that it's none of mine."

"It's the implication of disapproval," he says.

Julia's eyes twinkle.

"But Buzz," she protests, "you know I never disapprove of anything or anybody."

* * *

He drives home from dinner at Josh and Annie's though the alien looking, snowy landscape. The storm clouds have moved east and the huge sky is a chaos of moon- and starlight glinting off the whitened ground. The car's heater roars full blast, but still he shivers inside his bomber jacket. It was just the three of them tonight, but Tim's absence was palpable in the house. What was supposed to be a birthday celebration ended up feeling like a wake, though he took great care not to let the emptiness in his heart show. This time of year, with its pervasive gaiety and insistent preoccupation with families, is hard for Josh and Annie. They put up a brave front. They celebrate the season with as much fervor as anyone he knows. But regardless of the huge, extravagantly decorated tree, the roaring fire on the hearth, the carols on the stereo, their house feels empty, cold, and cheerless. They're two middle aged people with a shared sorrow that never goes away. It can be disguised, it can be ignored, but it can't be banished. Tim will always be their son. He will always be handsome, intelligent, funny, and charming. And he will always be seventeen years old. He will never provide them with a daughter-in-law, or grandchildren to dote on.

He knows Annie has assigned him the role of substitute. The almost-as-good-as-the-real-thing. She must feel this even more intensely now with his own mother dead and no family except for a few distant cousins he exchanges Christmas cards with but never hears from otherwise. But living for his mother has nearly destroyed any chance of happiness for him, and he can't consider shifting his allegiance to Annie and going right on like always. Her disappointment will be bitter, he knows. His sense of responsibility increases almost daily, sometimes threatening to make him physically ill. But it's way beyond the point merely of what he wants his life to be like. It's become a struggle for his survival. He can't let himself lose. Tim's dead. Somebody has to live the kind of life Tim dreamed of. That's his job if he can find the strength to do it.

* * *

He remembers the day everything went wrong like it was only yesterday. Just a few days earlier, he had graduated from college. His father had attended the ceremony alone. His mother was too ill to travel even as far as Phoenix. He remembers how his father looked that afternoon. Hale and hearty. Ten or fifteen years younger than his actual age. Like he hadn't had a sick day in his life, which was very nearly the truth. But only hours after returning to Hualapai from Phoenix, he collapsed. He was dead by the time the ambulance arrived at the house.

No one had ever expected his father to go first. It was inconceivable that this energetic, chronically healthy man with no history of heart trouble should die suddenly, leaving behind his frail, sickly wife, a woman people had been expecting to pass away any minute for the last thirty years. He remembers her quavery voice on the telephone that night telling him what had happened. He remembers hanging up and knowing exactly what it was going to mean. But most of all he remembers the day of his father's funeral. A scene at the graveyard in particular. The service was over. The crowd was beginning to disperse. And suddenly there was John Waggener, principal of Hualapai High School, smiling down at his mother in her wheelchair, murmuring condolences. Then Waggener turned to shake his hand and said he'd like to see him in his office the first thing Monday morning. There was a position in the English Department open for the fall.

He knew Waggener wouldn't have mentioned it in front of his mother if there was any question whether he would actually be offered the position. He knew from the man's smile that the interview would be a mere formality. He knew he could have the job if he wanted it and knew he would accept it from the way his mother smiled up at the two of them. He knew then that she'd live another twenty or thirty years regardless of her health, and in all that time he'd never leave her. He'd be in late middle age by the time he'd finally be on his own, and he'd never experience the life he had always dreamed of. He knew it was a kind of suicide, but what else could he do?

When he got to John Waggener's office the next morning, the contract had already been typed. There was no interview. They visited for a few minutes. Then he signed it. It was suicide, just as surely as if he'd shot himself to death. Just as surely as what Tim had done five years before. But what choice was there?

VI

He steers the van along the dirt road. Ramshackle houses line both sides, weatherbeaten frame houses, their paint blistered and peeling, their shingles cracked and curling, here and there cardboard taped into place where windowpanes should be. And front yards without lawns. Front yards of bare dirt or clotted with tumbleweeds. Broken glass sparkles in the dust of the yards. Ancient, decaying Chevrolets and Plymouths sit up on concrete blocks, their innards hanging greasy and tumorous underneath. Mangy looking dogs wander the streets. Impossibly skinny cats slink through the weeds, nap on dusty doorsteps.

It's only a few blocks from his own house but it might as well be another country. Except that he knows who he's seen all day inside these houses. Former or current students of his or their parents, grandparents, cousins, aunts, nieces, nephews. In his eight years of teaching he's been associated with almost every family in the county. Which is why he's a natural for this duty though it's not the reason he volunteered. He volunteered just like he has every year because he really has no choice. His memories of this annual project go back to grade school, when he would ride down these same streets and stop at these same houses with his father, the back seat and trunk of the Pontiac heaped with cardboard boxes. When his father died and Father Patterson showed no interest in continuing the effort, Annie Weekes took it over. And each year Buzz drives. Each year Josh supplies a van from the dealership, and the three of them share a hurried breakfast. They meet a few other volunteers at the parish hall who help them load the parcels. Then Josh goes off to work and Buzz and Annie hit the road.

Beside him Annie sits silent, her lips tight, worry lines around her eyes. These manifestations grow worse with each stop they make. She doesn't like visiting these neighborhoods. He knows it makes her feel guilty about her large, beautiful home, her new-every-model-year Cadillac, her Arabians, her swimming pool, her annual vacations in Paris, Acapulco and Hawaii. But regardless of her discomfort, or perhaps because of it, she spends weeks every fall soliciting donations for these holiday food parcels, spends hours packing the cardboard cartons in the parish hall, spends still more hours bargaining for hams and turkeys with the local supermarket managers and then carting the haul all over town to rest in the refrigerators and freezers of her collaborators until the big day, and more often than not ends up paying the difference between the money she has collected and what she actually spends out of her own pocket.

It's never enough. He knows that even more than the blight of these neighborhoods, the helplessness of the pathetic mothers, aunts, and grandmothers, the grimy children, bent over old men, drunks of all ages and descriptions, and squalling babies, this is what drains all the usual good humor from her face. Annie can work herself into a stupor preparing these food parcels every Christmas, but it's never enough. She knows perfectly well how these people live all the other weeks of the year. He has never understood her fervent, unwavering support for all things Republican because if anyone ever had the soul of a bleeding heart liberal, it's Annie. It's why she and Julia get along so well, though Julia's so far beyond liberal she's practically a communist.

All day long they've knocked on these shabby doors. All day long he's lifted the heavy cartons out of the back of the van and followed Annie into these houses. All day long he's observed her never-failing patience and courtesy. He's seen the bright smile directed indiscriminately at all and sundry, heard the warm voice wishing everyone they encounter a happy holiday. But the later it gets the less of her cheery nature remains when they climb back into the van.

It's not enough. No more than the similar parcels she organizes at Thanksgiving and Easter, the used clothing drives she runs out of her garage, the free vaccination clinics she volunteers at, the fundraising campaigns she chairs for the American Cancer Society and the March of Dimes and all the rest. It's at times like this that he can still be astonished by the depth and breadth of guilt she feels, after all these years and totally undeserved, about Tim.

Nothing she can do will bring him back, of course. But it's worse than that, because apparently nothing she can ever experience will convince her that she's done sufficient penance for whatever it is that she thinks she did to cause the death of her son. Nothing she can do to help these people have a merry

Christmas will permit her to have one herself, though he knows that when Josh and he sit down at the table tomorrow noon she will be all smiles as they gorge themselves on her sumptuous cooking; knows that they will hear her singing carols to herself in the kitchen as they wait for the meal to be served; knows she'll continue to sing out there as she cleans up afterward, refusing all offers of help with shining eyes, as if all's right with the world.

He used to believe that he could fix all this. All he had to do was tell his story and everything would be fine. He only lacked courage—that was the whole problem. He despised himself for not releasing her from her prison. He's no longer certain of it. The truth, he senses, is every bit as problematic as everything she imagines. His failure goes far beyond an inability to tell it. And if he did, she would still—she and Josh would still—find a way to take the blame. He's worked with enough parents to understand. Telling the story would accomplish nothing. They would simply exchange one heartache for another. Everything would go on as before. It's that futility that breaks his heart.

Like Annie, he feels Tim's absence keenly every Christmas. This year is no different. Even his mother's absence, new this year, isn't enough to distract him from it, isn't enough to blunt the pain of remembering that last Christmas with Tim. But there's something more bothering Annie today, and he knows what it is. She's his self appointed mother surrogate and she's convinced herself that there are important things going on that he's not telling her about. She's obviously spent the last several weeks expecting today to be the day. What better time for them to have that long awaited heart to heart? What better opportunity for him to tell her all about the girl she's certain he's been seeing, to ask her advice about the plans they're making together? He knows it's been on her mind ever since they left her house this morning. Every time they've gotten back into the van together, she's expected him to bring it up.

* * *

Dr. Sundine greets him at the door with a big grin and a slap on the back. Dr. Sundine hangs his jacket in the hall closet and steers him toward the kitchen, from where he can hear voices and hearty, masculine laughter. He isn't ready for this. But Julia was so excited he couldn't dream of turning down her invitation. Still, he is completely and totally unprepared. But it's too late to worry about that now because here they go, Dr. Sundine propelling him gently through the doorway into the brightly lit room, appliances and countertops gleaming like it's an operating theater.

He can't look. He resolutely keeps his eyes turned to the floor, finds Julia by the sound of her voice, kisses her Merry Christmas on the cheek just like he used to kiss his mother, just like he kissed Annie Weekes not two hours earlier as he left her recovering from the day—Josh, bless his heart, was giving her a foot massage. Finally, there's no avoiding it any more.

Robert he recognizes from the photo on the Sundine's mantel. Robert is taller than he imagined. Six-three at least and broad shouldered with it. And Robert is better looking in person, with that luxuriant silver hair and mustache to match, and those laughing eyes just like his sister's. Julia has never referred to her baby brother as gay, simply as a bachelor. If she has ever used the word gay in any connection with men of a certain kind, she hasn't done so in his hearing. He assumes this is out of sensitivity for his feelings—whatever those might be. They've never discussed his inner life. He's certain that she knows about him, certain that she and Dr. Sundine both are supportive, but what he has never told her she can't be held accountable for, should his sexuality ever become an issue at work. Unlike with Annie, this lack of candor has nothing to do with any possible cowardice on his part. It's simply practicality. It may not be illegal for a gay man to teach school in the State of Arizona—not explicitly. But it's as good as.

Robert's "friend", Michael, he's never seen a picture of. He only learned of Michael's existence recently. "Thank God Robert's new friend Michael is such a good influence", is what he thinks he recalls Julia saying. But Michael doesn't look like a good influence at all. He looks like a Viking warrior. To-night he's wearing one of those brightly colored ski sweaters with reindeer in the pattern. His eyes sparkle at Buzz as they're introduced. Buzz wonders what Julia has said about him to the bachelor and his friend.

* * *

It's a cold, moonlit night and he stuffs his hands deeper into the pock-ets of his bomber jacket, thankful for the plaid scarf that Julia insisted on wrapping around his neck before he left her house. She and Dr. Sundine are at home washing dishes and will meet them at the church later. In less than three hours it will be that fabled "midnight clear", and indeed, no sooner than he's had the thought, Mary Miller begins to sing that very carol and the rest of them join in, voices thin and small in the still air at first, but growing more confident after the first few bars. He wonders what Robert and Michael think of this, such a small town kind of thing to be doing. He wonders what kind of fabulous party they're missing back in New York in order to be here on this dusty street corner, in the bright circle underneath this streetlight atop a cracked wooden pole leaning a good eighteen degrees out of vertical. The two of them sing out with enthusiasm, as if there's nothing in the world they'd rather be doing.

He wonders how many others in the caroling party notice Robert and Michael holding hands. Trevor Weitzmann, for instance, standing beside him, singing away in a clear, surprisingly mature baritone. Trevor must have noticed the two tall, handsome strangers get out of Buzz's car in the church parking lot earlier. What does Trevor think of all this?

"Didn't expect to see you here," Buzz tells him, after they finish the carol.

"Why not?" Trevor chuckles. "Think you Christians should have all the fun? Besides, mom's as Episcopalian as you are, so technically I'm not Jewish. Ask any orthodox rabbi."

"I seem to remember attending your Bar Mitzvah."

"Oh, that," Trevor says. "You know, Mr. M., you have an awfully nice singing voice."

"Actually, you do."

"Think so? You should hear me on 'Hava Nagileh'."

Mary Miller begins to sing again. It's the one about the manger. The melody is too sweet. The familiar sentiments of the lyrics are almost cloying. It gets to him anyway, and as he starts to feel a lump rising in his throat he hears Trevor sniff, just once, in the shadows next to him. Suddenly, Trevor reaches into the pocket of Buzz's bomber jacket and grabs his hand. Just for a moment.

They sing into the cold night, their breaths rising like clouds into the halo of the street light.

* * *

Midnight. The sanctuary is packed. It blazes with candle light. The pipe organ roars. He stands next to Dr. Sundine, sharing his hymnal, though God knows the words are familiar enough neither of them should need it. Julia is on Dr. Sundine's other side. Robert and Michael fill out the pew. There won't be this many people at church again until Easter. The ladies of the altar guild have been busy all day. The dark woodwork gleams and the brass fixtures shine. Greenery hangs everywhere, along with glossy, deep red ristras and huge holiday themed banners of multicolored felt proclaiming all the sentiments of the season.

It's strange not to have his mother beside him. She never missed midnight service on Christmas Eve no matter how sick she was. He remembers how each year he would bundle her into her warmest clothing, carry her out to the car, and drive gingerly to the church, terrified of jostling her. He'd carry her into the sanctuary, where Annie Weekes always saved room for them in her regular pew. His tiny mother. In her whole life she'd never weighed more than ninety pounds. The last few years she was frailer than that. Carrying her had been almost like carrying a child. She didn't like being carried that way, with everyone watching. But it was always too crowded in the sanctuary on Christmas Eve for her wheelchair to be manageable. It was much easier to carry her.

He knows he's not the only one noting her absence. He feels the eyes of people all over the sanctuary on him as the carol ends and they sit down. They're not just remembering his mother, either. His father was rector here for over forty years. He's been dead for nearly a decade, but they still remember. The older ones especially. His father married them, baptized their children, then married the children, too. And always there was his mother, a tiny, almost silent figure. Always so frail. Always so sick. People hardly expected him to come along. Why, she was nearly fifty by then. It was a miracle, people said when he was born healthy and his mother didn't die of it. An honest to God miracle.

The candles blaze, the choir sings. Then it's the handbell group, high school students mostly, their bells polished and gleaming, their white gloves spotless, intent looks on their faces as they study their scores and wait for their cues. The silvery notes soar up into the vault and echo there.

He's going to cry if he's not careful. He's been holding it off all day, but he's not sure he can for much longer. He sees Annie a couple of pews away, dabbing at her eyes. Josh is beside her, blowing his nose into a handkerchief.

The bell choir finishes its numbers. The organ starts to roar again, and they're all on their feet for the last carol. Bill Roberts, particularly handsome tonight, leads the lay readers and members of the vestry down the aisle, all singing. Acolytes escort them, looking like an honest to God heavenly host, not young boys and girls of the town. The choir follows in their white robes and red satin stoles, hymnals held in front of them like weapons of war. The ushers pass candle flame down each pew, and as the procession reaches the rear of the sanctuary all the lights are turned out.

He blinks back tears and wonders where next December will find him. Anywhere, he thinks. Anywhere but here.

VII

He has always been ambivalent about Valentine's Day. It goes back to all those times in his boyhood when he didn't dare express his true feelings while everybody around him was screaming theirs at the top of their lungs. In adulthood his mixed emotions about the holiday, though harking back to those earlier ones, have a more practical basis. February 14th is the first day his employers can legally issue employment contracts for the coming school year. The town's remote location, not to mention its other less than ideal qualities, makes retaining teachers difficult. In addition, the district is a poor one. Salaries are lower than in most other districts in the state. Teachers often leave simply to get higher paying jobs. The district has every reason to solicit continued employment as early as possible. You either sign within the thirty day window or take your chances on being hired somewhere else. And it's a serious risk. Other districts won't even begin interviewing for positions until June or July, and there's a teacher surplus all over the state.

Up until now this trap he's in has been purely symbolic. With his mother alive there was no thought of leaving town anyway. But this year his predicament is all too concrete. Either he signs the new contract or he faces the very real possibility of not teaching anywhere next year. In which case he'll have to find another way of making a living. With a degree in English Literature, God help him. What could be more useless than that in the real world? With his teaching experience he's more expensive for another district to hire than someone just out of college and in many places that will disqualify him long before things reach the interview stage.

Why not sign, get a job somewhere else, and resign when he's in a secure position to? Because breaking a teaching contract for anything other than "good cause" is illegal under state law. And determination of good cause is left up to the employer. Here it's generally considered to include pregnancy, serious illness, or the transfer of a spouse. Sympathetic as everyone would be in his case, they can't set a precedent by treating him differently. The infraction is a misdemeanor only, but the penalty potentially includes the loss of the teaching credential. It could end his career.

He lies awake waiting for the alarm to ring knowing that it's time to face the music.

* * *

The day is a glimpse of purgatory for any high school teacher. The students simply won't focus on anything but hearts and flowers. He knows this and has scheduled a major exam. He is generally popular with the students, but this one day they truly despise him. Inside his classroom, if nowhere else, he has a will of iron. When quarter grades come out a few weeks later, he'll remind them of this day. "This," he'll say, handing them their report cards, "is your Valentine's Day greeting from me." The smarter, more mature ones will grin ruefully. The less academically inclined ones will fume. Within a week or two all will be forgiven. By then they'll be looking toward spring break and graduation beyond.

Just before the end of sixth period, the dreaded P.A. announcement comes booming out of the speaker: "teachers, before you leave work for the day, please pick up your contracts from the school secretary."

* * *

He doesn't open the envelope until he's in his car. The terms are exactly as he expected. He can sign right now, take the document back inside, hand it to the secretary, and have the business done for another year. It's harder not to do that than he expected. Not because he's actually having second thoughts, but because he's never been more anxious about the future.

* * *

The showroom is festooned with big red hearts hanging from clusters of red helium balloons. All the cars on display are red, as well. And all the salesmen are wearing red neckties.

"Sorry to keep you waiting," Josh greets him. "Phone call from regional headquarters. Everything's an emergency for those guys. Come on in and take a load off. Looks like you've had a rough day."

"Imagine all those seventeen and eighteen year olds on a day like this," he grins.

"I'd rather not, thank you," Josh grins, "but what the hell, it's just another opportunity to polish your halo, isn't it?"

"That's right," he laughs, "be sarcastic. Anyway, I didn't come here to complain about my job."

"Didn't think so," Josh says. "I know what day it is as well as anybody. Been expecting this visit. Wish I could make it easier for you, but no matter what I tell you there's Annie to think about."

"Josh, I'm sorry," he says.

"Hell, boy, don't start that. Of course you're not staying in town. Only an idiot would expect you to. Only an idiot and my dear wife, that is."

"I'll tell Annie myself," he says. "I don't expect you to do that for me. I just wanted to give you fair warning."

"Appreciate it, son. She's going to be pretty broken up about it. Been trying to prepare myself."

"I'd give anything for it to be different."

"'Course you would, Buzzie. We all would."

VIII

It was worse than he expected. Annie listened to him silently, slapped him so hard he tasted blood in his mouth, and led him without a word to the front door, which she slammed behind him. She hasn't spoken to him since. All these weeks—it's as if someone died.

Someone had.

So when Bill Roberts called Wednesday night and said that Josh would like to meet with him Saturday morning, he wasn't surprised. Something had to be done. Things between Annie and him couldn't be allowed to go on like this right on through the end of the year and his departure for parts unknown.

When he pulls up in front of the church he sees a white Mercedes parked there. Its presence alarms him. Bill hadn't said anything about Dr. Sundine being present. He knows the announcement of his plans upset Annie terribly, but what if they're about to tell him it literally made her sick? How can he face that?

It's all he can do to get out of his car and go inside.

* * *

"Morning, Buzz," Bill smiles. "Josh and Paul are waiting in the vestry."

"Is it Annie?"

"No, it's not Annie," Bill says. "She's still not speaking to you, but I'm convinced she's about ready to make her peace with it. No, this is about Josh."

"Oh, my God."

"Easy, Buzz. There's nothing wrong. Or, I should say, there's nothing new. He just needs to—well, there's a question he wants to ask you. I've been working with him for several months now. This is something he needs to do so he can finally move on. You could really help him do that, if you will. You're probably the only one who can. But since I don't know your side of things, I have no idea what it will require on your part. That's why I wanted to speak to you alone first. I think you know what his question is, and if you don't feel like you can answer, it's probably best for you to leave now. I'll go in and give him your apology."

So here it is. After all this time. He gets it. He needs to move on, too. It's not as simple as just leaving town.

"No," he says. "No, Bill, I'll come."

* * *

Josh and Dr. Sundine are sitting drinking coffee. They look up as Bill leads him into the room.

"Morning, Buzz."

"Morning, Dr. Sundine."

Josh rises from his seat.

"Thanks for coming, Buzzie," he says, gathering him into that familiar embrace. "Sorry I haven't been able to bring her around."

"It's my fault," he says. "I should have handled it better."

"Nonsense, boy. Isn't your fault. She just made up a story for herself about how things was going to be and she can't let go of it. Just give her a little more time. It's going to be all right. You'll see."

"Buzz, why don't you sit next to me," Bill suggests.

Buzz settles himself into a club chair he recognizes as one from Josh and Annie's den two remodelings ago.

"We're all here," Bill says, "because Josh has a question to ask you, Buzz. And he feels, and I agree with him, that it's probably best if you two don't try to address the matter by yourselves. Paul and I are here to support you both. And I want both of you to understand that whatever is said here will be kept by all of us in strictest confidence. All right?"

"Yes," he says.

"Right, Padre," Josh grunts.

"Now, Josh, just pretend that Paul and I aren't here, and talk directly to Buzz."

"All right."

He watches as Josh fidgets for a moment. He could interrupt him. He could still leave. He's not sure what's stopping him.

"You know what this is about, Buzzie," Josh says. "You and me, we've never talked about what happened to my Tim. We've just gone on for all these years, but, well, with you fixing to leave town and everything, I just. . .hell, son, you may not know any more about it than I already do. But I'd really appreciate it if you could—if it wouldn't be too hard on you. . ."

"It's O.K., Josh," he says. "I'm afraid it's not a very nice story. I have to apologize for that right now. Before I even start. And for not telling you sooner."

"Nothing for you to apologize for, boy."

"It's nice of you to say, Josh. But you don't really know that. Do you?"

Josh shrugs.

"I guess you'd have to say," he says, easing into it, feeling absolutely unequal to what he knows he's about to do, "it started before either of us could talk, really. Josh, you and Annie always insisted that Tim and I were inseparable even as toddlers. I know. That's ancient history. But I just want to remind everyone of that—that Tim and I were always best friends."

"We get it, Buzzie," Josh says.

"Well, this part of the story started the summer after our sophomore year. That's when I, well, I realized that I didn't just love Tim like my friend, you see, but that I was in love with him. I just woke up one day and knew it. And I was pretty upset about it. I really was. I mean, a thing like that. It was the worst thing possible. Everybody knew that. Tim could tell right away that something was wrong. And you know nobody could ever keep a secret from him. I shouldn't even have tried. But under the circumstances I felt I had to. I just knew that if he found out what was in my heart, what I was really thinking about when we were together, he'd hate me. There was no way I could have faced that. So I kept my mouth shut. It didn't take him very long to work it out of me, though.

"That's when the miracle happened. At least it seemed like one at the time. It turned out that he was in love with me, too. He'd understood his feelings for a long time, he said. And when I told him how I felt, it didn't take him long to plan our way out. We just had to be smart and make the right plans and everything would be fine. We were good students. We were on our way to college. Our parents had already decided that for us. So all we had to do was get ourselves accepted to the same college. We'd be roomies. After that we'd make sure to get the kind of jobs that would allow us to live in the same place—we'd be together always. It wasn't magic, it was just a question of good planning. He made it sound so simple.

"It was like heaven, being in love with Tim. Sorry, Josh, I know how that must sound. I know what you must be thinking right now. It's not the kind of thing you want to hear about your son. But that's how it was. It was the first time in my life I'd been truly happy. I hadn't really had a reason to live before that. I mean, I just got up every morning and did what I did. But being in love with Tim made it seem like there was a purpose for everything. I believed we were the luckiest boys in the world. We knew we had to be careful, of course. We couldn't expect anyone to understand our feelings for each other. We both made sure we had girlfriends all the time. For cover. I've always regretted that. It was dishonest. They felt things, those girls, even if we didn't, and that wasn't fair. I hated lying to those girls about how I felt, and I hated the jealous feelings I got just seeing Tim with a girl even though I understood that it didn't really mean anything about him and me—and us. But other than that, it felt like heaven. I've never experienced anything in all the years since then that made me feel so happy or alive."

He stops, shocked at how far into it he's gone, how much he's disclosed. He closes his eyes. He doesn't dare look any of them in the face. Any minute now somebody's going to say something. Something awful. Something that will destroy him, now that he's finally about to escape. And the only way he can think of to keep that from happening is just plunge on.

"Heaven. Yes. Heaven. But it was already over. I just didn't know it. Because there was a man. A grown up, I mean. See, in the last few months before I figured myself out Tim had been feeling very sad and depressed. Sure that I could never feel the way about him that he did about me. And that man had taken an interest in him and comforted him and made him feel good about himself, and when Tim confessed to me what had gone on between them I was heartbroken. I don't mean I blamed Tim. I want you all to know it wasn't like that. I understood how it could have happened, and I didn't think less of him for it. I was just heartbroken imagining him with someone else. Thinking of him so lonely and sad he'd do that. So desperate and unhappy that he couldn't help letting himself be manipulated.

"But it was worse than that, really. Because Tim hadn't been able to break things off with him. He was still going to see that man a couple of nights a week. The man had taken some photos of him, and Tim believed that he was prepared to show them to you and Annie, Josh. Blackmail, pure and simple."

Once again, he wants to stop but is afraid to. He wants to believe he's alone at home in the basement with his weight set, grinding out the reps and going over it again in his mind. That's how he's coped with it all these years. Anything but this.

"Now it turned out that the man had only gotten involved with Tim in the first place because Tim was close to me. It was always about me. The man wouldn't let Tim go until Tim brought me to him. Tim didn't tell me that part for a long time, but I could tell he was hiding something and I finally got it out of him. Tim said I didn't have to go, but of course I did. I had to do whatever it took to get Tim free. That was all that mattered to me. Tim said the man had always been nice to him. Gentle. Loving, actually. I know it doesn't seem possible, but that's how Tim said the man made him feel, and Tim said it really wasn't anything to be afraid of. He didn't try to convince me to go. I don't mean that. He told me over and over again not to, but he knew how stubborn I was. And I was hoping, you know, that if I went to the man he would keep his promise to leave Tim alone after that. That's what I couldn't stand. Tim with that man because the man couldn't have me. I couldn't let that go on. I would have done anything to protect Tim. I even thought about killing that man. I really did. But I couldn't figure out how to do it and get away with it, and I knew if I got caught it would kill Mom. She was so sick and so weak. I had to protect her, too. And Dad, of course.

"So I went. There was nothing else I could do. I went. I thought it would be just like Tim had described it, but it wasn't. The man wanted something else from me. And I gave it to him. To protect Tim. To protect everybody. I knew what would happen if you found out, Josh. You'd end up in prison. Or in the gas chamber. I had to protect everyone. So I let him do those things. Terrible things. Sometimes I still have nightmares. After all this time. It was torture, really. There's no other word for it. Torture. There was pain. God, there was pain. He had—these instruments and things. It wasn't pretend. He really wanted to hurt me."

"Stop, Buzz," Bill Roberts says. "You don't have to do this. We've heard enough. Josh knows what he needs to know."

"No," he says. "No. You have to hear it all. I have to tell all of it. I can't stop now. I can't. If I don't get to the end of it. . ."

"At least let me give you something," Dr. Sundine says. "I've got my bag here."

"I'll be fine," he insists. "I'm going to finish this and then I'll go home and go down in the basement and lift weights. That's what I always do when it gets really bad. I just lift weights until it doesn't hurt so much. That's what I've always done—for years and years. . ."

"That's how you got that build," Bill Roberts says.

"The worst thing of all," he says, "the very worst thing, was the way he would talk to me. The horrible things he'd say. He said he had to torture me like that. He had to toughen me up. He had to make a man of me. I still thought I was in love with that filthy little cocksucking pansy—sorry, Josh, but that's what he said—and this was the only way to do it. There I'd be, tied up, gagged, clothespins clamped on my nipples, lead weights hanging from—God, but what really hurt worse than anything was him saying all those things. He'd fuck me in the ass for what seemed like hours on end, and the whole time he'd be talking like that. He said that giving me his sperm that way would eventually make me a man. That's what he said.

"I tried to be tough. Not for him—for Tim. I knew I had to be tough or Tim would find out how bad it was. I was terrified of that. But he started noticing the marks. All over me. 'Timbo,' I'd say, 'you know it's wrestling season. You know I'm always beat to hamburger during wrestling season.' But you could never keep a secret from Tim. At least I couldn't. He went to see the man, to tell him he had to stop. But he just laughed at Tim. He showed Tim the pictures he'd been taking. Me, tied up, gagged, the clamps on my nipples, the lead weights hanging from—he showed Tim those pictures, and I thought Tim was going to lose his mind. He was going to get one of your guns out of the safe, Josh. He was going to—I had to beg him not to. 'It's senior year, Tim. In a few weeks we'll be out of here. We'll get away and we'll never come back. We'll tell our parents they have to come visit us.' I begged and I cried, and he promised not to do anything.

"Next time I went over there, the man had a special surprise waiting for me. Lots of girls had pierced ears. Everybody knows about that. But I had no idea you could pierce—God, whoever thought of doing something like that? It hurt so bad I thought I was dying. And it bled so bad I thought if the pain didn't kill me I'd bleed to death. He said, 'don't you dare take that out. You'll get an infection. You'll have to have surgery. You might even be ruined for life. You leave that thing in there until it heals up.' I said, 'how am I supposed to pee?' and he just laughed at me. I still have the scar. When Tim saw that—what the man had done to my—when Tim—he nearly went crazy. He felt guilty. He thought it was all his fault. I never blamed him, Josh. I promise, I never did, not once. But he felt so guilty. He told me he didn't think he could go on living. That's how guilty he felt. I didn't want to go home that night, but I had to. Mom was really bad that week, and Dad was out of town. I was so afraid of what might happen to her if I stayed with Tim. I never should have left him alone. God, if I had just stayed there with him. Josh, I'll never forgive myself. As God is my witness, I never will. I will carry that to my grave, the way I let Tim die like that. Alone."

"Buzzie, stop now," Josh says. "Annie and me never, ever blamed you. And I don't now."

"Buzz," Dr. Sundine says, "roll up your sleeve. This will just sting for a minute."

"No," he says.

"Yes, Buzz," Bill says.

"It's not going to put you out," Dr. Sundine says. "It's just going to calm you down a little, that's all."

"Buzzie, who did these things? Who was it hurt you and my boy?"

"Josh, don't," Bill says.

"It doesn't matter any more," he says. "It's all ancient history now. Josh, Dr. Sundine, you remember what a terrible week that was. First Tim. And then Coach Wilson had that terrible wreck. Drove his truck off that bridge. People thought he must have fallen asleep at the wheel or something. But that was no accident. No."

"Ray Wilson?" Josh says. "Coach Ray? He did all that?"

"I told him, Josh. The day after we found Tim hanging in the barn I went and told him he had to get out of town or I would tell everybody what he'd done. Didn't matter about his damn photos. He could show them to the whole

world. I didn't care any more. Tim was dead and I might as well be dead myself, and there was nothing he could do to make me feel any worse. I told him
I'd see that he spent the rest of his life in prison. Tim always said I was hopeless
at poker 'cause I could never bluff. But I bluffed Coach Wilson and he didn't
call me on it. I didn't plan on what happened next. Honest to God, I didn't.
I thought he'd just pack up Betty Sue and the little boys and leave town. Get
a job somewhere else. I was stupid right then. I didn't think about him going
somewhere else and doing the same thing to some other boys. It never crossed
my mind that he might do it again. Not until years later did I think of that. I
was sure he'd learned his lesson. He'd just go away and start over somewhere
else. Keep his nose clean there. That's how crazy I was right then."

"Coach Ray Wilson," Josh says softly, amazed.

"He coached us to the state championships in football that year," Buzz
says. "He coached me to the state championships in wrestling. He coached me
to the state championships in discus and javelin, he coached me and coached me
and coached me, and all the time he was. . ."

Then he can't say anything else.

IX

He knows confession is supposed to be good for the soul, but it's not his
soul he's worried about.

"It's bad."

"I'm not surprised," Dr. Sundine says. "You recently relived a series of
events that were extremely traumatic. If any of us had known the story we'd
never have put you through that."

"It's all right," he says. "It needed to happen."

"But perhaps not that way. I think you needed to be facilitated by a professional over a period of weeks or months."

"It's over now."

"Obviously it's not," Dr. Sundine said, "or you wouldn't be here. So tell
me. What's going on?"

"I'm having trouble sleeping. Sometimes I'm afraid to leave the house. I'm
concerned that my performance at work is suffering because I often find it difficult
to concentrate. I don't actually black out, but I seem to lose track of short periods
of time. God knows what's going on in my classroom while I'm out of it like that."

"All typical symptoms of trauma."

"But the trauma was years ago."

"And you've never really dealt with it. I wish you'd agree to see a therapist."

"What would a therapist tell me that I don't already know?"

"I can't tell you that. I'm not trained in the field."

"Surely you have some idea," he says. "An educated guess."

"A therapist would probably try to help you realize that those events can't hurt you any more. That they're truly in your past and you can leave them behind."

"Like I said: I already know that."

"There's knowing it and there's knowing it," Dr. Sundine says.

"Yes," he says. "Exactly."

* * *

After his appointment with Dr. Sundine he meets Bill Roberts for lunch.

"I don't mind telling you I was worried when you disappeared like that," Bill says. "I was about to organize a search party. But Julia Sundine said you'd already made plans to travel over spring break."

"Good thing I had," he says. "Complete change of scenery took my mind off the whole thing. I didn't fall apart until I got back home."

"I've never felt so worthless in my whole life as when I was listening to your story, Buzz. Here I've dedicated my life to helping people but I couldn't think of a thing to say or do that would help you."

"Pretty much a hopeless case," Buzz laughs uneasily. "You shouldn't worry about me."

"But what if there's some kid in my congregation right now going through something like you did?" Bill asks. "That's what kills me. Not that I couldn't help you that day. You're a grown man, and you'd already survived it. I'm not making light of what you may still be going through. I'd never do that. But I can't help thinking about that kid out there somewhere who needs help."

"You mean Tim," he nods.

"Yes," Bill nods. "Some boy like Tim."

"You'll just have to keep your eyes and ears open," Buzz says. "I'm convinced they give off signs. I work with kids the age we were when it happened. I know now that Tim and I must have shown signs that something was wrong, as careful as we were not to. But people didn't think about that kind of thing happening. And certainly not to boys like us."

"Well, I know better than that now."

* * *

"You can't miss prom," Julia says, scooping mashed potatoes into a serving bowl. "The students will be horribly disappointed. They're so worried about you already."

"Why? What are they saying?"

"They think that while you were out of town for spring break, the woman you've been seeing broke up with you."

"Good God."

"Buzz, you're a complete enigma to them," she says, handing him the bowl to take into the dining room. "You give them nothing to go on. About your personal life, I mean. So they can only understand you in terms of their own experiences and feelings. It's not surprising, really, that they've concocted a story like that."

"I guess," he says, setting the bowl of potatoes down next to the platter of roast beef. It's as if she's appointed herself his new guardian angel now that Annie Weekes has made him an outcast. This is the fifth Sunday dinner in as many weeks she's invited him to.

"I'm not saying you have to make yourself an open book," she says, setting a butter dish on the table. "I'm not saying you have to do anything."

"Except go to prom."

"Yes, except that. It would be different if you weren't leaving at the end of the year. The seniors would be disappointed, of course, but this is about the whole school. You can't let them down."

* * *

He won't let them down but he won't pretend, either. He could get in touch with an old friend from college, perhaps, and have her drive up for the weekend to be his prom date. He did that the first several years he was teaching. And spent the rest of the year fielding questions about the woman and his relationship with her. It's not an option this time. He'll fly solo, but he'll give them their show. He rents the sharpest tux he can find on a quick Saturday trip to Las Vegas and pulls out all the stops with the accessories.

Each year's seniors have to outdo their predecessors, of course, but it's only a high school gymnasium. And there are no miracle workers in the student body. Still, they've done a creditable job of transforming it into a small town teenage girl's vision of the ultimate romantic paradise. Then there's the band. All that can be said about the band is that it's the finest the senior class budget can afford. Which, admittedly, is pretty dismal, but the adolescent imagination is a powerful thing.

For many of these kids, this night will be the one against which all other nights are measured. This is not news to him, but being reminded so vividly of it makes him almost suicidal with despair. He dances with the few girls brave enough to ask him, but mostly he stands on the sidelines with some colleagues, gossiping and ignoring as much as he can of the action on the dance floor. Which, truth to tell, is pretty innocuous. Since the adults present are officially there as chaperones they have to pretend to be strict. But it's the cops stationed outside who are bearing the brunt of things. Kids who are truly intent on misbehaving don't even come inside the building.

The evening's high point, the crowing of the queen and her king, even manages to be an anticlimax of sorts: who else could it be but Giselle Anderson, head cheerleader and senior class vice president, and Trevor Weitzmann, Mr. Everything of the school? Trevor, he thinks. Yes Trevor. The one kid in the whole crowd who could hold his own anywhere in any company at all. He wouldn't be out of place at the Scottsdale Country Day School prom. He's just that good looking, that charismatic. But it's more than just that. Trevor has polish. He has that serene confidence Buzz would give anything to possess himself that makes it possible for him to fit in anywhere. That, more than Trevor's intelligence or self discipline, will lead him to great things.

Or maybe it won't. Trevor may be an archetype, but it's impossible to tell what he's an archetype of. Adolescence in America is as inscrutable as the riddle of the Sphinx. Despite all the hyperbole of senior year, he knows that when people are eighteen years old—or still seventeen in Trevor's case, since his birthday in November is just a few weeks before Buzz's own—it's far too early to tell who they'll turn into in adulthood. The boys are especially unpredictable. Their ingenuity at finding ways to go off the tracks is astonishing. But the girls manage to sabotage their futures, too. He recalls all too well the golden boys and girls of yesteryear who are big zeros now despite being blessed with the potential for amazing success. It's enough sometimes to make him think that he's wasted his whole career.

X

"This place won't be the same without you," Julia says, watching him box up his books.

"Just think of it this way," he smiles. "You'll finally get a shot at those Honors English 12 classes."

"You know the really smart kids terrify me."

"They terrify me, too," he says. "Every single day. The trick is never to let them know it."

"But Buzz, they're like wild animals. They smell fear."

"That's ninth graders you're describing," he laughs. "The twelfth graders are more like noble savages."

"As if that's an improvement," she says. "Honestly."

"Honesty has nothing to do with good teaching."

"I'll do a needlepoint sampler to that effect," she says. "So, are you excited?"

"I should be, shouldn't I?"

"If I were moving to San Francisco. . ."

"You were so right to insist that I go there for spring break. The first morning when I looked out of the window of that hotel and saw Alcatraz looming out of the fog I knew I really had no choice."

* * *

He can't remember time ever passing so slowly. Every other year, with his future forever on hold, the time passed quickly enough. But this year has been different. There have been days, many of them, when it seemed this year would never end. Even this final week of classes, with everything in the world to get done, has dragged by. He should be about a hundred and ten years old by now, he thinks. But finally it's the very last class of the very last day. He's written their grades on their report cards and handed them out and now he's signing yearbooks. Of all the chores, all the rituals, this one seems the most pointless. Nothing is going to be the way his students believe it will starting tomorrow morning, but this is truer with regard to their future relationship with their memories than anything else.

He's been signing yearbooks all week. Not just for his seniors. There's been a steady stream of woebegone juniors, disappointed that they won't have him as a teacher next year. Kids he doesn't know. Kids whose older siblings he taught in the past. His departure from the school is more momentous than he would have expected. It's humbling. It's also a little sad that such a trivial thing can seem so significant to them. That's small town life for you.

When Trevor Weitzmann hands him his yearbook it's all he can do not to say no. He'd write one of his trite little tried and true epigrams but knows Trevor won't settle for that. So he writes instead, very briefly, about the difficulty of putting one's feelings into words.

* * *

Resplendent in his own cap and gown—it is a local tradition for faculty members to wear academic regalia at graduation—he leads his assigned row of seniors to their seats on the football field. The podium has been set up in the west end zone so that everyone present stares into the setting sun. Yet another tradition. Even in sunglasses he can't keep from squinting.

After the pledge of allegiance and the invocation, John Waggener asks him to stand to receive the thanks of all present for his years of service to the school. He's moved by the tribute. But mostly he's embarrassed by it.

In his speech as salutatorian Trevor Weitzmann thanks him by name, and this makes him feel even more awkward.

* * *

The teachers on the field move forward and form a receiving line as the seniors receive their diplomas. One by one the kids, not his kids any longer but citizens of the world now, move past him, glassy eyed with excitement or triumph or relief or fear. They shake his hand. Some hug him. He congratulates each of them. Some thank him. Some can't speak.

He feels strangely detached. There's too much happening. He can't let himself feel it.

Bill Roberts pronounces the benediction. Principal Waggener declares the seniors graduates. Pandemonium breaks out. The bleachers begin to empty as the crowd—the entire town, it seems—storms the field.

* * *

"Ha," Trevor grins, "thought you'd sneak out of here. Well, not so fast, Mr. M. Mom wants a photo of us together."

Trevor is flanked by his parents. All three of them are grinning a little goofily, he thinks. But he probably is, too.

"All right," Trevor says, taking him by the shoulders and steering them into position side by side, Trevor's arm draped across his shoulders.

He feels awkward standing there grinning at the camera.

"One, two," Grace Weitzmann chants, "three."

The flash blinds him for a moment. He hopes it won't give him a migraine.

"One more to make sure," she says.

"We'll do without the three count, mom," Trevor says.

"Don't distract her, son," Martin Weitzmann says. "You know what happens when you make her nervous."

"One, two," Grace says, "two and a half—ha, Trevor, got you—two and three quarters."

"Mom."

"Three."

Once again that flash.

"Buzz," Martin Weitzmann says, just the slightest catch in his voice, "we can't thank you enough for all you've done for our boy."

"That's true," Grace says. "We're surely going to miss you around here."

Buzz absolutely, positively can't speak.

"Mr. M.," Trevor says, folding him into a hug that's surprisingly forceful—a grown man's hug, strong and determined, a hug that moves him far too deeply, "thanks for everything. Thanks for being the best teacher ever. I won't forget you."

* * *

"Thanks for coming by, Buzz," Josh says. "Know you're real busy right about now."

"Never too busy for you," he says. "I hope you know that."

"Got us some breakfast. From Rita's Diner."

"Looks great."

"Well don't just stand there. Sit down and dig in."

He doesn't need any more encouragement than that.

"You don't look too bad this morning."

"Huh?"

"All them graduation parties. Figured you'd be red eyed and fuzzy tongued this morning."

"Didn't go to any," he says. "I guess my heart wasn't in it."

"Probably done the same thing myself. So, you all packed and ready?"

"I'm just going out for a few days," he says. "Find a place to live and then come back for my stuff."

"Makes sense."

"I wish Annie would agree to see me."

"Won't be long now," Josh says. "Two of us'll be out for a visit before you know it."

"I hate leaving it this way."

"Done all you could," Josh says. "So have I. She'll make her peace with it in her own time. She's seeing Bill Roberts every week, but I'm not supposed to know that. It isn't about what all you told me, you know. Still haven't shared that with her. Not in any detail."

"Whatever you think is best," he says.

"Got a little something for you," Josh says, handing him an envelope. "Before you look inside, need to say something."

"All right."

"I'm a pretty successful businessman, wouldn't you say?"

"Well, sure."

"I know it's only a dinky little dealership in a small town, but I've been at it a long time. It piles up you know?"

"You've done very well," he says. "You're also very generous with what you have. Everybody in town knows that."

"Neither here nor there," Josh says. "Plan always was, of course, that Timmy would never want for anything. His children, either. None of Annie's and mine would ever be in want. They'd always have what they needed. Maybe not everything they wanted—within reason, you know?"

"Understood," he nods.

"Well, it's just been sitting there and sitting there. Every year the investments add to it and every year Annie and I put in more, by the grace of God. Got more than we know what to do with, is the thing. Last us forever, pretty much. I could quit work tomorrow and spend the rest of my life sitting on a beach in Mexico drinking *cerveza* and catching fish. Thought about it plenty, last little while."

"Annie wouldn't let you."

"You've got that right. So what's in the envelope—no, don't open it. Not until you're back home. Don't want to have to fight with you over it. But you need to understand, son, that you're all I've got left in the world of Timmy. You're the man he loved. I think I always knew it, even before you told your story. And there's nothing too good for you. So that in the envelope is to help you get started on your new life. 'Cause when I come out to San Francisco next fall to visit you, I want to see you doing well and living comfortably."

"Josh, I can't take money from you."

"Can't, Buzzy? Can't? Way I see it, you have to. Not giving you a choice, you hear?"

XI

He rounds the last corner and heads up the hill. Blocks behind, him Castro Street is waking up for Friday evening. Cooper and Ned have assigned him his own parking space at the office, but most days he walks down the hill to the bus stop instead of driving. It will probably be different as autumn comes and the weather grows less ideal. But he loves walking, loves riding the bus, loves everything about his new life. The city, this home he spent all those years yearning for without even knowing it, intoxicates him.

He'll grab a quick shower and change of clothes. He's supposed to be meeting Nick Romanovsky for dinner. They'll probably go dancing from there. It's not a date. Nick's not the type for that. And anyway, Buzz isn't sure he's ready for that chapter of his life to open. Everything in its time. But it's good to have a buddy here in a new city. Someone to show him the ropes. Nick and Cooper seem to be taking turns with that. Their friends T. and Big Steve have welcomed him with open arms as well. Like Buzz, T.'s the son of a pastor. He gets Buzz more clearly than any of the others. It's an astonishing new experience for him, having true friends. People he can be completely open with. People who have been through many of the same things he has. It's the way things might have been with Tim someday if they'd managed to make their escape. With his thirty year old heart and brain he's no longer certain they'd have made it permanently as lovers, but they would always have been friends.

As he nears the house he notices someone sitting on the front steps. Probably a friend of Adam, his downstairs tenant. Adam is extremely social. And extremely unreliable as to plans and schedules. Buzz has found more than one forlorn young man sitting there waiting. He feels sorry for them. Adam's special, but not that special. Almost any one of them could do better, he thinks.

But then whoever it is happens to glance in his direction. At first he thinks it's just a coincidence—it's not that unusual a physical type in San Francisco, in this neighborhood, in the dusk.

No, it can't be, because—for all kinds of reasons. The last he heard, Trevor Weitzmann was on his way to Northwestern. That's for starters. But he spies the Porsche lurking at the curb a few paces farther up the hill. That

Arizona license plate clinches it. His last two strides turn into a stumble, like he's been drinking. Damn that seismically compromised stretch of sidewalk.

That mane is pulled back to a pony tail, and those shoulders loom wider than he recalls, but the eyes haven't changed. He'd know those eyes anywhere. Those eyes are lethal. And the circumstances don't help matters.

"I thought you'd never get home," Trevor grins.

"What are you doing here?"

"Waiting for you. What's it look like?"

"But. . ."

"Moved into the dorm at Berkeley last weekend. Classes start Monday. Thought it would be a good time to look you up."

"Berkeley?"

"You've heard of it."

"Well, yes."

"It's a university. People go there to get educated. You knew I planned to continue my education. We talked about it. More than once, as I recall."

"Yes, but."

"So," Trevor gets to his feet. "You are going to invite me in, aren't you?"

"Of course," he says.   "What's all this stuff?"

"I'm making you dinner."

"Huh?"

"Have you lost a lot of brain cells since moving to San Francisco? Because I have to say you seem very confused."

"It's just. . ."

"Just what?"

"That seems like an awful lot of stuff," he says. "For dinner, I mean."

"Well," Trevor grins, "If you're a very good boy, and I have no reason to doubt you will be, I'm planning to make you breakfast as well."

Cooper Luxemberg:
September, 1978

"We dated a few times," Nick said, staring out across the dance floor at Buzz and his new boyfriend, Trevor. "Then that one showed up. Do you think it's serious?"

"Everything a Jewish-American Prince does is serious," Cooper laughed. "By definition. Even if his mother's Chinese."

"You would know," Nick grunted.

"About Chinese mothers?"

"Don't play dumb."

"Just maintaining the stereotype," Cooper said.

"Which one?"

"Take your pick," Cooper said. "Jewish-American Prince, musclebound dummy, empty-headed pretty boy——I embody dozens of them."

"Speaking as a Jewish-American Prince then," Nick said, "explain to me how you can have a Chinese mother and even be a Jew."

"Simple," Cooper said. "Join a Reform congregation. They're very big on mixed marriages."

"All I know," Nick said, "is I'm going after Trevor if Buzz gets tired of him. He looks like lots of fun."

"And more trouble than he's worth," Cooper said. "Anybody who ever dated me could tell you how it works."

* * *

Cooper grasped the concept of Lance Garrison's new project just by looking at who else was in the room. Kirk de Havilland was a zillion-aire trust fund baby. Blond and Nordic looking in the fashion of Nick Romanovsky's non-existent younger cousin, he'd recently won the tall class at the Mr. California, having packed a ripped and shredded two hundred forty-five pounds onto his six foot two inch frame. He was just back from his honeymoon and sported a lazy grin, a deep Caribbean tan, and hair bleached by the sun to a shade lighter than his usual. Sean Eastman was an inch shorter than Cooper and managed to look way more impressive

than ought to be possible at "only" two hundred pounds. With his luxuriant chestnut hair and clear gray eyes he gave off a boy next door vibe. But
once the clothes came off the story changed to "Eagle Scout gone horribly
wrong". His pierced nipples, tattooed cock, and shaven scrotum hinted at
scandalous inclinations. Cooper had lost track of the rumors about Sean.
A dishonorable discharge from the Mounties; a lifetime ban (for unspeci-
fied offenses) from the U.K. ordered personally by his distant cousin, the
Queen; a buyout under questionable circumstances of his contract by the
professional rugby team back in Toronto; dismissal from the cast of a CBC
kiddie program for "sexually precocious" escapades—only God Himself
knew if any of this was true.

They had each posed for Lance Garrison in the past. They had all prepared for the shoot in their own ways, and the results were unmistakable.
Lance was obviously pleased at the condition they presented on arrival for the
first session. That day of shooting went perfectly.

* * *

"It's inspired casting," Nick said the next Sunday at brunch. "A Viking
warrior, a sultry exotic, and an All-American."

"Who just happens to be from north of the border," Cooper laughed.

"The best all-American boys are," Jared Bartok chuckled.

"In any case," Nick said, "it's the ultimate threeway, a blazing hot
musclefest."

"But relentlessly tasteful," Scott Bailey said. "Lance's work is always
artistic."

"That's right," T. agreed. "Lance never puts a foot wrong. He knows
exactly how to showcase his talent."

"And if Kirk and Sean are in the same condition you are," Big Steve said,
"the result will be a remarkable photo essay."

"They'd have to be," Nick said. "Lance wouldn't expose a single frame of
film otherwise."

"He told us he believes it's going to be his best work yet," Cooper said.

* * *

"We going to fuck?" Sean asked. "Like ever?"

"Huh?"

"We're not in escrow, Coop," Sean laughed. "It's just a photo shoot.
Hell, we're practically doing porn."

"No, we're not."

"Three naked guys? All those wrestling holds? I know what I'd call it."

"What Lance does is art," Cooper insisted.

"Of course," Sean said, "but you and I both know what the guys who look at those pictures are going to be thinking about. And you can't tell me you haven't at least imagined taking the action farther than Lance directs."

"All right, sure," Cooper grinned, "I'll plead guilty to that."

"So what are we waiting for?"

"No offense, Sean," Cooper said, "but. . ."

"Don't even try to tell me I'm not your type," Sean said. "I know better. You're like a sexual Statue of Liberty. 'Give me your tired, your poor, your huddled masses. . .'"

"It's not that," Cooper said. "I just always got the impression that you're more of a commercial property."

"And you never pay for it," Sean said.

"Never have," Cooper said. "Not saying I never would. . ."

"Asking for a freebie, are you?"

"I wouldn't do that," Cooper said. "A man's got to make a living."

"Awfully gracious of you," Sean laughed, "but as it happens, I'm not as mercenary as you think."

"Mercenary's a big word for a hustler."

"McGill University," Sean said. "Philosophy major, literature minor. Straight B's. Bo's the hustler. I'm just the wingman."

"Right."

"All right," Sean said, "sometimes I do go on a call with him. And in that case, sure, I take a cut. But the rest of the time, I'm just another fun-loving San Francisco bachelor."

"Really."

"So what are we waiting for?"

* * *

It was a long time since Cooper had slept with a guy so close to his own level of muscular development. Sean was twenty pounds lighter than Cooper, more or less, but as sharp and defined. When Cooper held him, there was no question that he was holding a gym rat like himself. And in addition to Sean's superb physique, he'd logged lots and lots of what Cooper's friend, Ashby, who was married to an airline pilot, called "flying time." The combination of amazing body and remarkable technique blew Kent out of the water. Kent was cute as it was possible to be and as enthusiastic as you'd expect of such a relentless go-go boy. But that was just the point—go-go *boy*, when Sean was unmistakably a man. It was no contest.

Except Cooper knew it wasn't a contest in any sense. When faced with two guys like Kent and Sean, you simply adjusted your schedule to accommodate both. Kent might complain—almost certainly would in fact. But Sean was far too realistic for that.

* * *

"What's he like?" Nick asked, sipping his Calistoga.

"Who?"

"Sean," Nick said. "Half the town's wondering what would possess Cooper Luxemberg to pay for sex and the other half wants to know how you talked Sean into gratis fucking."

"Really?"

"So spill."

"He's good," Cooper said.

"Of course he's good," Nick said. "You can tell that just looking at him. The question is, how good?"

"He's one of those rare guys who's exactly as good as he looks like he would be," Cooper said.

"He looks like he'd be amazing," Nick said. "Perhaps even life changing. Did he change yours?"

"Let's put it this way," Cooper said, "pay him if you have to. Though in your case I don't think the issue of money will come up."

"Really."

"You won't be sorry," Cooper said.

"You might," Nick said.

"What's that supposed to mean?"

"That twinkie you've been seeing," Nick said.

"Not really seeing him," Cooper said.

"All right," Nick said. "That twinkie you fuck the living daylights every time he can get his hands on you."

"What's this got to do with Kent?"

"He saw you leave the bar with Sean last night," Nick said. "He was ready to burn the place down."

"His problem," Cooper said.

"Until he makes it your problem."

"You don't really think I can't handle a kid like that," Cooper scoffed.

"I know you think you're invincible," Nick said. "I thought that about myself, too."

"What are you talking about?"

"I thought it was just a run of bad luck at first," Nick said.

"Now you're being ridiculous," Cooper said, "Mr. Undefeated Warrior of the backrooms and sex dungeons."

"It's all well and good if what you're looking for is hot sex."

"What else is there?"

"How the hell would I know?" Nick asked. "And that's exactly the point. What if there actually is more than fucking?"

"You're spending too much time around Big Steve and T.," Cooper said. "Not to mention Scott and Jared and Matt and Ashby. All the happy couples."

"Anything wrong with that?"

"No," Cooper said. "As long as you don't let it warp your perspective."

"Keep talking," Nick said.

"It's like this," Cooper said. "There are guys like them, who are wired to pair off and settle down. And there are guys like you and me, who are wired for the hunt."

"Great," Nick said. "Throw my own theory back at me."

"You're kind of the prototype," Cooper said.

"But what if I'm wrong?" Nick asked. "What if there aren't guys like them and guys like us? What if there are just guys?"

"Jeez," Cooper said. "What's got you in such a funk?"

"New guy at the office," Nick said. "Fresh out of law school. 'Thirties matinee idol kind of handsome. Medium height. Slim."

"You're describing our friend, Dr. Ashby Sainte-Claire," Cooper said.

"Same type," Nick nodded. "Exactly."

"What about him?"

"Well, he's perfect husband material," Nick said. "I really should be going after him."

"You work together," Cooper said. "There's got to be a rule about stuff like that."

"I know that," Nick said. "As a type, I mean."

"You're all depressed over a hypothesis?" Cooper asked. "This is worse than I thought."

"Turns out the one thing I have in common with him," Nick said, "is wanting the wrong kind of guy."

"Uh-oh," Cooper said. "Don't tell me."

"Had a heart to heart with him a couple of days ago," Nick said. "Turns out he's got this major case on your buddy, Sean."

"Who's definitely not the marrying kind," Cooper said.

*　*　*

Nick's lamentations were becoming ever more frequent, detailed, and comprehensive. Cooper was as keen an observer of the scene as Nick was. He recognized the same phenomena Nick identified but also knew that they were only excuses. If what Nick really wanted was to settle down with someone, none of the people or circumstances he deplored truly constituted obstacles. The real problem was the one thing Nick never mentioned—his continuing belief that T. was Mr. Right and there was no acceptable substitute. There was no question that T. was remarkable in every possible way. But was he really someone for you to hold yourself hostage to? Was Nick's predicament inevitable and inescapable? This was the kind of box guys put themselves in when they focused on "relationships". In the process, they made themselves ripe for exploitation. Any day now, some cute, calculating twinkie was going to figure out that approximating T. was the way to Nick's heart. Nothing good could come of that, but at the first sign of it Cooper was prepared to take steps.

*　*　*

Several factors made Sean the perfect fuck buddy for Cooper. First of all, his busy schedule as a hustler—because as far as Cooper was concerned, that's what Sean was despite his evasions—meant he'd never be underfoot. Cooper's buddy, Stone, had been like that, present when wanted, invisible otherwise. After Stone ran off to Buenos Aires with a sugar daddy, Cooper never stopped missing him. Their arrangement had been darned near perfect. A hustler who took enough of a shine to you that he didn't expect to be paid was worth his weight in gold.

Too, Sean represented an opportunity to keep Chanel Rococo in check. After maneuvering Cooper into Kent's bed and promoting their "romance" in its initial stages, she quickly soured on the whole thing, coming to see Kent as more than a photogenic diversion for Cooper—as an actual obstruction in the path of her ultimate goal. She might demean Cooper as a musclebound oaf or little more than a handsome face, she might insist on treating him like a slow-witted younger brother or poorly trained mascot, but her true intentions couldn't have been clearer. She wanted Cooper as her consort. That would never happen. But Cooper didn't try to talk her out of it. She wouldn't listen in any case. He knew that showing was far better than telling. So bring on Sean. An additional rival for Chanel to stew about was all to the good. And in this instance, the rival was someone whose stalwart masculinity made a statement Cooper knew she was sure to be offended by. With stakes like these, he couldn't worry about being diplomatic.

Kent, too. Kent was starting to be as troublesome as Chanel was, and in an uncannily similar way. For gay San Francisco's reigning diva and the pre-eminent go-go boy of the age—Nick Romanovsky's only somewhat ironic designation for Kent—to share almost identical psychological profiles was surprising. But there was no getting around it. Grandiose and self absorbed, they proved beyond doubt that narcissists came in all shapes and sizes. Weekly they grew more strident and demanding, leaving Cooper wondering if it wasn't time to cut them both loose. The case for keeping Chanel was simple: like her or loathe her, and Cooper entertained both sentiments more or less simultaneously, she remained the best available source of local gossip. And gossip, through Cooper refused to spread it himself, was important. He needed both the information itself and an understanding of how people reacted to it. From Cooper's perspective, access to Chanel and her network of "informants" could be replaced eventually, but only with a great deal of effort. As far as he was concerned, this was effort he could better expend working out, selling homes, or finding sex. So despite her many drawbacks as an associate, he was inclined to keep Chanel in his orbit. But Kent was another matter. The woods were full of willing twinkies. They almost literally grew on trees. As a species, they shared a penchant for falling out of those trees and into his path. Really, Cooper only had to take his choice. Kent had seemed like a reasonable selection at first. To be objective about it, he kept getting cuter. Not to mention his technique continued to improve, and it wasn't all down to Cooper's tutoring. And in the months since meeting Cooper, Kent's definition had visibly improved if not his mass. Still, he was starting to get really annoying. It wasn't a question of finding a replacement. In Cooper's existence, sex was a constant. The variable was whose bed he'd be occupying at any given time. So cutting Kent loose really would be without consequence. For Cooper.

For Kent there would be consequences, certainly. And the most serious one, at least potentially, wasn't the most obvious. Kent was cute enough that being "abandoned" by Cooper wouldn't be more than a minor inconvenience, carnally speaking. But there had been a chance, Cooper believed, that he might teach Kent some things beyond the realm of bedroom acrobatics. He still might. It was true that Kent wasn't a particularly apt pupil in any other regard, but Cooper might yet be able to share some snippet of wisdom here or there, unlikely as it seemed, that would matter to Kent in the long run.

Bringing Sean into the mix might be just the thing to snap Kent to attention.

Using Sean to keep Chanel and Kent in line meant, well, using Sean. People used each other all the time. Cooper couldn't begin to guess what purpose Sean might put him to, but he assumed they'd both consider it a fair exchange. And the sex, if their first couple of encounters were anything to go by, would be spectacular.

So Cooper had no qualms about what he was doing. Chanel and Kent deserved whatever came their way. As for Sean, he wasn't a drag queen or a go-go boy. He was a man. That meant he'd be able to figure arrangements out for himself and do what he needed to do.

"This isn't the way to my place," Sean said as the Jaguar grumbled up Market Street.

"Not where we're heading," Cooper said.

* * *

"I thought nobody ever got to see the batcave," Sean laughed, following Cooper down the stairs.

"Bedroom's this way," Cooper said.

* * *

"Now that I know all your secrets," Sean said, surveying Cooper's bathroom, "aren't you afraid I might blab?"

"I know a secret of yours, too," Cooper said.

"Really?" Sean yawned. "Any chance you're up for seconds?"

"Bedroom hasn't moved," Cooper said.

"I like a stationary bedroom," Sean said. "Better traction."

"Right," Cooper said, hugging him from behind.

"My secret, huh?"

"I know who you're in love with."

"Don't flatter yourself," Sean said.

"Didn't say it was me, did I? If I thought that, you'd never have gotten through the front door."

"So that's the trick," Sean laughed.

"It's Bo," Cooper said.

"You know how it works," Sean said, "at least by observation. So there's a guy who says he's in love with you, but you're in love with somebody else. And that somebody else doesn't return your feelings. You can never have him."

"I was under the impression you could have Bo just about any time," Cooper said.

"Sex isn't about feelings," Sean said. "Aren't you some kind of expert on that?"

"I don't know," Cooper said. "Am I?"

"As good as Bo," Sean said.

"Does that mean I should be doing it for money?"

"Very funny," Sean said. "That's your worst kept secret."

"All in the past now," Cooper said.

"Thing is," Sean said, "all that sex with Bo just makes it worse. It's like we're all part of some cosmic daisy chain where nobody ever gets the guy he wants. The only thing you can do in a situation like that is to go fuck your brains out."

"Come back to bed," Cooper said, inhaling the scent of Sean's hair.

"Am I talking too much?"

"No," Cooper said. "Just come back to bed."

Will Crawford

I

"Thanks for agreeing to see me, old man."

"What are you talking about?" Will asked. "You know you're my favorite uncle."

At fourteen years younger than Pa and twelve years older than Will, Uncle Harris was either a younger, better looking version of Will's father or an older, better looking version of Will himself, depending on your perspective.

"Mean to say. One doesn't like to presume."

Uncle Harris had been a Rhodes Scholar and later went to work for the State Department. The list of his postings read like a gazetteer. Will's mother's most frequent complaint about her brother-in-law was that he didn't "talk like normal people". Other perennial favorites were, "he really ought to marry and settle down," and "it's simply not appropriate for a man to be that handsome." His mother's criticisms were a motivating force behind Will's deep affection for his uncle and indeed most of Will's preferences.

"One can hardly call it presumptuous," Will said, his poet's ear dictating that he'd ape his uncle's speech whether he intended to or not. "It's a noteworthy event when we're in the same hemisphere."

"Time of the semester, old man," Uncle Harris said, a little hangdog. "Know how it is. Papers and exams and what all."

"Don't be silly," Will said. "Family always comes first."

"Right," Harris chuckled. "Quote your mother to me, old man."

"Couldn't resist it," Will said.

"You'll already have sussed that this visit is Dougal's idea."

"Nothing new there."

"Busman's holiday. Emissary by trade. Occupational hazard. 'But you know how to talk to the boy, Harris'. One would rather not carry the water for him, of course, but one feels obligated."

"You make this sound like a scene out of Henry James."

"Dougal's favorite author," Uncle Harris sighed with an expression of pro-found disapproval. He had dated a distant cousin of Isherwood's, family legend asserted, and thus it was to be expected that he had opinions about literature. A real gentleman, so went the family ethos, didn't have opinions about anything. Or if he did, he pretended not to. A real gentleman had convictions, invariably of the most conventional nature, and thus so universally understood that they didn't need to be mentioned. "Thing is, old man, this book of yours. This slim volume of verse one received by post."

"Did you like it?"

"Most edifying, old man. Most edifying indeed. Showed it off to one's friends. Presented a copy or two as gifts. Real talent, all that."

"Thanks," Will said. He hadn't seriously doubted his uncle would be complimentary, but until he actually heard it spoken, well. . .

"Thing is, it rather put the wind up your Pa. You ken?"

"I anticipated it might," Will admitted.

"Good lad," Uncle Harris said. "Then one's mission isn't quite so. . ."

"No," Will said. "I get it. Pa's concerned lest it signify some unexpected turbulence."

"Just so. Exacerbated, one hates to say, by the happy tidings of a second slim volume soon to follow. Impending literary career. All that. Heartfelt congratulations, by the by."

"I see," Will said.

"Do you?"

"Perfectly, I'm afraid."

"Thing is, young Will, you and your Pa made an agreement."

"He's going to hold me to it, is he?"

"Good faith on his part."

"He is going to hold me to it," Will said. Well, of course. It had been foolish to hope for any other outcome. Pa never let anyone off the hook.

"Not as if he's proposing to disown you if you don't pay up. Nothing that serious. Ruth would insist on it, so he couldn't. You know that. More a betray-al of trust kind of thing. Family tradition. Generations of honorable behavior. Raised you to be a man of your word. Letting down the side. Uneasy silences during holiday dinners or other festive gatherings. Unspoken disappointment you'll always be able to read in his expression."

"Right."

"What I mean to say. One finds Dougal's eyes particularly eloquent."

"Yes," Will said. Not to menton the way Pa made his nostrils flare in moments of high emotion.

"Not the end of the world, young Will," Uncle Harris said. "Just a simple exchange of *ars longa, vita brevis* for *ars gratia artis,* accent on the *vita*—as in the making of one. Think of William Carlos Williams dashing off those divine verses of his between house calls. Think of Charles Ives selling all that insurance whilst conceiving of those fiendishly clever sonatas and symphonies. Think of Albert Schweitzer. . ."

"Organist, wasn't he?"

"World famous," Uncle Harris nodded. "Constructed his own instrument out there in the bush. Fabricated it out of indigenous materials, one seems to recall. Played Bach and Buxtehude for the African tribesmen."

"In between lancing their boils and delivering their babies," Will said.

"Kind of thing," Uncle Harris nodded. "Saw some of Churchill's paintings in London recently. Quite fine, really. Surprisingly better than one expected. Special exhibition, you know. Charity do."

"Right."

"One does trust," Uncle Harris said, "that one's favorite nephew will do the right thing. Word to the wise."

"Is it the right thing?"

"Sorry. Not much good at metaphysical speculation, old man."

"I was afraid you'd say that."

"So one can tell Dougal?"

"That I'll be in touch."

"Best to have it cleared up before you trek home for the holidays."

"By the end of the week," Will promised.

* * *

The agreement had been that Will's father would pay for two years of graduate school so he could get his M.F.A. in creative writing and seriously try his hand at poetry. And here he was, one semester away from graduation, a gaggle of awards and prizes to his credit, his first collection of poems already published and his second due out right around Valentine's Day, and at least the beginnings of a literary reputation. The reviews had been gratifying, the reactions of his professors even more so, and topping everything, the rampant jealousy of his fellow students. He would never forget the way they seethed.

No money in it, of course. Absolutely not a cent. But that's not the purpose of poetry, apparently.

There could be, of course, no agreement of the sort Will and Pa made without a *quid pro quo*. His uncle's visit was Will's Notice to Perform.

So the very first thing Monday morning, Will went out and registered for the LSAT, and Monday evening instead of making his way to his favorite pub and sitting for a couple of hours nursing a pint and talking poetics with his grad school buddies, he stayed home and wrote letters requesting application materials from the sort of law schools his father would approve of. It wasn't a very long list. Pa was nothing if not a snob. Tuesday morning, he dashed off a note to his father detailing these efforts and wrote a second one to his uncle expressing the same thing in slightly less austere terms.

It occurred to him as he slid all of his missives through the slot at the post office that all he had to do, really, was muff the LSAT. With an exam score low enough there wasn't a law school in the hemisphere that would take him and he'd be free to dedicate his life to his art. But his mother would cry. She was never more theatrical than when pretending to be disappointed in her offspring, and this occasion would top the charts. His grandmother would purse her lips and stare off into the distance. His younger brothers would sneer, and worse than that, his father would know. Because Pa's instincts about such things were legendary. His father and his uncle—both of them would know that he had cheated his way out of the agreement.

If anything, Uncle Harris' eyes were even more expressive than Pa's. That's what clinched it. You could almost convince yourself you were willing to risk your father's disapproval, but not your favorite uncle's.

* * *

Will wouldn't go as far as a total capitulation, however. Face must be saved, after all. Pa's face as well as his own, Pa, who took enormous pride in the supposition that he had raised his sons to be manly enough never to tolerate such bullying as he perennially subjected them to. A show of rebelliousness had to be made or Will would never be able to look the man in the eye. Or his younger brothers, with their deep voices, platoons of female admirers, and record of athletic accomplishments stretching back to grade school. A show just sufficient to demonstrate the requisite level of testosterone in Will's bloodstream: this was a matter about which there had always been much unspoken skepticism on the domestic front. Even dotty old Grandpere MacLeod had expressed misgivings. So Will turned aside any thought of Princeton and Columbia and the prestigious local institutions his cousins on his mother's side had entered, and set his sights on the West Coast. But mere geography might not demonstrate sufficient intractability on his part, so Stanford, with its sterling reputation, was unfortunately out of the question. He finally hit on U.C. Hastings. The school itself was unimpeachable, so Pa couldn't look down on it, but its location on the fringes of San Francisco's perennially seedy Tenderloin district sent just the right message, Will thought.

II

"The great thing about the neighborhood I live in," the girl wearing granny glasses and a tie dyed babushka kind of thing said in an accent straight out of Brooklyn, "is that it's still 1967 there."

"Cool," her equally chic companion mooed.

Will had just dropped his mother off at the airport for her flight back to Philadelphia. They taxied out from her hotel but he was taking a bus back into the city, his first independent act since arriving. He was furious with himself for his comprehensive acquiescence. What was the use of being twenty-three years old and a published author if you still allowed yourself to be treated like a child? In just this few days his mother had arranged his whole new life for him. She had chosen the apartment, made out the check and signed the lease, rented the furniture and supervised its delivery, interviewed candidates and engaged a cleaning lady, made his plane reservations for Thanksgiving, Christmas, and Easter vacations, gone shopping for his linens and kitchen things, and he hadn't managed a single word of protest. She left everything in a state he would have had to describe as perfect if he'd been someone else.

It was, he mused, exactly the way she managed his father's life. Arranged down to the last obsessive detail. Pa's response was to ignore her almost completely, pretending to believe the sterile perfection surrounding him was an act of God. But that wasn't an appropriate response on Will's part. You couldn't ignore someone from a distance of three thousand miles. They'd never be aware of it. The point would be lost but the aftermath of his mother's meddling would remain. If a tree falls in the forest and there's no one to hear it, the tree is still lying on the ground until someone drags it away and chops it up. In the few days remaining until his law school classes began, Will was going to have to give some consideration to the art of subversion. But before that, there was the matter of his godfather to attend to.

"They only think the Summer of Love is over, you know," babushka girl asserted. "We're going straight to my place. You'll see."

"Cool," the companion said, gazing out the bus window.

* * *

Pa had met Forbes MacWhirter at Andover. They shared rooms there and later at Yale. When Pa returned to Philadelphia for law school Forbes tagged along, so the story went, though Will had always thought the account made rather short shrift of Forbes's law school record, which, truth to tell, seriously eclipsed Pa's. The day after Dougal and Ruth's wedding, Forbes headed off to France, returning to Philadelphia just long enough to play that crucial role in Will's baptism and close up the apartment where he and Will's father had kept bachelors' hall. Next he moved to San Francisco. There, as in Philadelphia, he'd been recruited by the top law firms. But he had elected instead to enter private practice. His trust funds supported him nicely while his practice was picking up steam.

Generous, though his mother pronounced them excessive, gifts had come for Will every Christmas. On his birthdays, too. The birthday gifts were hand delivered right up through his thirteenth. These visits from his godfather were some of Will's best memories of his childhood, not least because of his parents' exasperated reaction to the presence of their guest, as if they regretted their selection of Will's godfather almost as soon as they had enlisted him for the duty. Each time Forbes MacWhirter arrived on the Crawford doorstep, Will's mother's perpetually tight jaw grew noticeably tighter and Pa's intake of alcohol, strictly limited at all other times, skyrocketed, while his mood veered toward bellicosity. Only Uncle Harris, who always managed to appear for Will's birthdays, too, seemed to enjoy Forbes MacWhirter's company.

Will hadn't selected his law school because of his godfather's presence in the same city. At least not consciously, though as a poet of what he liked to think was a decidedly avant garde sensibility he knew he had to have some suspicions of himself on this score. But when he realized his parents must think he had, he was all the more pleased with his choice.

On the telephone, Forbes had offered to pick him up. But Will insisted on getting to his godfather's house on his own. He loved exploring the city, he said. He hoped this made him sound intrepid, cosmopolitan even. As it turned out there wasn't very challenging topography between his apartment and Forbes' neighborhood. He only had to change buses twice. Forbes lived on a curving block in the shadow of Coit tower. Compulsive about punctuality, Will arrived on the spot much too early and had to circle the neighborhood on foot half a dozen times before he dared walk up to the elegant looking front door and ring the bell.

Its subdued clang elicited a chaos of barking inside which turned out to have been produced by a surprisingly small number of dogs for the volume of noise involved—a pair of liver and white Springers. Mother and son, he was informed later.

"My dear boy," his godfather greeted him as the dogs capered at their feet. "Welcome, welcome. My god, you're all grown up. And you look exactly like that uncle of yours. Harmon?"

"Harris."

"That's him." A vigorous nod. "Taciturn chap. Rather military in demeanor, though I don't remember hearing anything about actual service. The resemblance is uncanny."

"Uncle Harris is taller than me," Will pointed out, trying not to grimace at the vigor of Forbes's handshake, "and has broader shoulders."

"Yes," Forbes agreed, propelling him through the entry hall into a living room that looked like a museum exhibit of Bauhaus artifacts. "You're unmistakably a Crawford, but you're built like your mother's people. I have to give your parents credit for teaching you how to dress. That's the old St. Cuthbert's tie, as I live and breathe. I believe your great-great grandfather MacTavish had a hand in selecting the pattern originally. They certainly had style in those days. Dougal had half a dozen of the things. He wore them everywhere we went. Literally everywhere. Used one as a belt once when his suspenders failed. The number of men in this city who believe they can show up just anywhere wearing blue jeans and a t-shirt—it's inexcusable. I mean, the opera? Sometimes I despair of the human race."

"Mother threatened to throttle him with it the last time he tried to put one on."

"I'm not at all surprised to hear she hates it," Forbes smiled. "She's compelled to, you know. For any number of reasons. Some of them even subconscious, though I realize it's indelicate to suggest she has one of those. That's exactly the sort of domestic detail I love knowing about my old friends' establishments. It makes them smaller than life, I always think. Now, we've got time for a drink before we leave for dinner. I've made a reservation at a little spot that's a favorite of mine. Nothing fancy, mind you, but the best *boeuf bourgingon* this side of the Atlantic."

* * *

"I was sick when I realized I'd be missing Ruth's visit," Forbes said.

This was so patently false that Will was surprised he was able to say it with a straight face. Perpetual and bitter, the feud between his mother and godfather was one of the minor elephants in the Crawford living room, dwarfed, not to mention obscured, by the herd of others, but nevertheless a hardy beast and immune to any and all attempts at domestication. Not that there were many. Ironically, those few overtures that had been made came by way of Uncle Harris, himself the object of much of her enmity. Will's mother certainly had taste. He had to give her that. Show her a man of intelligence, culture, and good looks, and she'd practically spit fire at him. She was especially vitriolic when the object of her ire was a bachelor. In her mind, bachelors apparently justified genocide.

"My secretary is usually totally reliable," Forbes said. "I can't think how she got the dates so scrambled."

The godfather Will thought he recalled would never have been reduced to such a transparent excuse for what, after all, was nothing more significant than a minor social awkwardness. In fact, snubbing Will's mother was, given their relationship, practically obligatory. She'd have been furious if Forbes hadn't done it. But Will wished he'd at least been willing to own up to doing it on purpose. Still, he was inclined to excuse it. Forbes had never disappointed him before that he could remember.

"Mother expressed similar regrets," Will told him, just to see what, if any, reaction he might elicit by matching his godfather's lack of candor. The answer to that question was none whatever, apparently.

"So," Forbes said, making a slight adjustment to the alignment of his flatware, "all settled in are you? Where did you say your apartment was?"

"Actually, I'd like to talk to you about that," Will said. Enlisting his godfather in his crusade seemed to have a great deal to recommend it.

"Oh?"

"Just how difficult is it to break a lease here in San Francisco?"

"That depends entirely on the lease," Forbes said. "Is there something unsatisfactory about the apartment?"

"Nothing at all," Will said, "from mother's perspective."

"I see," Forbes smiled, apparently pleased at this declaration of independence, with its whiff of filial disloyalty. "I could help you with that, I suppose. Not that it would be appropriate for me to take your side in a dispute with your parents."

"Heaven forbid."

"Sarcasm, Will, is the response of the weak."

"Is it?"

"Surely you know that," Forbes said. "I mean, I would have thought, you being a poet."

"It certainly makes me feel weak," Will conceded.

"Now this lease," Forbes said. "I'm sure I could help you work something out with the landlord. But I'd rather you thought of my intervention as a last resort. Surely your own ingenuity is up to the task."

"I'm ingenious?"

"Please, my boy. False modesty isn't the thing at all. Not in these parts, at least."

* * *

The minute Will stepped off the bus on Haight Street he realized that the girl from Thursday afternoon had been speaking the truth, unlikely as that seemed. Here, eight years and two presidents later, the Summer of Love still flourished everywhere he looked. Flower vendors, street musicians, panhandlers, and tourists dressed in imitation of all the above thronged the sidewalks, and the disembodied wailing of Grace Slick throbbed in the patchouli scented air. He set off down the block at what proved to be an unsustainable pace given the crowds thronging around him. Everywhere he looked some exotic vignette or other caught his eye. The neighborhood seemed as alien yet picturesque as a working class quarter of Prague or Montevideo. This, it suddenly struck him, was what he had come to San Francisco to find. After twenty minutes or so of meandering, he stopped into a macrobiotic bakery and sat at a tiny bistro table savoring herbal tea that tasted like an infusion of lawn cuttings and a seven grain granola and carob muffin that had the texture of sawdust. The scene unfolding around him was so evocative that he was moved to pull out his trusty notebook and attempt a snatch of verse.

It was everything the neighborhood where his mother had installed him was not. The yeasty argot of the natives, larded as it was with ridiculous hippie-isms, was nevertheless piquant and strangely charming. The squalor, bizarrely magnetic. The competing aromas emerging from the doorways of vegetarian restaurants, exotic and mouthwatering. He simply had to find a way to live here. As an antidote to his legal studies it seemed an absolute necessity. And he couldn't think of a more perfect riposte to his mother. Not that he'd fit in in such surroundings. He knew that all too well, conscious as he was of the spectacle he presented bent over his notebook with his English schoolboy hair-cut flopping across his forehead. His painstakingly trimmed 1930's mustache and his costume of chinos and a polo shirt selected to match his eyes made his appearance tragically bourgeois.

Well, he was bourgeois. There was no escaping it. What could be more bourgeois than a first year law student? Unfortunately, the answer to that was probably a young poet who'd had the good fortune to be published by a major New York house and have his book reviewed in the *Times*. He was hopelessly out of place, a private school boy slumming as a supernumerary in *La Boheme*. Attempting to disguise it would be a fool's errand. Yet regardless of appearances, he knew that in his own way he was as free a spirit as any of the people he saw around him. He wrote poetry without any punctuation marks. Occasionally, even, without any verbs. But faced with all this street theatre, that seemed insufficient justification. What he lacked was an authentic way of expressing the gentle anarchy of his soul in everyday life. These natives were living their freedom. Or at least giving a convincing impression of doing so.

He went back the next day determined to be disappointed in the neighborhood and its inhabitants. He had had time to talk himself out of his infatuation. But this expedition was unsuccessful.

III

The young woman set her lunch tray down across the table from Will.
"Do you mind if I join you?"
"Not at all."
With her raven hair cut in a style reminiscent of Twiggy, circa 1965, and her eye makeup evocative of 1930's Berlin, she couldn't have looked less like a law student. Nevertheless, Will recognized her from a couple of his classes. And for confirmation, here she was in the lunchroom, a place no member of the general public would have sought out either for its atmosphere or its cuisine. At first glance, the contents of her tray seemed almost theatrical in their

eccentricity. Then Will got it—she must be vegetarian. He should have known as much from that mascara.

"You live in my neighborhood," she said. "I see you there all the time."

"Really? What street do you live on?"

"Ashbury," she said.

"Oh," he said, feeling himself start to blush. "I don't actually live around there. I just like the vibe."

He grimaced internally at that word. He'd sensed himself about to say "ambiance" and veered off in a panic, finally ending up in exactly the state of embarrassment he'd been intent on avoiding.

"Really," she said, nibbling on a breadstick. "You always seem so habituated."

"Do I?"

"Like a native," she nodded. "Sitting at your regular table, scribbling away in your little notebook like Fitzgerald in Montmartre."

So she'd been observing him. Will loved observing people but didn't much like the idea of the tables being turned. Particularly not by young women, who invariably terrified him.

"I never really was a fan of Fitzgerald," he said.

"Thank God," she smiled. "I'd probably hate you if you were. I'm Yvette."

"My name's Will."

"I know," she said, pulling a copy of his second book out of her bag. "I was hoping I might get you to sign this."

"My God," he said. "That."

"It's not a tarantula," she laughed.

"Of course not," he said. "I just never expect to encounter it in real life. But I'll be happy to sign it for you."

"So if you don't live in the Haight, where do you live?"

"That's a long story," he said. "And pretty boring, I'm afraid."

* * *

Yvette hadn't been exaggerating about the location of her apartment. She lived in the heart of what he had come to think of as the holy land, though she referred to it as "ground zero". He had walked by the house countless times without suspecting there was a fellow student in residence there. The façade hinted of quasi operatic grandeur inside, and that had undoubtedly once been the case. But the structure was now little more than a tenement. Yvette's apartment consisted of what had been one of the grander upstairs parlors, complete with wood burning fireplace, and a few adjoining rooms. The first time he visited there, Yvette's roommate was moving out. Roxanna had joined a commune of vegan Esperantists. Yvette claimed she sensed a lesbian undertone to the enterprise. Will quipped that he thought "lesbian Esperantist" must surely be a redundancy, and Yvette immediately adopted the phrase for use as an under-the-breath epithet.

"What a shame your lease runs for the whole year, Will," she said, listening to Roxanna drag her steamer trunk down the stairs. "We'd make fabulous roomies."

* * *

Before he knew it, Yvette and Will were inseparable. He'd never had a female friend before. Over the years he'd known a few girls who were the daughters of his parents' friends. And some girls from church, who barely counted. That was that. His schools, even as early as first grade, had been male only. He had found an all-male atmosphere so comfortable that when he started university he maintained a voluntary segregation. There had been female acquaintances at university, of course. Plenty of those, some of which might have turned into true friendships if he hadn't been so determined to elude them because of the possibility of misunderstandings. But women terrified him. The only ones of whom he had intimate knowledge were his mother, his aunts, and his girl cousins. They were a bloodthirsty and avaricious breed—practically a different species. One that haunted jungles constantly on the trail of prey. He couldn't imagine having anything to do with them by choice. But Yvette differed from them as surely as penguins differed from wombats. She never made him feel as if he were somehow not living up to her expectations. That had been a more or less perennial difficulty for him in his prior dealings with her gender—expectations. But the thing he liked best about her was her disdain for conventionality. He had never before encountered a female who didn't make a cult of conformity. He considered his own impulses in that direction the very worst of his character flaws.

* * *

"Of course you are, darling," Yvette said when he finally worked up the courage to tell her about himself. "All my best friends are homosexuals. It's always been that way. Ever since I was a little girl. Honestly, I have no idea what straight men are good for."

"I'd have thought that was obvious," Will said.

"Yes, but afterward they insist on talking about their feelings. They want you to respect them in the morning, and they get all mopey if you don't call within a day or two. Really, it's so tiresome of them."

It was the first time he had had that conversation with anyone. He had come close on numerous occasions but always pulled up short at the crucial moment. He supposed at least a few of those friends had read between the lines but not one of them ever referred to the matter afterward even in the most oblique way. At the time this had been both a relief and a disappointment. Something about Yvette had given him the confidence to take it past the goal line. Her reaction both surprised and gratified him. When he thought about it afterward he was more surprised at her lack of surprise than anything else.

* * *

"But how can you love opera, Will?" Yvette asked, grimacing at the taste of her herbal tea. "I mean, how can you possibly?"

Will shrugged.

"I don't understand it. You have marvelous taste in everything else. But opera? It's all about sappy young women who glory in their own stupidity and weakness and the even sappier young men who adore them in spite of how useless they are. It's inexplicable. Real men wouldn't look at girls like that twice."

"I know," he said. What he actually thought, however, was that the real men he knew seemed addicted to, rather than repelled by, female folly. It was one of the most baffling things about them.

"And of course, those sappy young women and sappier young men we are supposed to believe in and empathize with are invariably portrayed by fat, middle aged individuals with no sex appeal whatever. It couldn't be more absurd. Talk about your willing suspension of disbelief."

From his first glimpse of her, Will had known she would have opinions. So far she hadn't let him down. He imagined she even had opinions in her sleep. They were always interesting and generally well founded. But it was exhausting keeping track of all of them.

"As a modernist poet, you surely know better."

"It's as deplorable as you say," Will admitted. "It's as bad as my grandmother's addiction to *The Guiding Light* and *Search for Tomorrow*. But I can't seem to help myself."

"You know, if I had any doubt about your being gay," she said, "this would certainly put it to rest."

"I think it's about the tunes mostly."

"Well," she said, "if your godfather insists on taking us."

"He's going to be crazy about you."

"Yes," she nodded. "Middle aged homosexuals always are."

"I never said he was homosexual," Will said. "Did I?"

"Sorry, darling," she said. "I just assumed."

"But I suppose he is," Will said. "Yes, now that I think of it, he must be. Stupid of me never to have figured it out."

"Not really," she said. "I believe we're all happier thinking people of that generation don't have sexual feelings at all. Especially our parents."

* * *

"I had no idea you were such a dark horse, my boy," Forbes MacWhirter said a few nights after the opera when Will met him at his club for drinks. "That Miss Grossman of yours is a real corker. Smart as a whip but charming in spite of it. And what a looker. Can't imagine Ruth approving of her on any account."

The question hadn't occurred to Will. As far as he was concerned, never the twain would meet. He was a little dismayed to hear his godfather speculate on it. It was almost as distressing as the realization the Forbes had jumped to the conclusion that Yvette and he were a couple in the conventional sense of the term. Shouldn't one homosexual recognize another?

"It's not the Jewish thing," Forbes continued. "At least not entirely, you understand."

"Yvette's not Jewish," Will said. "At least I don't think so. She's certainly never mentioned it. She's a socialist, of course."

"She's Jewish," Forbes said. "All the best socialists are. And vice versa, for that matter."

"Anyway, it hardly matters what Mom thinks," Will said. "Yvette and I are just friends."

"Nonsense, my boy," Forbes frowned. "Men and women your age are never just friends. Somebody always has an agenda. Invariably an unholy one. I hope in this instance that's not you. Or wait, perhaps I do hope it's you. That would certainly simplify matters."

"But she knows about me, you see," Will said.

"I'm sorry. I don't think I follow you."

"You know," Will said, "that I'm gay."

"Gay?" Forbes looked baffled.

"That's right," Will said. "Gay."

"Oh," Forbes said, faintly surprised, "I suppose you mean homosexual. Really? I wouldn't have thought. You seem so—well, I mean, you've always had such backbone standing up to those goons, your brothers. Always punch well over your weight, has been my impression of matters. Tough little bugger in your own quiet way."

"Nevertheless," Will said.

"Well, there certainly seems to be a lot of that about lately," Forbes said. "Even here at the club. Jonathan Lewis was saying just the other day that his younger brother, Adam, had taken it up. So it's in the very best families. That means no one will be able to criticize you on the grounds that it's déclassé. Not that you'd care about that. Or admit to it if you did. You young people are such fascists about egalitarianism. Even our younger members here exhibit the tendency, unfortunately. To egalitarianism, I mean. And I'll grant you, adopting that predeliction is one way of keeping Miss Grossman in line. She can hardly make inappropriate demands on your person as long as you stick to your guns about being an avowed homosexual. So I rather find I have to congratulate you. Most ingenious, my boy, most ingenious."

* * *

"That big old poof said what?" Yvette howled.

"I'm not making it up," Will said. "I almost wish I were."

"No, I don't suppose you are. Still, talk about the pot calling the kettle black."

"But he wasn't calling me anything," Will protested.

"He was, too. He was implying that you're just like him. A duplicitous queen."

"How is coming out to you being duplicitous?"

"He's claiming to be a straight man, right? But Mrs. Thingamabob obviously believes he's gay, or she wouldn't be using him as her walker."

"Her what?"

"Escort, darling."

"He told me they're very old friends."

"I'm sure they are," Yvette said, "by now. But really, if he were what he claims to be he'd probably have been named co-respondent in her divorce. And they certainly wouldn't be friends after that experience."

"She's divorced?" Will asked. "Because I seem to remember him telling me she's a widow."

"All women like Mrs. Thingamabob are divorced," Yvette nodded. "If she's actually presenting herself as a widow, it will be because her ex-husband subsequently became a deceased one."

* * *

Their classmates seemed to take for granted that Yvette and Will were lovers. Will had made no public declarations that might disabuse them of this belief and didn't feel inclined to. He knew it was hypocritical of him. Generally, he considered hypocrisy the blackest of sins, but he made a conscious decision to risk perdition in this instance. The climate of the school mitigated strongly against honesty. It wasn't just the students who gave the impression that they might greet the presence of a gay classmate in their midst with hostility. A few of the professors were openly prejudiced. Will wasn't about to jeopardize his career plans over it. So he was ruthless with himself in terms of preserving the appropriate heterosexual demeanor. When they were alone together, Yvette was hysterical at this, suggesting with tears of mirth in her eyes that the stage was his true calling. At the same time, her public treatment of Will, relentlessly flirtatious as it was, served to give the impression that he was quite the ladies' man. She let it be generally known that she had to be on her guard at all times, lest his eye, not to mention his other parts, wander. Yvette found it entertaining in the extreme pulling the wool over the eyes of the ex-frat men that constituted the majority of their fellow students.

"It's far too easy making monkeys of those apes," she said. "Almost to the point that it bores me."

* * *

"I so sorry, Meester Veel," Mrs. Matuszak said, shaking her head with a vehemence Will feared would dislodge her wig, "so, so sorry, but heffing geef you noteess. Two veek, yais?"

"What's the problem, Mrs. Matuszak?" Will asked. If he truly had to have a cleaning lady, Mrs. Matuszak was the ideal one. She did as little as possible to his apartment, and thus he never had trouble finding anything. Some weeks she never showed up at all. The best thing was he wasn't sure she even knew where the vacuum cleaner was kept. His mother had turned her nose up at all the Hispanic and Chinese women she interviewed for the post. Only an Eastern European woman, an unmistakably white individual, was an object truly worthy of her exploitive impulses. This was what she got for her trouble and prejudice—a cleaning woman who didn't clean. The perfection of the arrangement stirred Will's deepest impulses toward both justice and anarchy. So this news was distressing. Replacing Mrs. Matuszak would be difficult. He hardly dared attempt it. He heard disheartening stories about the industriousness of the Chinese ladies the other tenants in his building employed. He heard their vacuums running day and night.

"Eez vee heffing moove," Mrs. Matuszak said. "My daughter hoozbant he loozing chob. Vee find sheeper apartment for moove to. But izz too far. Too much bus for me. Heffing geef noteess. Two veek, yais?"

"I'm very sorry to hear about your trouble," Will said. "Where is your new apartment located?"

* * *

His godfather had described him as ingenious, but Will didn't credit it at the time. Still, he surprised himself by rising to the occasion, though he wasn't at all certain where the inspiration came from.

"So let me get this straight," Yvette said, stifling a yawn. "Mrs. Matuszak and her family move into your place on lovely Nob Hill. Which your parents prepaid the lease on. The new tenants pay you enough in rent that you can split rent and utilities with me and come out even. I get the new roomie of my dreams, Mrs. Matuszak *et famille* spend less than they thought they would have to for a decent place to live, you emigrate to colorful Haight-Ashbury and in the process subvert your mum. Everybody wins."

"Yes," Will nodded. "That's how it works."

"Darling, you're a genius. It's like something Rube Goldberg would have come up with."

"Until something happens and Mom finds out. Then there'll be hell to pay."

"We'll cross that bridge together."

He'd like to see that, actually. His mother and Yvette locked in hand to hand combat, or at least the female equivalent of it.

The plan had one more thing to recommend it. For the next ten months he'd have the luxury of being able to pretend to himself that he'd put one over on his parents.

* * *

"Darling Will," Yvette giggled in the doorway, watching him shove his newly acquired thrift store furniture around the tiny space. It was like a disassembled Chinese puzzle he couldn't figure out how to put back together. "I had no idea you were leaving all those things with Mrs. Matuszak and her tribe."

"That furniture was specially selected for that apartment," Will said, "and prepaid for the year. There's no way it would all have fit in here even if I wanted to bring it. What else could I have done? The agency wouldn't take it back, and I couldn't leave it on the street."

"Those people must think you're Father Christmas."

"They think they're taking advantage of a spoiled and stupid rich boy," Will said. "Which, coincidentally, is exactly what my parents think of me as well. Perhaps it's true."

"Well, I think you've deceived them all as to your true nature in a particularly admirable way."

IV

"This is so exciting," Yvette squealed, staring at the small volume he'd just slid across the table toward her. "My roomie is a published author."

"I already was one when you met me," Will pointed out.

"Yes, yes, of course," she nodded, "but three books is more than twice as impressive as two books. It's exponential, really. One book is a fluke. No offense, Will, but anybody can write one book. Two books simply means you hadn't run out of things to say by the time you got to the end of the first. But three books constitute a budding career. I have an uncle in publishing. I know about such matters."

"Yes, well," Will shrugged.

"Tell me again why you're wasting your life in law school," she said, leafing through the thin volume.

"I love law school," he protested.

"You keep saying that. But how am I supposed to believe you if you can't convince yourself?"

"Well, at least I don't hate it as much as I did at first."

"There's that," Yvette conceded.

"That's not all," Will said. "The book, I mean."

"Oh?"

"I'm doing a reading. At City Lights."

"Darling, how fabulous. An event. Now I have an excuse to go shopping. Not that I ever need one. Still, one always shops better with a specific purpose in mind. I'll buy something divine to wear. All your fans will be amazed at your glamorous girlfriend. And between your talent and my looks, any of your rivals who happen to attend will want to kill themselves. Just rush right over to either of the bridges and jump off. It's going to be a triumph."

"I'd settle for a Volkswagen."

* * *

It wasn't until after midterm exams that Will gave serious thought to what selections he'd present at his reading. He had done readings previously, both back home in Philadelphia and while studying at Northwestern. Chicago audiences were highly academic, as you'd expect in the home of formalist criticism. They had clear expectations. They wanted poetry that called attention to itself as poetry, poetry that gloried in its display of authorial technique. And since that was the kind of poetry he wrote, his appearances there had always been love fests. Philadelphia audiences were altogether different. They were more hygienic in their approach to the art. They'd listen politely to anything anybody decided to label a poem, no matter how sublime or abysmal, and applaud enthusiastically at the end simply because appreciating poetry was like flossing your teeth—it was good for you. Everybody knew it made you a better person. Questions about artistic merit were the province of experts, and most Philadelphians seemed to think the less said on the subject the better. San Franciscans, he suspected, were more cerebral than either of the other groups and smug in their estimation of themselves as the hippest of all Americans except, perhaps, New Yorkers. He had to anticipate that they'd be a difficult audience to win over.

As he read back through his favorite pieces from his books, he realized to his dismay that none of them would do. Really they wouldn't. Somehow there was too much artifice in them. They were beautifully crafted. There was no question about that. He had taken great pride in it when he wrote the poems and he still did. But they struck him as being strangely like items on display in a museum. They might be poetry, technically speaking, but they weren't art. They might sit prettily on a shelf, but they didn't live or breathe. They lacked something crucial which he very much feared might be authenticity. They didn't illuminate, they obfuscated. And thus they were the opposite of real poetry. He had to admit it. They were schoolboy exercises, nothing more. It was his worst nightmare. Pa, it seemed, had been right. And nothing was worse than that.

Still, he was committed. He had agreed to the date. His publisher had sent out multiple press releases. Flyers had been printed and posted all over the city. He'd be minding his business at the bus stop and the next thing he knew he'd notice someone staring at one that seemed to have sprouted there overnight, and he'd feel like a fraud. Once or twice he nearly spoke up, identified himself as the poet and told onlookers not to bother. He just had to face it. He was going to have to go out in front of the public and give them something that he was no longer proud of, that didn't truly represent what he had always believed and still wanted to believe about his talent. He was no better than one of those guys on the street corners selling fake Rolexes. He was probably worse, come to think of it. He had options. He'd still have a roof over his head whether he ever wrote another word or not.

* * *

"Know quite well one shouldn't cast aspersions," Uncle Harris said, setting his suitcase on the stand. "Your godfather, all that."

"Cast away," Will said, still smarting from—what, exactly? At the very least, putting his foot in it the last time he saw Forbes. It hadn't at all been the reaction he was expecting. It had been the move of a coward, revealing himself to the man only because he thought that what he was disclosing was something they had in common and thus doing it without risk. And though the resulting misunderstanding was almost certainly his own fault, it felt far better to blame Forbes. Which made Will less than the man he wanted his uncle to think him.

"Mean to say, horse's ass," Uncle Harris said, beginning to unpack. "Harmless enough, one has to admit. And certainly charming. Yes, by all means. Tick that box. But, has to be said, charming in a flashy, almost middle class kind of way. That 'everybody look at me' sort of charm. One of them in every year at every school. Bank on it. Taggart Murchison in my time. The divine Tag. Really had to keep oneself on a short lead with that one stalking the corridors. Still, with that sort of individual on the loose one can all too easily

imagine the young Dougal being taken in. Too impressionable, one's forced to
conclude from careful consideration of family lore. And Forbes. One's seen
photos. Yearbook, what? The hair alone. Sheer perfection. Schoolboy glam-
our of the highest order. Take stern stuff to resist that. At that age one always
likes to have good looking friends. It's a sort of validation. Still, never saw the
point of him somehow. Goes against the grain: agreeing with one's sister-in-
law. Can't tell you how distressing one finds that. No telling what it might
lead to. Never admit to it in any case. Bad form. Even worse strategy. Worst
possible, really. Still, coincidences will happen. However bizarre, however
unlikely. History—full of examples. Most instructive, history."

 "I wouldn't have agreed with you about him," Will said, "until recently."

 "Really? Something happen to prompt this change of heart?"

 "Incipient maturity, I suppose."

 "Yours? Or his?"

 "God knows," Will laughed.

 "You, on the other hand," Uncle Harris said. "Genuine article. Real
thoroughbred. Flourishing. One can tell. Shiny coat, bright eyes, tail carried
high, just so. Mean to say. Absolute pick of the litter."

 "Thanks," Will said.

 "Always have a capital apetite as well. Never have to be coaxed to eat.
Really tore into the prime rib this evening. Happy to see it. Good apetite—
always a sign that a man is truly sound. Philadelphia last week. One saw that
brother of yours. Fergus, you ken. Green salad for an entree. Green salad, I
tell you. Vinegar and oil dressing. Few oyster crackers on the side. Water with
lemon. Saddest looking luncheon one had witnessed in this hemisphere. And
thinning hair. At his age, I ask you. Blame your mother. MacLeod tribe full of
men who lost their hair. Shame—all one can say. Never really a handsome boy,
Fergus, but presentable at least. Spoils the effect. Could be ten years older than
you. Hardly feel like his uncle, somehow. More like a prefect encountering a
weedy new boy. Thank God you take after the Crawfords that way. Magnificent heads of hair, all the Crawfords. Great Grandpa Crawford, case in point.
Full head of hair at age ninety-three. Looked amazing in that casket. Made one
proud. And that other brother of yours, Madison. Young man really must get
control of himself. Thirty pounds overweight if he's an ounce. Perhaps even
thirty-five. Hardly weaned yet and carrying all that around. That's the MacTa-
vishes for you. Metabolisms like tree sloths. Dougal really should have married

that Fiona MacAlistair. Told him so at the time. Didn't listen. 'Mind your business, squeak.' Didn't realize I was right until it was too late."

"You wanted him to break up with Mom?"

"Hadn't met Ruth yet. Fiddled around playing hard to get and let that Robbie Stewart sweep the fair Fiona off her feet. Can't play hard to get up against a narcissist. They don't comprehend what you're about."

"Do we know anybody but other Scottish families?"

"Not really. Some Jews, of course. Unavoidable, really. Law's full of them. So's my trade, funnily enough. Convenient excuse for doing what one ought to in the first place. Scots aren't God's Chosen either, even if we think we are. Never saw the harm in Jews. Funny people. Smart. Hard working. Friendly, if one approaches them with proper respect. Always know where you stand with a Jew. Don't know why our tribe makes such a case of them. Take my advice you'll find a nice Jewish girl. Make fabulous wives. Very sensuous, what one hears. Ruth will have kittens of course, but Dougal will thank you. Not aloud. Wouldn't expect that. But make it worth your while in his own way. Magnificient grandchildren is the thing. Smart, handsome, driven."

"I didn't mean anything by the suggestion, you know."

"Say no more."

"You and Forbes just always seemed to hit it off. Back in the old days."

"Extraordinary," Uncle Harris said. "Never thought it would come back to haunt one. Simple courtesy, really. Good manners. Nothing more than that. Understand why one's nephew might have misconstrued it, however."

"I wouldn't have mentioned it in the first place except I thought the two of you would enjoy catching up."

"This hotel," Uncle Harris said, "most satisfactory, old man. Always more comfortable in hotels. Far better level of service. Need clean towels, one only has to call housekeeping. No heavy negotiations required. No possibility of embarrassment. Or hurt feelings. Best of all, more privacy. And this one in particular. Close to all the attractions."

"I'm glad you like it."

"Yes. Most satisfactory. Sure to enjoy the stay."

* * *

Yvette drove her LeCar with truly Parisian verve. It was just short of terrifying the way she attacked the hills and all but refused to brake for down-grades. She never upshifted until the engine absolutely screamed for mercy.

The tires, the brakes, the suspension, every component complained at the top of its lungs. Stop signs were mere suggestions. She carved up traffic like a Thanksgiving turkey. A journey as her passenger, no matter how short, though not relaxing by any means was certainly cathartic. A parking space had been reserved for them, and the tires shrieked as she steered into it. He could smell burning rubber through the open window.

"Darling, you'll be scintillating," Yvette said, kissing him on both cheeks.

If anything scintillated, he thought, it had to be her eyes.

"Scintillating" was her new pet word. Will wasn't certain how it could justifiably be applied either to his person or his work but accepted her use of it as affectionately motivated. While she went off to work the crowd a bookstore functionary ushered him to a small office in the back to wait. There was an overflow turnout, the boy assured him, and he didn't know whether to laugh or flee. On the bulletin board they had tacked an extra copy of the publicity shot his publisher had sent. He stared at himself. Fake reading glasses because on these occasions he had to have something to hide behind. Preppy clothing because whenever he wore anything else he felt like he was in costume for Halloween and the resulting self consciousness made him an even worse performer. Floppy English schoolboy haircut because Will had no imagination when it came to such things. This was his persona, for better or worse. The audience would be judging that as surely as they'd be judging his work. Perhaps even more so. The evening couldn't end well. That was inconceivable.

* * *

He had learned some things from his previous readings. It was important to keep the pitch of his voice in a low register. The higher he allowed the pitch to drift, the faster and less intelligible his delivery became. It was a nervous thing, really. Keeping the pitch low required him to concentrate on slowing down and breathing deeply, and breathing deeply calmed him, and everything went—perhaps not beautifully, but better than it would have otherwise. Then, too, he must at all costs fight the temptation to read with "expression". His old high school literature teacher, Mr. Carpenter, had read with expression. His readings of poetry were beautiful. Inspiring, really. More than once during Will's school days whole classes of students rewarded these performances with standing ovations. Mr. Carpenter was, to Will's mind, the Platonic Ideal of a teacher, the teacher he would have wanted to be had he ever entertained such a lunatic notion as becoming one. But Will was no Mr. Carpenter and he knew it. When he attempted to read with expression he merely sounded as if he was verging on hysteria. Besides, reading with expression seemed to claim a significance for his work that he was daily more convinced it didn't deserve.

Most of all, he reminded himself as he took his place at the lectern and adjusted his fake reading glasses, he must never, ever look at the audience. That was for comedians and politicians, if indeed those were two different species.

* * *

"My boy," Forbes MacWhirter beamed, shaking his hand like he was pumping water from a well, "what a triumph. I had no idea you were so talented."

This despite the fact that Will had presented him with copies of his previous books as birthday presents. He'd even inscribed them. Obviously they hadn't been read.

His friend, Mrs. Pangbourne—Yvette referred to her as Forbes' beard— smiled a sour little smile. Her taste in poetry probably didn't stretch even as far as Whitman. And she undoubtedly believed she was slumming. Will supposed she was. She'd been told she was attending a reading by a real poet.

"I only wish your parents had been here tonight," Forbes continued. "What a sharp stick in the eye for Dougal. And Ruth would have been livid at all that applause. Those two never could abide the successes of their offspring. Least attractive thing about them."

* * *

"Young Will," Uncle Harris said, "like you to meet Ned Westerleigh. Dear friend and fellow aesthete."

Mr. Westerleigh was rather a duplicate of Uncle Harris one generation removed. Tall, broad shouldered, straight backed, silver haired, handsome in an unmistakably aristocratic fashion.

"It's very nice to meet you, Mr. Westerleigh."

"Ned, my boy. You must call me Ned. 'Mr. Westerleigh' is reserved for civilians."

"Ned."

"Pleasure is all mine. Always appreciate true talent. Particularly when it's connected with a close friend like Harris. I find I'm quite strongly prejudiced in favor of all Crawfords."

"He hasn't met your brothers," Uncle Harris laughed.

* * *

"Didn't I tell you, darling?" Yvette said, starting the LeCar with a roar and a lunge. "You scintillated."

"You're not just saying that?" Will asked, frantically scrambling to get his seat belt fastened. Not that it would do much good in the event of the inevitable confrontation with a city bus.

"You know me better than that."

Did he? He still wasn't absolutely sure of her.

"Meet anybody nice tonight?"

"Not that kind of crowd, was it?"

"I'd have thought it was exactly that kind of crowd," Will said

* * *

As it turned out, several of Will's classmates had attended the reading. And even Professor Steinberg, who complimented him obliquely on it in his lecture the next morning. He was turning into a law school luminary with his glamorous alleged girlfriend and his literary reputation. He could feel his classmates' envy stalking him through the hallways. It was almost like old times back in graduate school. Those had been the days. Unfortunately, in the wake of his "triumphant" reading he felt more than ever like a fraud. He could hardly stand to pick up his notebook. The idea of writing made him faintly queasy. This sensation grew more, rather than less, intense over the few days after the event. He couldn't bring himself to mention it to Yvette, who was still glowing with pride.

* * *

"One finds," Uncle Harris said, contemplating his coffee cup, "that the work holds up perfectly well. Any dissatisfaction with it—chalk that up to maturity. Or to your own changing perspective on things, my best guess. Next book to reflect that shift, one expects."

After dinner they had come back to Uncle Harris' hotel room, where he was in the middle of packing for an early morning departure.

"If there is a next book."

"Entirely up to you, old man. Shouldn't abandon it out of pique. Never a good idea to make a decision like that out of emotion. Focus on one's studies, revisit the question later. Fresh outlook, all that. Certain to be a success at the law of course. Still, one suspects one hasn't seen the last of the poet."

"You always give such good advice," Will said. What he actually meant in the place of "good advice" was "praise". If only he had the guts to express himself more forthrightly.

"One tries. Truly. Weighty responsibility. No escaping that. Super visit. Have to say. Hate to leave so soon. Never here for long enough. Love this city. Can't think why one doesn't live here."

"You don't live anywhere that I can tell. You're constantly on the go."

"Base of operations, mean to say. *Pied a terre.* Lovely old buildings here. Some neighborhoods one might almost be in Paris. Except for the hills."

"Is there any reason you couldn't locate here?"

"Give it some thought. Simply must. One finds the climate so congenial. To say nothing of the local flora and fauna. Especially the fauna. Have to say, quite a remarkable young woman, your Miss Grossman."

"She's crazy about you."

"Mutual, certainly. One hopes the old paths cross again before too long, what?"

"About Yvette," Will said.

"Yes?"

"I hate to seem ungrateful for advice. Especially coming from you."

"Like a second helping of dessert, young Will. One isn't obligated to partake just because the tray is passed."

"It's just that in my case I'm afraid it would have to be a nice Jewish boy."

"Ah," Uncle Harris nodded. "Ruth terrified about your cousin Arch along that line. One knew she was barking up the wrong tree. Never convince her. Didn't even attempt it. Really had her teeth into it. Trenchant commentary on the subject of how your Auntie Victoria's responsible for it. Load of rot. Even Freud eventually gave up on that tack. Grannie Crawford raised five sons. Treated us exactly alike. But we didn't all turn out musical."

"Right."

"Not stringing Miss Grossman along, I hope."

"She's aware of the situation. She has interests of her own."

"Good man. Decent thing. Sorry, but one has to ask."

"I'd have had to take your temperature if you didn't," Will grinned.

"It's not an easy life, I'm afraid," Uncle Harris said. "Fact must be faced. Nothing to be gained—turning one's back on the essential truth of matters."

"I never supposed it would be."

"Still, you'll find that authenticity has a great deal to recommend it. Profound satisfaction over the years. Moral clarity—yes, you heard that. Moral. Most of the disapproval one hears expressed isn't based on morality at all. People do so hate anything unconventional, what? And set against that? The examined life sort of thing. That silly queen Forbes won't ever admit it, you know. Not even to himself. Can't forgive that—willful obliviousness. Others might, more charitably inclined, but one simply can't find it in oneself to excuse it. Not because of what he said to one all those years ago. Or even what he did. Let bygones be—easy enough. No. That refusal to confront reality's the thing. Cowardly. Unforgivable. Know you noticed. Saw it in your eyes."

"I suppose."

"By the by," Uncle Harris said, pulling a small parcel wrapped in brown paper out of his attaché case.

"What's that?"

"Copies of your books. Property of my friend, Ned Westerleigh. He'd appreciate inscriptions."

"Certainly," Will said. "It'll be my pleasure."

"Told him as much."

"Who is he, anyway?"

"Old friend."

"Yes, but."

"Patron of the arts," Uncle Harris said.

"Seriously."

"Seriously."

"And?"

"Sells real estate," Uncle Harris explained. "Best there is at it. If you're ever in the market, give him a ring."

"Of course."

"All for now, young man. Too long a story. But—chapter one: Great Uncle Niall. London. The Blitz. Eagle Squadron. Ned Westerleigh. All that."

"I see. How will I get the books back to him?"

"He'll be in touch. Ask you to tea I shouldn't wonder. You'll be sure to be properly impressed with the views from his place. Won't you?"

"Right," Will said.

"Ridiculously proud of you, young Will," Uncle Harris smiled. "Deliriously. Poetry. School. Other thing. Mean to say, shaping up nicely. Kind of man one can be proud to know, relation or not."

* * *

Will returned home from his farewell evening with Uncle Harris to find a giant in the kitchen. Taking up most of the space, actually. A blond giant, half Mr. Universe and half Viking chieftain, staring intently into the open refrigerator. A naked giant. Proportionately naked, which Will tried his best not to notice too obviously though he was certain he was failing to give an impression of sufficient disinterestedness.

"Oh, hi," he said, turning to greet Will. "Yvette says she's hungry. Where are the Hershey's Kisses kept?"

So apparently he wasn't a rapist, burglar, or axe murderer. A plunderer almost certainly. And inexcusably handsome. It wasn't just the flattering light, Will silently acknowledged.

"Freezer compartment," Will stammered, involuntarily imagining himself as the plunderee.

"Thanks. I'm Kirk, by the way."

"I'm Will."

"Ah, yes," he said, reaching into the freezer compartment. "The poet."

"Huh?"

"Met Yvette at your reading."

"You were there?"

"Nice stuff."

"Thanks."

"Better get these in to her. Before she goes into a coma."

V

The problem with Kirk de Havilland was that he was perfect.

"I swear to God I'm going to get to the bottom of it if it's the last thing I do," Yvette said at least once a day. Either that or "He's not going to get away with it. And you can take that to the bank." She was convinced that there had to be something terrible that Kirk was concealing. Some inner flaw as gruesome as his exterior was splendid. And she was determined not to get rid of him before she had a chance to unearth it. Will believed this was the only reason she was still dating Kirk. It wasn't as if he was her type. Her type was intellectual and artistic and otherworldly and undernourished and politically obsessed and eccentric at least if not genuinely disturbed. So her ongoing dealings with Kirk lacked any of her typical motivations. She was as capable as anyone of indiscriminate fucking, but to Will's knowledge she never let those guys make her breakfast. Yet within a couple of weeks Kirk had completely reorganized their kitchen and their diets. Stumbling into the kitchen and encountering that astonishing vision preparing an *omelette aux fines herbes* or somesuch culinary masterpiece felt to Will like making a daily visit to the Twilight Zone. When he ran that description past Yvette she rolled her eyes.

The second problem with Kirk, though Will would have jumped off the Golden Gate Bridge before admitting it to anyone, was that Kirk was his type. Not that he'd known it until actually laying eyes on the paragon. That first dizzying moment in their dimly lit kitchen was the epiphany he'd been await-ing since childhood. And every time he recalled it he was mortified. To have become instantaneously infatuated. And with that big bundle of cliches. Hand-some beyond any possible justification, musclebound, charismatic, unmistak-ably not stupid. It was far too obvious. Not to mention juvenile. Like Will's brothers slobbering and drooling over *Playboy* centerfolds. And he and Yvette learned very soon—and totally by accident, because Kirk didn't say a thing about it—that Kirk was rich, too. Not just upper middle class or even up-per *upper* middle class, not *nouveau riche* which they could have laughed about since for all practical purposes that's what they were themselves, but old money big money rich. Literally stretching back centuries. His family didn't deposit money in banks; they bought the banks. And assorted other enterprises such as shipping lines, mining companies, and railroads.

After a couple of months of close observation Kirk remained as flawless as he had been on first sight, and Yvette's continued fervor to unmask him raged unabated. As for Will, the impact Kirk had on him could only mean that Will was inexcusably shallow. It was not a pleasant thing to learn about himself.

But it was worse than it sounded. Will had known he was gay since before he knew there was a word for it. It wasn't something he was proud of, but he had vowed early on not to let it ruin his life. Uncle Harris had apparently found a way to navigate it, and Will took that as his sign. As long as his inclination remained abstract, a matter of perfect grooming and impeccable manners and aesthetic tastes in all things, it wasn't so bad. And he'd managed to get through St. Cuthbert's and university and even graduate school without any serious em-barrassments. He had discreet little crushes, of course. More or less perpetu-ally. But you didn't have to act on them or mention them to anyone. Most of the time he pretended not even to think about them. It made for a lonely exis-tence but at the same time it was probably what had propelled his writing, and if that was the price you paid to create art, even mediocre art, so be it. Yvette sensed all this about him, and though she teased him about it from time to time, she seemed to understand and even respect it. She occasionally complained that he was allowing life to pass him by, to which he generally replied that she was living enough for both of them. And though that denoted a fundamentally unsatisfactory situation, she liked the sound of it enough not to meddle unduly in his celibacy beyond making a suggestion every now and then that he cut loose and find somebody nice and get his ashes hauled.

When he contemplated the possibility of being gay in more existential terms, Will was still incapable of envisioning it except in the most genteel and domestic of manners. A snug cottage behind a white picket fence on a street of similarly quaint houses. Roses growing in the garden, Labradors sunning themselves drowsily on the velvety lawn, Will sitting on a terrace drinking coffee and composing poetry, and tantalizing smells issuing from the kitchen where someone nice bustled away while Mozart played on the stereo. As if wrapping himself and his beloved in layer upon layer of bourgeois clichés could make the scene respectable.

As for the beloved, the presumed centerpiece of the tableau, Will's imagination invariably faltered at that point. The best it could come up with was someone very much like him. Average looking or perhaps average plus, similar enough to him physically that they might conveniently share clothing, well behaved, articulate but a little reserved, unfailingly considerate, intelligent, refined in his tastes. Someone, in other words, who'd never think of making awkward demands, of embarrassing himself or Will in public, of calling attention to them in any way. Someone people would look at and judge as appropriate, both as an individual and as half of a couple. Or if not exactly appropriate, because people's sensibilities were awfully sensitive about certain things, at least more or less inoffensive. Will could just about give himself permission to go that far.

That spectacle lurking in the kitchen like a gladiator in the off season was something else altogether. Nobody between the ages of thirteen and a hundred of either gender could look at a guy like Kirk and *not* think about sex. He was a prodigy. He was rampant. He was an erection on two spellbinding legs. Despite Kirk's expertise in the kitchen and with all known implements involved in housekeeping, there was nothing domestic about him. And he was about as bourgeois as a barbarian warrior. You looked at him and you imagined rape and pillage, not cucumber sandwiches in the rose garden or freshly disinfected bathroom fixtures. For him to have immediately become Will's reigning fantasy said something about Will that he'd rather have remained unaware of. The idea that being gay included a component of such unbridled carnality—that was fine and good for people who went in for it. It just made Will feel queasy. And like he couldn't look at himself in the mirror.

He battled his unexpected and unwelcome obsession with Kirk on two fronts. The immediate threat was that he would unconsciously say or do something that would tip Yvette off. If she figured it out he'd never hear the end of it. She never missed an opportunity to subject him to gentle ridicule and she'd take full advantage of the opening. It was one of her less attractive habits. Though he had to admit to finding it highly entertaining when she trained her sights on their classmates or neighbors, it truly stung when the barbs were aimed at him. More serious than that, however, was his awareness that once she was in on the secret it would be much harder for him to ignore it himself. Discussing it with her—and there'd be no escaping those conversations—would make it more real than ever. His mortification would be inescapable.

The situation with Kirk wouldn't last forever. Yvette was bound to get bored with him sooner or later whether she solved the mystery of his "true nature" or not. She complained at least once a day that having him around was like being on a steady diet of Black Forest Cake. Though Will thought of Kirk more in terms of raw meat, he saw her point. You could only consume so much of anything before it lost the power to satisfy you. Instead, it would make you sick. You'd find yourself craving something else. Anything else. Even something you would ordinarily have turned your nose up at. Though there was no sign of it happening, sooner or later Kirk would exit the scene. Will just had to hang on.

But even then Will's battle wouldn't be over. Because getting the genie back into the bottle wouldn't be easy. Kirk had awakened him. Yes, that made two more metaphors, and Will knew that thinking of his predicament in terms of metaphors was intellectually lazy. But it was the only way he could stand to think about his feelings. Examining them literally was simply too distressing. It meant admitting to himself that he was enthralled, enslaved, stupefied. That he was incapable of controlling himself. That he was at the mercy of his unruly parts despite his poetry, his education, his professional prospects, his obsessively cultivated respectability. Already his weakness had grown bigger even than Kirk. Everywhere he went he saw men who had a similar, if not as intense, effect on him. A motorcycle cop on the street. A delivery man stepping out of his UPS truck. A young man stocking shelves in the supermarket. A jogger loping down the street in the fog. A bodybuilder he encountered on the bus. Worst of all, a few of his fellow students had somehow taken on the power to distract him. Now that he'd been confronted with the reality of what these men could make him think of, make him feel (if only in silence), nowhere in the city was safe. And he couldn't imagine that changing just because he woke up one morning to find that Yvette had sent Kirk on his way.

Then the unthinkable happened. Will recognized immediately that he had no right to be surprised by it. Yvette's commentary, which had started off swaggering and trenchant—"*whoever said size doesn't matter was an idiot*"—suddenly turned goofily cryptic and then trailed off into silence, as if she'd been struck dumb. And she nearly had. Will realized an instant before she stammered her confession what she was going to say. She had fallen in love. It was too unlikely, too absurd, really, not to be true. Which meant that Will was trapped indefinitely.

When Will looked into Yvette's eyes, he saw certainty. She had always known her own mind. Her opinions and preferences were like the steel reinforced concrete skyscrapers were built out of. You could rely on her convictions like you could rely on the ground beneath your feet. Of course this was San Francisco where the ground often shook, sometimes alarmingly. But it always settled back into place more or less, and once it did you could depend on it again. Something similar had happened in this case. Something that transformed Yvette's initial skepticism about Kirk into faith. Now, that faith burned in her like a pure, unflickering flame. Will would be a fool to question it. And not just a fool but a hypocrite. He felt the fire himself.

So Kirk wasn't going away anytime soon. Perhaps not ever. Will would have to look for salvation through some other means. For the first time since his schooldays, poetry provided no solace. He'd start to compose and before he knew it there would be the beginnings of a half assed ode to you know who. Oh, the ridiculous metaphors. The overheated imagery. In Will's current condition, writing poetry was like tossing gasoline on a burning house. He groped for an alternative. Finally he got desperate enough to go with the obvious solution. So far he'd been working just hard enough to get by in his classes. Now that changed. The first time he outscored Yvette on an exam, she was amused. The second time, she was incredulous.

"What the hell has gotten into you?" she demanded.

"Wouldn't you like to know?"

"Answering a question with a question," she fumed. "Law school's obviously bringing out the worst in you."

Finally one weekend just after final exams Kirk and Yvette went away together and in their absence Will couldn't contain himself any longer. He composed a long, turgid poem that made him blush as he re-read it. He titled it "Rhapsody in Blond" and told himself it was good to have gotten it out of his system. He knew he hadn't when he tried to burn the thing in the back yard and couldn't strike the match.

There was one positive result of Yvette's acceptance of her new status as Kirk's girlfriend. It allowed Will a latitude that he hadn't previously granted himself. He could ask questions now. There was nothing suspicious in wanting to know all about the man his best friend loved. He was careful not to try and get it all at once as if he'd been compiling a list. He'd throw out a question here, a supposition there, a couple of days later an assumption Yvette would refute and which would lead to further discussion. He might feel safe in his newly acquired disguise of interested friend, but it could still go wrong. So though he actually did have a list, he presented his inquiries as if at random.

"We know so little about him," he said a few days after the initial scene had been played. "For instance this roommate he's always talking about. Have we ever seen him? I'm not sure he even exists."

It seemed safer to ask questions about Kirk through a sort of metonymy. His apartment. His car. His friends. Etc.

"Evan?" Yvette nodded. "He exists all right. I've met him."

"Really? You never said."

"Big as life."

"As big as Kirk?"

"Nobody is," Yvette laughed. "But bigger than you, certainly. And every bit as real."

"And that story Kirk told us about him?"

"I know," Yvette nodded. "It did sound far fetched at the time. Never around because his career as an international model keeps him constantly on the go."

"Exactly," Will nodded.

"I can't claim to have actually counted the stamps in his passport," Yvette said, "but he certainly looks the part."

At this news Will's heart plummeted. That Kirk had recently assumed semi-permanent status in his life was bad enough. But another one? If Evan was even half as spectacular as Kirk, Will's life would hardly be worth living.

"The rest of it," Yvette went on, "all that stuff about how they were roomies at St. Dunstan's and fraternity brothers at USC: that's documented fact. And by the way, Evan's family owns hotels. Four and five star ones. They're not as rich as the de Havillands, but at that level what's the difference?"

* * *

Will hadn't completely lost his mind. He understood that the reason he didn't stand a chance with Kirk wasn't that Kirk was taken. He got the whole thing about straight guys. He'd put a lot into his refusal to be a victim of his orientation. But a thing like this certainly made him feel like the heroine of a tragic opera. Dying ostensibly of consumption but in actuality of unrequited love. A guy like Kirk loving him back? Right.

In fact, the more he thought about it, it seemed almost as unlikely that they'd even be able to co-exist. What red blooded American male would tolerate his woman's deep friendship with one of those? It was probably a miracle Will hadn't already awakened in the dumpster out back. Up until now, Yvette and he and presented themselves as "just roomies" and "platonic friends", and Kirk hadn't expressed the least suspicion that there might be more to the story. Will walked on eggs the whole time. But now, with Kirk's departure indefinitely delayed and an unforeseen degree of intimacy between Yvette and Kirk unfolding daily, anything might happen. If worst came to worst, Will would do the decent thing. You couldn't put a girl like Yvette in a position of having to choose. And besides, Will didn't want to face being the loser.

* * *

"Kirk's not like that," Yvette said.

"All straight guys are like that," Will said. "My brothers hate that I'm gay."

"I thought you weren't out to your family."

"It's assumed," Will said.

"You don't have anything to worry about," Yvette insisted. "Kirk's different. He's his own man."

This was difficult for Will to believe. If anything, Kirk seemed to exemplify the type of guy who tortured gays for entertainment.

"You know that for certain?" he asked. "You've discussed it with him?"

"As a matter of fact, yes."

* * *

"No big deal, Will," Kirk grinned. "It's not the taboo you think it is. At least not as far as I'm concerned."

"What?"

"I won't insult you by saying some of my best friends are gay," Kirk said. "That's always a sure sign somebody's a bigot, isn't it? And in my case it wouldn't be true. But I've known plenty of you guys. School. Fraternity. Sports teams, believe it or not. Always a few of you around. Never had a problem with any of them. Gym I go to—half the guys there are gay. Not a limp wrist in the bunch. Snap you like a twig if they think you're looking down on them. Damn right, too. Why should they tolerate disrespect? Great guys. Wouldn't mind at all having them for friends. Just haven't made the effort, I guess. Me, I mean. I understand why they haven't. Too risky. Haven't actually put out the welcome mat. Cordial enough, but still. Have to be a little more obvious than that. Anyway, Yvette's bosom buddy, you're just going to have to get over it. I'm not going to strangle you in your sleep or take all the stuff out of your room and burn it out on the sidewalk."

"If you say so," Will mumbled, reeling.

"Way I see it," Kirk said, "we have to get along. For Yvette's sake."

"You're right."

"I know in your own way you love her as much as I do," Kirk said. "I've never known a girl like her. Intellect and sense of humor of a guy with those looks and the kind of plumbing I prefer. No wonder we're both crazy about her."

VI

"You're gay, right?" Evan observed. Kirk's best friend and roommate actually existed.

"Yes," Will confirmed. This wasn't a coming out scene. His orientation had been a subject of discussion for this group on several previous occasions.

"No offense, but in that case why are you always hanging out with us? We must bore you to death. Why aren't you out being gay? Far as I can tell the whole thing's more or less theoretical."

"Evan," Yvette protested.

"No," Will said. "It's a fair question."

"What I mean is," Evan went on, "you're a great guy and all. It's fun having you around. Always welcome and all that. But isn't it a waste of your time?"

"I don't understand," Will said.

"It just seems like you'd rather spend your time out looking for. . ."

"He can do whatever he wants, dude," Kirk said.

"Sure he can," Evan said. "Just trying to look out for him, right? And
sooner or later everybody wants to get laid."

* * *

"He didn't mean anything by it," Yvette said the next morning on their
way to classes. "He's a nice guy. Really."

"I know," Will said. "They both are."

"You and I have talked about it lots of times. How I'm the love-'em-and-
leave-'em type. Or at least I was until I met Kirk. And you're Mr. Stay at Home."

"Yes," Will agreed.

"It's only natural," she went on. "Those two take for granted that a handsome young law student should be getting lots of it. Whatever it consists of."

"I understand," Will said, though he was a little baffled by the *handsome*
part. "Believe me, I do. From their point of view I should be out on the chase
every night. Just like Evan himself."

"Well, maybe not just like Evan," Yvette said. "He's kind of an exceptional case."

"No kidding."

"But you could at least dip your toe into the water."

* * *

Evan Whitney was the kind of guy Will's mother hated on sight. In fact,
he was so good looking and charismatic that she probably would have hated him
blindfolded, presumably based on her sense of smell. Kirk was ridiculously
handsome, too, but Ruth Crawford would have overlooked that based on his
stupefying physique, which she would have labeled "musclebound" and "grotesque". That would have been enough to dispense with him. But Evan, though
broad shouldered and undoubtedly athletic, was close enough to her idea of how
a normal male was constructed that she'd have been free to turn the full power
of her critical eye on everything above his neck. And there, Will knew, she'd
have found more than enough to disapprove of. She might well have gone up
in flames from the heat of her enmity. He made his living modeling, for God's
sake.

Evan and Kirk were private school boys, having graduated from St. Dunstan's, which from what Will had been able to gather was a St. Cuthbert's clone located somewhere up in Marin. They had roomed together there and after that at USC. Despite their looks and athletic background no one could dismiss them as dummies. They were, unfortunately, exactly the kind of men Will dreamed about. Obsessively, it had to be admitted. Yes, they were the men of his dreams. There was no use denying it. Except for that one disqualifying factor.

The possibility that he might someday encounter their gay analogue was what kept him from committing suicide. At least that's what he told himself. The idea that such a paragon, once located, might actually return Will's interest was, he feared, as unlikely as glaciers reclaiming the Mohave Desert. It said something about the power of the survival instinct that he was still alive.

* * *

"We're not taking no for an answer," Evan said. "Are we, Kirk?"

"Um, no," Kirk said. "No, we're not."

They were both dressed to go out.

"But what's the question?" Will asked.

"So go pretty yourself up or whatever it is you gay guys do," Kirk said.

"And no dilly dallying," Evan said. "There's no time to waste."

"What are they talking about?" Will asked, turning to Yvette. "I mean, do you have any idea?"

"What does it sound like?" she smiled.

"Oh, no," Will said. "No, that's a terrible idea. The worst ever."

"Don't worry," Evan grinned. "It's going to hurt us a lot more than it's going to hurt you."

* * *

Will stumbled along between them, inhaling the mixed scent of their colognes. If this wasn't the most bizarre predicament he had ever been in he at least couldn't remember what had exceeded it. Being taken out to a gay bar by two straight guys wasn't the kind of thing he lay awake dreaming of. And these two—how in the world would it all end? They were nice enough, but he couldn't imagine them in a room full of gays without something terrible happening. In fact it seemed inevitable, given their overall gorgeousness, that some enormity or other would take place. And since he was the reason for this misbegotten expedition, he'd be held responsible for whatever resulted. What would happen if a drag queen asked Kirk to dance? What if somebody groped Evan in the men's room? What if chaos erupted and the police had to be called and all three of them got arrested?

* * *

"You see," Evan said, sipping his drink, "there's nothing frightening about the place. Right, Kirk?"

They'd been in the bar for well over an hour. Will had been to the men's room twice just for something to do. But insane as it seemed, Evan and Kirk were as happy as kids on a school field trip. They had taken to the place like fish to water. The pool might be unfamiliar but it was unquestionably wet. And apparently deep enough. Evan had already made friends with the drag queen who sat in state beside the jukebox, and Kirk had charmed the bartender into an astonishing degree of attentiveness.

"It's true," Kirk said. "Just guys hanging out drinking and shooting the bull. Isn't a bad way to spend an evening when you come right down to it."

"Except for the smoke," Will said, miming a cough. He was looking for any excuse for an early departure.

"You're just not used to it," Evan said. "You think this is bad, you should hang out with models. Those gals are worse smokers than nurses."

"I can't imagine," Kirk said, "why we didn't think of this sooner."

"That's right," Evan nodded. "If Will had just spoken up for himself, we'd have known."

"Really," Kirk said, "I can't think of a better Tuesday night place."

"Shoot a little pool," Evan said. "Play a game of darts. Makes a nice change from having to pretend to be interested in everything the girl wants to tell you about before she'll let you take her home. Might just have to make a regular thing of this. Right, Kirk? Keep you out of trouble with Yvette, too."

"Yes, indeed," Kirk said. "Not really what we're here for, though."

"Oops," Evan grinned. "That's right."

"Got to get to work," Kirk said. "Find Will a nice boy to kiss. What about that one over there? He's handsome, wouldn't you say?"

He was handsome. Will had to admit it. He'd been hoping they didn't notice him sneaking peeks.

"Good shoulders on him," Kirk continued. "Goes to the gym."

"He's been staring at you," Evan said.

"He's been staring at you," Will insisted.

"We'll never know who's right," Kirk said, "unless someone makes the first move."

"Shall I do the honors?" Evan asked.

"Don't you dare," Will muttered.

So that's how Will met Ronnie. Ronnie was great looking. Ronnie was funny. Ronnie was experienced, thank God, because Will hardly knew anything about what went on between guys once the lights went out, and it was great to get that part of it over with at long last. But apart from being a serviceable set of training wheels, Ronnie didn't have much to recommend him. It was a relief, really, when he dumped Will on the fifth date.

Will chalked it up to Ronnie's much talked about short attention span, which might even have been the truth.

About the time that fizzled out, Evan went off to Asia to model underwear, and in his absence Kirk and Yvette went through some sort of mysterious cooling off which left her mopey and at loose ends. That gave Will an excuse not to think about dating for several weeks.

* * *

"What happened with that Jim guy?" Kirk asked, mixing his protein shake.

"What?" Will asked, spreading cream cheese on his toast.

"That guy, Jim," Kirk repeated, several decibels louder.

"Didn't your mother ever teach you not to talk while the blender was running?"

"What did you say?" Kirk asked, turning it off. "You really shouldn't mumble. Bad habit for a lawyer, seems like."

"I'm sure," Will agreed.

"So," Kirk said, sitting down across from him. "That guy Jim. You two were all hot and heavy last I knew."

"Long story," Will said.

"Got all day," Kirk said.

Which was true. Now that he had finished college, Kirk didn't seem to do anything except go to the gym and figure out ingenious ways of spending the quarterly allowance from his trust fund. Not that Will was critical. He had to admit that the apartment had never been cleaner. And Kirk wasn't even living there. At least not officially. He and Evan had an apartment over on Russian Hill. But he wielded a mean dust mop. Among other implements.

"Evan said he ran into the two of you a couple of times. Told me you looked really tight. But you haven't mentioned him the last week or so."

"We're taking a time out," Will said.

Of course, it wasn't that simple. At first, Jim had seemed like Mr. Right. He was an attorney. He'd just passed the bar exam and gotten on with a firm that had offices on California Street. He drove a Saab and had an apartment in Cow Hollow. He'd read Will's books and liked them. They had similar politics and similar taste in clothes. They were compatible sexually from what Will could tell. And Jim had passed the Yvette and Kirk test with flying colors. Evan hadn't attended that dinner party—he was on a shoot in the Bahamas modeling swimwear. But he'd awarded his seal of approval a couple of weeks later when Will and Jim ran into him out dancing. He was with a matched pair of tall, busty blond girls, one of whom had actually been named Barbie.

Will even got to the point of leaving a spare toothbrush at Jim's place. That, it seemed to him, indicated that things were getting serious.

* * *

"The thing is," Jim said, sipping his herbal tea, "jeez, Will, I really don't know how to say this."

"Oh, come on. How bad can it be?"

Which, Will knew the moment it came out of his mouth, was probably the stupidest thing he could have said.

"See," Jim said. "That just makes it harder, you know?"

But Will didn't know.

"What does?"

"You sitting there being so reasonable. And looking at me like that."

"Looking at you how?"

"Those puppy dog eyes of yours."

Will couldn't imagine what he was talking about. Jim must be thinking of somebody else.

"I don't mean to do it."

"Of course you don't. But it always makes me want to fall for you," Jim said.

"Is there something wrong with that?"

"That's what I'm trying to tell you," Jim said. "God, I wish I could be more like you are. More sure of myself."

This was not how Will saw himself by any means.

"You're just so confident. Like you've got everything figured out."

"You know," Will said, sensing some sort of accusation in the air, "I may give that impression. But in actuality I'm not that squared away."

"Oh, it's not an impression," Jim said. "I see you with your friends. So at ease with them. So matter of fact about it. How I wish I could be that carefree about things. But I'm not sure I'm even gay, you know?"

"You're what?"

"You heard me," Jim said. "It's just so confusing. When we're together you make it seem so simple. But it isn't. Not for me. When we're apart I have all these doubts."

Will didn't know how to feel about it. If Jim had been telling the truth, Will was probably better off without him. Who needed a boyfriend with unresolved issues like those? But what if Jim hadn't been telling the truth? What if his "confusion" was just a convenient excuse? What if the real reason was that Will wasn't good looking enough, or charming enough, or interesting enough, or good enough in bed?

The list of his deficiencies grew longer each time he revisited it. He didn't dare talk to Yvette about it. She'd throw things at him.

* * *

"It's a shame," Kirk said, the next Sunday when the subject was discussed over brunch. "He seemed like such a nice guy. Those shoulders."

"Well," Yvette said, "if they can't find their way out of the closet, fuck 'em."

"I did," Will laughed, a little lightheaded.

"You know what I think?" Evan asked, grinning at Will in a way that gave him serious jitters.

"Tell us, please," Yvette said.

"I think Will can do a hell of a lot better than Jim."

* * *

"There's really only one cure for it," Evan said, running a hand through his luxuriant hair while scanning the bar. "Get right back on the horse. I'm afraid you've left it too long already. You really must tell your uncles the minute these things happen to you. No sulking quietly in your room. None of that licking your wounds stuff. Being dumped is like finding out you have cancer. The sooner you start treatment, the better your chance of a cure."

"Listen to him, Will," Kirk nodded. "He knows. We've both been there."

"Dumped," Evan nodded. "Thrown over. Ditched."

"Cheated on," Kirk said, "emotionally abused. Ignored."

"Taken for granted."

"Like I believe any of those things have happened to either of you," Will said.

"Taken advantage of," Evan repeated.

"All that stuff," Kirk nodded.

"And more," Evan said. "Much, much more. What about that one?"

"Good spot, dude," Kirk said. "Pecs on him are almost as big as yours. Bet he's a real good time."

"I thought we were trying to find someone for me," Will said.

"Ha, ha," Evan said. "See, we're cheering you up already."

"So, who's going in?" Kirk asked, setting down his drink.

His name was Chuck and his pectoral development was impressive. He wasn't much of a conversationalist, but, he assured Will, he was a great listener. After three dates Will decided he was the verbal equivalent of a black hole. Your words went into his ears but nothing came back out. No sympathy, no expression of interest, no reaction, even. But even that wouldn't necessarily have been a fatal flaw. It turned out that he was exclusively a bottom, and though Will tried his best to be accommodating he couldn't really see himself in the required role.

* * *

Outside the restaurant windows, gay San Francisco and its ancillaries trudged past on the teeming sidewalk. Will looked at his watch again. He held it up to his ear to listen just in case it had stopped. It hadn't. How long did one wait before facing facts? What would the etiquette books say?

"Will?"

He looked up. It was Evan, flanked by interchangeable brunettes. He seemed to be majoring in group activities these days. Behind the trio, a blond girl craned to see what they were all looking at.

"Oh, hi."

"Dining alone on Friday night?" Evan asked. "That's unusual."

"Looks like I've been stood up."

"Bob? Good old Bob stood you up?"

"Maybe not," Will said. "Maybe he's just unavoidably detained."

"How detained would that be?"

"One hour and thirty seven minutes," Will said looking at his watch in what he hoped was a convincing representation of disbelief, though the scene seemed dismally predictable.

"Oh, little one," Evan shook his head. "Even in gay that's too long. Well, it's certainly a good thing the girls and I happened by."

"Is it?"

"Saw you from outside. So down at the mouth. Can't have that. We'll join you for your belated meal. You don't mind, do you?"

"Suit yourself."

"Girls, have a seat. This is my very good buddy, Will, and somebody's just been mean to him. So we have our work cut out, cheering him up."

* * *

"I don't know what's wrong with the gay men of this city," Evan said at brunch the next Sunday, punctuating the thought with his fork, which had a hunk of cantaloupe impaled on it.

"It's a scandal, is what it is," Kirk agreed. "Calf development like that. And he still turned out to be a creep."

"He was wearing white after Labor Day," Will said, "as several habitués of our favorite watering hole took great pleasure pointing out. After the fact, that is. When it was too late for the insight to be of any practical use. But they found great significance in it."

"Doesn't signify, darling," Yvette said. "Bob's Australian. They celebrate Labor Day on the first of May."

"May is the dead of winter down there," Evan said. He had just returned from a photo shoot in Fiji, modeling fragrances. Will had had to have that one explained to him. "Did a layout for swimwear on Bondi Beach year before last. Nearly froze my tits off."

"Never you mind, darling," Yvette said. "Plenty more fish in the sea."

"And Jolly Roger here," Evan said squinting his left eye closed. "At your service. Keelhaul you a live one."

"Keelhaul," Kirk mused. "Is that some new thing you gay guys are doing? Sounds kind of kinky."

"Mostly it's wet," Evan said.

* * *

Tory, Will's friends agreed, was his best prospect yet. As the cousin of the roommate of two different girls Evan had dated, his pedigree was a known factor. Will wasn't so sure of the gang's assessment, but Tory's dark wavy hair was almost too glossy to credit and his laugh rumbled agreeably. Not that Will had a choice in the matter. He'd be giving it the old college try if only to keep Evan and Kirk at bay.

"You'll see, darling," Yvette promised. "Relationships go better in the fall. In the summer people are too distracted. They can't concentrate on you. The warm weather makes them restless."

"What warm weather?" Will asked. "I spent all June freezing to death, and July wasn't much warmer."

"It wasn't that bad."

"How would you know? You spent six weeks in the Caribbean with Kirk."

For Halloween, which was their third date, Tory and Will wore three piece business suits and told everyone they were Republicans.

* * *

"Now that's a turkey," Kirk said, setting it in the middle of the table.

Yvette had decreed a pot luck for the gang's first Thanksgiving together. Will contributed a green bean casserole. His mother detested green bean casserole, so he'd really had no choice of what to sign up for. Tory brought half a dozen pies. Yvette made stuffing, mashed potatoes, and a Waldorf salad. Evan brought half a dozen girls and a dozen number of bottles of wine.

* * *

Christmas Eve, Tory showed them all how to make a sumptuous seafood stew, which he said was traditional in his family.

"You never told me he cooks, darling," Yvette said.

"He cooks," Will grinned.

"When are you going to make an honest boy out of him?" Kirk asked.

Tory shrugged, blushing slightly.

"You already would have if there was a brain in that cute head of yours," Evan said.

* * *

New Year's Eve, Evan hosted them to dinner at a restaurant overlooking the bay. He was leaving the next morning for six weeks on the French Riviera, where he'd be shooting layouts for men's fashion lines.

"When I get back," he told Will, "I want to hear that you and Tory have moved in together."

* * *

"About our plans for Valentine's Day," Tory said.

"Uh huh?"

"Gosh, Will, this is really hard to say."

Will's heart fell.

* * *

"He says he loves me," Will said, "but he's not in love with me."

"What does that mean?" Kirk asked, looking baffled.

"It doesn't mean anything," Evan said. "It's just doubletalk."

"He thinks of me as a friend."

"No," Kirk said. "I think of you as a friend. He thinks of you as someone he's spent the last six months having sex with but isn't willing to commit to."

"It's not that simple," Yvette said.

"Of course it is," Evan said. "What are you, a girl?"

"As a matter of fact, yes."

"Sorry," Evan said, "forgot."

"Forgot she's a girl?" Will asked.

"Forgot she was in the room," Yvette complained. "And I reject the notion that Tory's a bad guy. Sometimes the chemistry just isn't there."

"If there's sex," Kirk said, "there's chemistry, believe me. That's how guys work. There was sex, wasn't there, Will?"

"Plenty."

"Good sex?"

"I thought so."

"And you were there so you should know," Kirk said. "Tory's just being chickenshit."

"It's his loss," Evan said, "entirely."

"Idiot," Kirk said.

"You can't really call him an idiot," Yvette disagreed. "He teaches microbiology at State."

"Fool, then," Evan said. "Hunky but ultimately clueless."

"Those deltoids," Kirk nodded. "Those trapezius. . .trapezii?"

"Listen to me, Will," Evan said. "You're handsome, smart, funny. . ."

"Trustworthy," Kirk said. "Considerate. . ."

"Patient," Evan said, "a great listener. . ."

"Well hung," Kirk said.

"Really?" Evan asked.

"Very impressive," Kirk nodded. "Almost as big as you."

"Well hung," Evan said, "and let's not forget, handsome. You will not get down in the dumps over that guy. We'll find you someone better."

"Maybe you should just let Will find a boyfriend for himself," Yvette suggested.

"We'd never stand in his way," Kirk agreed.

"Certainly not," Evan shook his head.

"But if we just happen to find Mr. Right, you don't mean we should just keep him under wraps, do you?"

It was Kirk at his most emphatic.

"We get closer every time," Evan said. "Don't we, Will?"

"Closer to what?" Will asked.

"Closer to our target, of course," Evan said. "Your ideal boyfriend. Mr. Right himself. But before this chapter of your life closes, Will, I would like to know what Tory uses on his hair to make it shiny like that."

* * *

Will found Jon himself. Evan was in Argentina modeling for jewelry layouts, and Kirk was preoccupied getting ready to compete in a bodybuilding contest. Contrary to his own expectations, Will just went out and did it. He had no idea how. He couldn't have explained it to save his life. Nor could he remember ever feeling more pleased with himself. Jon wasn't like anyone he had dated before. He was tall, for one thing. As tall as Kirk and Evan, while Will had been more or less eye to eye with his previous boyfriends. And Jon was a strawberry blond. Will had always been curious about strawberry blonds.

* * *

"He what?" Yvette gaped.

"He has a wife," Will said. "And an ex-wife."

"My God."

"He's going back to one or the other as soon as he figures out which."

"Fucking breeders," Evan said.

"You're a breeder," Will said.

"Right," Kirk nodded, "but guys like that give the rest of us a bad name."

"I can't believe it took him six months to figure all this out," Yvette said.

"Men forget about their wives all the time," Evan said. "And their ex-wives? Unless they're paying alimony or child support, it's like they never existed."

"I hate seeing you so miserable, darling," Yvette said, "but if that's the kind of man he was, good riddance."

"I suppose so," Will said.

"Never mind," Evan said. "Kirk and I are on the case."

"You know," Will said, "I think I need to take a break from all this."

"Perhaps you do, darling," Yvette said. "Clear your head. Get in touch with yourself. Take some time to gain perspective on all you've been through."

"I don't know," Evan said. "It sounds like giving up to me."

"Not really," Yvette said. "Just taking stock."

"You're sure you're not giving up, Will?" Evan asked.

"Don't worry," Kirk said. "Three of us won't let that happen."

"I really think it's best," Will said.

"You know," Kirk said, "I took a break like that once."

"You did?" Yvette looked shocked.

"I was on time out when I met you," Kirk said, "and look at us now. Fixing to get engaged."

"We are?" Yvette looked even more shocked.

* * *

"So how's the time out going?" Evan asked.

"I hate it," Will said.

"What's it been? Three months?"

"Four," Will said, "going on a decade."

"That bad," Evan nodded. "Well, you want Kirk and me to help out you only have to say the word."

* * *

"Man's a genius, of course," Uncle Harris said.

"Ned? Oh, undoubtedly," Will agreed.

"Mean to say—this flat."

The apartment Ned Westerleigh had found for Uncle Harris was amazing. There were swoon worthy views from every room. The original architectural details were not only exquisite but perfectly preserved. The wood burning fireplace was in working order. Will couldn't imagine a setting more appropriate for a man like his uncle. The California Street cable car was just close enough to be convenient but not so close that the rumbling and clanging of its passing would be obtrusive, and there was something comforting about having a cathedral in the vicinity, whether one thought of oneself as devout or not.

"Well, considering what good taste both of you have," Will said, "I shouldn't be surprised. But still, it's a little overwhelming."

"A very wise man once gave me some advice I've never forgotten," Uncle Harris said.

"Yes?"

"Always hold out for the very best."

"I see," Will said, taking a quick inventory of his uncle's wristwatch, shoes, ring, and haircut. He'd love to know if the advice was meant to apply to boyfriends, but couldn't bring himself to ask.

"One's made it a kind of watchword," Uncle Harris said.

But if you decided to apply Uncle Harris' credo to the hunt for the man of your dreams, weren't you risking ending up old and alone? As far as Will knew, neither his uncle nor the redoubtable Ned Westerleigh had managed to find a mate as yet.

* * *

"This is Sean," Kirk said.

Will had noticed him when the three of them first entered the bar. He was on top of a speaker box doing bodybuilding poses.

"He's from Canada," Evan said. "His brother is a Mountie."

"He was a Mountie himself," Kirk said.

"Briefly," Sean said, looking a little ill at ease.

"He goes to my gym," Kirk said.

"Funny," Evan said, "he goes to my gym."

"He goes to our gym," Kirk said, "And as you can see. . ."

And Will certainly could see, because Sean's gym shorts and sneakers constituted the entirety of his wardrobe.

". . .when he goes to the gym he really goes to the gym."

VII

"You want what?" Will asked.

"Relax, darling," Yvette said. "I'm not expecting you to wear a gown. I just have no patience with the whole bridesmaids thing. And I won't give my sisters and cousins the satisfaction. Kirk is going to have his best man by his side. I want mine."

"I can't imagine what your mother's going to think."

"Mummy loves you, darling."

"On principle, I mean."

"Well, yes," Yvette said. "Principle, as you put it. The principle in force at this time is, the de Havilland attorneys recently consulted with the Grossman attorneys and the outcome was highly satisfactory. It seems there's this interesting little trigger to the trust fund."

"Kirk told me," Will nodded.

"And Mummy is as mercenary a woman as you'll find in a month of Shabboses. When Uncle Mortie walks me down that aisle she'll be purring like a kitten. As long as Kirk's under the *chuppah*, she won't care who else is waiting for me there."

"Uncle Mortie's giving you away?"

"Pop's not invited," Yvette said, "unless he agrees to leave That Horrible Woman at home. And he won't. Obviously. So yes, Uncle Mortie."

"Oh, sweetie," Will said, "how awful for you not to have Pop there."

"You wouldn't say that if you'd seen the check he wrote us," Yvette said. "Trust me. Money can buy happiness—temporarily."

* * *

"You don't think that's weird?" Will asked. He wasn't completely certain Sean had heard his explanation of Yvette's request. Concise as he tried to make it, it might not register. He had noticed that Sean's attention always began to wander the minute Will opened his mouth.

"It doesn't matter what I think," Sean said, staring into the mirror.

Of course it mattered. But Will didn't say so. He was always walking on eggs with Sean. It was like one false move and he might disappear in a puff of smoke.

"That barber took too much off, dammit. I can't get it to lie down flat."

"It looks great," Will said. "Very masculine."

"Nobody's wearing it this short."

"They will be once they see you," Will assured him. Sean needed lots of assurance. With a face like that and eyes like that and hair like that and a body like that, Will couldn't understand why this would be so, or, for that matter, how it was even possible, but he was happy to oblige. He just wished that whatever he managed to stammer would someday be enough to do the job once and for all.

"Maybe there's something else I can use on it," Sean mused. "I'll ask some of the guys at the gym."

"Yes," Will said. "I would."

"You just said it looks great."

"It does, Sean," Will said. "That's not what I meant. Just for your own peace of mind, you know? Since it seems to bother you so much."

"As long as it doesn't have a strong scent," Sean said. "It always bothers me when hair products are too heavily scented."

Will supposed it went with the territory. You had a boyfriend as hot as Sean, this was what you put up with. It only made sense that a guy who looked like that would have a lot invested in his appearance.

"Yvette knows what she wants." Sean said. "Everybody gets that. So just relax. It'll be easier in the long run to go along with her."

"You're probably right."

"It's actually kind of a cute idea."

"Do you think so?"

"It doesn't matter what I think," Sean said. "But yes, cute."

"Well, good," Will said.

"You know, I've been thinking," Sean said.

Will's ears pricked up. This might be his cue. He was continuously on the alert for signs of commitment on Sean's part.

"Yes?"

"All the guys at the gym are getting tattoos," Sean said.

* * *

Will's eyes swam. Yvette had insisted it would be a mistake cramming for finals and the bar exam simultaneously. He was determined to prove her wrong, but as Kirk had warned him, the flesh was weak. Between Sean's unpredictable timetable and Yvette's distraction over the wedding, he hardly seemed to get anything done. And finals were due to start in just over a week.

"You look beat."

"Evan," Will looked up from his notes. "I didn't know you were back in town."

"Leaving again tonight," Evan said, sitting down across the table from him. He usually didn't frequent establishments like this. Or even this part of town. "Won't be back until just before the big day."

"Where to this time?"

"Zimbabwe," Evan said. "Which my agent informs me is in Africa."

"It is," Will said. "Used to be called Rhodesia."

"How long ago?" Evan asked.

"Pretty recently."

"No wonder I couldn't find it on my globe."

"Really."

"I thought it was because Africa is so small on my globe," Evan mused.

"What's the shoot?"

"Italian sports car thing," Evan shrugged.

"You'll look great behind the wheel."

"Tell me something, Will."

"Yes?"

"Who do you know that drives naked?"

"Nobody."

"Right," Evan nodded. "That's what I was thinking. Money's great. No problem there. Just seems strange."

"I've never been to Italy," Will said. "Perhaps nude driving is the thing over there."

"Perhaps," Evan said. "Listen, should I be worried?"

"I don't think so. Yvette and Kirk seem fine to me."

"Not them," Evan frowned. "You, dummy."

"Me?"

"Thing with Sean," Evan said. "Heard he's seeing other people. Not just gossip—Kirk told me there have been sightings."

"He always has been," Will said. "From the first. He was real up front about it."

"You O.K. with that?"

"Last I knew," Will said, "you were the world champion at seeing lots of people at once. Why the concern all of a sudden?"

"Those are just women," Evan said. "You're my buddy."

"I'm trying to be O.K. with it."

"Don't try too hard," Evan said.

* * *

"So here's the plan," Kirk said. "My grandparents have a house on Aruba. Beachfront property."

"I know," Will said. "I've seen pictures, remember?"

"Right after the wedding—I mean right after, you know? Redeye to Miami directly from the reception and on to the island the next morning."

"Yes."

"You and Evan, see? He's been there lots. He knows how to talk to the staff and everything. Then, after a spending a few nights at an undisclosed location, Yvette and I will join you there. It's going to be so great. Just the four of us. Sun, sand, seafood. Two weeks. Can you swing that?"

"I'm not starting my job until July first. Apparently the city has no money to pay me any sooner than that."

"Perfect."

Except it wasn't really. Because Will didn't see how leaving Sean on his own for that long could possibly be a good idea. Will would be out of sight and out of mind.

* * *

All of Will's classmates, Yvette included, were planning to take time off between graduation and the bar exam. But he wanted the test over with. Pass or fail, he had to put it behind him so he could concentrate on things with Sean. And if he didn't pass this time, he'd know what to study for next time. That had been the plan.

Now that he was checking back over his answers, he felt relieved. He'd made the right choice. The exam didn't seem that bad. Perhaps it was because he wasn't sure he cared one way or other. Or maybe he just hadn't been paying close enough attention. At any rate, it had been easier than he'd expected. He closed the test booklet.

Yvette had multiple job offers from major firms. Firms whose names listed long strings of WASP sounding partners and ended with "and somebody Jewish", firms with prestigious addresses in tall buildings, firms that did work for major corporations and extremely wealthy families. Will hadn't gotten any offers like that despite the fact that his class ranking was slightly higher than hers. He hadn't gotten any offers at all, though he'd been to plenty of interviews. Apparently, he didn't interview well. This was not a surprise. He had always suspected that when the time came he'd interview like the failed poet he was. There was only one thing to do. "No, darling," Yvette had insisted. "Don't go into the public defender's office. Standing up for the oppressed is such a cliché nowadays. It's becoming almost chic. Go into the prosecutor's office instead. Nobody wants that job. They're all afraid people will think they're fascists. Think about it. Ingratiate yourself with the police, some of whom, incidentally, are extremely hot. It'll be a fantastic opportunity. You can subvert the entire department from within. You'll be by far the best looking boy there and get all kinds of dates and drive Sean out of his mind with jealousy." Except for the part about Sean, it sounded like good advice. Making Sean jealous seemed about as realistic a goal as building an igloo in the Sahara. Will had barely gotten in the door for his interview before they offered him the job. And they didn't blink at his request to have a few weeks off before starting. At first he thought it was because of how impressed with him they were. But it turned out to have something to do with their fiscal year.

The best thing about it was how angry Pa was at the news. Will had been expected to come back to Philadelphia and join a firm there. This was never mentioned, of course. He was supposed to get it by osmosis. "It's about that poetry of yours, isn't it?" Pa fumed. "That stupid poetry. You believe you find inspiration in that Babylon by the Pacific. I thought you were starting to take adult life seriously. And now this."

The fact was, though he'd never tell Pa this, he hadn't written so much as a line in over two years. That chapter of his life was apparently over.

* * *

"So what do you think of the place?" Will asked.

"It doesn't matter what I think," Sean answered from the bathroom.

Will stuck his head through the doorway. Sean had taken his shirt off and was staring at himself in the mirror. Will supposed that if he were built like Sean he'd spend lots of time doing the same thing.

"Of course it matters what you think," Will insisted. "That's why I brought you here. To get your opinion. Something wrong with your nipple?"

"Guy at the gym got one of his pierced."

"What?"

"Pierced," Sean said.

"I'm not sure what you're talking about."

"Like a pierced ear," Sean said.

"No," Will said, "a nipple is nothing like an ear."

"Same principle, though," Sean said. "You end up with a ring or something like that stuck through it. Guy at the gym has a barbell."

"I had no idea anything like that existed."

"Supposed to enhance the sensation in it," Sean said, fondling himself absentmindedly.

Will couldn't imagine Sean's nipples needing their sensation enhanced, said anatomical features apparently being, in his case, hard wired to his cock. Touching one or the other of them had an effect similar to when a fighter pilot turned on his afterburner. More than once, sensing that Sean's attention might be wandering, Will had given the left one—the more sensitive of the two—a little tweak and they were off to the races.

"Well," Will said, "I think it's a terrific apartment. Lots of room. Lots of privacy. Nice neighborhood."

"Thank God."

"I don't understand why you dislike Haight Ashbury so much."

"It's the most pointless neighborhood in the city. It used to be cool, but now it's nothing but tourists and aging hippies. The Summer of Love was over a decade ago."

Will didn't know whether this was Sean's authentic take or just something he had heard from one of his hyper fashionable friends. He could never be sure who he was hearing when Sean said something. Will secretly hoped to be adopted by the gang Sean ran with, but so far there was no sign.

"So what do you think?" Sean asked.

"About what?"

"Should I get my nipple pierced?"

Will almost said, "it doesn't matter what I think, Sean," but thought better of it. It would probably sound catty. There were a couple of really catty guys in Sean's gang and Will knew he didn't approve of them. Will stared at Sean's nipple, trying to formulate a response.

"Won't it hurt?" Will asked.

"I'm sure," Sean nodded. "When they first do it, it's bound to be painful."

That did it. Will imagined the scene, Sean lying on his back bare-chested, his arms spread, his full, smoothly shaven pecs satiny in the light from overhead, waiting as the sharp instrument was prepared—really, Sean's pecs were his best feature. And that was saying something.

* * *

"Can't tell you how proud," Uncle Harris said, releasing Will from what seemed an unusually fervent hug. They'd just gotten to his building. Will had picked him up at the airport in Yvette's LeCar, which he hadn't stalled once. This was a record and seemed particularly auspicious given the significance of his passenger.

Uncle Harris just got better looking, Will thought. He wasn't a particular fan of older men, but Uncle Harris was an exceptional case. He might be in his late thirties, but he could pass for ten years younger. If Will could just figure out how to look like that, he thought, his worries about Sean would be a thing of the past.

"Really," Uncle Harris continued, "one always has such hopes for the succeeding generation. Generally unfulfilled, unfortunately. But in your case, young Will. . ."

"That's a pretty heavy responsibility to take on," Will said. "Not sure I'm up to it."

"Hogwash."

"I've always been able to depend on you for encouragement."

"One certainly hopes so. Now please promise you'll keep your pecker up, so to speak. Deep breaths, all that. Ruth and Dougal. Arriving late tonight. Suite at the Fairmount. Rental car. Whole production. Know those two aren't your favorite people."

"Mom and Dad aren't so bad," Will admitted.

"At a safe distance, no," Uncle Harris said. "Dougal suggested we meet them for brunch before the ceremony. Talked them out of it. Too hectic, one insisted. Really, one didn't want them spooking you on your big day."

"Spooking me? I'm not a horse."

"Well, dampening your mood."

"At this point," Will said, "what are they going to say? I'm graduating with honors from law school. If that's not enough to make them happy, and I strongly suspect it won't be, it's their problem, not mine."

"That's the spirit. Meet them afterward. MacWhirter's place."

"That'll be a scene," Will laughed. "Noel Coward by way of Berthold Brecht."

"Kind of thing," Uncle Harris laughed. "Plenty of opportunity to abuse you there. Ruth always prefers to do that in front of witnesses."

"Right."

"And then the wedding on Saturday evening. Enough togetherness for one weekend, one feels."

"More than enough."

"One's thrilled to attend. And honored. Big fan of both of them. Have to say: not sure why Ruth and Dougal are invited."

"Because they were going to be in town anyway," Will said. "Seemed the only thing. Tried to talk Yvette out of it. Her mother insisted. The de Havillands have invited thousands, it seems. Kirk described it as equivalent to the population of a small town. And Mrs. Grossman was glad to have reinforcements."

"As long as no one felt obligated."

"Rest assured."

"Ruth especially baffled, you ken?"

"I'm sure. Bridesmaid but not the bride," Will said.

"Kind of thing," Uncle Harris smiled. "One's other nephews were expected to have provided a grandchild or two long since."

"Just one more thing she'll never forgive me for, I suppose," Will said.

"Never is a very long time."

"No, really," Will said. "She's not the kind of woman to change. And as for me, it's no phase."

"Never thought," Uncle Harris said. "Still, one does have to ask. One has friends who have—no, one can't say they actually changed. More they made certain accommodations. Certainly don't appear to be happy about having done it. Stayed married all the same. Path of least resistance. Child or two apiece. One has several godsons, actually. Delightful young chaps. Apparently one's chums thought it would simplify things just to go along."

"Did it?"

"One's never asked. Shockingly Bad Form even to allude to certain things. One's supposed to have forgotten anything and everything that chanced to happen prior to the joyous nuptials."

"I suppose."

"But you mark my words," Uncle Harris said, "nothing simpler than being who one really is. Nothing more satisfying, either. One's own experience—no hypotheticals, what?"

"Yes."

"Still, don't let them get to you," Uncle Harris said. "Pater and Mater, you know. The old P. and M. Grisly at the best of times. One knows what it's like to feel unappreciated. Not the end of the world."

"Of course not."

"Free for dinner this p.m., young Will?"

"Kept the whole evening open for you."

"Most gratifying. One wishes one had more nephews of your sort."

"Too kind."

"Not to say one's disappointed with things as they are. Quite the contrary, in fact. Eminently satisfactory."

* * *

"Darling, is there time, do you think, for me to slip off to the euphemism?"

"Do you really need to?"

Yvette crossed her eyes.

"All right," Will said, "I'll save your place inside if you don't get back before the processional."

"Stupid Mummy," Yvette said. "She would insist on champagne at brunch. As if there's not going to be enough drinking the next little while. Always goes right through me. She knows that, the silly cow."

"Go," Will said, "don't waste time talking about your mother."

"Speaking critically about Mummy is never a waste of time," Yvette said over her shoulder. "Thought you'd have realized that by now."

Will felt himself sweating inside his academic gown. Underneath the funereal garment he was wearing dress pants, white shirt, tie. He'd followed the dress guidelines to the letter, only to arrive that morning for the ceremony and find that no one else, literally no one, had done so. Now they were all comfortable and he was roasting. There was a lesson for you. The same one, apparently, that he continually failed to learn.

"Everyone quiet, please," a bullhorn squawked. "The dean would like to say a word."

"Wonder what word it will be," Joey Steinberg muttered.

"If only," Will grinned at him.

"Just once," Joey said, "I wish somebody actually would, you know? Say only one word."

"Sssh, you two," Alice Watson hissed.

"And so," the dean droned, "no matter where your journeys chance to take you, may you never forget all that this place has done for you."

"Or where you keep your checkbook," Joey whispered.

"Not to mention your ballpoint," Will chuckled.

"What did I miss?" Yvette asked, huffing.

"Not a damn thing," Joey said.

"Except these two cutting up," Alice complained.

"Cutting up?" Yvette asked. "The very idea. And without me."

Finally, the line began to move.

* * *

"Congratulations, young man," Forbes MacWhirter said, motioning him through the doorway.

"Thanks."

"The others are already here."

The spaniels capered at his feet, and he almost tripped. He always seemed to lose his footing around his godfather.

"There's our boy now," Uncle Harris exclaimed.

"Come sit by me, dear," his mother said. She and her hairdresser had selected something a couple of shades redder than Will was accustomed to seeing on her. It was really rather strident. He wasn't sure it suited her. But, he thought, it was only fair to give members of the public an indication of the essential volatility of her nature before they discovered it by accident. Considering how accident prone she was.

He kissed her cheek and made a safe landing on Forbes' sofa.

"Really proud of you, son," his father said with what passed on that face for a cheery grin. "Quite proud, I must say."

It wasn't the greeting he'd expected. Not by a long shot. He'd been bracing himself for something terse. Perhaps even trenchant. He hadn't graduated head of the class by any means, and there was his new job ripe for criticism. But his father had obviously been drinking. You had to hand it to Forbes. He stocked the most expensive liquor on the planet. Pa's condition wasn't such a surprise now that Will thought about it. Pa always had to stay good and drunk to tolerate the presence of his old buddy, Forbes.

"Yes, dear," Mom said. "We certainly are. Very, very proud of you."

So she'd been drinking, too. All the better.

"Get you a cocktail, young man?" Forbes offered.

"No thanks," Will said. "Just need to catch my breath for a minute."

"I should think so, too," Forbes said. "Your uncle has just been filling us in on the whirlwind that is your life of late. The bar exam yesterday, graduation this morning, Miss Grossman's wedding tomorrow. I don't remember having that much energy when I was your age."

"Well, I do," Mom said. "I certainly do. And dear Dougal running himself ragged trying to keep up with you. I thought I'd never get his attention for long enough that he could propose to me."

"Speaking of weddings," Forbes said. "Anything looming on that front for you, young man?"

Will could hardly believe he'd heard the question. Out of the corner of his eye he saw the sour expression on Uncle Harris' face.

"Not at the moment," he said.

"No hurry, of course," Forbes said, perhaps sensing Will's discomfort, perhaps merely oblivious to his *faux pas*. "Just that a dashing young attorney like you can't lack for opportunities. Simply not possible."

Dashing? For a moment Will wasn't certain he hadn't expressed his incredulity aloud.

"I'm sure he doesn't," Dad said, walking over to the bar to freshen his drink. "No son of mine would. His brothers were both married virtually the minute they finished university. Barely held it off that long, those two."

"And Will's certainly as eligible as either of them," Forbes agreed.

"Eligible," Mom said, "I'll give you eligible. Handsome, considerate, intelligent, artistic, and an attorney. I don't know what's wrong with the women of this city. My boy is far more eligible than most of the young men one comes in contact with these days. He's positively a catch."

"Mom," Will protested.

"Will, dear, I don't know why you always squirm like that when you're being complimented."

"I've noticed that about him, Ruth," Forbes said. "Even when he was a little boy it made him uncomfortable to be praised. I've never for the life of me been able to understand it."

"He's like Harris that way," Pa said.

"Oh, I don't know that I think he's very much like Harris," Mom said. "You always say that, dear, but I've never seen it."

Even Forbes seemed aware that this comparison was problematic.

"Speaking of the wedding, Will," he said, "I assume you have plans later this evening. That's why I made the dinner reservation for four only."

Will was tempted to lie, but with Uncle Harris in the room he couldn't bring himself to.

"Actually, I'm not seeing any of the wedding party tonight."

"No?" Forbes raised an eyebrow. "I'm astonished. When a de Havilland gets married this whole city practically grinds to a halt. I can't believe there's not a major do planned. I hope there's not a problem about you know what."

"None at all," Will said. "As it happens, Kirk has a Jewish great-grandmother on his father's side."

"Really?"

"A Rothschild," Uncle Harris nodded.

"Thank God," Forbes said, though it wasn't clear if it was because the specter of anti-semitism had been dispelled or simply that the name Rothschild had been invoked. "But now—tonight?"

"Yes, dear," Mom said. "Surely there's a function of some sort. You mustn't miss it on our account."

What she meant, of course, was that she'd be thrilled to tell her friends that he'd skipped an affair thrown by the de Havillands in preference to spending time with his mother. And Will couldn't give her that satisfaction.

"I'm not invited."

"How dare they snub you like that?" she fumed.

"It's not about me, really," Will said. "Mrs. de Havilland disapproves of the wedding arrangements, is all."

"You mean?"

"Yes," Will said. "I'm afraid so."

"Well, I certainly don't blame her for that. It's a stupid idea, I must say. Somebody needs to spank that girl. Just because she's the bride doesn't give her the right to do such a thing."

"Such a thing" meant dashing the hopes of dozens of young women that they might get to be bridesmaids at an event which should by all rights have been the wedding of the year, considering the ramifications of Kirk's family.

"I only hope it won't make my dear boy here look too ridiculous. Still, it doesn't seem fair to take it out on him."

* * *

Will spent several minutes circling the block looking for parking. He wasn't fond of driving Yvette's LeCar. Its bright yellow finish seemed awfully extroverted for a vehicle so underpowered it could hardly get out of its own way. San Francisco's hills were a constant threat to its survival. Whenever he drove it, Will thought of a dinghy braving a tropical storm. The one thing he appreciated about the car was how easy it was to park if you were ever fortunate enough to locate a space. When he finally found one, it was right behind Evan's Austin-Healey.

To his further surprise, Will found Evan perched on the front steps.

"Lost your key?" Will asked.

"Thought I'd wait out here to see if anybody showed up."

It was extremely uncharacteristic of Evan not to have made himself at home.

"When did you get in?"

"A while ago."

"How was it?"

"Great money," Evan said, following him into the foyer and up the stairs. "Kind of boring."

Evan didn't usually get bored. Evan generally kept other people from being bored. Evan invariably mentioned the girls he had met. Will supposed he must be jet lagged.

"How was graduation?"

"Great money," Will said, opening the front door of the apartment. "Or at least the prospect of it. But kind of boring."

"Ha, ha," Evan said, plopping down on the sofa. "Very funny. And after the ceremony?"

"Came back here for a nap. Ended up oversleeping. Did some laundry for the trip. Cocktails with my godfather and my parents. Then I went out."

"With Sean?"

"Well, I was hoping to run into him. Somehow I kept showing up at places he'd just left."

"You two didn't have plans?"

"Not firm ones. I wasn't sure how soon I'd be able to get away from my parents."

"Yes," Evan nodded, closing his eyes, "that's always an unpredictable kind of thing."

"You want anything to drink?"

"I'm fine," Evan said. "Listen, don't let yourself be too bummed about missing the shindig this evening."

"I'm not."

"It isn't personal, you know. Mrs. D.H. gets these bees in her bonnet every now and then. I could tell you stories. Kicked the Governor of California out of one of her pool parties because she didn't like his shoes. I was there. I saw it. She didn't give him a chance to take them off, just told him to leave. When he ran for re-election, she hosted a fundraiser and no harm done. Raised half a million for his re-election campaign. So you're in good company. And Kirk was furious when he heard you'd been left out. You'll always be family to him."

"I know that," Will said. "I just feel bad that Yvette and her mother-in-law-to-be are already mixing it up. I should have turned down that gig and made her rustle up some bridesmaids."

"Don't be silly. It if hadn't been that, they'd have tangled over something else," Evan said. "Those two will spend the next fifty years fighting like alley cats. And they'll love every minute of it."

"You'd know that better than me."

"Trust me. They're practically the same person. You know the dynamic that sets up."

"You're not one of those guys who believe in the theory that all men marry their mothers, are you?"

"I don't know, am I?" Evan pondered. "In that case, I guess you'd have to marry someone like your father."

"I might as well just kill myself right now," Will said. "You sure you don't want anything?"

"No," Evan said. "Don't let me keep you up. I'm just going to sit here for a while."

"All right," Will said. "See you tomorrow."

* * *

When he got up the next morning, Will noticed that the sofa had been slept on. Other than that, there was no sign of Evan.

"By all means, darling," Yvette yawned, "head off to your brunch. And give my love to Ned and Uncle Harris. I'm so happy they'll be at the wedding."

"I feel bad deserting you."

"Any minute now Mummy's going to show up. Or the dressmaker. Or the hairdresser. Or the makeup girl. Or—I don't know who else there even is. Somebody, that's for certain. You'd better get out while you still can."

"I love you, you know."

"I do know, Will darling."

* * *

Ned Westerleigh lived in the penthouse of one of the tallest buildings on the tallest hill in the city. Prior to Will's first visit, Uncle Harris had warned him about admiring the view, but he didn't need to be coached. It was still one of the seven wonders of his world. The housekeeper had set brunch up out on the roof garden. The morning was overcast, but the view managed to be dazzling nevertheless.

"So, young man," Ned said, pouring him a mimosa, "all graduated."

"I suppose,"

"Still ambivalent about your choice of profession?"

"Pa's choice of my profession."

"Know the story," Ned said. "As a younger son of a younger son, you understand."

"But I thought your father held a title," Will said.

"He did," Ned nodded, "but only after his older brother died childless. It wasn't until I was serving in World War II that my father succeeded. My brothers and I grew up without any expectations at all. Aristocratic but penniless, just like a brood of sisters in some silly Victorian novel. Papa had made elaborate plans for each of us. Maurice was to marry an American heiress, Arthur was to enter the church and eventually become Archbishop of Canterbury—that sort of thing."

"And you were supposed to come to the colonies and sell real estate?" Will asked.

"Something very like that," Ned smiled.

"Different world, eh?" Uncle Harris smiled.

"You know, Will, a law degree needn't be a life sentence," Ned said. "You can always go back into literature if you choose. And as to your new position, well, I believe you'll find that in this country at least, the flash boys who go into those top firms always pay a price for it. Meanwhile, look who ends up on the bench."

"Who?"

"Men who started out in the prosecutor's office," Uncle Harris said. "Imagine how Dougal will feel when you're the youngest ever judge on the California Supreme Court."

"I don't think that's very likely," Will said.

"Well, when I look at you, Will," Ned smiled, "I see a man in a black robe handing down sentences. Stiff ones."

* * *

In any other company, Yvette's family would have been the rich ones. Her mother's people were Park Avenue furriers, her father was a neurosurgeon, Uncle Mortie was the biggest produce wholesaler in the Midwest. That Horrible Woman, despite Mrs. Grossman's complaints about gold diggers, made a comfortable living selling high end Manhattan real estate. But the de Havillands eclipsed all that by a wide margin. The run up to the wedding had been, among other things, a crash course in Kirk's pedigree and financial ramifications. This was highly illuminating. That Rothschild was far from the only prominent name that featured. There were Roosevelts, there were Morgans, there were Vanderbilts, there was a lone Rockefeller, and, farther back, there were the names of great European houses.

"It's like a Kennedy wedding," one of the ushers gushed.

"Bite your tongue," Evan snapped, "those *nouveaux riches* wouldn't get a foot in the door at a function like this."

Evan should know, Will thought. His own background was almost equally rarified.

"You look great tonight, Will," Evan said, staring into the washroom mirror next to his.

"Thanks," Will gulped.

"Really," Evan nodded. "Extremely cute. Sweep Sean right off his feet."

* * *

Will had been on the point of inviting Sean to the wedding as his date. But as so often seemed to happen when Sean was involved, events overtook him. By the time Will worked up the nerve, Kirk had asked a bunch of his gym buddies to usher, and Sean was on that roster. There had been some concern about how such a crew would look spiffed up in formal wear. Mrs. de Havilland had even used the term "roughnecks". But Kirk's tailors knew exactly how to cut those tuxes. Sean and company were spectacular, if a little bulky. Will had previously met all but one of them.

"This is Bo," Sean smiled.

Bo was the largest of the bunch. Without actually seeing the two of them side by side Will couldn't be certain, but it was just possible that Bo was even larger than Kirk, something that hardly seemed possible. He was ridiculously handsome, and when he spoke he sounded like a long haul French truckdriver.

"Very nice to meet you," Will said, determined not to wince at the pressure of his handshake.

"*Enchante*," the giant smiled.

There was something familiar about the way he smelled. It took Will a moment to identify it as the scent of the stuff Sean had recently started using on his hair. He looked more closely, and sure enough, Bo's do was under ruthless control and sported that same high shine. Will wondered if underneath Bo's formal wear one of his nipples was pierced. He decided he didn't really want to know.

* * *

Coming up the aisle on the arm of Uncle Mortie, Yvette was ravishing if not exactly herself. Will anticipated much hilarity when they all sat down together to look at the wedding photos.

Just as the couple took their places under the chuppah, Will happened to glance at Evan. From his expression, he might as easily have been standing at the side of a grave. He sensed Will's eyes on him and snapped immediately back into character.

* * *

The Episcopal bishop and the rabbi were old friends, it turned out. Will had met them both "backstage" and almost laughed out loud at the way they finished each other's sentences. They were apparently old hands at these functions. They made short work of it. A wedding that couldn't begin until after sundown on a Saturday in June couldn't last long without causing an unreasonable delay to the reception.

* * *

"Will," Stan Grossman greeted him.

"Dr. Grossman."

"Great to see you."

"You, too."

"You remember Alicia."

"Of course. How are you?"

"You were the handsomest bridesmaid I've ever seen," she laughed, kissing his cheek. "I'm so proud of my stepdaughter."

"Not a word about this to Brenda," Dr. Grossman grinned. "Don't want you implicated."

"Mum's the word."

* * *

Will had never seen Kirk so drunk. He had never seen Evan so quiet. In an evening strangely packed with false notes, these were the most glaring.

* * *

"Your father and I are leaving, dear," Will's mother greeted him. "We have a very early flight tomorrow. Sorry we couldn't spend more time with you."

"You weren't too mortified by the proceedings, I hope."

"It was actually rather sweet," Mom admitted, "and you looked so handsome up there."

"Mom, you're not tearing up."

"Something in my eye, dear," she laughed. "Nothing to concern yourself with."

* * *

"Will, honey," Mrs. Grossman said. "What a wonderful wedding. Thanks for everything you did to keep my baby on track. I'm not sure I ever expected to see this day."

"She made a lovely bride," Will said.

"Didn't she just? I told her and told her that gown was a big mistake. And then the minute I saw her coming down the aisle, I knew how wrong I had been. Thanks for talking me through it."

"I really didn't do anything," Will said.

"And it was so nice of your parents to attend. They're such lovely people. Truly lovely. It's no surprise, of course, because look at you, dear. Anyway, please make sure to let them know how much Yvette's Grannie and I appreciate it."

"They had a wonderful time."

"They must be so proud of you, Will," Mrs. Grossman said. "I know I certainly wish Yvette's brothers were more like you."

"Be careful what you wish for," Will said.

"Oh, you're such a wit."

* * *

"How the hell did you pull that one off?" Will asked.

"You know I don't take no for an answer, darling," Yvette grinned. "I just promised Mummy not to invite them and then turned around and did. After swearing them to silence. I knew that when the time came, she'd be too distracted even to notice they were here. As long as we were reasonably discreet, at least."

"Typical Yvette," Kirk said. "The master manipulator."

"And thank God I am," Yvette laughed. "It's the only way everybody wins."

* * *

"Real panache," Uncle Harris beamed, shaking his hand. "Carried it off. Grand style."

"Sorry not to have had more time with you."

"In town for several weeks, young Will," Uncle Harris said. "May still be here when you get back from the honeymoon."

"Hope so," Will said.

"We should go change," Evan said. "It's almost time to leave for the airport."

The hulking Bo followed them into the men's room

"He's taking our tuxes back for us," Evan said. "And driving us to the airport."

Will noticed that smell again.

* * *

"Have a good time in Jamaica," Sean said.

"Aruba."

"Right."

"I'd send you a postcard, but I have no idea where you'll be staying after Monday."

"No sweat," Sean said

"We'll get together when I get back."

"Sure," Sean said. "Call me."

But how was he to manage that? This was the problem with boyfriends of no fixed address and no permanent place of employment. Keeping track of them was maddening. Will couldn't bring himself to mention it. He thought of this predicament as an indictment against him. Men like Kirk and Evan never found themselves stymied in such a manner. And it wasn't because they were straight. They had some power he lacked. They got what they wanted. He leaned in for a kiss and got Sean's cheek instead of his mouth. He couldn't be sure it was an accident and didn't dare make a second attempt.

* * *

"I've never flown first class before," Will said. His seat seemed as roomy as an armchair at his grandfather's club.

"I always do," Evan said. "It's in my contract. And before you say anything about how spoiled I am, there's a very good reason for it. If I'm not able to rest on the flight I don't look my best when I land. Looking spectacular on arrival is my bread and butter. Simple as that. I make no apologies for it."

"No," Will said. "I get it. In your case it's a business expense."

"Better looking flight attendants, too," Evan said.

"Are those a business expense as well? No, forget I asked that."

"What a dirty mind you have." Evan laughed.

* * *

"Did she tell you?" Will asked, once they were in the air and it seemed that they weren't going to crash right away.

"He did," Evan said. "I can't believe it."

"Me, either," Will said. "I knew something was up, but I had no idea what it could be."

"I mean, I know it's what people do," Evan said. "Get married. Have children. Kirk's always talked about wanting to be a dad. It's—I can't explain it, really. It's like until now the whole thing didn't seem real. They've just been play acting or something. I guess that's probably more about me than it is about them."

"No," Will said, "I know what you mean. I felt the same way. When she told me, I was so stunned by it that I almost couldn't act excited. God knows what she thought."

"I wouldn't worry about that," Evan said. "They're excited enough about it, I don't think they've even registered our reactions."

"She does seem remarkably off balance," Will said. "All during planning for the wedding I was waiting for her to go off the rails and she didn't. It's like now she's making up for lost time."

"They're talking about two godfathers instead of a godfather and godmother."

"Mrs. D.H. will have kittens," Will said. "Again."

Contrary to his expectations, Will slept on the flight. He dreamed about Sean. In his dream, he and Sean weren't just a couple of guys who got together every few days for sex. In his dream they were real, honest to goodness boy-friends. In his dream, Sean said, "I love you, Will."

When Will woke up, Evan grinned and said, "I'm not even going to ask."

IX

"You're in luck, Mr. Crawford," the chief clerk said. "There was a resignation on Nick Romanovsky's team just last week. Looks like you're taking that slot. I know you originally interviewed with Amy DeAngelis, but apparently Nick won the toss instead. You'll like him. He's a real guy's guy."

Will had no idea what to make of that last statement. Amy DeAngelis had reminded him of Yvette, and he'd spent the last several weeks in happy anticipation of working with someone who could be a friend as well as a colleague. But "a real guy's guy"? He had visions of loud, tasteless ties with cigarette ash clinging to them, thinning hair in an unfashionable cut, and having to pretend he cared about football. He almost resigned on the spot. But a job was a job. And quitting would have required explanations to everyone he knew. Actually, a different one to everyone he knew. It would be far too much work.

"He'll be in court most of the day today," the clerk said, "so why don't I show you to your office? You can start getting yourself organized, at least."

* * *

"Will Crawford, huh?"

"Yes, Mr. Romanovsky."

Nick Romanovsky wasn't at all what Will had been expecting—a burned out hack with bad taste in clothes and questionable hygiene. He was a blond, powerful looking giant, a sort of grown up Kirk with a mustache, and he was dressed like a guy in a full page advertisement for suits in *Gentlemen's Quarterly*. Will had spent the day anticipating all kinds of difficulties associated with his new position but the possibility that he might end up having a crush on his boss was nowhere on the list. He squirmed involuntarily in his chair.

"Name's Nick," he grunted, staring at Will's file like it might be something toxic. Or at least incriminating. "Mr. Romanovsky is my dad."

"Nick."

"What made you want to join the prosecutor's office?"

"Well," Will said, weighing the risk. "Mostly, I think I wanted to piss off my family."

"What's that?"

Nick riveted him with piercing blue eyes.

"Say," he said, "I know you."

"I don't think so," Will said, baffled.

"Sure I do. You hang with that pack of twinkies that follows Christopher Melendez-Greene everywhere."

What this said about Will's new boss was both astounding and fascinating.

"Not exactly," Will said.

"What's that mean?"

"Guess you'd say I never quite made the cut," Will said, feeling himself start to blush.

"No?" Nick said.

"It wasn't really about joining their club," Will elaborated. "More just a particular guy I'm, well, interested in."

"Huh," Nick nodded. "Well, you'd better get one thing straight—if you'll pardon the term. You won't be able to handle this job and keep up with that crew."

"Never expected to," Will said.

"All right," Nick said. "Suppose you tell me some more about pissing off your family."

* * *

By the end of his first week in the prosecutor's office, Will knew he owed Yvette big time for advising him to apply there. It wasn't like law school at all. And it wasn't like the work his father and brothers did in their firms. It wasn't dull and soul destroying by any stretch of the imagination. He had been in meetings with hot police officers, with slimy, stereotypical defense attorneys, some of them hot, too, but in a different way than the cops, and with creepy and sometimes frightening defendants. Yvette would have insisted it was like a television series. Uncle Harris, on the other hand, would have said it was like opera, and Will supposed that was as apt a description as any. Opera by some Russian social realist composer terrified of being sent to Siberia.

The proof of his unexpected satisfaction was that all through that week he found himself composing poems at odd times during the day. His legal pads were full of marginalia that looked to him like drafts for his next published collection. It was too soon to tell if any of this new work was good. But the fact of its existence amazed him. He began to think of coming to work in the prosecutor's office as occasioning some kind of artistic rebirth. He seemed to recall Uncle Harris predicting it.

When he wasn't in court, Nick Romanovsky stalked the hallways of the department like a titan. The story about him was that he'd been promoted to Assistant City Attorney faster than anyone else in the history of the office, and it wasn't hard to see why. His charisma and his dynamism were prodigious. His intellect was staggering. The imposing physique and dazzling good looks were just a bonus.

Where, Will wondered, were the guys his own age of that quality? Then he thought of Sean and felt guilty at this disloyal sentiment.

* * *

Nevada Beige or Navaho White? Will simply had to repaint his new apartment before moving in but couldn't decide on colors. Or much of anything else. Fiestawear or that cute Romanian pottery he'd seen at Cost Plus? Oriental rugs, or just bare hardwood floors? Solid color bed linens or patterns?

Everything had to be perfect. Eventually Sean was going to resurface. And when he came over, the apartment had to be part of Will's renewed sales pitch.

* * *

"Will, darling," Yvette's voice came over the telephone, "we're finally back."

"Welcome home."

"I can't believe it's been three weeks since we've seen each other. Do you realize that's the longest we've ever been separated?"

"Actually, it's not," Will said. "You two spent six weeks down there on one of your earlier trips."

"Did we?"

"You did."

"Well, this time felt longer than any of the others."

Will thought this was a strange sentiment for a newlywed to express but didn't point it out. The time seemed to him to have flown past. That's what happened, he supposed, when you spent all your time obsessing over a guy. You lost track of the things and people that were really important to you.

* * *

"Still here?" Nick Romanovsky grunted from the doorway to Will's office. He made it sound like an accusation.

"Just wanted to read through a couple more briefs before I went home."

"Seven o'clock on a Friday," Nick said. "Last one here. Haven't had enough yet?"

"I must have lost track of time."

"If you're not careful, you'll give the department a good name. Come on, I'm buying you a drink."

* * *

"Sean Eastman, huh?" Nick said, sipping his club soda. "I must say, I admire your taste. But he seems like he'd be a pretty tough nut to crack."

This was gratifying and dismaying at the same time. And how did Nick know Sean's last name? Will hadn't even known Sean's last name until hearing Nick say it just then. How futile that made the whole thing seem, a half assed little affair with a guy he knew no better than that.

"Let's drink a toast," Nick suggested. "To the chase."

* * *

After weeks of humiliating himself in his search for Sean and right when he was on the point of giving up for good, there he was one evening in a bar Will had just discovered around the corner from his new apartment. Will told himself it was kismet. And when Sean smiled and actually allowed himself to be kissed briefly on the mouth in greeting, Will felt his cup running over.

* * *

"I think I liked that other place better," Sean said. "You know. The one you showed me a while back."

"I thought you didn't like it."

"I don't think I said that," Sean said. "Did I?"

"I guess not," Will admitted. "You just didn't seem very enthusiastic."

"That place had better views," Sean said. "Didn't it?'

"I suppose."

"Guy at the gym was talking about views the other day. He said it's particularly important to look for a place with good views."

Will tried his best not to take this implied criticism to heart, but it really felt like being back at square one.

* * *

"What the?" Will asked, astonished.

"A couple of the guys at the gym did this," Sean said, "as kind of an experiment. Makes your junk look bigger."

As a matter of fact it did, not that Sean's junk needed any help.

"Isn't it tricky?" Will asked. "Shaving down there? You could give yourself a nasty cut."

"You get the hang of it," Sean said. "It's really starting to catch on. Every time I'm in the showers at the gym, I notice more guys have started doing it."

"It must itch like hell when you get stubbly."

"You have to do it regularly enough so that doesn't become a problem."

Will wondered if he was expected to adopt the practice himself now that Sean had endorsed it so highly. He wasn't sure how he'd incorporate it into his regimen without killing himself.

* * *

"All right, everyone," Nick said, "that about wraps things up. Thanks for meeting on such short notice. Will Crawford, please don't leave. I need to speak to you."

The others wasted no time exiting the tiny conference room. The fresh paint fumes were overpowering, and Nick, though charismatic, had conducted the session in a particularly intimidating manner. Will wondered if he was about to be fired.

"What's up?" Will said.

"Doodling all during the meeting is what," Nick said.

"Sorry," Will said, "didn't mean anything by it."

"Hand that pad over, please,"

"It's just notes over the meeting, really."

"And marginalia, I see."

"I'm sorry," Will said, "I didn't know it would be a problem."

"It's not," Nick said, "just made me curious, is all."

"I see."

"Right," Nick said, after scanning a couple of pages. "Are those iambic hexameters?"

"I'm not really good at them yet. I mostly do free verse."

"Ned Westerleigh told me about you."

* * *

Yvette's office had a view of California Street. Seven stories down Will could see cable cars gliding silently up and down the hill. His own office didn't have a view of anything. It was in a basement. He tried not to let himself think of the contrast between his setting and Yvette's as a metaphor for their radically different career trajectories. As long as he was actually at work, he loved his job. But at times like this he came close to convincing himself that other people thought of him as a failure. His brother had said as much last week when Will called him on his birthday.

"Darling, I know," Yvette said, grinning sheepishly. "I'm the most awful sellout. I can hardly look at myself in the mirror."

"Don't be silly," Will said. "You deserve the success. You worked harder than anyone in our class."

"I don't deserve it at all," she shook her head, "but it's sweet of you to say so."

"So where would you like to go for lunch?"

"Actually," Yvette said, "lunch has come to us. We have a person here who comes around each morning and takes lunch orders. Can you believe it?"

"Really," Will said. "What did I order?"

"Barbecue pork fried rice, Mongolian beef, General Tso's chicken, Taste of Three Ingredients. And some spare ribs."

"All your favorites," Will lauged.

"You know, I haven't had decent Chinese since that night a week before the wedding. That crazy night when you and Kirk and Evan serenaded me right there on Union Square. It was like being in a movie. I felt like Audrey Hepburn."

"Does Chinese food agree with junior?" Will asked.

"We'll find out," Yvette said, picking up her phone. "Darling Mrs. Lee, Yvette de Havilland here. My guest has arrived and we're ready for lunch. Yes, thanks so much."

"I'm impressed," Will said.

"You've seen me order lunch before," Yvette said.

"Well, yes," Will said, "but not on such a high floor."

"Incidentally, you'll be happy to know that Evan is flourishing."

"I'm sure."

"We spent three days in Nice with him just before coming back to the States. The women, Will. Eating out of his hand, they were."

"I know," Will said. "I'm sure it was even worse than on Aruba."

"It was," Yvette nodded. "Far, far worse."

"That's Evan for you."

"I know he's as shallow as they come, but you have to admit he's always been a good friend to Kirk."

"No question about it," Will said.

"Still, sometimes I despair of him, you know. I mean, now that Kirk and I are married and getting ready for the baby to come, it's really time for him to think about settling down. But what kind of girl wants to take on a bad boy like that?"

"Any kind, I'd think," Will said.

"That's just the problem, isn't it? It's too easy for him. All the women in the world to choose from and not a discriminating bone in his body from what one can tell. He's a tragedy waiting to happen. He'll marry the very worst girl imaginable and spend the rest of his life paying the price. It's exactly what happened to Daddy."

"That Horrible Woman isn't so bad," Will said.

"Not talking about her," Yvette said. "He got lucky there. I'm talking about the one before her. And the two before that."

"I see,"

' "Ah, there you are, Mrs. Lee, come in, come in. This is my best friend in the whole world, Will Crawford. He's with the Public Prosecutor's office."

Mrs. Lee was not the grandmotherly figure Will had envisioned, but a glamorous thirty-two year old in a three hundred dollar suit.

"Happy to meet you, Will."

"Pleasure's all mine," Will said.

"Just let me clear some space on this desk," Yvette said. "By the by, how are things with Sean?"

"About the same," Will said. Admitting how little progress he'd made felt like a personal failure. "He's just moved into his own apartment. That seems like a good sign. At least he can commit to a six month lease. I'm supposed to be going over to see it soon."

* * *

"First of all," Nick said, "this is not a formal performance review. The two of you need to understand that before we go any farther. I just called you in so we can have a casual discussion about how you feel you're doing at the end of your first two months here in the prosecutor's office. Until your bar exam results come in I have to sign off on all your work. And our bosses expect me to supervise you closely. They get nervous unless they know I'm meeting with you regularly and not just saying 'hi' when I happen to run into you in the corridor."

"Fine," Angelina said.

"Suits me," Will said.

Angelina Suarez-Carrasco was from New Jersey by way of Stanford Law. She graduated high in her class and was then recruited by the kind of firms that had hired Yvette. She'd opted for prosecutions as the first rung of the ladder she envisioned taking her to the United States Senate. In other words, she had more than enough drive and ambition for the two of them. Will let her go first. He always did. He'd figured that out his second day working next door to her.

"I've got four cases in preparation for court dates," she said. "Four."

Will knew she had repeated the number to emphasize the fact that Will currently had no cases in preparation for trial. It was like a tennis player shouting the score each time she won a point.

"Excellent, Angelina," Nick said. "Everyone here recognizes how hard you work. Preparing cases for trial is extremely difficult and time consuming work and you're to be commended for your dedication. Now, Will, how about you?"

"No cases in preparation."

"None?" Nick asked. "Really? None at all?"

Will saw the gleam in Nick's eye and sensed that his gamble was paying off.

"That's right," Will said. "None. But eleven dispositions so far. And another seven pending."

"Actually," Nick said, "twelve dispositions and another six pending. But you may not have seen the paperwork on *People vs. Murray*, since it came in just before I headed downstairs. Nice work, Will."

Next to him, Will could feel Angelina seething.

"Seriously. You're to be congratulated," Nick said.

"Thanks."

"I don't see why," Angelina said. "All he does is cut deals. That's not practicing law. It's like hosting that stupid game show."

"It's called plea bargaining," Nick said, "and I don't suppose they think very highly of it at Stanford Law. They certainly hated it where I attended. But the taxpayers of this state hold it in high regard, whether they know it or not. Would you like to know why?"

Angelina glowered.

"Your four cases going to trial, Angelina, might not result in a single conviction. In a court trial you always run the risk of an acquittal. Will, on the other hand, has sent six defendants to prison and six others are either on probation or received suspended sentences. A one hundred per cent conviction rate, in other words. The name of the game show isn't 'Let's Make a Deal,' as you suggest, but 'A Bird in the Hand.' In each case, Will got a clear admission of guilt for the record and he saved boatloads of money by keeping the cases from going to trial. It's not elegant, by the book practice, but it's cost effective and fast. It's results."

"All I know," Angelina said, "is I'd be ashamed to practice law that way."

"Perhaps you would," Nick said. "It's certainly not the way I used to think about law. Will, why don't you describe your background to Angelina?"

"My background?"

"What does that have to do with anything?" Angelina asked.

"Go ahead, Will," Nick said.

"Well, my father is an attorney—he'd tell you he's a very prominent one. My grandfather is eighty-three years old and he still takes cases occasionally. My great-grandfather was a justice on the Pennsylvania Supreme Court, and he literally died in his chambers one afternoon during a brief recess. It was an appeal of a homicide conviction. Then there's my mother's family. . ."

"I think we get the picture," Nick said.

"Gee, Will," Angelina said, "how proud of you they'd all be."

"Well, they should be," Nick said, "because he's doing the people's business effectively and efficiently. With the work load we handle around here, we simply can't afford to have you going about it the way you are, Angelina. When you've been around for a few years, you'll be assigned the kinds of cases that require the approach you're taking. Cases that are important enough to warrant taking to trial. But for right now, I need you to consider taking a page from Will's book."

"So why all the talk about his illustrious family of lawyers?"

"Because they inform his work here. Don't they, Will?"

"That's right," Will said, smiling back at Nick. "Every time I get a new case, I spend a few moments thinking about how all of them would handle it. And I do the opposite."

X

Sean was probably a lost cause. Will's trip to the Caribbean had interrupted his pursuit of Sean at what was apparently a critical stage. On his return, Sean was nowhere to be found, and when he finally resurfaced he seemed barely to have noticed Will's absence, which seemed like a grave setback. Will's efforts in the eight weeks since then had been fruitless. The best that could be said was that with San Francisco's version of summer now at its peak, Sean's deltoids were on more or less permanent display. The part of Sean that might have made him consent to becoming Will's actual boyfriend was as elusive as ever.

Will was beginning to suspect, however, that the whole thing had been a fool's errand from the start. Sean's physical perfection hadn't lost its appeal by any means. If anything, it hadn't yet reached its apogee. And Sean's personality, what there was of it, was pleasing enough. He was obviously well educated, though Will knew none of the details. He was unfailingly considerate, if easily distracted. But there were other things about him that gave Will pause. Things that had probably doomed the project before he ever embarked on it. Willing something to be so can't make it so if fate has turned its thumbs down. And as hard as Will tried to master his own bourgeois conditioning, he had to admit that a guy who performed in live sex shows, however sporadically, might not be the best possible marriage prospect. Facts that hadn't been faced remained facts.

Despite that, Will was seriously contemplating a last ditch effort that Friday evening when the buzzer sounded. Hoping against hope, he dashed across the room and pressed the button.

"Yes."

"Will?"

It wasn't Sean, and for a moment Will considered concealing his identity and pretending that the party downstairs had pressed the wrong button. For a moment. He knew people did such things, but he wasn't one of them.

"Yes."

"It's Evan. Can I come up?"

Of all people. Will was surprised Evan knew where he lived. It was no secret, of course. But Evan had been out of the country when Will moved in. His sudden arrival meant that he must have asked. And Will couldn't imagine Evan bothering.

"I'm buzzing you in."

* * *

It was simply wrong for a man to look that good eating penne primavera, Will thought. The play of muscles under the hairless skin of the forearms was inspirational, as was the shine of candlelight off the smooth, glossy hair. The eyes were downright dangerous. Evan was the worst kind of straight guy—beautiful and flirtatious. He was just back from a stint in Paris and Milan, where it had been his job to look exactly that miraculous wearing designer clothing or merely posing as an accessory for a young woman who was. Getting paid, and paid ridiculous sums, because of how you looked seemed to Will to be a sort of validation just short of divine. But the future of Evan's modeling career was in some doubt. He had finally logged enough hours in the gym that he had outgrown the high fashion ideal to a degree that there was no longer any possible fudging it. Those shoulders seemed substantially more impressive than Will recalled from even a few weeks previously. Evan's agent was said to be suicidal over the size of them.

Evan alluded to none of this over dinner. Will knew about it from brunch with Yvette and Kirk the previous Sunday, at which he'd been miserable—hung over from the night before and desolate at the turn his relations with Sean had taken. Yvette noticed but didn't say anything. Kirk was strangely oblivious. Will assumed Kirk's oblivion was intentional, some newly raised defense against knowing too much about his wife's homosexual best friend. This was, of course, totally out of character. Will hadn't expected getting married to change Kirk that much, but there was no question about it. Kirk was guarded these days, almost like a stranger. He'd been like that ever since Yvette and he returned from their honeymoon. In addition to gossip about Evan's modeling, there had been talk that morning about his new job. Someone was opening a nightclub "for ladies only" which would feature young men performing exotic dance routines and stripping down to g-strings. Kirk had auditioned as well but wasn't hired. He was "muscle bound". He insisted that he had only gone to the auditions to give Evan moral support, but Will sensed that he was truly miffed at the rejection, though he expressed enthusiasm at Evan's success.

Tonight, Evan's conversation during the meal was prosaic, mostly about parties he had missed while out of the country which Will wouldn't have been invited to and wouldn't have attended in any case. The gulf between straight and gay seemed to widen daily, and Will no longer harbored any illusions about straddling it. He had reached the point where it didn't seem like much of a loss, being more or less superfluous to the entire heterosexual world.

"We should get our desserts to go," Evan suggested when the waiter arrived with the special, hand written cards that emphasized the restaurant's old world charm.

"Oh?"

"Let's take them back to your place," Evan said. "We'll have coffee. We'll talk."

It seemed bizarre that looking and smelling like that Evan had nothing of greater moment on his agenda than coffee and dessert at the cramped apartment of a frustrated, lonely homosexual of no more than average looks and little discernable charm. This was hardly an objection Will felt prepared to raise, however, so he simply asked for his favorite cheesecake with dark chocolate mini-chunks.

* * *

It had been a long week. Will was still new enough at his job to find it exhausting. Nick Romanovsky was not only the stuff of wet dreams, he was the sternest of taskmasters. Every night Will came home feeling like his head was about to explode if some other part of him didn't first. And there was still the matter of that party later that he was kind of—almost—invited to that Sean was almost certainly seriously considering the possibility of may-be dropping by. If entertaining Evan didn't prolong itself unduly, Will still should be able to make it. That's what he thought about on the short ride back to his place.

He knew he was supposed to be impressed with Evan's new car. The Austin-Healey was a thing of the past. Kirk had explained repeatedly that this was an extremely special variety of Alfa-Romeo, one not available in North America through official channels, very fast and exotic. Will seemed to re-member that a minor tuneup was supposed to cost something on the wrong side of a thousand dollars. Indeed, everything about Evan implied high maintenance costs. Will had grown up around enough money that he didn't find such ex-travagance intimidating, merely imprudent.

What he couldn't help noting was Evan's sexy, unselfconscious manner at the controls. He flicked up and down through the gears like a racing driver. He didn't wrestle with the wheel, he almost caressed it. Will could all too easily imagine him exhibiting the same serene flair on the back of a polo pony, at the tiller of a racing yacht, or in bed with a young woman of the European aristoc-racy. In that respect, Evan was much like Will's two first cousins, Hamish and Colin, though ironically it was Uncle Harris, the lavender sheep of the family, who most exemplified the type.

* * *

"A man who's serious about coffee," Evan grinned, as Will got the beans out of the freezer compartment, the grinder out of the cabinet, the gold plated filter insert—guaranteed for life—out of a drawer. "Except I recently spent two weeks in the Caribbean with you, and you never touched a drop."

Will had been hoping Evan didn't remember this. How could this display appear anything but pathetic? Will, fully equipped to serve gourmet coffee brewed using the finest implements in the unlikely event anyone ever spent the night under his roof.

"If you don't mind," Evan said, "I'll handle this. You go put on some music."

"It's for when I entertain," Will explained, mortified at how lame he knew he sounded.

"You've been hosting parties and not inviting me? Not sure what to make of that."

Evan's grin was an offensive weapon, Will reminded himself for the thousandth time. And time was ticking away. Even now, Sean was probably in his tiny bathroom—Will had been in the apartment exactly once since Sean moved in three weeks ago, one inconclusive time—painstakingly shaving his chest in preparation for whatever his evening was to bring. Will put Ravel's *Bolero* on the turntable—not loud, but loud enough. If that music wasn't enough to scare off a straight guy, Will was out of tactics.

"That's *Bolero*," Evan called from the kitchen. "I love *Bolero*."

* * *

"Damn, I make a fine cup of coffee," Evan said into the awkward silence when the record ended. "How's that Fresca?"

"A particularly good vintage," Will quipped.

"Glad to hear it. Should we have our desserts now?"

"I'll get them," Will said.

"And another cup for me, please."

Will went into the kitchen. He rifled through a stack of Fiesta bread plates for just the right colors. Music crashed on in the living room. Rachmaninoff's Second Symphony, of all things.

"You have to let me borrow this record," Evan called. "Mine got broken."

"How do you break an LP?"

"Frisbee accident."

Will decided that a request for further explanation would only heighten the absurdity. He got out forks and napkins, refilled Evan's coffee mug, loaded the tray and went back out. In his absence from the room, Evan's powder blue pullover had been removed, neatly folded, and draped over one arm of the sofa. The a-shirt he had on underneath shone unnaturally white against his deep tan. On him, the skimpy thing hardly seemed like a garment at all, just the implication of one.

"Warm in here," Evan said. "Hope you don't mind."

* * *

"That place makes the best desserts," Evan said, licking the tines of his fork. "And believe me, I know. When you only get dessert once every couple of months, you have to make it count."

"Right."

"Why haven't I ever seen your apartment before?"

"I don't know. I haven't been in it that long. I'm barely unpacked."

"You've had Yvette and Kirk over."

"A couple of times," Will admitted. "You're out of town a lot."

"That's true," Evan mused. His tone indicated a concern that the explanation might be more complex than that, but only a slight one.

And of course, his suspicions were right on the mark. It wouldn't have occurred to Will to invite Evan over. It wouldn't have occurred to Will that Evan would be the least bit interested in this or any other apartment he occupied.

"You're here now," Will pointed out.

"I am," Evan nodded. "The bathroom?"

"That way," Will said, wincing inwardly at the condition of his towels. He had meant to get out clean ones before leaving for the party in the almost unimaginable event that Sean agreed to come home with him. "You can't miss it."

"Don't go anywhere," Evan grinned.

But what if he did? Just get up and slip out while Evan was in the bathroom. What could be simpler, really? There was still just about enough time. But he was dressed all wrong for the party. His teeth weren't brushed, and God knew what his hair looked like. And what on earth would Evan make of it if he up and disappeared from his own apartment? He'd certainly say something about it to Yvette and Kirk. There would have to be an explanation, and there was no telling what kind of awkwardness he'd face the next time he encountered Evan.

Not even that threat would have been enough to dissuade him if he hadn't already been feeling more than a little trepidation. What if there was a repeat of last week's performance? Or something even worse? Sean's gang had achieved no little notoriety over the past several months for their performances. But until last weekend those had entailed nothing more outré than some dancing, naked horseplay, and pretend wrestling. It was all good fun, and they were certainly hot enough guys that no onlooker could have objected to their hijinks. But last weekend the host was Christopher Melendez-Greene himself, he of the outrageous reputation, so Will shouldn't have been surprised at the no holds barred turn things took, with Sean splayed in an X on the platform, his wrists shackled but his legs left free. It was an arresting image, muscular, powerful looking Sean laid out like that, and Will couldn't help but be a little titillated at his implied vulnerability. But that was just the beginning. What followed was Sean's ravishment by a succession of bodybuilders, each one larger and more impressive than the last, and finishing with that Bo character Will had met at Yvette and Kirk's wedding, an absolute giant even larger than Kirk himself. Will still hadn't gotten over his revulsion at the sight of Sean being used like that. He had always though of Sean as a serious top, and there he was to all intents and purposes being gang raped and begging each of those guys to give it to him more and harder, appearing to glory in being dominated and brutalized.

Even if they had only been acting, it hinted at something inside Sean Will couldn't understand and wasn't sure he wanted to.

* * *

It really was like a straight guy to show up unannounced and expect the evening to revolve around him. Will listened to the flush and then the sound of water running in the basin. A moment later, Evan emerged. Will wasn't absolutely certain, but Evan's hair looked freshly combed. And Will thought he caught a whiff of mouthwash. Surely these preparations pointed to an imminent departure.

"You know," Evan said, "this isn't a bad little place you have. Yvette says you're embarrassed by it, but you shouldn't be. The location is fantastic. And the building has loads of character. You could make it really nice with a little effort."

"Thanks, I think," Will said. "You must have a better imagination than I do."

"Just a different perspective," Evan said. "Could I have a glass of water?"

"Sure."

"No, don't get up. I'm familiar with the layout of your kitchen."

He returned a moment later carrying a tumbler decorated with the image of Donald Duck, a bonus gift from some long forgotten fast food purchase.

"Looks like I found where you keep the good china and crystal," Evan laughed.

"God, no," Will moaned. "You opened the wrong cabinet."

"Or the right one. I always suspected you of having a silly streak. Yvette insists that you do. Now I know."

"Please," Will said, "let me get you another glass."

"Not on your life," Evan said. "In France, as a matter of fact, they're crazy about *Le Donald*. You know, you're extremely cute when you blush."

Which only made Will blush more intensely.

"I have a confession to make," Evan said, riveting him suddenly with cerulean eyes.

"Oh?" Will gulped.

"I kind of have a crush on you."

"You what?"

"The whole time we were in Aruba I could hardly keep my hands off you. You must have noticed."

Will had noticed no such thing. And he'd been all but incapable of keeping his eyes off Evan. What he had noticed was Evan's hands all over Kirk, and vice versa. So much so that he'd had to bite his tongue more or less continuously to keep from mentioning it to Yvette. It was her honeymoon, after all. Not the time to engage in the kind of speculations what he was witnessing brought to mind. Yes, that was definitely what he had noticed while they were in Aruba.

"But, I. . .I mean. . .you're straight."

"I am?" Evan laughed. "That'll come as a surprise to all my ex-boyfriends."

"Huh?" Will had spent over two years hearing in minute detail all about Evan's dozens of conquests. But there had never been the least indication that the girls weren't girls or had been otherwise fictitious. He felt like he was being pulled beyond the looking glass.

"Don't tell me you fell for that straight guy routine," Evan laughed. "I mean I know Kirk and I were laying it on pretty thick, but surely Will, a guy as smart as you must have seen through it."

"I don't. . ." Will stammered

"I've discussed this with Yvette and Kirk, you know. They think we'd make a terrific couple."

"Is that why you're here?" Will asked, "because they think we'd make a terrific couple?"

"Of course not, you goof. I'm here because I'm crazy about you and I decided it was time to do something about it."

Will frantically groped for some argument to refute this. He called upon all his legal training and experience, but it was too late. Before he got another word out, he was in Evan's arms and no longer capable of rational thought.

Cooper Luxemberg:
May, 1979

"Good morning. I have Fausto Villanueva on the line for Cooper Luxemberg."

Bella Steinberg's father was so rich and important that his administrative assistant had his own secretary. With his pale, flawless skin, dark, soulful eyes, and sleek, "latin lover" hair, Fausto might look like a star of Mexican television, but Cooper knew better than to underestimate a man with an M.B.A. from Wharton and a law degree from Yale. Fausto had grown up in a wealthy Puerto Rican enclave north of Manhattan, so he and Cooper shared an accent.

"This is Cooper."

"One moment."

"Cooper, good morning."

"Morning, Fausto. To what do I owe the pleasure?"

"Sol would like to do lunch. This week, if possible."

"Let me check my calendar," Cooper said. He knew he was open at midday all week, but it didn't hurt to give the impression that his affairs were more complicated than that. "Fausto, how does Thursday sound?"

"We'll make it work. My secretary will call when we know where we're meeting you."

* * *

Sol Steinberg began his pitch the moment their drink orders had been taken.

"Let's talk about this house Bella wants you to find for her."

"I was surprised when she called," Cooper said. "I thought she was happy with her apartment."

"She is," Sol affirmed. "You did a great job getting it for her. But her mother and I raised her to—well, I know it's not fashionable to speak in these terms nowadays, but somebody has to be realistic. The thing is, she'll never really be happy as anything but a wife and mother. She loves her work at the gallery, of course. But she's thinking more and more of settling down. I know the two of you have discussed her plans."

There it was. Cooper hadn't expected it to come into the open so quickly. But Sol had never been the type to waste time.

"Not discussed, exactly," Cooper said. "Mostly she talks and I listen."

"Yes," Sol nodded. "She talks and you listen, but what is it you think you hear?"

"The same thing you do, I expect," Cooper said.

"Exactly," Sol nodded.

Out of the corner of his eye, Cooper saw Fausto's intent expression. He seemed more interested in the scene than Cooper would have expected.

"Tell me," Sol said. "How would you describe my daughter, Cooper? Would you say she's beautiful?"

"No question about it," Cooper said.

"Intelligent? Charming? Fun to be around?"

"All those things," Cooper agreed.

"Then I'm afraid I don't understand the difficulty."

"Sol," Cooper said, "I want you to know I've always been completely honest with Bella."

"I suppose you're referring to your homosexuality."

"I am," Cooper said.

"I have to say I fail to understand what that has to do with my daughter's interest in marrying you."

"Just about everything, I would have thought," Cooper said.

"And you'd be wrong," Sol said. "My sex life never got in the way of my wife's happiness. Estelle is far too sensible a woman to let it. Our arrangement has worked beautifully for over thirty years now."

"Your arrangement?" Cooper asked. Sol couldn't be saying what it sounded like.

"That's right," Sol nodded. "You don't think I keep Fausto so close to me due to constant concerns I might suddenly need legal advice, do you? You don't think it's his M.B.A. that keeps me warm at night? No. Arrangements like Estelle and I have make the world go around. Marriage would hardly be possible without them. Only mistake I made was buying a property without a guest house. I hate having to troop clear over to Fausto's place several nights a week in all sorts of weather. Bella's not going to make that mistake. You hear that, Cooper? A property with a guest house so you can keep your amours ready to hand. I insist on it. You, your boyfriend, and Bella will all thank me."

"Duly noted," Cooper said. He noticed that Fausto wasn't smiling.

"Very well," Sol said. "Now I'm leaving. Fausto will fill you in on the terms of the settlement I'm proposing while the two of you have a nice lunch."

* * *

"I had no idea," Cooper said, squeezing lemon juice over his grilled sole.

"You and I don't move in the same circles," Fausto said. "It's not much of a secret, really."

He had ordered a shrimp cocktail and a caesar salad.

"How long have you two been an item?"

"It depends on how you count it," Fausto said. "When we first met, I was a junior in college. Then I went on directly to Wharton and Yale Law. We'd been 'together' for seven years when I moved to San Francisco eight years ago, but in all that time we'd only actually spent the equivalent of a few weeks in each other's company."

"You moved here to be near him?"

"It was our agreement," Fausto said. "That story Sol tells about my rich parents is a load of bullshit. I grew up in Hell's Kitchen. I put myself through college waiting tables and turning tricks. That's how Sol met me. He liked me and he decided he wanted to make things easy for me."

"So you stay with him out of gratitude?"

"Certainly I'm grateful," Fausto said. "Graduate school and law school paid for? A high paying job? My apartment on Nob Hill? That's a lot to be grateful for."

"Sure," Cooper said.

"He continues to be generous," Fausto said. "In addition, he gives me a reasonable amount of freedom. He allows me my diversions."

* * *

Two hundred fifty thousand to be placed in a trust the day after Bella and Cooper's wedding. The capital to be Cooper's free and clear the day of their fifth anniversary. Another hundred thousand to be paid Cooper on the birth of each child. Cooper wasn't in the least tempted, but he couldn't help being impressed at the lengths the Sol Steinbergs was willing to go to in ensuring Bella's happiness.

"Does Bella know about this offer?" Cooper asked.

"No," Fausto said. "And Sol would appreciate it if you don't tell her."

"Of course I won't," Cooper said. He'd never get rid of her if she knew about the kind of money involved. She'd hold a gun on him if necessary. "One more question, though."

"What's that?"

"Does she know about you and Sol?"

"I don't think so. She's pretty sure he has someone on the side. But she envisions more of a Barbie doll."

"Right."

II

"I wouldn't be your friend," Big Steve said, "if I wasn't honest with you."

Around them, the gym was as busy as it ever got.

"Understood," Cooper said.

"It's been over a year since the Western States," Big Steve said.

"Right."

"You're bigger and more ripped than you were then. You came back from that contest and started working harder than ever."

"I'm glad it shows," Cooper said. He couldn't think of a more meaningful affirmation than praise from this idol and mentor.

"Point is," Big Steve said, "you're ready to enter a national level contest."

Cooper had been waiting a long time to hear that.

"The guy who beat you last year just won his first national level title," Big Steve continued. "Not sure he would have come in first if you'd been there."

"You're serious," Cooper said.

"You know me," Big Steve smiled. "I only bullshit with people I don't take seriously."

"So you think I should make definite plans for next season."

"Didn't say that," Big Steve said. "I'm giving you information, not advice. It's your call. If you decide to go for it, it will mean working out harder and dieting more strictly than you ever have."

"You're not sure I can do it."

"Don't put words in my mouth," Big Steve frowned. "I know you can do it. I wouldn't be discussing it with you otherwise. What I don't know about is your priorities. Maybe a high placing in a national contest isn't the most important goal for you right now. Maybe your focus belongs somewhere else. Your career, for instance. Maybe a better time for this conversation would be next year. I don't know that. All I know is you're ready to take the next step."

* * *

"The thing is," Cooper said, "I'm kind of seeing someone."

It had been a couple of weeks since that surreal lunch. He'd met Fausto tonight at his second favorite bar, which, it turned out, was Fausto's second favorite bar as well. Cooper was surprised that they'd never run into each other there.

"Boyfriend, huh?"

It wasn't exactly true. He never went home from the bars alone unless he wanted to. And he'd been seeing Kent off and on for—hell, for over a year now, though they weren't really an item, just fuck buddies. Then there was Sean, whom he was still seeing sporadically and who, in a rational universe, would be somebody's husband by now. Finally, there was that certain percentage of the gay male population of San Francisco Cooper hadn't yet bedded.

"Sol would tell you to discuss his offer with your boyfriend," Fausto said. His eyes were scanning the bar. Shopping for diversions, Cooper assumed. "Come up with an arrangement you can both live with."

"What would you tell me?" Cooper asked.

"That he won't hold it against you if you turn the offer down," Fausto said. "Really."

"That's off the record, you understand," Fausto said. "I never said such a thing. All he really wants is to see Bella happy."

"Does he really think Bella will be happy married to a gay man?"

"He wants to believe Estelle is happy married to a gay man. That's very important to him. Bella marrying you would kind of validate that."

"But is Estelle Steinberg truly happy with her life?"

"You'd have to ask her that," Fausto said. "She's never discussed it with me. But as far as Sol is concerned, he doesn't want to believe this is anything more than a business proposition. Nothing personal."

"This is all way too subtle for me," Cooper said.

* * *

"How did you like my new trick?" Kent asked, soaping himself.

"Great," Cooper said. "Didn't quite catch his name, I'm afraid."

"Not that kind of trick," Kent frowned. "I meant that thing when I. . ."

"I know what you meant," Cooper said. Kent's shower had abysmal water pressure. The landlord ought to be fined.

"Made you shoot really hard," Kent laughed.

"I always shoot hard," Cooper said, wondering if Kent's shower was bad enough to require him to begin entertaining Kent at his house. So far he'd held the line, and he wasn't inclined to make changes. Still. This shower.

"God," Kent said. "You don't give an inch, do you?"

"I give eight of them, actually."

"More like nine," Kent corrected him, "but that's not what I'm referring to."

"I'm aware," Cooper said.

"So?"

"What?"

"Jesus, Cooper."

"Kent?"

"What?"

"Is the sex good?" Cooper asked.

"Of course."

"Would you even say it's great?"

"You know the answer to that, Coop."

"Say it."

"It's great."

"Kent, say 'the sex is great, Cooper'."

"The sex is great, Cooper."

"Got to talk to your landlord about the water heater," Cooper said.

"That's all?"

"What?"

"The sex is great and your water heater sucks?" Kent sulked. "That's the end of the discussion?"

"I'm sorry," Cooper said, "is there a discussion here?"

"Apparently not," Kent said.

"You seem to think there should be," Cooper said, "so all right. You want to stop seeing me, all you have to do is stop seeing me. Simple as that. You don't need anybody's permission."

"I don't want to stop seeing you," Kent said.

"I didn't think so."

"I just want. . ."

"What, Kent?" Cooper asked. "What do you want? A boyfriend? There are all kinds of guys who'd like to be your boyfriend. I can think of three or four of them that you're already having sex with regularly. So what's the problem? Let one of those worthy gentlemen sweep you away to his castle. Just make sure the plumbing at his place is up to code before you agree to anything."

"Are you breaking up with me?" Kent asked.

"Breaking up with you?" Cooper asked. "Where did that come from?"

"Fuck, Cooper," Kent said. "You just told me to find a boyfriend. That sounds like breaking up to me."

"I said, *if* a boyfriend is what you want, there are candidates available. Lots of them."

"You're impossible," Kent fumed. "Arrogant, narcissistic, cold-hearted."

"Yet you never seem to get tired of me fucking you."

* * *

"Will I see you tomorrow night?" Kent asked.

"I have opera tickets," Cooper said, stepping into his shoes.

"Exceeded my quota for the month?" Kent asked. "Is that the problem?"

"There's no quota," Cooper said.

"It sure feels like there is," Kent said.

"It's not like you'll be sitting at home by yourself," Cooper said. "You never do."

"What if I did?" Kent asked. "How would it make you feel?"

"Repeat after me," Cooper said. "Fuck buddies."

"No." Kent shook his head.

"Say it."

"No."

"Your choice," Cooper shrugged. "You want something *meaningful*, you know where to look."

* * *

"God, Coop," Sean panted as Cooper slid out of him. "Am I glad I ran into you this afternoon. It's been too long."

"What's wrong?" Cooper laughed. "Bo not keeping you satisfied these days?"

"Bo's a terrific fuck," Sean said. "No question about it. But he only fucks me when one of his clients requests it or when he thinks it'll help keep me in line. When you fuck me, there's no agenda. You fuck me because it's what you feel like doing at the time. Believe me, it makes a difference."

"You're welcome."

III

"I have a table reserved at Harry Gordini's," Chanel Rococo announced, traipsing gingerly down the steps of the opera house in her stiletto heels.

"Just the thing," Holly Montezuma enthused, "to revive us after a grueling night at the opera."

It was almost as if she was the one who had died at the end of the third act.

"Exactly what I was thinking," Marina del Rey purred.

"I'll hail you ladies a cab," Cooper said.

"Not so fast, handsome," Chanel snapped. "You can't expect us to go to Harry Gordini's unescorted."

"How unsuitable," Marina del Rey sniffed.

"How ungallant," Holly asserted.

So in spite of himself, he was stuck.

* * *

"Why, what in the world?" Chanel gasped. "Just look at that."

"What dear?" Holly asked.

"There. At the piano," Chanel said. "Where the hell is Johnny Domino?"

"He's not playing tonight," Marina said. "Didn't you notice the lobby card?"

"Her contacts must have fogged up during the last act," Holly suggested. "*Tosca* is her favorite opera, you know."

"I thought *Salome* was her favorite opera," Marina said.

"That was last week," Holly explained. "The week before that it was some German thing."

"*Die Tote Stadt,*" Chanel hissed, "by Erich Wolfgang Korngold is and forever will be my favorite opera. My true friends all know that."

"Pipe down, you guys," Cooper said. "We're about to get thrown out of here."

He knew that wouldn't happen of course. He just didn't like them being so conspicuous. He was tying to cultivate a classier reputation than that. Turbulent scenes involving drag queens he was escorting didn't help.

"They wouldn't dare," Marina said. "I've been thrown out of much finer establishments than this."

"Who is that red-haired creature at the keyboard?" Chanel asked. "Does anyone know?"

Cooper hadn't paid attention to the figure at the piano when they entered the club, but now he did. It must be that kid Elizabeth and Ned, Cooper's business partners, had been raving about lately. Cooper couldn't remember his name. Some kind of prodigy, apparently.

* * *

"This is just too dreary," Chanel said, forty minutes and two rounds of drinks later.

"Oh, I don't know," Holly said. "He actually seems very talented."

"And he's certainly cute," Marina said. "Notice how the light plays off that dark red hair."

"He's a toad," Chanel insisted. "And he's boring."

"Easy, girl," Cooper said.

"I think it's time for someone to liven up this funeral," Chanel said, rising unsteadily from her seat.

"Don't," Cooper said.

"I believe I will, thank you," Chanel laughed.

"I'm warning you," Cooper said.

"Warning me?" she asked. "Really? What are you going to do, big boy? Something absolutely dire? Keep on never, ever fucking me, for instance? That'll bring me to my knees. Except you don't let me give you blow jobs, either. Sometimes I'm not sure you actually have a penis."

"Chanel," Cooper growled.

"Let her do what she's going to do," Holly said, as the three of them watched her lurch away from the table. "Let her become the prima donna she believes is her destiny. Let her hang herself by the neck with her own entrails if that's what she's intent on."

"Yes," Marina hissed. "Let her slash her own throat from ear to ear. Let her take up that poisonous asp in her delicate, claw-like hand and raise it to her milk white breast. . ."

"Some people we know might even venture the opinion," Holly said, "that whatever is about to happen is inevitable sooner or later, seeing as a certain young lady has grown too big for her britches lately."

By that point, Chanel had reached the piano and was conferring with the musician. She turned to face the audience, favoring all present with the sunniest of smiles.

"This is too droll," Marina giggled. "She's actually going to try and sing."

"Sing? I'm surprised she can even stand," Holly gloated. "Blind drunk like that."

The pianist began to play. Cooper thought he recognized the tune. Yes. It was that aria, "Marietta's Lied". He had ransacked the city for a recording of it the week before Chanel's birthday. She took a deep, expressive breath and began to sing in a surreal falsetto. Suddenly her voice cracked. She whirled, snarled something at the pianist, and dumped her drink all over him.

"Naughty, naughty," Marina said. "She'll have to be punished for that one."

"History in the making," Holly declared.

"Get her out of here, Cooper," Harry Gordini shouted. "Get her out of here now."

IV

"Hey, Buzz," Cooper said, entering the office through the side door.

"Morning, boss."

"How was your weekend?"

"Saw you at the opera," Buzz said. "But you didn't see us. We had balcony seats."

"You should have tracked me down at intermission."

"Trevor's scared of drag queens."

"He may be right," Cooper laughed. "I'm reconsidering my position on that issue."

"Listen, I know you're showing properties at noon," Buzz said, "but I've got a pair of live ones in the conference room. Do you want to see them, or should I give Ned a call to come in?"

"What about Elizabeth? Isn't it her turn for an up?"

"Stepped out," Buzz said. "Early lunch with Stewart. Hair appointment after that."

"I've got time for them, Buzzy. Just give me the lowdown before you bring them upstairs."

"Gay couple. Forrest Reynolds and Morgan Lundquist. Here from New York for a few days and thinking about relocating. I'm not sure how seriously. May just be a whim."

"What's your hunch?"

"My hunch is, you could sell icebergs to Eskimos, you can sell these guys a house. Forrest is about my age. Dark wavy hair, pirate king mustache, and one of those Tristan Bentley cornball accents. Morgan is several years younger, extremely blond, and looks like he's been more or less living at the gym since he hit puberty. It seems he did a photo shoot with Lance Garrison yesterday and they're taking the rest of the week as a vacation."

"A shoot with Lance? Really?"

"Yes, Coop. That good. High placing at the Mr. Manhattan recently."

"Well, we can always use more of those around town," Cooper said. "They interested in anything in particular?"

"Forrest seems to think he can't go on living until he's seen that property in Pacific Heights just across the street from the wedding cake house. The flyer is, of course, prominently displayed in our front window, thanks to Ned."

"Really? The Peterson-Jones place? Are they aware of the price?"

"They are."

"And?"

"Something tells me that unlikely as it seems for two men their age, they might actually be able to afford it."

"Right," Cooper said, "just give me two minutes."

"Coop," Buzz laughed, "your hair is already perfect."

Forrest Reynolds

I

Forrest is already awake when Miss Betsy comes in, but Bobby Lee is snoring to beat the band.

"Rise and shine, boys. Rise and shine," she singsongs, smiling toothlessly.

The first morning Forrest was here, he was surprised at the sight. Without her false teeth she looked so strange. It wasn't just the toothless mouth smiling at him. The whole shape of her face was different. He almost laughed out loud but he didn't think she could tell. She was having to work too hard trying to wake Bobby Lee up. Last Sunday, when Daddy and Mother and Amelia and Elyse came out from town after church and they all had dinner together, he told them about it while Miss Betsy was busy putting Dad Reynolds down for his nap. Daddy smiled and Mother bit her lip to keep from laughing. He doesn't think Amelia heard at all. She was too busy watching the old roan horse out in the back field and dreaming about National Velvet. And Elyse was lying down on Miss Betsy's bed for a nap.

"Son," Daddy said, "someday you'll be old yourself and you'll have your little quirks, too, and you won't want people laughing at you."

"But Daddy, I didn't laugh."

"That's right," his smile widened. "That's what I'm telling you. Just go right on not laughing at your grandmother. Of course, you can smile all you want."

"I'll try to remember."

And that got him a big hug from Mother.

"You're a good boy, sweetheart."

Forrest doesn't know how good he really is, but he's been following Daddy's advice ever since. He never laughs at Miss Betsy's teeth or funny slippers, but he smiles lots. Bobby Lee hates it because she's now telling all her old lady friends, who she talks to on the telephone every afternoon while Dad Reynolds is down for his nap, about what a handsome young man Forrest is and so well behaved and always smiling and pleasant to everyone. Bobby Lee says it makes him gag. But Forrest doesn't care. He always does what he's told when he's staying at the farm because he doesn't want Miss Betsy or any of the aunts telling Daddy and Mother that he's been impolite or disobedient. He doesn't want to embarrass his parents like that in front of family. Strangers are different. They don't matter to him so much, though Daddy would say he's got it backwards and that you should be even more polite to people you don't know.

Bobby Lee says Miss Betsy's an old bat and he hates her. She is an old bat, no question. But Forrest doesn't think Bobby Lee really hates her. She's old and sometimes she acts funny, and Forrest is sure she doesn't understand him. Or Bobby Lee. But she's their grandmother. And he doesn't hate her. Maybe he'd feel differently about it if he had to live here with her like Bobby Lee does. He knows he wouldn't like that much.

"Bobby Lee Reynolds," Miss Betsy screeches frantically, "now, you rise and shine, you hear?"

Bobby Lee snores on, but Forrest knows he's awake now and pretending to be asleep only to torment her. She finally leans over the side of the bed and grabs Bobby Lee by the shoulders and tries to pull him up, but he's too big and she's too old and weak and he flops back down. She grabs one of his ears next.

"Ow, ow, ow," Bobby Lee howls, eyes wide with pretend agony. "Ow, ow. That hurts, Miss Betsy. Stop it."

"I'll stop it, young man, when you stop plaguing and tormenting me and start doing what you're told the first time you're told, like your Cousin Karl here."

"I'm Forrest, Miss Betsy," he says. Cousin Karl lives in Nashville and is sixteen years old. She doesn't hear and he supposes it doesn't matter, but Bobby Lee sticks out his tongue at him and he grins back. Miss Betsy slaps Bobby Lee but it's more loud than hard.

"Bobby Lee Reynolds, don't go sticking out your tongue. How many times have I told you?"

But Forrest can see the twinkle in her eyes, and he suspects she enjoys Bobby Lee's acting up almost as much as Bobby Lee does. On the phone to her old lady friends, she always says that Bobby Lee's all boy and will be the death of her yet. But without Bobby Lee to complain about, Forrest thinks she'd go crazy.

"You two get dressed and go down to the barn and get me some milk and eggs so I can fix your breakfast. You hear me?"

"Yes, Miss Betsy," Bobby Lee whines.

She closes the door behind her.

"Rise and shine, boys," Bobby Lee mimics her, pulling his lips in over his teeth so he even looks a little bit like her.

Forrest keeps smiling.

* * *

Down at the creek house, Bucky, the hired man, gives them a gallon of milk to take back up the hill. They have already gathered a dozen eggs. Forrest hates the way those mean old hens peck his hands as he takes the eggs from the nests. Bucky is tall and broad shouldered and wears his blond hair greased back in a D.A. that Miss Betsy says is indecent. His big blue eyes are always a little bloodshot and he has a dragon tattoo on his right forearm. Miss Betsy hates the tattoo even more than the haircut. There's always a cigarette hanging from one corner of Bucky's mouth. Miss Betsy doesn't like Bobby and Forrest following Bucky around the place while he does his work. She says they get in his way and bother him and he's too nice to tell them to leave him alone. But Bucky's not nice at all. Anybody can see that just looking at him. And what Forrest really thinks is that Miss Betsy is afraid he'll teach them things she doesn't want her grandsons to know about. He's already taught Bobby Lee some amazing words he learned in the navy. Every once in a while, when Bobby Lee knows Miss Betsy is listening, he'll cut loose with a stream of them just to get a rise. It's unbelievable how she can screech. This morning, Bucky gives them a yellow-toothed grin. Forrest wishes he wouldn't smile, because until you see those yellow teeth he's handsome as a movie star. He asks them how hot they think it'll get today.

"Hot as the devil's wife's pussy," Bobby Lee says.

Forrest doesn't know what that word means, but he's pretty sure it doesn't have anything to do with a cat. He doesn't think Bobby Lee knows, either. Something scandalous, certainly.

They all laugh very loud. Bucky reaches out and tousles Bobby Lee's hair, something Forrest is glad Bucky never does to him. The idea of Bucky touching him makes him really nervous.

"Now you two get your candy asses back up the hill before that old lady has a stroke," he says, boxing Bobby Lee's ears and giving Forrest a wink.

Forrest grins back and picks up the milk pail. Bobby Lee's carrying the eggs, and they head up the hill toward the farmhouse, Bobby Lee whooping like a banshee at the cows to make them stampede. They don't pay him any mind.

* * *

Breakfast isn't like Forrest has at home. Since Mother goes to work early, Daddy, Amelia, Elyse, and he are on their own, which usually means shredded wheat with maybe a banana sliced on top. Occasionally they have french toast. Daddy considers french toast his specialty. In the wintertime, Daddy gets up early and makes oatmeal or Cream of Wheat. On Saturdays, he makes waffles.

But as far as Miss Betsy is concerned, none of that is breakfast. So Bobby Lee and Forrest sit down to scrambled eggs and sausage and homemade apple sauce and biscuits and gravy. Forrest isn't crazy about biscuits with gravy on them, so he eats his biscuits buttered and smeared with blackberry preserves. He remembers going out with Bobby Lee and picking these very blackberries last season. They got covered with chiggers from the tops of their heads to the soles of their feet, and he scratched for weeks afterward. The preserves are good, and the blackberry cobblers Miss Betsy makes every few weeks from canned berries are good, too, so maybe all that itching was worth it.

While they eat, Bobby Lee finds the sports section and reads out the baseball statistics from yesterday's games. Forrest pays close attention because he knows he'll be quizzed over them later by Dad Reynolds, who suspects that he doesn't like baseball. Dad Reynolds is right about that, though Forrest is careful to play the sport well enough to keep anyone else from being suspicious. Daddy says he has the makings of a fine little shortstop, and Daddy is legendary in these parts for playing shortstop in high school and then going to Vanderbilt on scholarship and becoming a collegiate All-American. In the background they hear Miss Betsy, who never has breakfast herself until everyone else in the house has been fed, back in Dad Reynolds' room fussing at him about something. Her voice rises and falls, and though Forrest can't make out the words the tone is unmistakable. He wonders if she has always fussed at Dad Reynolds like this and if Dad Reynolds has always ignored her.

Bobby Lee drones on with the stats, pushing his food around on his plate with his fork but actually eating very little of it. Forrest decides to try some of Aunt Libby's watermelon rind preserves on his next biscuit. He can hear the tractor out in the south field. Uncle Fred is always out on the tractor before Bobby Lee and Forrest are up, and Aunt Libby is already in town because the Piggly Wiggly opens early in the summer and she's on first shift this week.

Forrest finally gets bored listening to Bobby Lee and finds the section of the paper with the funnies in it. He starts reading them and just as he's finishing "Peanuts", Miss Betsy comes into the kitchen.

"Bobby Lee Reynolds," she shrieks, "you haven't eaten a bite of breakfast, and here I need to get these dishes done and start fixing lunch. Now you finish up right smart."

"Yes'm," Bobby Lee says, not looking up from the newspaper.

"Look at your cousin. He's cleaned his plate already."

Bobby Lee sticks out his tongue at Forrest.

"You're not still hungry, are you, Karl?" Her faded gray eyes look worried. "It's a long time until lunch, and I won't have you going out of this house hungry."

"I'm full, Miss Betsy."

"His name is Forrest, Miss Betsy," Bobby Lee says, "Forrest Campbell Reynolds."

Miss Betsy ignores him.

"Well all right," she says, but she stands there looking at Forrest like she's afraid he's about to die of starvation. He knows you have to eat one more bite while she stands there watching you or else she'll never believe you've really had enough. So he reaches for another biscuit.

"Bobby Lee," she sighs.

"What?"

"Why didn't you tell me I'd forgotten to put out that crabapple jelly that Miss Sophia Robinson brought by yesterday afternoon? You boys love crabapple jelly."

"Sorry, Miss Betsy."

"And look at me when I speak to you, boy."

"Yes, Miss Betsy," he says, not raising his eyes from the sports page.

"You could learn something about manners from your Cousin Karl."

"I'm sure I could, Miss Betsy," Bobby says, "if he ever came to visit us all the way from Nashville."

"Your Cousin Karl doesn't live in Nashville, you idiot," she screeches. "He lives just over in town. You know that."

"Cousin Forrest lives just over in town," Bobby Lee says, "but Cousin Karl lives in Nashville."

"Well of course," Miss Betsy says. "What kind of idiot are you, getting those two mixed up? I swear I don't know what's going to become of you. Your poor teachers over at the school will need tranquilizers before you ever live to graduate to seventh grade. Either that, or they'll take to drink. Now you two finish up right smart so I can start cooking lunch in here, and don't forget to feed the chickens before you head to the hills."

"Yes, Miss Betsy," Forrest and Bobby Lee say in unison.

* * *

Forrest's father's family, the Reynoldses, have lived in this county since just after the Revolutionary War, though it was part of North Carolina then and not Tennessee. There wasn't any Tennessee at all in those days. Forrests' great-great-great grandfather fought in the War Between the States, and Dad Reynolds himself was Justice of the Peace for nearly fifty years until Miss Betsy made him give it up five or six years ago. She said since he was blind as a bat and deaf as a post he ought to give somebody else a chance at it. Everybody thought it would probably go to the oldest of Forrest's uncles, Uncle Davis, but he said he was too old to learn all that legal talk and the seat went outside the family for the first time since the 1830's. Miss Betsy was mad as a wet hen over it, even though she's only a Reynolds by marriage.

Her people are the Campbells, and they never amounted to anything much according to what Forrest has been told. They never had enough money to own any slaves and they didn't send anybody off to any of the wars until World War II, and they're Holy Rollers. The Reynoldses have been Baptists since the Presbyterian Church in the neighborhood shut down back in the 1850's, and when Miss Betsy married Dad Reynolds, her family turned their backs on her and said she was going to burn in hell for all eternity for forsaking the One True Religion, and she won't have anything to do with them—most of the time. They're just the next thing to white trash. At least that's what Great Aunt Edith Forrest says, and she knows everything about everybody in these parts.

Anyway, Miss Betsy married Dad Reynolds when she was sixteen and he was thirty-four, and they had seven sons. The two oldest, Uncle Davis and Uncle Gardner, still live around here. The three middle ones all live in Nashville. Daddy and Uncle Fred are the youngest of the seven. They're identical twins. Uncle Fred's wife, Aunt Libby, is Mother's identical twin. Forrest's Great Aunt Edith says that makes Bobby Lee and him a lot closer than just first cousins, but he didn't really understand much of her explanation about it. Seems if Daddy and Uncle Ned were just brothers but not twins and Mother and Aunt Libby were just sisters but not twins, that would make Bobby Lee and Forrest double first cousins, but apparently there's no word in the English Language for what the two of them are because of the twins business. Anyway, for two such closely related boys they don't look much alike. Bobby Lee has kinky red hair and freckles and he's shorter than Forrest is and not exactly chubby but not exactly not chubby either. Without the smooth black hair and blue eyes of the Reynoldses or the curly black hair and brown eyes of the Forrests, Bobby's more like Miss Betsy's people, who all have that red hair and are short and stocky. All Forrest got from the Campbells are his light gray eyes. Bobby's are green. Nobody has any idea where that came from.

Bobby Lee and Forrest may not look anything alike, but they have the same birthday. Bobby Lee was born about two hours before Forrest was, and he never lets Forrest forget that he's older. Bobby Lee has one older sister, Mary Jane. She's thirteen, and she's spending the summer with Cousins Mary Alice, Mary Louise, Mary Sue, Mary Laura, and Mary Julia in Nashville. Forrest has two younger sisters. Amelia is seven. All she ever thinks about is horses. The Forrests have always been great ones for horses. That's what Great Aunt Edith says. Elyse is only four, so nobody's certain yet what her great passion will be. Daddy says he hopes she'll grow up to be an airline pilot. Everybody thinks he's joking when he says it, but Forrest has a hunch that he's not.

Mother's family, the Forrests, live in town. Dad Forrest was a doctor. Uncle Sonny was killed in France in 1944, and Uncle Ellis ran away to live in New York before Forrest was born, and nobody's heard from him since. It's some big family secret nobody ever talks about, though Miss Geneva, Forrest's grandmother, still keeps his picture on her dresser and every once in a while you'll hear her get all weepy about her poor baby and whatever happened to him and how she'd give just about anything to see him again one last time before she dies. Miss Geneva lives in a big white house about a block from Mother and Daddy and Forrest and the girls in the middle of town. Her sister, Miss Edith, lives next door to her in the house where their mother and father, Great-Grandfather and Great-Grandmother Ferguson lived. Miss Geneva and Miss Edith's sister, Miss Bertie, lived with Miss Edith until a year ago when she fell and broke her hip and had to go live in a rest home. But she'd been crazy as a coot for years before that. It wasn't just Forrest who thought so.

After he got home from the war, Uncle Fred decided he'd stay on the farm because nobody else was interested in working it. The other uncles had gotten jobs in Nashville and didn't really want to come back once Dad Reynolds got too old to farm. By then, Daddy was already close to graduating from Vanderbilt, and after that he went to law school at UT. Uncle Ned and Aunt

Libby had gotten married right out of high school, but Mother and Daddy waited a long time, until Daddy was through law school and Mother was through medical school and her internship and was ready to practice. She took over Dad Forrest's practice in town, though he kept coming in and seeing a few patients each day until the year before he died.

* * *

After they feed the chickens, Bobby Lee and Forrest go out to the woods. There's what Bobby Lee says is an old Indian burial ground about half a mile behind the house. It's actually across the fence on Uncle Gardner's property. Bobby Lee's got a whole collection of arrowheads or at least what he says are arrowheads, though they don't look much like it to Forrest. There's other stuff Bobby Lee says the Cherokees left behind, though Forrest thinks it all looks like a load of junk, and he's not sure there were ever Cherokees around here. One time Bobby Lee found what he insisted were Indian remains, but Uncle Horace had a look at them on his next trip down from Nashville and told him he'd found the bones of a heifer, probably a Gurnsey.

Bobby Lee still thinks he'll hit the jackpot sooner or later, so every morning they go out and sift through the brush back there and find more of what he calls "artifacts". He's sure someday it's going to make him rich and famous, but all Forrest can see that it's accomplished so far is that they have to clean the ticks off each other every night before they go to bed. This morning they go out like usual, and Blackie, the old Collie mix, goes with them and they're not rooting around for more than about five minutes before Bobby Lee starts whooping away and yelling that he's found it, he's found the main gravesite. But they just look like chicken bones to Forrest, and pretty fresh ones at that, and he decides that Bobby Lee must come out and plant the stuff so he can "discover" it later on when there's somebody around to be impressed. The cousins from Nashville come down every once in a while, and those big city kids will swallow pretty much anything.

"They're just chicken bones," Forrest says, as Bobby Lee grins and holds out some of the "remains".

"Since when are you a forensic scientist?"

They have been reading a book about forensic science at night before they go to bed. They take turns reading aloud. Bobby Lee thinks he would like to be a forensic scientist when he grows up. He'd get to help solve crimes. He plans to track down Jack the Ripper and the True Kidnapper of the Lindbergh Baby.

Forrest doesn't have any idea what he wants to be when he grows up, but being a scientist of any kind doesn't sound like fun.

"You don't have to be a forensic scientist to recognize chicken bones. You just have to be alive and kicking. Hell, ain't no trick to it at all."

Mother would have a stroke if she heard Forrest using language like that. "Ain't" is a pet peeve of hers.

"You just don't get it, Forrest," Bobby Lee complains.

"I guess not."

Forrest is about to remind him of the time he found an old Mason jar that he insisted was a sacred vessel used in religious rites when old Blackie starts barking fit to kill. Bobby Lee falls all over himself trying to get up off the ground because it sounds like old Blackie's snake bark, and snakes are the one thing in the world Bobby Lee's afraid of. Blackie stands there barking his fool head off and Forrest is looking for the snake himself, not because he's afraid of them but because he's afraid that if there really is a snake it might get hurt. But he doesn't see one anywhere, and old Blackie finally stops barking, and before Bobby Lee has a chance to get back to work unearthing any more remains they hear Miss Betsy ringing the dinner bell that hangs by the kitchen door. That means she's seen the mail carrier down at the end of the road and it's time for them to run down there and bring the mail back. She sits by the living room window every morning looking through her binoculars for his Ford because she enjoys getting letters almost as much as she enjoys calling her old lady friends on the phone.

When they get back to the house for lunch, Dad Reynolds is sitting in his chair in the living room watching T.V. Dad Reynolds never misses his programs. On weekdays he watches *Search for Tomorrow*, and *The Guiding Light*, and *The Secret Storm*. There are other programs Forrest doesn't know the names of. Bobby Lee and he are not allowed to sit in there and watch the programs with Dad Reynolds because Miss Betsy says they're about things that aren't fit for children. Forrest tried watching *The Guiding Light* one day when he stayed home from school with the flu, and it was just boring. But even if Miss Betsy would let them in there, Dad Reynolds doesn't appreciate company while his programs are on, and anyone in the room with him has to be completely silent because he can't have his concentration disturbed. Great Aunt Edith says that the people on those shows are more important to Dad Reynolds than his own family. He certainly spends more time with them, and he talks about them like they're real. He knows everything about everybody on those programs but he can never remember Forrest's name or even that Amelia and Elyse are his granddaughters. And he gets the cousins from Nashville completely mixed up, not remembering which one of his sons any of them belong to. Even though today is Saturday and there's nothing about a baseball game that could harm boys like Forrest and Bobby Lee, they're still not allowed in there while Dad Reynolds is watching. So they sit in the kitchen while Miss Betsy serves Dad Reynolds his lunch on a T.V. tray, and when she comes back in she says grace and Bobby Lee and Forrest eat. There's cold ham and cold fried chicken and there's mashed potatoes and gravy and shuck beans and yellow squash and baked apples and fried corn and four kinds of pickles and hot cornbread with butter and molasses. Miss Betsy makes fresh biscuits every morning and fresh cornbread every day for lunch. She never serves white bread at her table except when they have sandwiches.

Bucky and Uncle Fred eat in the kitchen with them, talking about the cows and the tobacco crop the whole time. They chew with their mouths wide open and Miss Betsy doesn't say anything about it. But if Bobby Lee or Forrest do it, well, she just has a fit, fussing and sighing like it's the end of the world.

Uncle Fred may be Daddy's identical twin, but they don't look much alike. Uncle Fred works outside all day, for one thing, so his skin is tanned a lot darker than Daddy's. He's starting to have wrinkles, too. He's got several teeth missing, and the ones that are left are real yellow like Bucky's. Daddy's are perfect and white. And Uncle Fred's a little chubby around the middle. Daddy's very careful to keep fit, only eating dessert on special occasions and never using sugar in his coffee or iced tea. And nobody's ever seen Daddy in public when he hasn't shaved, but Uncle Ned goes around stubbly all week. He shaves on Sunday for church, and maybe once during the week if he has to go into town for something. Otherwise he says it's too much trouble. And finally, Uncle Fred almost never combs his hair, except for church, and Daddy's more careful about that than anything.

Anyway, they sit and eat, and Miss Betsy keeps trying to get them to eat even more, and when she finally decides they've all had enough she gets out a fresh peach cobbler, which she serves with vanilla ice cream from the Piggly Wiggly. Then Uncle Fred and Bucky go out in the front yard and smoke for a while before heading back to work, and Bobby Lee and Forrest have to lie down upstairs for their food to digest.

* * *

After their rest, they go down to the barn. Forrest can't remember ever seeing it freshly painted. Uncle Fred is only running four dozen head of dairy cattle these days, and the part of the barn where they are fed and milked is kept spotless. But the rest of it is full of junk, dirt, wasp nests, and hay. There's even an old Model A Ford up on blocks. It hasn't been driven since gas rationing in World War II. Bobby Lee has plans for that old car. He's decided that he and Forrest are going to restore it when they get their licenses and then they're going to drive it all over the county and sometimes all the way to Nashville. That does sound like fun, but Daddy's promised Forrest an M.G., and he thinks that sounds like a lot more fun and a lot less work than the old Ford.

Most of the space in the barn is full of huge stacks of baled hay reaching up to the floor of the loft. Even more hay is stored up there. Bobby Lee and Forrest have spent weeks building a complicated network of tunnels and bunkers out of hay bales. It's too hot to stay in their fortress for long, even if the flashlight batteries don't give out, but they come down every day after lunch for a while at least, and if they can't stay hidden for very long there's still the loft itself and the large piles of loose hay on the floor of the barn that they can jump down into.

Bobby Lee always tries to do flips and twists on the way down. Forrest prefers to concentrate on his landings, trying to figure out what is the best position to have his body in when he hits. Bobby Lee makes three or four jumps to every one of Forrest's, because after each one Forrest likes to sit and think through the jump, trying to remember what it felt like at various points in the fall and planning the next one in detail before heading back up the rickety wooden ladder.

Bobby Lee screeches like a crazy man every time he jumps, but Forrest is silent. Someday he's going to bring Daddy's movie camera with him and carry it with him on one of his jumps. He thinks it would be neat to be able to play a movie of it over and over again. And in slow motion. When he told Bobby Lee this plan, he said Forrest would probably just break the damned thing.

This afternoon, Bucky's forking hay to the cows and after Forrest's fourth jump he sits in the hay to watch. Bucky has his shirt off, and he's covered with sweat. His big muscles move under his shiny skin like they have minds of their own. Watching Bucky with his shirt off always makes Forrest feel a little nervous. He gets a funny feeling way down in his stomach and it's hard for him to catch his breath. He doesn't think Bobby Lee has noticed. And he doesn't know why he can't keep himself from staring at Bucky. Every time Bucky turns

toward him, Forrest sees his nipples, which are very dark and very, very large.
They stick out in front of his chest muscles. You can even see them sticking out
like that under his t-shirts. None of the boys or men Forrest sees when he goes
to the city pool has nipples like that. He also wonders why Bucky doesn't have
any hair on his chest. There's light golden hair on his arms and a little line of it
running down from his belly button and inside his jeans. Bobby Lee once told
him that muscle men shave the hair off their chests so their muscles will show
up better. Bucky has big muscles, all right. Forrest finally gets so nervous that
he can't watch Bucky any more, so he goes back up into the loft planning his
next jump.

When it gets too hot to stay in the barn any more, they go down to the
creek to cool off. There's a swimming hole that is shaded by tall trees, and the
water's deep enough that you can jump out of one of them and land right in the
middle. It's the only time all day when Forrest feels really cool. In the house
there are only electric fans, not air conditioners like people have in town. He
doesn't like it much, all the sitting around and sweating and feeling like it's too
hot to do anything. But the swimming hole is all right. And since it's just the
two of them, they don't follow the rule about keeping their drawers on. They
just go into the water buck naked. Bobby Lee likes to dive into the water over
and over and make as much noise and commotion as he can. Forrest likes to
float on his back and look up through the dense branches at the sky. He stares
up trying to see as far as he can into it. He stares so long that after a while he
can't be sure how far he's seeing. One minute it will seem like he can see forever into the clear blueness and the next minute it will seem like he's looking
at something completely flat. Like there's nothing up there but a giant picture.
After a while, staring up makes him feel a little dizzy. He knows he can blink
and turn his head and the dizziness will go away, but he still has the feeling that
he's really small. Sometimes he imagines that there's somebody somewhere else
looking up at exactly the same time he is and thinking the same thoughts, and if
Forrest could find him they would be friends.

Forrest likes the city pool better than the swimming hole. There aren't
any trees in the way of the view and you don't have to worry about water moc-
casins. He's allowed to ride his bicycle over there in the afternoons, and he has
a right smart good time. There's almost always somebody there that he knows
from school, and there's a snack bar. Miss Geneva and Miss Edith pay him
enough for chores and odd jobs he does around their places that he always has

enough for a cokecola and a moon pie. There's a lifeguard there, Ruby Minifee's big brother, Beau, who reminds him a lot of Bucky. Except when he smiles his teeth aren't yellow, and his muscles aren't as big. They're pretty big, though. Beau's going to be a senior this fall.

Forrest floats on his back in the cool water that smells of weeds and wet sand and minnows, and Bobby Lee eventually gets bored splashing around and just floats, too. It gets quiet enough that all you can hear are the birds singing and every once and a while a car driving by on the county road.

* * *

After supper Miss Betsy and Aunt Libby sit in the living room listening to Lawrence Welk on the television. Aunt Libby crochets but Miss Betsy doesn't on account of her arthritis. They talk softly, which Forrest knows is so that he and Bobby Lee won't be able to hear, because Bobby Lee is very bad about repeating things he's not supposed to know. Uncle Fred and Dad Reynolds sit out on the front porch and smoke. Bucky always leaves as soon as supper is over. He excuses himself from the table and goes down to his little stone cottage by the creek and half an hour later Forrest will hear him start up his 1940 Ford coupe and roar off toward town.

Bucky's got two four-barrel carbs on that V-8 and dual exhausts and Baby Moon hubcaps. He's had the car painted bright yellow, and there's red and orange flames painted on the side to look like there's a fire under the hood. When Forrest is at home in town, sometimes Mother lets him walk over to the courthouse square after supper and he sees Bucky's car parked there. He's got some buddies who bring their cars, too. They all sit on the hoods of their cars and smoke. You can see the tips of their cigarettes glowing in the darkness like lightning bugs. Forrest has never gone close enough to hear what they talk about. Sometimes they'll get into their cars and start the engines and sit making them go "vroom vroom" like they're getting ready for a drag race or something, but Forrest has never seen them actually have one. Daddy says they go out in the country to do that, and sooner or later they're going to get caught and lose their licenses.

Later that evening, Uncle Davis and Aunt Helen stop by and a while after that it's Uncle Gardner and Aunt Jesse. Uncle Davis and Uncle Gardner are the oldest of Miss Betsy and Dad Reynolds' sons, and they're pretty close to being old men themselves. Cousin Kenny and his wife, Sue Ellen, come over, too. Sue Ellen is pregnant again, and that gives the women in the living room something to talk about, and something *not* to talk about, too. Sue Ellen has been pregnant three or four times now but she and Kenny still don't have any kids. So the women all talk about baby things but they don't talk about the question they're all wondering about, which is will the baby live this time?

By now, there's quite a crowd of men on the porch sitting and smoking. Dad Reynolds always smokes cigars, and Uncle Davis and Uncle Gardner have their pipes, and Uncle Ned and Cousin Kenny smoke Camels. From where Bobby Lee and Forrest are sitting out by the fence that keeps the cows out of Miss Betsy's front yard, they can hear everything the men say. Dad Reynolds doesn't talk at all. He just sits and smokes his cigar until it goes out, and then he chews on the stub until it's too soggy to keep. Finally he throws it into Miss Betsy's rosebushes. Every once in a while somebody will say something that makes him grunt. It's the only way anybody can tell he's still awake. Miss Betsy will come out in the morning to tend her roses, and she'll find that cigar butt and she'll go whooping into his room and Bobby Lee and Forrest will hear her in there hollering at him right smart about how many times she's told him never to do that again. And the next time he's out there with the uncles he'll do the same thing.

The moon comes up over the hills and Forrest can tell that it's going to be full tonight. The bugs are chirping away and the grass is wet with dew and he wishes he was back in town in his bedroom. He's going back to town tomorrow. Two weeks out here on the farm is about all he can stand of Miss Betsy and Dad Reynolds and even Bobby Lee. He'll miss them some. He'll probably come out for another week just before school starts. But he gets awfully bored without his friends and the public library and the city pool. He misses the color television and Mother's piano, even though she makes him practice for an hour every day. And he misses Daddy and Mother and his dogs, Miss Lucy and Skeeter. They're Dalmatians. Miss Lucy is Skeeter's mother. Sometimes he even misses Amelia and Elyse. It's only eight miles into town, but when he's staying out here on the farm it seems like a lot farther.

It's completely dark now, and Miss Betsy comes out on the porch to ask the men what flavor of ice cream they want with their angel food cake, and if they want Hershey's syrup on top of it. Forrest hears old Blackie barking out by Miss Betsy's vegetable garden, and he figures he'll miss that old dog more than just about anybody out here.

* * *

When Miss Betsy comes in to wake them up, she's already got her teeth in and she's wearing her church clothes. She tells them to hurry up right smart, and for once Bobby Lee does what she says. Miss Betsy doesn't fix a big break- fast on Sundays. Instead she makes her own special sticky rolls, with thick, gooey topping of brown sugar and cinnamon and chopped pecans. Forrest eats four of them and Bobby Lee eats six, and then they go back upstairs to put on their ties.

They all pile into Uncle Fred's BelAir, except for Dad Reynolds, who stays home and reads the Nashville paper. He's a Deacon Emeritus of the church, which means he doesn't have to attend services any more. The Reynoldses have been pillars of the Shady Creek Baptist Church for generations, and when they arrive there are all kinds of people that Forrest has to say good morning to. He has to shake hands with the men and he has to let all the old ladies kiss him and tell him how tall he's gotten and how handsome he is and how much he looks like his father. Forrest doesn't like all this social stuff much, but he tries to be nice.

Finally they go into the church basement for Sunday School. Aunt Jesse is their teacher. The lesson this morning is about Samson. Forrest has heard this story lots of times, and he likes the part about how Samson kills the lion with his bare hands and then kills all those Philistines with the jawbone of an ass. One afternoon earlier in the summer Bucky said Miss Betsy could kill you the same way, which Forrest thought was pretty funny once he figured it out. What he has never been able to understand about the story of Samson is why the strongest man in the world would get himself mixed up with a woman like that and Reveal the Secret of His Amazing Strength. He can't imagine Bucky doing anything like that, for instance. It just doesn't make any sense. Forrest doesn't see how a guy like that—Aunt Jesse tells them that Samson was handsome as a movie star, too—would have any use for a woman at all, but he doesn't ask her to explain it because the last time he asked her a question in Sunday School she told Miss Betsy and all the aunts about it and they laughed and kidded him for weeks afterward. He decides this week's lesson is obvious enough not to re- quire further explanations and well worth remembering. Don't have anything to do with women.

After Sunday School is over, Aunt Jesse tells them to hurry up and get themselves to the sanctuary right smart so they won't be late and disturb the worship of the people already in there. But when they go inside and sit down by

Miss Betsy, Forrest can't see a solitary soul worshipping, though there's a whole lot of gossiping going on and all the men are still outside smoking. You can see and smell them through the open windows.

Forrest misses the pipe organ at St. Stephen's Episcopal, where Mother and Daddy take him and his sisters on Sundays. Here there's only a beat up old upright piano Miss Betsy says hasn't been tuned since God was a little boy. Miss Betsy and Bobby Lee and he sit fanning themselves like there's no tomorrow and the men all start to come in from outside, clearing their throats and coughing. Then the choir marches into the loft behind the pulpit. Aunt Helen is the choir director. Then the preacher, Brother Sykes, comes in and Uncle Davis is with him. Uncle Davis is the song leader. They all put down their fans and pick up their hymnals, and they sing "Onward, Christian Soldiers".

After that, Deacon Robertson prays for about an hour, mumbling and grumbling about all our Many Blessings and seeking for the Lost Souls and bless our governor and senators and turn these United States from our Sinful Ways and back into the One True Path. Then Uncle Gardner gets up. He's Super-intendent of the Sunday School, and he gives a report about how many people were present this week and how many were on time and how many brought their Bibles with them and how much money was in the Sunday School collec-tion. After each of these items is announced there are gruff sounding Amens from the men in the sanctuary but the women just keep fanning, because it's not reverent for a woman to say Amen in church except at the end of a prayer.

Next there's a special number from the choir. It is called "The Fight is On", and the sopranos screech and the altos sound like they're moaning and the tenors look like they're about to have strokes on the high notes, and the basses rumble and grumble, and at the end the men in the sanctuary all say Amen again.

Then Brother Sykes gets up to preach. He's already sweating, and he thumps his fist down on the pulpit and waves his big black Bible up in the air. His sermon is about "Ye Shall All Likewise Perish". Daddy says that he doesn't have respect for a clergyman who shouts and who doesn't have a college degree and hasn't been to divinity school and doesn't preach about anything but hellfire and damnation, but Miss Betsy insists that Brother Sykes is a True Man of God and preaches like One Inspired. Forrest thinks he just looks and sounds like a maniac. And he doesn't know when to stop. He goes around and around in circles like a bird dog getting ready to lie down, saying the same things over and over again, only louder each time. He preaches for a long time and then he gives the invitation for people to walk down the aisle and be saved. Everyone sings all five verses of "Just As I Am Without One Plea" three times through and nobody comes forward, so while the piano keeps playing, Brother Sykes leans over and whispers something to Aunt Helen. She nods and goes over to whisper to the pianist, who nods, too, and then Brother Sykes asks everyone to close their eyes and pray for the Lost Souls Among Us, and while they are all standing there melting and praying, Aunt Helen starts singing "His Eye is On the Sparrow." Nobody gets saved, and after a long, long benediction everybody goes home.

* * *

When they get back to Miss Betsy's, Mother and Daddy and the girls are sitting in the living room with Dad Reynolds. Mother tells Forrest that he's grown an inch and Daddy says he's gotten very tan. Amelia's too busy looking at her picture book of horses to notice he's even there, and Elyse goes on pretending that she can read the funnies. Everybody comes over for lunch. Miss Betsy and the aunts head to the kitchen to put the food out. Miss Betsy fixes a plate for Dad Reynolds and takes it back to his bedroom where he's waiting for it. Daddy and Mother and all the aunts and uncles sit in the dining room at the big table. There's a small table for Bobby Lee and Forrest and the girls. Miss Betsy won't sit down at the table. She'll bustle in and out of the kitchen and everyone will try to get her to have something to eat, but she won't. She'll fuss around until everybody is finished, worrying about is the okra too soggy and is the roast beef too tough and is the gravy lumpy and are the potatoes too cold? Everyone will tell her that everything's fine, but she'll act like she's not sure she should believe it and everyone will have to eat just a little bit more of everything to prove that it's all delicious. Later on she'll have a plate out in the kitchen.

While everyone's eating, the aunts talk about old Mrs. Sutherland who died three weeks ago. They say over and over again to Mother that they know she did everything she could. Mother points out that Mrs. Sutherland was 98 years old and had been bedridden since her last stroke twelve years ago and nobody could have saved her, and the aunts all look shocked. Miss Betsy says one more time that everyone knows Mother did all she could and everybody knows what a fine doctor she is. Forrest knows it's making Mother angry, but she acts like she's not.

Finally it's time for dessert. There's Miss Betsy's coconut layer cake and Aunt Jesse's specialty, a Mississippi Mud Cake, and Aunt Helen has made three pies—peach, apple, and pecan. Bobby Lee says he'll have some of all three, and Miss Betsy boxes his ears and says she doesn't know what they're going to do with him. But everybody ends up trying a little of everything anyway.

After dessert, Forrest goes upstairs to get his stuff. Bobby Lee goes with him. When they come downstairs, everybody's gathered around Daddy's Buick like they're setting off on a trip to the moon. Forrest has to kiss Miss Betsy and every last one of the aunts. Bobby Lee leans in through the car window to say goodbye. Forrest says he'll probably be back for a week just before school starts, and Bobby Lee says that'll be great.

II

Forrest's hand trembles slightly as he reaches up to push the buzzer. It's not the first time he's done this, but it doesn't get any easier. If anything, this time is a little worse. Maybe it's because he's thought all along that this would be the place and he only went to those other addresses for practice. Anyway, here he is in front of a shabby looking old place around the corner from Bleeker waiting to be buzzed in and all he can think about is the last letter he got from Bobby Lee and how after this he'd best not call Forrest a candy ass again.

He is buzzed in. He bolts through a squalid lobby and up the stairs toward 4B hoping he's right and he'll find the man there. He soaks up details like a sponge, because in his letters Bobby Lee always demands details and Forrest feels so guilty having the time of his life in New York while Bobby Lee's off in the God Forsaken, Snake and Viet Cong Infested Jungle. Bobby Lee is addicted to capitalization as a means of emphasizing things, but God knows some things are bad enough without help like that. The only way Forrest can escape his guilt is doing whatever Bobby Lee asks him to do in those pitiful letters. He knows he's being manipulated, but he really is a candy ass. Telling Bobby Lee no is unthinkable.

Hence this quest. It would never have occurred to Forrest. And had anyone other than Bobby Lee suggested it, he'd have said a fast no, thank you. It's been over a quarter century since Uncle Ellis up and left home, and just because he is believed to have come to New York doesn't mean he did. He could have gone anywhere in the wide world. He could have come here and left for somewhere else. He could be dead by now. When Forrest raised these objections to Bobby Lee, they were dismissed out of hand. If Uncle Ellis had died, the family would have learned of it somehow. And where, if not New York, is a runaway southern faggot to go? Just about anywhere north of the Mason-Dixon Line, Forrest would have thought. Not to mention Sunny California. And who ever said Uncle Ellis was gay?

But Bobby Lee remained adamant. It came through loud and clear in his next letter. So Forrest reluctantly agreed to initiate a search. He assumed that the task would quickly prove impossible and he'd be off the hook. Several weeks later, here he is. At 4B he knocks on the door and holds his breath. Inside the apartment some three hundred pound soprano is screaming her guts out backed by a full orchestra. If Rik were here he'd know what opera, which act, the title of the aria, and probably the identity of the singer. But Rik doesn't know anything about this little adventure. Rik follows Forrest around too much already. Forrest isn't in the market for a puppy, or, for that matter, a boyfriend who impersonates one.

The man who opens the door is tall and broad shouldered. His black hair is wet, presumably from the shower. He's wearing a red satin robe that's open at the chest, revealing a build that was athletic not too horribly long ago. He's enveloped in a dense cloud of some obnoxious cologne. He looks about ten years too young for the role, but his features are distressingly familiar and his eyes exactly match Forrest's.

"Good afternoon," Forrest stammers.

"Where are the things?"

"Things?"

"My grocery order."

"Your grocery order?"

The man glares for a long moment. Then the eyes soften a little.

"You're not the boy from Gristede's."

"No," Forrest shakes his head as much to clear it as to emphasize the denial.

"Well then, who are you?" the man asks, expression changing from exasperated to merely curious.

"My name is Forrest Reynolds. I'm from Pulaski, Tennessee. My mother's name is Julia Emily Forrest Reynolds, and ever since I came to New York I've been trying to locate her older brother, Ellis. None of the family has heard from him in many years."

During this speech, Forrest has kept his eyes locked to the man's, and he's seen enough there to know, even without the family resemblance, that this is the man he's looking for.

"That's a very interesting story, I'm sure," the man says, after a long, awkward silence during which he seems to loom larger and larger in the doorway, "but I'm afraid I'm very late for an appointment and can't discuss it with you just now."

"I know. I apologize. I should have called first."

Forrest knows Bobby Lee will never forgive him if he doesn't get inside the apartment, if only for a few moments. But as he stands there on the dark, smelly landing, he can see the man digging in his heels. He figures it's a lost cause. Bobby Lee can just come here himself and try to do better. The man and Forrest stare at each other for a long moment, and then he hears the buzzer inside the apartment.

"That will be the boy from Gristede's. I'm afraid you'll have to excuse me."

Forrest knows exactly how it feels to be dismissed by a peevish southern would-be aristocrat. In such cases there's no arguing and no chance of an appeal. He doesn't waste his breath attempting another, more effective apology. He simply turns and goes back down the stairs. On the way he passes the boy from Gristede's going up, though boy is hardly the appropriate term to apply to that two hundred pound Puerto Rican wrestler (with the face of an angel, incidentally) toting that carton.

* * *

A letter comes from Bobby Lee. The first part of it is barely comprehensible. Bobby Lee has just come in from his third patrol in as many days, and he writes in a demented kind of stream of consciousness that makes Forrest feel guiltier than ever about being safe in New York. After three pages of that, there's a shift. He's writing a couple of days later. He's had a shower, some hot food, and some sleep, and there have been no more patrols. He feels better, except he's just gotten Forrest's letter about that botchup down in the Village. He agrees that Forrest has found Uncle Ellis. He disagrees about tactics. He advocates Forrest camping out on Uncle Ellis' doorstep until he's invited inside.

Having faced the man himself, Forrest refuses to try it. For all kinds of reasons. Who are they, after all, to invade his privacy? To just show up and insist he become their uncle? What do they really know about what happened in Tennessee all those years ago, and do they have the right to force him to recall it? But since Bobby Lee won't be argued with about any of this, Forrest writes back as if he's planning to make another attempt almost immediately.

He figures the best he can do is buy some time and make up whatever story he has to later on.

* * *

No more than thirty seconds after Forrest gets in the door from playing rugby, the buzzer rings. Rik shows up earlier and earlier these days: fifteen minutes before they're supposed to meet for dinner, thirty minutes before they agreed to leave for the movies. Occasionally Forrest even finds Rik waiting downstairs in the mail alcove, having beaten him there. The cute Jewish boy across the hall would know what to do about all this. Forrest hears him at least once a day telling his mother not to call him so often, his girlfriend to get off his back, his older brothers to mind their own business, his father to For God's Sake Stop Kvetching. Forrest doesn't mean to overhear. His neighbor is apparently incapable of answering his telephone without opening the front door of his apartment first. He seems to prefer talking on the phone from the landing—the cord is easily long enough to reach well out into the hallway. Forrest admires his assertiveness, his lack of reserve. Not to mention his cute little straight boy ass. Forrest enjoys elaborate reveries in which that ass plays a starring role.

Forrest never felt like a southerner until he came to New York. Back home he always felt like a displaced alien. But up here there's no question he's a foreigner. He is not sufficiently assertive except on the rugby field, or, some would say, in bed. He is reserved to a fault, and he suffers Rik's excesses in silence, in return for which, like the good southern boy he is, Rik insinuates his attentions rather than expressing them explicitly. Forrest knows all too well what Rik really wants, but because Rik never actually comes out and says it Forrest doesn't tell him to get lost. This, apparently, is what Rik means when he describes them as best buddies.

He buzzes Rik in and goes on taking off his clothes. That's why Rik comes early, obviously. To catch Forrest in some stage of undress. It occurred to him last week that if he'd only oblige Rik, the boy might settle down a little. By the time there's a knock on the door, he's down to his jockstrap. It's the most of his skin Rik has ever seen or ever will. Not that Forrest is particularly modest. And it's not even that Rik's not his type. Forrest simply won't be manipulated past a certain point.

He opens the door. It's not Rik, and he feels himself blushing down to his toes.

"It's the boy from Gristede's," the man announces, striding in without a by your leave. He's wearing a navy blazer, white flannels, a sky blue oxford cloth button down, a scarlet ascot, a pair of boat shoes that match the blazer, and once again too much cologne. His coal black hair is brylcreemed within an inch of its life.

How long has it been since the Saturday when he refused Forrest admittance to that Greenwich Village walkup? Six weeks? Seven? There have been four letters from Bobby Lee since then, full of admonitions and remonstrances. And here the man is, dead in the center of Forrest's living room, taller and broader of shoulder than Forrest seems to remember, and doing a pirouette. Tarzan of the Apes as Dame Margot Fonteyn.

"The boy! From! Gristede's!" he repeats, grinning manically. And as Forrest shuts the front door, he notices that the man does indeed have a bag from said emporium in his left hand. In his right hand there's a bunch of yellow roses. Yellow roses are a particular favorite of Mother's. Apparently this is some sort of signal. A peace offering, perhaps.

"Well, hello," Forrest says, knowing that his smile is a sheepish one and wishing to heaven he had some clothes on.

"Hello yourself, chile."

"You'll have to excuse me. I just got back from a rugby match,"

"Rugby. Such a manly game, I always think. I don't suppose you have anything to put these in, do you?"

He brandishes the roses and looks around the minimally furnished apartment. Only an incurable romantic or a helpless drunk would describe it as bohemian.

"As a matter of fact, I do," Forrest says, relieved to be presented with this simple task. He heads for the kitchen, where he knows Rik left a cut glass vase he found at a flea market last weekend. Rik "forgets" things here so later on he can return to fetch them. He thinks he needs excuses for coming around. Forrest may not be interested in being Rik's boyfriend, but he enjoys Rik's company well enough. He finds the vase and rinses it out. He runs water into it and takes it out to the living room.

"The very thing."

Forrest can't tell if this utterance expresses genuine delight or exquisite sarcasm.

"Now, don't worry your pretty head about me. You go and do your primping. I'll be fine here."

"A friend of mine will be coming by," Forrest says over his shoulder.

"Oh, dear. Is this a bad time?"

"Not at all. Just buzz him in, won't you?"

"Why, certainly, dear chile."

* * *

When Forrest comes out of the bathroom Rik has arrived. These two guests are sitting on opposite ends of the serape covered sofa staring at each other, and all four of their eyes are as big as saucers. Rik's a short boy and frail besides. With his delicate features and silky blond hair pulled back in a pony tail, he looks like somebody's twelve year old sister. Some three hundred pound soprano is screeching away backed by a full orchestra on Forrest's turntable. The first thing Rik always does when he arrives is put on some opera. He doesn't have his own stereo yet, not because he can't afford one but because Forrest won't tell him which components to buy, and so he has to listen to his opera in Forrest's living room.

"There you are," the man who might be Uncle Ellis shouts over the music, "here's your little friend."

"Hey, Rik boy."

Rik doesn't speak. He smiles up languidly.

"Did you know that his people are the Knoxville Tiptons?" perhaps Uncle Ellis asks.

"Indeed," Forrest says, patting Rik's head. "I did know that."

"A fine old Tennessee family. Connected to several governors of that fine state and a senator or two."

Rik's obviously eating this up. It's exactly the kind of adulation Forrest won't give him.

"Now shoo, chile," maybe Uncle Ellis says, dismissing Forrest with a limp wristed wave of his large, masculine looking hand. "Finish your toilette. We can't lollygag around all day. I have things! To show! You two!"

* * *

After this meeting, Rik wants to know the Whole Story. He, too, capitalizes obsessively. Perhaps it's a southern trait. It's obvious from the questions he asks that Uncle Ellis or whoever he is hasn't told him anything. But Forrest doesn't know what to say. He can't expect Rik to accept the gentleman as a kind of *objet trouve*. All he's certain of is that the truth, at least as he knows it, won't do. That long lost uncle business will drive Rik into a frenzy. Dinners and excursions together—that first afternoon it was the Frick Collection and then dinner at Tavern on the Green—wrapped up in a gossamer net of refined conversation won't satisfy him. He'll insist on tearful scenes of reunion in which Uncle Ellis acknowledges Forrest as his kin, something he hasn't even done privately so far, and recounts the entire epic of his exile. And though that would give Forrest lots to write Bobby Lee about, he doesn't think, now that he's met the man, that he'll stay around for that kind of spectacle. Nor would Forrest want to participate in it. So, hoping that Rik hasn't noticed the family resemblance, Forrest makes up a tale about an old college buddy of Daddy's who sent word with his graduation present that Forrest should look him up on his arrival in the city. Mr. Worthington.

A letter comes from Bobby Lee congratulating Forrest on his strategy. Pique the target's interest, then disappear and let him find you. Bobby Lee declares Forrest a genius. Maybe he is. But it was hardly strategy. When he left that Greenwich Village walkup with his tail behind his legs, he figured it was all over. He never expected the man to show up on his doorstep nearly two months later. Or ever. But Bobby Lee's happy. Though you couldn't say he's satisfied. He wants details. He demands narrative.

* * *

Forrest and Rik sit next to each other on the train, and Rik is as pale as a ghost. A year and a half in New York, and this is his first time on the subway. He believes far too much of what he's heard about it, and he's terrified. Anywhere he can't go on foot he goes by taxi or bus. Forrest has told him many times that both of those alternatives take far longer, but Rik simply arranges his life accordingly.

They'd be on the bus this afternoon, except they're behind schedule. Forrest's fault. When Rik came by his place to pick him up, he took one look at the jeans and rugby shirt, wailed, "you can't! go! to High Tea! looking! like that!" and refused to leave Forrest's apartment until there had been a complete change of attire. Forrest acquiesced, thinking all the while that ever since they encountered Mr. Worthington, Rik, who spent his first eighteen months in the city ruthlessly suppressing his accent, is nowadays speaking broad Tennesseean once again, and in a heavily inflected, copiously italicized, elaborately punctuated dialect that often makes Forrest want to spank him.

So here they are in their suits and ties and shiny black shoes as the train pulls into Christopher Street station. Rik follows Forrest up the stairs to the street, muttering ostensibly to himself but just loud enough for it to be audible about the Black Hole of Calcutta. On the sidewalk he stops to look around. Not only is today his first adventure on the subway, it's his first expedition to the Village. It's clear from the look on his face that he doesn't approve. They walk along grimy sidewalks and there's something at every quarter from which he has to avert his eyes in horror, but at least he doesn't complain aloud. At Mr. Worthington's door, as Forrest pushes the buzzer, Rik gives him a look that says "He! Can't! Possibly! Live! HERE!", and Forrest grins back. All too obviously, Rik was expecting something more Sutton Place than this, or that Greenwich Village truly looked like one: thatched roofed stone cottages nestled among the Cotswolds or somesuch bullshit.

They're buzzed inside and trudge up the stairs to 4B. Mr. Worthington stands in the open doorway, all got up in a double breasted gray suit. Music and his perennial scent billow out onto the landing, and with a swashbuckling gesture he motions them inside and closes the door before kissing their cheeks. The apartment, which Forrest is seeing for the first time, is exactly as he's imagined it, with Victorian furniture and threadbare oriental rugs. Its other features include a table lamp with a base in the shape of Michelangelo's *David*, a crystal chandelier in the dining alcove, knickknacks clotting every flat surface, crocheted doilies everywhere else, and enough ball fringe to trim the perimeter of a soccer field. There's even a trio of Siamese cats who yowl reproachfully as Rik and Forrest supplant them on the emerald green velvet, diamond tufted loveseat. Among the dozens of ornately framed photographs, Forrest can see none of anyone he might be related to.

"Dear! Dear! Boys! Don't! You! Both! Look! SPLENDID!"

"What! A! Lovely! APARTMENT!" Rik croons up at him.

"It's not much, I know," Mr. Wentworth sighs, with a look on his face— well, imagine Rhett Butler rather than Scarlett pining for Tara, and you've got the picture. "But it's home."

"Well!" Rik continues gushing, "I Think! It's Just! DARLING!"

"Thank YOU! Dear! CHILE!"

Forrest has no idea what kind of uncle Bobby Lee was hoping to unearth when he insisted on this quest, but he's reasonably certain of one thing. Bobby Lee wasn't expecting an auntie. But that's what this man, despite his fading matinee idol looks and the build of a washed up offensive lineman, seems to want to be. Forrest is already turning the phrases he'll use to describe this little tableau in his next letter to Southeast Asia.

Once tea is poured and cucumber sandwiches, miniature salmon quiches, brandy laced fruitcake slices, petit fours, napoleons, and bourbon balls have been served, Forrest begins to relax a little. The Siamese eat their own quiches off their own china plates, hissing and cackling away intently under the Queen Anne cocktail table. In addition to the tea, their host plies them with champagne served in Waterford flutes. Forrest can just hear Rik oohing and aahing over it on the way home.

* * *

The weekly letter comes from Bobby Lee. In it are a pair of polaroids of Bobby Lee and his buddy, Gregg. Gregg's a tall, stalwart looking boy with a mischievous grin and a dragon tattoo taking up most of his left forearm just like the one sported by the late Bucky Greene. Forrest wonders exactly what the two of them are to each other. Bobby Lee's letters hint of nothing more than good comradeship. Maybe that's exactly the case. But knowing Bobby Lee like he does, maybe it's not. The two photos, one with their arms draped across each other's shoulders, the other sitting side by side on the hood of a jeep, both of them bare-chested in both shots, offer no clues.

Bobby Lee's letter offers little news beyond the information that he's still alive, he's bored silly and at the same time terrified, and the exact number of days remaining before he leaves that particular hellhole. Like his other letters, this one is full of questions. Questions about Uncle Ellis. Bobby knows nothing of "Mr. Worthington". Forrest hasn't told him about that manufactured identity. Forrest writes about everything else. The Sunday afternoon high teas which have become an institution for the little trio. The nights at the opera and ballet. Their host considers musicals vulgar, being written and performed in English. Plays, because they lack both singing and dancing, are too boring to be endured. The symphony is even worse because there's nothing to watch except some old conductor and perhaps a soloist. Other than these events, Forrest knows nothing about the man or his life. All he talks about is the opera, the ballet, the weather, the shopping, and where he's taking them next. Forrest thinks of him as an actor playing a role for an audience of two and can't help but wonder what goes on after the curtain falls. Mr. Worthington gives no hints.

* * *

"That young James Richardson Tipton," Mr. Worthington muses, studiously avoiding eye contact. Forrest waits for him to continue. Whenever the two of them are alone together for even the shortest period of time, this is Mr. Worthington's theme. He takes a sip of tea and a slow drag off his Gauloise and looks around the room, exhaling languidly. This afternoon they're at Rumplemeyer's.

"Well," he says, "I'm sure I don't have to tell you."

He stubs out the cigarette, and gray tendrils of smoke drift between them. Forrest decides he must have been rehearsing for years how to stub out a cigarette just so.

"Tell me what?"

Even though Forrest plays dumb, he knows what all these hints are aimed at. He'd have to be an even bigger fool than he actually is not to. At some point during the last few weeks, Mr. Worthington apparently decided to play match-maker. Forrest is willfully obtuse, and not merely because he has no romantic interest in Rik. He finds it intolerable for Mr. Worthington to insert himself into his affairs. If Mr. Worthington were to come clean about Uncle Ellis it would be different. Forrest would listen to these little epithalamiums with a better spirit. But as it is, Mr. Worthington seems to be in clear violation of their unspoken agreement.

"Why, Forrest," he sighs, eyes wide, "I'm sure his charms aren't lost on you. And they are considerable, I have to say. Such a pretty little thing. And so refined. Don't expect me to believe you haven't noticed."

"If you like the type," Forrest says. Considering everything Rik has apparently told Mr. Worthington about their friendship, it should be pretty obvious that Rik's not his type or he'd have done something about it already.

"He's charming. And ever so well mannered. And from such a fine old family. Yes sir, that young James Richardson Tipton would make someone a fine little. . ."

"Holy cow," Forrest says, cutting him off in mid-flight. "Is that the time? I have rugby practice."

* * *

Rik comes out of the kitchen dabbing ever so daintily at his brow with a dishcloth. Forrest has not been allowed to help with the shopping or cooking, though he did split the cost of the groceries. He hasn't been consulted about the table setting or the floral arrangement. Rik knows about such things and Forrest doesn't. Forrest knows about things like playing manly sports and riding the subway. At least that's the script they're working from at present. And the one contribution he's made to the evening is providing the venue. Rik considers that the street he lives on is unchic, though Forrest is not sure how his own address is an improvement.

"We'd better change," Rik says. "Don't you think?"

His change of clothes is hanging in Forrest's closet.

"You go ahead. I think I'll wait a bit."

"Forrest," Rik protests. He omits the exclamation point he'd ordinarily shove in there because Forrest warned him he'd be locked out on the fire escape otherwise.

"There's plenty of time."

"No, there's not," Rik insists, looking at his watch.

"You don't think that he'll be on time? Do you? Come on, Rik boy. Get real."

Rik looks exasperated. He exhales histrionically, but he doesn't argue. He goes into Forrest's bedroom and starts pulling off his clothes. Forrest can tell Rik's upset because he doesn't once look back to see if he's being watched.

Forrest stands surveying his latest acquisition. It's a set of antique sterling silver picture frames. He found them in a little shop on Grove Street. They're not really his kind of thing, but the minute he saw them he had an idea they just might do. In them he's mounted family photos. One of all five of them, taken a couple of years ago for the St. Stephen's Parish Directory. Another of Mother and Daddy. One of Bobby Lee in his dress uniform. Forrest has arranged these on top of the bookcase. It's impossible to miss them from anywhere in the room.

* * *

After the dinner, after listening about a hundred times to "*Ebben? Ne andro lontana*" from Catalani's *La Wally*, after hours of soporific conversation, it's time for Mr. Worthington to make his departure. Forrest has watched him like a hawk all evening, and though Mr. Worthington would never admit having done it, every so often he's looked across at those pictures on the bookcase. But he's never quite risen to the bait.

"Dear! Dear! Boys!" he sighs, as Rik helps him on with his coat. "What! A Perfect! Evening!"

He kisses them both goodbye and is gone.

"Do you really think he had a good time?" Rik asks after a long, reverential silence.

"Of course he did," Forrest snorts, beginning to clear the dinner table. "And if he didn't it's his own fault."

"That's your problem," Rik sighs.

Forrest may have broken him of gratuitous exclamation points and indiscriminate italicization, but he still sighs.

"What's my problem, Rik boy?"

"You have no poetry."

"No poetry? No poetry?"

"That's right," Rik says, eyes wide and solemn.

"'Won't you walk a little faster?' said a whiting to a snail/'There's a porpoise close behind us, and he's treading on my tail'. Poetry, Rik. The very finest. Come on, I know you know this one. 'See how eagerly the lobsters and the turtles all advance/They are waiting on the shingle, won't you come and join the dance?'"

Rik tries his best to look disgusted.

* * *

Bobby Lee writes from the war. He can stand the suspense no longer. It's time for the denouement. He insists that Forrest gets off his ass and do something—anything—to bring it about. He must contrive a scenario that will force Uncle Ellis to tell all. But Bobby Lee hasn't met the man. He only knows him from Forrest's letters. And Forrest has apparently failed to convey exactly how difficult a case he is. Slippery as an eel. Wise as an owl. Sly as a fox. A menagerie of animal similes.

When the moment comes, several weeks later, it's not due to any machination on Forrest's part. They're having brunch at the Four Seasons. They're on their way to a matinee at the Met: *Carmen*. And while Forrest is distracted by a spectacular man three tables away, Rik tosses the bomb.

"Did you know that Forrest's parents are coming to New York?"

There's a long, awkward pause. Forrest wishes that at some random moment during the last year he had smothered Rik with a sofa pillow.

"No, I didn't. Forrest, you didn't mention a thing about it."

"Sorry." Forrest can actually see discomfort in those usually inscrutable eyes. "I forgot to mention it. I had the letter just this morning. Mother's coming up for a medical conference. And Daddy never misses a chance to visit New York."

Forrest knows it must look like a trap, but it's honestly not. He simply left the letter out where Rik could see it and stupidly answered his questions about the contents without thinking of the consequences.

"I'm sure you'll be thrilled to see Judge Reynolds again," Rik enthuses. "He's just been appointed to the Tennessee Supreme Court, you know."

"No, I didn't. Forrest, you haven't done a very good job of passing things on."

All Forrest can do is gulp. The whole thing is about to get completely out of hand. He could shoot himself for not having prevented it.

"Admit it," Rik says, "You can't wait to see them."

"Why, certainly."

"I mean, since you were the judge's best friend in college. His roommate. The best man at their wedding. I'm sure they're just as excited as you are."

There's another long silence.

"I'm sorry," Forrest says. "I wanted it to be a surprise. Rik wormed it out of me."

"Yes. Little Rik. Such a persistent chile. Not to mention cryptic."

But of course it's not Rik he's talking about.

"Tell me again when they're due to arrive."

"Two weeks from tomorrow," Forrest says.

"Well then, we've plenty of time to anticipate this reunion."

* * *

Two evenings later they're sitting over coffee after an evening of "reimagined" Chekhov in a Soho storefront. Forrest is wondering how soon he can get away because he has early chem lab in the morning. He's just about to say so when Mr. Worthington hauls out a couple of small packages. It's not Sunday afternoon high tea, the typical occasion for presenting gifts, and Forrest immediately suspects something's up.

"Now my dears, you must open these at the same time."

Forrest looks at Rik and Rik looks back. Forrest tears into his package while Rik picks genteelly at his. In a small black leather case, Forrest finds a set of platinum shirt studs and cufflinks. They're obviously not new, but it's still an extravagant gift. He's about to protest when Mr. Worthington speaks.

"And now the sad news, dear boys."

The level of melodrama in his voice would do justice to a basso at the Met.

"I shall be leaving soon. Very soon, as a matter of fact. And I just wanted you to have these things to remember me by."

"But why are you going away?" Rik sputters. "Where are you going?"

"The West Coast," he sighs, looking no longer tragic but suddenly near euphoria. "Palm trees! Moonlit nights on gleaming white beaches! California! Dear Chile!"

"California!"

Forrest decides just this once to forgive the exclamation point.

"But why?" Rik wails.

"Why, work! My Dear! Work! An actor must have work, and at long last I've been offered work! A pilot! For a weekly series! On a major network!"

An actor. It's the first he's mentioned it. Forrest feels like he's being offered a discount on the Brooklyn Bridge.

"Who knows?" Mr. Worthington speculates. "It might even lead to Motion Pictures."

"That's wonderful!" Rik gushes. "Just think!"

Forrest is thinking, all right.

"Don't you think it's wonderful, Forrest?" Rik insists.

"Amazing," Forrest nods.

"Of course we'll miss you terribly," Rik says.

"And I you."

"When do you leave?" Forrest asks.

"I fly out! In the morning!"

"No!" Rik moans. "So soon? Oh, no! That means you're going to miss seeing Forrest's parents."

"Yes," Mr. Worthington says, avoiding eye contact. "I'm afraid so."

"What a shame," Rik sighs.

"Indeed. It's my only regret about this sudden opportunity. The timing is unfortunate, as you say."

* * *

In the two months since Uncle Ellis left, Rik has settled down a little. His speech patterns are nearly back to normal. So is his diet: no more lady fingers dipped in sherry for breakfast. They still come to the Met, but less often since it's on their own dimes now.

"Just look at him," Rik sighs.

It's intermission, and Rik's tongue is hanging out at the sight of a man across the foyer. He's almost exactly Forrest's height but somewhat broader shouldered. He's blond and wears his hair in the style of an upper class English schoolboy. Forrest can't help wondering what he'd look like dressed out for a rugby match. He's in a tux tonight and so are his five buddies. They're a sleek, prosperous looking, undeniably handsome bunch of professional types—Forrest imagines them as stockbrokers or attorneys—probably on the cusp of turning thirty.

"Isn't he fabulous?" Rik sighs.

"Are you coming?"

"I think I'll wait here."

"Can I get you anything?"

"White wine."

Forrest leaves him there, staring and sighing, and heads for the line at the bar. It's a long opera and consequently a thirsty crowd.

"Are you and your friend enjoying the opera?"

Forrest looks over his shoulder. It's the blond man with the shoulders. Forrest turns the rest of the way around and smiles. Not only does he look like a refugee from Jolly Olde, his accent is straight out of a Noel Coward play. Forrest imagines Rik swooning over it.

"Well, my friend is."

The blond nods as if he understands perfectly.

"I've seen the two of you here before. With an older gentleman."

"My uncle. He recently moved to Los Angeles."

"And you two are. . . ?"

"Friends," Forrest stammers. "Pals. Buddies. Chums."

"Because it seems one of my chums is wild about him."

"Then let them be introduced," Forrest grins. "By all means."

"You and I might have dinner soon. And make plans to bring them together."

"Great idea," Forrest says, feeling lightheaded.

The blond reaches into the pocket of his jacket and pulls out a platinum card case and an equally impressive looking pen. He extracts a card from the case, writes on the back of it, and hands it over.

Forrest reads the front of the card first. "Dr. Phillip Haverstraw, M.D." There's a Park Avenue address and a phone number. On the back of the card, in neat, architectural printing, there's a different one.

"I'm afraid I don't have one to give you," Forrest says.

"Then perhaps. . ." The good doctor takes out another card. Forrest gives his name and telephone number, and the lights dim in the lobby to recall the audience to their seats for the third act curtain.

"Dinner. You promised."

"And I always keep my word," Forrest says.

* * *

The postcard is waiting on the hall table when Forrest comes in from his physics final. It's been forwarded from his old place. He can hear Phillip rummaging around in the bedroom, presumably packing. They're flying to Tennessee tonight to spend Christmas with Forrest's family. Bobby Lee will be there. He called three nights ago from San Francisco, just off a military flight, exultant at having gotten back from the war in one piece.

The postcard is of some resort in Mexico Forrest has never heard of. The handwriting is spidery, like that of an old maid aunt. He says he's having a wonderful time and misses both his Dear Boys. It gives no information of a practical nature. It mentions nothing about a weekly television series on a major network. It says only that months after leaving, he's still alive. Since that's more than he told anyone the first time he disappeared, Forrest supposes it's a sign of progress.

Rik would want to hear about this, but Forrest doesn't have his new number. They haven't spoken since last spring, and Forrest only heard about his move from mutual friends. He won't bother looking Rik up because it really doesn't matter. The postcard may be postmarked Mexico, but the charade is over. Because Forrest was down in the Village visiting a classmate last week, and he spotted a familiar face. Forrest wasn't sure at first, because Uncle Ellis has changed. The hair is completely gray now and cropped short enough to be combed with a washcloth. And the mustache has expanded into a full beard. He was nearly unrecognizable. But then Forrest caught sight of his eyes as he gazed at a Puerto Rican delivery boy, and he knew he had his man. Forrest was very careful not to let himself be seen as he followed his quarry down Bleeker. He stayed well back. But there was no mistaking that stride and those clothes.

His address hadn't changed.

Forrest takes off his coat and hangs it next to Phillip's in the hall closet. "I'm home."

"Darling," Phillip emerges from the bedroom, boyishly disheveled from his labors. "How ghastly was it?"

"Not bad. I think I passed."

"There's a post card for you."

"I saw it, thanks."

He sees that glint in Phillip's eye that denotes unease.

"It's going to be fine."

"Easy for you to say," Phillip says, looking pensive.

"You've met them before. They adored you."

"On my own turf. This is different."

"Not that different," Forrest insists.

III

Forrest looks down into the grave. It's his third funeral in six weeks. It's all he can do not to cry, but he feels Miss Betsy's eyes on him and he won't let her see that. Everyone says she's blind as a bat these days, but he doesn't buy it. Mother apparently senses that things inside him are building to a crescendo. She squeezes his hand. He turns and tries to smile.

Uncle Davis was seventy-nine. He collapsed one morning a few weeks back. It was a stroke. All the Reynoldses seem to go that way. He never re-gained consciousness and he died four days ago. On the other side of the grave, Cousin Kenny and his latest wife flank Miss Betsy and Aunt Helen. Kenny looks slimmer and harder than he did the last time Forrest saw him. He looks older, too. Everyone present does. Staring into the mirror this morning in his old bedroom, Forrest could have sworn he was a thousand.

But not Miss Betsy. The last decade has changed her remarkably little. As if she's long since aged as much as she was ever going to. As if there was no room left anywhere on her face for more wrinkles and no remaining space for her internal organs should she shrink any further. Or as if some mad scientist in the neighborhood has finally invented suspended animation and they only bring her out of it for noteworthy occasions. People tell Forrest that she's still sharp as a tack. That she's forgotten nothing. They say it like they're proud of her. But Forrest hasn't forgotten much himself. He knows from bitter experi-ence that as sharp as her mind might be, her old tongue is sharper still. And she's not too particular about who she uses it on. And one other thing. Every time in the last decade until three weeks ago, she could have made it up to Forrest by treating Phillip the way he always wanted her to. She can't now. There are no more chances. Forrest can't forgive her. Not for that.

There's a pretty young preacher boy officiating today. Old Brother Sykes died of a heart attack three years ago. Smack in the middle of one of his famous hellfire and damnation sermons. And the church can't afford to pay a full time pastor any more. All they can get these days is a succession of twenty year old Bible college students who drive in from Nashville on weekends and for the occasional funeral. This one is sincere but not exactly what you expect a spiritual authority to look and sound like. He's not nearly as longwinded as Brother Sykes, that's for certain. Because unless Forrest has forgotten some part of this, it's just about wound up and they'll be out of here and on their way to Miss Betsy's for the luncheon before you know it. He would skip that but he won't give her the satisfaction of thinking he's afraid to face her. There's a final prayer. One of those homespun, extemporaneous, semi-coherent Baptist prayers. Before Forrest knows it everyone's saying, "Amen" and heading for their cars. Daddy walks toward the Jaguar, and Mother and Forrest follow him arm in arm. Amelia and Justin didn't make the trip because the twins have been sick. Elyse is in the middle of final exams. She's in graduate school at Vanderbilt.

"I was fine until we got to the grave."

Mother nods. Her eyes well up. Her tears are, Forrest knows, no more for Uncle Davis than his own. Daddy opens the rear door of the Jaguar for Mother. Forrest gets in beside him. Just as they're about to pull away, there's a rapping on Daddy's window.

"Mind if I hop in?" Bobby Lee asks.

"Not at all, boy," Daddy says.

He climbs into the back seat beside Mother.

* * *

Upstairs in Bobby Lee's old room, which as far as Forrest can see hasn't changed in the slightest detail since his cousin first left for the army, they sit on the bed with their plastic forks and heaping paper plates. Forrest pokes at his potato salad and wonders if he'll ever have an appetite again. He can tell it's Aunt Jesse's potato salad because she's the only woman in the family daring enough to include pimientos in her recipe. This kind of culinary adventurousness is described as "gourmet" in these parts. Forrest tries to remember how many funeral meals he's consumed under this roof. He can't begin to count them all. Indeed, he can't remember as far back as the first one. People have always been dying around here. Just like the sun always rises and falls and the seasons always follow each other in the same succession. He just never took note of all the mortality going on. It never seemed to touch him.

"You look pretty rough," Bobby Lee says.

"Feel about that way, too."

"One too many funerals lately."

His green eyes indicate clearly that he's not talking about Uncle Davis. And it's two too many funerals, but Forrest hasn't told anybody about Uncle Ellis yet. He doesn't know when he will. Mentioning it would require talking about the cause of death, and he doesn't know if he's up to it. The body was barely identifiable—that's how badly Uncle Ellis had been beaten. The police have made no progress in their search for the hustler who did it. He's not sure they're really trying.

"It really meant a lot to me that you called. Mother and Daddy flew to London with me, of course. And Amelia and Justin sent flowers. Elyse did, too. But none of these others acknowledged it at all. It was as if he never existed."

"Nobody even told me about it," Bobby Lee says. "Four days after I got back home I ran into your mother at the hospital. I was just coming out of Uncle Davis' room and there she was on her morning rounds. I asked after you and she said something about how hard you were taking things. I didn't have the least idea what she was talking about. And of course she had no idea I hadn't been told. When we got it all straightened out, she was mad enough to spit nails. She gave Mama such a chewing out over it that she's not through sulking yet."

"Well," Forrest says, "it surely was good to hear from you."

Bobby Lee looks out the window.

"So you've been back for two weeks now."

"That's right."

"Some way to spend your leave. Hanging around the hospital and now this."

Bobby Lee shrugs.

"You'll be climbing the walls by the time you have to go back."

Bobby Lee turns from the window, and Forrest can see him trying to make some decision. It's like he can see the gears turning in the deeps behind the eyes. He can almost hear them whirring away like parts of some exquisitely engineered machine.

"I'm not going back," Bobby Lee finally says, "but nobody knows that yet."

"What do you mean, you're not going back? Can you do that? Just quit?"

"You can when your enlistment's up."

"And is it?" For all Forrest knows about the military, it could be.

"Not exactly. But that's what I'll tell everyone."

"Won't they wonder why you didn't mention it before you got home?"

"You know it's not like that around here. They believe what they want to believe. And in this case, they'll want to believe that my enlistment is up."

"Even though it's not?"

Bobby Lee closes his eyes. He looks like he wants to go to sleep. For about a year and a half. Which is not like him at all. He was always the life of the party.

"So here's the real story," he begins.

"You don't have to tell me."

"I'm discharged. Not honorably."

"God."

"Not dishonorably, either," he says.

"What else is there?"

"A general discharge. And that's all I'm saying under this roof."

"All right."

"You know," he says, looking back out the window, "I was thinking maybe you'd like some company back in New York. Just for a week or so."

"Yes," Forrest says. "Of course. Come for as long as you want."

* * *

The plane hangs above the runway. Forrest's knuckles are white and he's sure his face is, too. He's sweating buckets and struggling desperately not to shit his pants. Phillip's last flight ended prematurely during a failed landing. The weather that night was perfect, just like tonight, and there were no apparent problems with his plane, a 727 just like this one. Almost everyone on board walked away. Almost. But not Phillip.

The plane hangs just feet above the runway. Forrest remembers standing at the gate waiting for the plane to taxi up. He remembers a loud noise like an explosion. He remembers flashing lights and sirens.

"Take it easy," Bobby Lee mutters next to him. "Easy, Forrest. Everything's going to be fine. We're almost down now."

But the plane hangs in the air, and Forrest remembers. All the years worth of memories, from the night he met Phillip at the opera until that last afternoon when he called on his way to the airport for his flight.

There's a thud and a judder and a bounce. They're down.

"See," Bobby Lee says. "We're here. Everything's O.K."

* * *

"Nice place," Bobby Lee says, looking around the living room. "Must have cost a bundle."

"Phillip had already been here for five years when we met."

"And lots of nice stuff," he says, eyeing a pair of Lalique cats. "So what now?"

"What do you mean?"

"Do you get to stay here? I know you make a ton of money working at that bank, but what arrangements were there? The mortgage on a place like this. . ."

"We paid off the mortgage back in March."

"And what? He left it to you? His family didn't make trouble?"

"No trouble. I have to ship some of the art back to them soon, but other than that they're peaches."

"So you're O.K. financially."

Forrest is O.K. financially. He's not O.K. in any other respect, but he's got a home, a stock portfolio, certificates of deposit and tax free municipal bonds. He's got a quarter interest in a house on Fire Island. The Miro over the fireplace is staying, as are the Picasso in entry hall and the two Dalis in the master bedroom. He's got a Jaguar sedan and a Mercedes convertible. And all of it's paid for. Every last thing. Phillip was very successful and didn't believe in debt.

"I'm fine."

Bobby Lee nods.

"That's good. Got to say, you look like hell. You need a shower and a good stiff drink. And then bed."

"It's not even eight o'clock."

"Don't argue. Where do you keep your liquor?"

"In the kitchen," Forrest says, "just through there. I think the bed in the study is already made up."

"Don't you worry about me. I'm used to sleeping in tents, remember? With critters crawling around under my cot all night. Shaking scorpions out of my boots every morning before I put them on so I don't get stung."

"God, Bobby Lee."

"There," he chuckles, "I finally got a smile out of you. O.K Listen. I didn't come up here for you to take care of me. So go take your shower and I'll get your drink ready."

* * *

"They caught me," Bobby Lee says the next morning over coffee and toast, "in the motel room with those two young men. Apparently somebody's jealous ex-boyfriend had tipped off the M.P.'s. They arrested me and dragged me off to the stockade without so much as a by your leave. I figured it was all over. Court martial. Prison for twenty years at least. My life completely ruined. But it turned out I got a few breaks. The guys were nineteen, thank God. I mean, I'm not in the habit of carding my tricks, you know? Although maybe I'd better start. So anyway, it was just dumb luck. There aren't any sodomy statutes in that state any more, and no money had changed hands. So the civilian authorities didn't want to hear about it. And my friends weren't military personnel. Did you know that the military consider it much worse when you fuck a fellow soldier than when you fuck a civilian?"

"I had no idea."

"Well, it's true. I'd never have gotten off if those two had been privates. Anyway, I called a friend of mine who'd been through something similar a couple of years back, and he gave me the name of the attorney who handled his case. It cost the earth."

"You'll let me help you with the costs, of course."

"Nope."

"Bobby Lee."

"Our mothers raised us to clean up our own messes, cous."

"Yes, but."

"But nothing. Anyway, I called the guy who got my buddy off and he got me off, too. No court martial: decorated war veteran, consenting adults, all that bullshit. They let me stay in a few weeks until my enlistment was up. End of story."

"That's amazing."

"No shit. As opposed to stepping in it. No benefits, but I've got money saved."

"Hell, boy, you can do anything you want now. Go back to school. . ."

"Yeah," Bobby Lee nods. "I can do anything the hell I want except what I want, which is to finish my twenty and retire. By then I'm sure I'd have made some plans. But now—fuck if I know."

Forrest knows the feeling. He didn't make any plans either, except the one about growing old with Phillip.

"There are jobs here, you realize," he says. "I mean, it's New York, right?"

"Sure, cous. I can stand on a street corner and sell flowers. Or fake Rolexes. I can operate a newsstand. I can wash dishes in a restaurant. No, thank you."

"There are real jobs you can get."

"Name one, Forrest. I've got a high school diploma and twelve years in the infantry, where I learned how to stumble around in the boonies carrying a gun, how to dig a foxhole, how to drink and cuss and spit, and how to pitch a tent. I don't have any skills anyone around here gives a shit about."

"It's not that bad. And anyway, you just need something to keep yourself going while you figure things out. Face it. You're going to have to tell Aunt Libby and Uncle Fred something sooner or later. But if you already had a job up here and looked like you were making plans, it might be easier to explain."

"There's nothing to explain. I decided I hated it in the army and I got out. It isn't a dishonorable discharge. There's no reason for anybody back home to be suspicious. They could find out easily enough, I guess. If they wanted to. But nobody back there wants to. Not really."

"But Bobby Lee."

"No, cous. All this openness and honesty—well, that's fine for a guy like you. You don't give a damn what any of them think. You never did."

"That's not true."

"O.K., maybe about a hundred years ago. I'm not saying it's bad that you don't care any more. I'm just saying it's not that simple for me."

"Yes, it is," Forrest says. "It is exactly that simple. At least it could be."

"No," Bobby Lee says, looking sadder than Forrest can ever remember seeing him. "No. You've done it your way, and I've spent years listening to them talk about you behind your back. Behind your parents' backs, too. They're never going to be able to say stuff like that about me. I won't stand for that. You're enough of a hero for one clan of southerners. I'm doing this my way."

"If you say so."

"You won't blow the whistle on me? I mean, I trust you with my life, of course. You know that. It's just that you might get it into your head to do something like that for my own good."

It's exactly what Forrest has been considering, and he hates it that Bobby Lee suspects.

"I won't say anything," he says.

* * *

"Sit down, cous," Bobby Lee says.

"What's up?"

Bobby Lee is sitting in an armchair drinking a Stroh's. Forrest flops onto the couch. He's just back from the gym. He's only been going back to the gym for a couple of weeks, and it makes him more tired than he ever imagined he could be.

"Need to talk to you about our plans for this evening," Bobby Lee says.

"O.K."

"Well," he says, after a long swig, "would you mind it too bad if we didn't go to that movie?"

"Of course not," Forrest says, "if you'd rather do something else. Or we can stay home."

"Forrest, I don't want you to take this wrong, but in the last three weeks we've been to the movies eight times and we've been to three plays, two art gallery openings, a poetry reading, and three concerts."

"I know I've been dragging you all over the place," Forrest says. "You're too nice to say so, but you hate all that stuff. We'll stay home."

It's been nothing so noble as trying to show Bobby Lee a good time in the big city. It's been pure selfishness. Forrest doesn't like spending any more time than necessary at home. He can't walk into any room without halfway expecting to find Phillip there. It's like being under siege. Memories come without warning. They explode like terrorist car bombs. They rain down like mortar fire. Forrest isn't safe anywhere. The streets and the bars and the theatres and shops and restaurants and galleries are bad enough, but nothing's as bad as the apartment.

"That's not what I meant," Bobby Lee says.

"So?"

"Forrest, I'm a grownup. I know my way around the city. And I'm going out by myself tonight. Get the picture?"

"Certainly. Whatever you want."

"I don't want you to think I haven't been having a terrific time. I'm just ready for a little adventure of my own."

"Sure."

"And so are you."

"No," Forrest says. "No, I'm not, thank you very much."

"That's your business, of course."

* * *

"Morning," the young man says.

"Good morning," Forrest answers, wishing he had something on. Anything. It was pretty stupid of him not to have foreseen the possibility of an overnight guest, with Bobby Lee cooped up for so long.

"I'm Jake."

He's wearing a pair of bikini briefs, and he's built like a brick shithouse. He must live at the gym. He has dirty blond hair and eyes the color of iced tea. Forrest can't speak.

"You're the cousin."

"Right," Forrest stammers, faking a yawn, "I'm the cousin."

"I hope you don't mind," Jake says, holding up a filter and the carafe, which is full of water.

"Not at all. Make yourself at home. He drinks it black, and he likes it strong enough to float a horseshoe."

* * *

The next morning, the guy's name is J.J. and he looks like the pretty half of a professional wrestling tag team. He expresses a willingness to forego breakfast for a quick round with Forrest before heading off to his job stocking shelves at a Grand Union somewhere in Brooklyn, but Forrest politely declines.

* * *

The next morning, the guy's name is Albert, which he pronounces in the French manner. In spite of this, Forrest suspects he's not from any farther away than Newark. But he's cute as a button and he makes a heavenly omelet. While they eat, he asks a lot of questions about Bobby Lee, who is not up yet.

* * *

Forrest has been dreading coming back to the island. He can't imagine a worse place to be, considering what's ailing him. Phillip and he had some of their best times out here. All those summers, counting the first one when they only made it out for two weekends before Phillip bought an interest in the house. It amounts to too many memories, and Forrest had unconsciously decided to sit out the whole season in the city. But when Harry called last week asking if Forrest was planning to use his room because if not he wanted to offer it to someone from his office, Forrest surprised himself by saying yes, he'd be coming out. He has no idea why he did that. But once he had, he felt strangely committed. Like when you agree to attend a family reunion you know will be misery from beginning to end. Once you say you'll be there, there's no backing out short of famine, war, or pestilence.

Bobby Lee didn't know about the place out here. When Forrest told him about the plan, he was like a kid at Christmas. On the way to catch the ferry, he kept pinching himself. Forrest sees a lot of familiar faces on the deck. Not people he actually knows, just people he recognizes from other weekends, other years. There are also, as is true everywhere in the city, hordes of men he's never seen before. After living in New York for as along as he has, he sometimes feels he ought to know everyone. This is, of course, stupid of him. He doesn't even know everyone in his building or everyone who goes to his gym. But even understanding this he is surprised by the sheer number of men he's never laid eyes on before. Refugees from America just as he is, just as Bobby Lee would be if he'd only agree to it. The specific names and biographical details differ from individual to individual but the essential story is pretty much the same. Like, Forrest supposes, eastern European Jews several decades ago, or Italians from the old country, Irish from the Old Sod.

Forrest and his people even have their own culture. The proof is right in front of him, an abandoned copy of a lesbian vampire science fiction thriller by a friend of a friend of the sister of somebody his buddy, Kevin, went to high school with or somesuch backstory, which is actually more interesting than the book itself turns out to be. While Forrest struggles through page after page of lurid description and turgid prose, all composed in the most up to date High Middle Gay imaginable and thus so excruciatingly *au courant* he almost feels the need of a translator, Bobby Lee works the deck. Forrest is sure that before the weekend is out people are going to be referring to Bobby Lee as Miss Congeniality.

* * *

"Look," Bobby Lee hisses into Forrest's ear.

Forrest looks, but he has no idea who he's supposed to see in the array of faces, heads, shoulders, t-shirts.

"No, cous, not that way. Over there."

He grabs Forrest's shoulder and turns him about twenty degrees to the right.

"See him?"

Forrest sees a room full of hims.

"Dark hair. Mustache. Black t-shirt. Shoulders like the broad side of a barn."

This narrows things down less than might be imagined.

"He's really something, isn't he?"

"If you like the type," Forrest says.

"He's been watching you," Bobby Lee says. "I think he wants you to ask him to dance."

"Think again, Jimbo."

"Seriously. He keeps looking over here."

"There are about three dozen guys within five yards of us. He could be looking at anyone."

"No," Bobby Lee insists. "I've been watching him. It's definitely you. When you went to the bar to get our drinks he followed you with his eyes. All the way over there and all the way back."

Forrest shrugs. He still isn't sure which guy they're talking about.

"I swear, cous. You need to get your tail over there and ask him to dance."

"In your dreams."

Forrest turns to look out at the water. Moonlight dances off it. Moonlight is the last thing he needs.

"Well," Bobby Lee says, "if you won't do it."

Forrest watches him set off. Then he catches sight of his friend Harry dancing with some blond guy who looks like every single one of his former lovers, not to mention his current one who stayed in the city this weekend because his parents, who don't know about Harry, are in town. Harry waves and looks sheepish. Bobby Lee has reached the other side of the room now and is whispering into the ear of a smoldering beauty of a twenty-three year old. Black Irish would be Forrest's guess. The young man nods. Forrest is pretty sure from Bobby Lee's grin what he must have said—Forrest is too shy to ask anyone to dance. Bobby Lee's meddling annoys him. He almost decides to slip into the crowd. But it's easier just to stand there and let it happen. It's just a dance.

* * *

On the beach at night alone. It was one of Phillip's favorite poems. Whitman. "On the beach at night alone." And Forrest is, with the Atlantic lapping
his bare feet in the darkness, cool sand wet and compacted against the soles. On
the beach. At night. Alone. Whenever he thought of the poem, Phillip once
said, he imagined this very stretch of beach. Forrest has no idea if Whitman
ever came to Fire Island, but for what he apparently had in mind when he wrote
the poem it's as good a locale as any. Phillip first became familiar with the text
in a musical setting by Ralph Vaughan Williams. A baritone sings it. It's the
second movement of *A Sea Symphony*. It started Phillip's lifelong love affair with
Whitman's poetry.

Phillip loved to leave the dancing and partying and dishing behind and
come down to the water like this. It was, for him, the quintessential Fire Island
experience: time out from all that frenetic activity to contemplate the meaning
of life for a few moments every now and then on a summer night. He believed
that gay life in Manhattan was heavily populated with philosopher-princes like
himself—that everyone did this in some way or another. And it was this inner
quest that energized all the rest of the culture he believed he and his gay brothers were building.

Forrest didn't make anything so grand of it. It was pure romance, that's
all. A solitary man—a handsome, smart, cultivated man coming down to the
water to dream a little. Sometimes Forrest would come with him through the
darkness. They'd stand hand in hand looking out into the blackness that was
alive with motion they could hardly see, that was discernable chiefly through
its sound. Mostly, though, Phillip preferred to come down to the water by
himself and stand gazing out into something he said was to infinity what a
cocktease is to a healthy young man. Forrest never saw that, though goodness
knows he tried.

The poem is about transcendence. Not a word Forrest is comfortable
with. Not that he has any special aversion to the concept itself. At least as Phillip understood Whitman to have meant it. It's just that the word got so ruined
by the hippies, misapplied in so many ways by so many people—Forrest's skin
crawls thinking about it. And then there are all those Baptists in his lineage,
with their own quaint, set in stone certainties about the cosmos. Particularly
the parts of it that can't be seen.

Forrest can almost hear the baritone singing those sublime words, the
orchestra surging and throbbing around him like these waters. He can almost

see Phillip huddled over the turntable back at their apartment, watching the shiny black disc spin. Phillip did that. He would sit staring at those surfaces, staring at the waving lines moving there in some strange way like this ocean. As if staring at those tiny grooves might tell him something that listening to the words and music alone couldn't. Phillip claimed that there were people who could look at the grooves on a record, even from clear across the room, and identify the music without hearing it or referring to the label. Phillip insisted it was true. Documented by science. Forrest never argued. Nearly anything you can imagine has happened somewhere sometime. Phillip never claimed to be able to do it himself or to know anyone who could. His faith in the medical literature was infinite.

Forrest remembers the first time he saw Phillip crouched like that over the turntable. It wasn't Vaughan Williams that night. It was Shostakovich. The Fourth Symphony. The one the composer withdrew from performance in fear of the Stalinist purges. Forrest didn't know that story at the time. He simply saw the man he had recently fallen in love with doing something he couldn't comprehend. He only heard wild, tortured music. Music he now knows hinted at anguish Phillip must have felt but Forrest never sensed in all those years of living with him.

Talk about alone. Remembering your inability ever to truly know the man you loved. It's enough to pull you step by step down the beach and into that water, never to come back.

* * *

"Look who I found," Bobby Lee says, sidling up through the glare of high noon to the table where Harry and Brad and Michael and Michael's new lover whose name Forrest can't ever remember and Michael's new lover's best friend who is called Ty or maybe Cy are keeping Forrest company, sitting and drinking and watching the oiled and bronzed bodies glinting out on the dance deck. Who Bobby Lee has found is about twenty and blond and classically handsome and built like a poster boy for heavy poundages and perfectly executed reps. His cobalt eyes may be sparking, but Forrest can smell farm boy reserve a mile away.

"Who?" Brad asks for all of them as they crane necks and raise hands to shade eyes for a better view of this marvel.

"Why, it's young Morgan Lundquist. That's who," Bobby Lee drawls, every inch the southern queen, a role he relishes playing for these Yankees. In the process he reminds Forrest excruciatingly of Uncle Ellis in full cry.

Forrest looks more closely in spite of himself. Closely enough that he begins to feel a little queasy, though he assures himself that it's nothing more than the heat of midday and a couple of drinks on an empty stomach in addition to not enough sleep the night before. Yes, sirree. Five feet nine inches or so, and say an even two hundred pounds of hard, exquisitely sculpted, corn fed muscle twink. Enough to make you beat your head against a brick wall. Enough to give women palpitations and make a grown man weep. If you like the type, that is. And obviously a new boy in town, because this kind of meat can become a legend in an afternoon but none of them has heard of him.

Brad makes the introductions and Morgan smiles politely and shakes everyone's hand. He's soft spoken and well mannered and apparently intelligent and just the tiniest bit shy, it seems. Exactly the kind of boy you'd think anyone's mother would be happy for one of her children to meet and settle down with.

"We really can't stay," Bobby Lee insists with a hauteur that won't be argued with as certain members of the party begin rearranging the seating to accommodate these newcomers. "We'll be late for our luncheon engagement."

Luncheon engagement? Forrest nearly spits up his drink. Nobody should be able to get away with Bobby Lee's level of pretentiousness. But these yankees seem to find it charming. Or at least harmlessly eccentric.

* * *

"What did you think of Morgan?" Bobby Lee asks the next morning over a late breakfast on the deck.

Unfortunately, Forrest has had yet another bad night, and his bitchery rears its ugly head.

"He looks like he'd be loads of fun. Is he?"

Forrest regrets the bitter edge of insinuation in his voice as soon as he hears it. It apparently amuses Bobby Lee.

"Why, it appears you've gotten the wrong impression, cous," he says, eyes wide with what he thinks plays as innocence. "That splendid young man is ever so refined and genteel."

"I'm sure," Forrest says. "That must be why he was wearing the skimpiest garment ever to masquerade as a swimsuit on this particular stretch of beach. And believe me, that's saying something."

"Aha," Bobby Lee laughs. "You noticed."

Forrest savagely butters a croissant. He knows first hand how trashy a boy that age can be. Even one that innocent looking. Especially one that innocent looking. He was one himself. And a paragon of depravity. At least until he met Phillip, who proposed on their first date and kept him on the shortest of leashes from then on.

"You can't judge a book by its cover," Bobby Lee says.

"Oh yes you can," Forrest says. "When a book has nearly naked muscle boys on the cover, you can be sure of what's going to be happening by the end of chapter three."

"Fair enough," Bobby Lee nods. "But see, he's just gotten here. Not to mention he's just come out. He doesn't really know anything about anything. We had a long talk about it last night. Or, well, maybe it was this morning after all. Doesn't matter. But honest to God, cous, that young man has this crazy idea about saving himself for Mr. Right."

"They all do," Forrest says, "when they first get off the bus. But by the time it's pulling back out of the station, they're having second thoughts."

"Now, now."

"Seriously, Bobby Lee. Half the guys on this island would tell you the same thing. But it doesn't keep them away from the Meat Rack."

"Well, I'm quite sure you know what you're talking about, Forrest. God knows you always do. But I tell you, this boy is too serious minded for all that. He's holding out for true love. In his case that's spelled with capital letters. And what do you call it? *Italicized?*"

"Just as long as he's not holding his breath," Forrest mutters, almost knocking over his tomato juice as he reaches for a napkin. "And don't come on like the Dowager Empress of Knoxville with me, boy, because I know better. You may be able to bamboozle these yankees with that routine, but I know just exactly how white trash you are because I am myself."

"Somebody's in a perfectly beastly mood this morning."

"And somebody else is stunningly observant."

"Somebody must have gotten up on the wrong side of the bed."

"And somebody else didn't get out of bed at all. At least not his own."

"Morgan wanted to watch the sunrise over the ocean."

"How romantic. Are you sure he doesn't put out?"

"God, cous, you sure can be a bitch."

He's right, Forrest knows.

"Sorry, Jimbo. I'm just not having a very good time out here. It was a bad idea to come, and I'm taking it out on you."

"The day I need or want an apology from you is a long way off," he smiles. This just makes Forrest feel worse.

"I know you're not enjoying yourself. But I appreciate your bringing me out here in spite of the fact that you knew you were going to be miserable."

A lump in Forrest's throat prevents any reply to this. A single tear falls onto his plate.

"You know that boy," Bobby Lee says, looking pensive. "Well, I mean, I'm not his type and he's not mine. We both got that right away. It meant we didn't have to work through a whole lot of bullshit. We could just sit down and talk."

"I'm glad you found someone for company."

"Exactly. Company. Now, he's truly a nice boy. Really sincere. And smart enough to know what he wants. But like just about everybody out here, he doesn't seem to have the first idea how to find it. I can't believe it, you know, cous? All these too, too slick city boys with their clothes and their grooming agents and sophisticated conversation so that I feel like I need an interpreter half the time. Not to mention the stuff I see going on out in the woods. Hellfire, it's like some kind of nuclear physics experiment or something. They're all such expert technicians. You almost expect to see them wearing lab coats. But try to get them on the subject of, well, any kind of genuine emotion, and they're like a bunch of cub scouts sitting around a campfire terrified of what's out there in the dark. I swear and vow, it's enough to break your heart."

He's right of course. It's exactly like that, and at the same time highly reminiscent of the final act of a Greek tragedy. Forrest has been watching it for years. It's what Phillip saved him from, after all. They never spoke of it, but Forrest knew.

"Cous, this boy could be better than that. If only the right man took him in hand, so to speak, I think young Morgan would grow into something pretty damned spectacular. You know what I'm talking about. Something your Daddy would call character."

"I'm sure that's true," Forrest says, remembering how Phillip did just that for him, a nineteen year old with too much in the way of looks and attitude for his own good.

"Yes, indeed," Bobby Lee says. "That's exactly what he needs. Some nice man to take care of him and keep him out of trouble until he finds his feet. Then that nice man will have a real partner, you know?"

And suddenly Forrest doesn't like the way Bobby Lee is looking at him at all. The hell of it is, Bobby Lee does know what he's talking about. Dangerous in the extreme, Forrest thinks, having someone around who knows him as well as Bobby Lee does. Every bluff is called. Every misleading statement is challenged, every evasion forcibly clarified. Worst of all, it's impossible for Forrest to lie to himself with Bobby Lee at his side acting like some kind of quaint, down home oracle, threatening to shout the truth from the housetops.

Forrest has been in love exactly twice. Before this. He doesn't count this time. He hasn't accepted it. He cannot and he will not. He might be living back in Tennessee today if Bucky Greene hadn't overturned that Farmall tractor onto himself. Forrest could so easily have ended up living an outwardly respectable small town life and sneaking off to see his boyfriend a couple of nights a week. Choosing the path of least resistance takes very little encouragement.

That's what Mother and Daddy were saving him from when they packed him off to Columbia. Not a lifetime as a victim of all that local oppression as they thought of it, but of secret meetings with other married men, of hanging around the truckstops on I-65, of anonymous sex in washrooms and adult bookstores up in Nashville, of being arrested by butch young plainclothes cops committing entrapment in small town parks.

Bobby Lee knows all this. Not that they have actually discussed it. They are southerners. If they ever speak of uncomfortable things they do so in such oblique terms as to make them all but incomprehensible to anyone who might overhear. The more crucial the matter the more desperately they strive to achieve complete opacity in every utterance that touches on it.

But Bobby Lee knows, and Bobby Lee is largely right about young Morgan because Bobby Lee carries in his own cells as much of Forrest's DNA as anybody walking the face of the earth. Because Bobby Lee knows the history of their family and all its various and convoluted tributaries far better than Forrest does or ever will. Because for the first seventeen and a half years of Forrest's life he spent more of his waking hours with Bobby Lee than anyone else. Because for all practical purposes Bobby Lee has absorbed both his biography and psychology by osmosis. Telling Bobby Lee anything would be redundant.

So Bobby Lee sees what nobody else sees. He recognizes signs and portents altogether inscrutable to everyone else who knows Forrest. And he knows what he knows. He must have sized Morgan up as a prime candidate for Forrest's next husband within five minutes of meeting him. And Forrest might as well attempt to halt the earth on its axis as try to prevent Bobby Lee from expressing his opinion on the subject.

Yes, Bobby Lee did see, so Bobby Lee knows. Within five seconds of laying eyes on that boy, Forrest was a seething volcano of lust, threatening to erupt without warning. Right there in broad daylight surrounded by half of gay New York. After not so much as a twinge of libido in all the weeks since Phillip died. And Morgan's eyes undoubtedly did tell him what the answer would be if Forrest ever asked the question. Why then is Forrest sitting alone on the deck at 3:00 a.m. instead of rampaging up the beach, knocking on each and every door, peeking in through each and every window, searching in and under each and every bed for the young Prince Charming? Pillaging this whole sleeping island? Because Phillip is out there in the dark. He waits on the beach, on the boardwalk, under the trees, hidden from the moonlight. He is right here next to Forrest. And for all Forrest knows, is reading his mind—these very thoughts. Phillip was there on the beach yesterday. He watched Forrest looking at Morgan. He knows what Forrest was feeling and thinking. Worst of all, he knew he was totally forgotten during that five or so minutes. He wasn't just dead, he had never existed.

How did that happen? How can Forrest be feeling these things so soon? Right out of the blue? And behaving this way? Didn't their love for each other and their years together mean anything? Doesn't Forrest know anything about loyalty? Doesn't Forrest have the decency to mourn for Phillip as he deserves? And how, knowing or at least suspecting the worst about himself, can Forrest go on living?

* * *

Forrest opens the door and starts taking things out of the closet. He hardly lets himself look at them. It's the only way he can bear this chore. He's mentally selected a dozen or so items of Phillip's clothing that he'll keep. The rest has to go. He sent Phillip's mother some things she had asked for at the funeral. But he's left the rest undisturbed, as if Phillip might walk in the door any minute and decide to change into this cashmere sweater or that corduroy sport coat. The therapist Forrest has been seeing says there's no hurry. But he has gotten to the point where he can't go on living in the apartment knowing these things are here. He's been sleeping in the guest room for weeks, which is bad enough, but even that's becoming increasingly difficult. And it's meant Bobby Lee is bunking in Phillip's study, on a hide-a-bed that should be in a museum. He hasn't once complained.

Forrest pulls shirts and pants and jackets out of the closet, and every scrap of fabric, every color and texture he encounters, reminds him of Phillip more vividly than a photograph could. He feels the knits and poplins and corduroys and twills and broadcloths run through his fingers and it's almost as if he can feel the shapes of Phillip's body inside the garments.

And the smell. Even now everything smells like Phillip. Not any single, identifiable scent, like cologne or soap or even sweat. Just an amalgam that signifies Phillip himself, the odor that always lurked tantalizingly behind all the other odors. When it first happened, Forrest didn't change the sheets on the bed for weeks because of Phillip's persistent smell on them. He didn't sleep in that bed, but he visited it every day, and every day the smell grew fainter. And when Forrest finally couldn't smell Phillip there any more he stripped the bed and laundered the sheets and sent them off to a charity thrift store. Now, clearing out the closet, he encounters that smell again, and it's as if Phillip never left. He clutches half a dozen dress shirts to his chest and cries like a baby. Phillip only took that particular flight to get home sooner from his conference. He was supposed to be on a later one, which landed without incident. On the phone, Forrest assured him that there was no need to change his booking, but Phillip was anxious to get home.

"*I can't wait to see you.*"

Those were the last words Forrest ever heard him say. He blinks back tears and fights down the sobs, terrified that Bobby Lee and Morgan will come home from their expedition to the park and find him like this. He sniffs and looks down at the crumpled shirts in his arms and it starts right up again. God help him when he gets to Phillip's sweaters. All those beautiful sweaters.

* * *

"I wouldn't have thought this was Bobby Lee's kind of thing," Morgan says, looking around the gallery.

The paintings are all of unidentifiable but unmistakably menacing objects done in grays, blacks, and grimy looking whites. Every once in a while you'll come upon a spectral purple or lurid green lurking in some corner, or a splash of blood red. All of it is laid on the canvas so heavily it looks like the artist might well have employed a soup spoon.

"It's not," Forrest says, avoiding the friendly, cobalt blue eyes.

Neither was the movie last night. French, with clumsily translated subtitles and heavyhanded, insistent symbolism, in gloomy black and white. Or the concert the night before. String quartets by Bartok. And last Saturday it was the opera. *Wozzeck*. God save us.

Morgan looks puzzled.

"He wants you to realize how cultured he is," Forrest explains, hoping it doesn't sound insufferably patronizing. But more importantly, he hopes it sounds like the truth. Which it doesn't remotely coincide with although it might if you tinkered with the personal pronouns a bit. Needless to say, Bobby Lee doesn't give a flying fuck what Morgan thinks of him. This marathon of high culture he's been subjecting them to for the last couple of weeks is for Forrest's benefit. Bobby Lee's all too transparently trying to prove what good husband material Morgan is. You can take him anywhere and he won't seem ill at east or out of place. Not only is he fabulous to look at in a pair of Speedos, he knows how to dress for all other venues requisite to urban gay life. He knows how to behave when he gets there, as well. Won't snore during the final act or embarrass you by laughing at some inopportune moment. Knows which fork to use when, when to keep his mouth resolutely shut—a skill Forrest himself has never come close to mastering—and how to turn down a proposition with grace. He seems incapable of the tiniest gaucherie and can even order dinner in French. What more could one ask for in a husband? But Forrest is having none of it, and he's pretending that he's an eyewitness to Bobby Lee's courtship of the young man.

"I don't understand," Morgan says.

"He's awed by your breeding and background," Forrest says. "We're not much more than jumped up white trash in our family."

"Neither are we," Morgan says, looking puzzled.

Forrest wonders for a moment if he's overplayed it.

"I thought," Morgan says, then shuts up, looking extremely ill at ease.

"Thought what?"

"Nothing. It doesn't matter."

"This really isn't my kind of thing either," Forrest says. "I mean, I like the impressionists. And the expressionists, too. Even the cubists. But this is just too. . ."

"Weird," Morgan finishes the sentence.

They stand there grinning at each other like a couple of conspirators, which is fun for the five seconds or so it takes Forrest to realize that he's playing right into Bobby Lee's hands. Again.

"Well," Bobby Lee says, smiling like the cat who caught the canary and handing them paper cups of white wine, "you two look like you're having a wonderful time."

Morgan's eyes are sparkling in his direction and Forrest tries not to meet them. As far as he can tell they're the most dangerous part of Morgan's anatomy. And that's saying lots.

"We are," Morgan says. "We were just talking about art history."

"Really?" Bobby Lee's grin grows wider. He winks.

Forrest ignores him.

"Isn't this stuff terrific?" Bobby Lee enthuses. "Such technique. Such composition. Which piece do you like best?"

"I'm not sure," Morgan says, glancing in Forrest's direction for help.

Forrest studies his wine glass like it's the Rosetta Stone. This is every man for himself.

* * *

Forrest lies on his back looking up through tree branches at the sky. He can hear Bobby Lee and Morgan laughing. He can also hear other, more distant voices and beyond them the generalized sound of Manhattan in midafternoon. But here, looking up at the sky, Forrest could be anywhere. He's trying, and failing miserably, not to remember. The last time Phillip and he were in England. One of Phillip's cousins was getting married and they went. Phillip described it as being worse than the fifth act of *King Lear*. Afterwards they stayed for several days at his Great Uncle Hugh's home in Gloucestershire, a huge old crumbling barn of a place that's been in the Haverstraw family since the thirteenth century—complete with resident ghost. Forrest was awed by so much history, though he never saw the ghost. Phillip seemed to take it all in stride, merely complaining about Uncle Hugh's refusal to have the late Victorian plumbing updated.

There wasn't much to do in that part of Gloucestershire, so they took lots of walks. And one afternoon they found themselves lying side by side in the grass at the edge of a field where the hay had just been cut. The view up through the branches of trees was just like this. The afternoon was just like this one, too, an unusually hot day for England.

Bobby Lee said he wanted a picnic in Central Park. Just like real New Yorkers have. Forrest doesn't know about that. He knows lots of New Yorkers who wouldn't set foot in the park for love or money, much less bring a hamper from Tavern on the Green. But here they are. Bobby Lee and Morgan are practically joined at the hip lately. Bobby Lee has backed off the overt match-making, but Morgan's still being invited on each and every one of the little excursions Bobby Lee plans with such care. Last weekend they went back to the island. Last night they went to the movies. Bobby Lee even asked permission to bring Morgan along the last time he and Forrest had dinner at Amelia and Justin's up in Yorkville. Morgan and Justin discussed foreign policy, Sonny and Sammy were crazy about their new friend, and Amelia was captivated. Forrest is sure that by now Bobby Lee has enlisted all of them in his little crusade. What it comes down to is that Forrest is under siege.

That afternoon in Gloucestershire, Phillip promised once again that he'd love Forrest forever.

* * *

The ferry is packed. Everyone is going back to the city. The last dull gleams of sunset light the end of Labor Day Weekend. Looking around the crowded deck, Forrest can't help thinking of a ship full of refugees. There's little of the zaniness and high spirits he remembers from last Friday on their way out. All that could have been a decade ago, so completely does it seem to have been forgotten. The trips back into the city at the end of the weekend are often subdued, but this one seems almost funereal.

It's only the fourth time Forrest has been to the island all summer, but Bobby Lee hasn't missed a single weekend since their first trip out in June. People tell Forrest that Bobby Lee has become quite the celebrity. Watching him work the deck this evening confirms it. Bobby Lee is not particularly handsome, he's no more than averagely built for this crowd, and he doesn't possess much in the way of urbanity. What he does have are a ready laugh and a way of listening to you like you're the most important person in the whole world. Apparently that's enough. He certainly hasn't lacked for companionship or invitations all summer. Forrest wonders how he'll translate it into a social life as fall comes to the city and everything moves indoors.

Bobby Lee wraps up a conversation with a sad faced beauty of either seventeen or twenty-three and heads in Forrest's direction, waving to a couple more people on his way. He plops himself on the bench next to Forrest and stares out at the water.

"I'm going to miss all this."

"Phillip always got that way when the season ended."

"Yes, well, he could at least expect to see these people back in the city. I mean, I'm sure there are lots of them you'd run into here and there."

"I guess," Forrest says. Though in his experience the people you know on the island aren't necessarily the same people you see in the city. He has heard of whole relationships between people based on spending the same two weeks at the same resort every year and exchanging little more than Christmas cards during the intervening months, and that seems to sum up his own life in New York.

"It really is time, cous."

Forrest snaps to attention. That's what Bobby Lee meant.

"When are you leaving?"

"Saturday morning. I already made my reservation."

"You don't have to go."

What Forrest really means is "*you can't.*" Or even more honestly "*don't leave me yet.*"

"Honestly, Bobby Lee, you can stay as long as you want."

"And I have," Bobby Lee says. "No offense, cous, but it's time for both of us to get on with our lives. You're obviously not going to do that as long as I'm in that apartment with you. And I'm not going to do it as long as I'm here in Never Never Land."

"What are you going to do?"

"Go back to the farm."

"You'll lose your mind."

"It's not that bad."

"It's not just the farm," Forrest says. "It's everything."

"Forrest, you're not listening. It's not that bad."

"Yes it is."

"Like you'd know what you're talking about," Bobby Lee says. "You've been gone for your entire adult life."

"Fair enough," Forrest says, "but so have you. It'll be fine for a week or so, maybe. I know what I'm talking about. You won't be able to just walk out the front door and see guys like you everywhere you go and know everybody else sees them, too. It's not like that back home, and it's not like that in Nashville. It's all one big closet. All you'll be able to do is hope and pray for invisibility. You've been around here long enough to know what I'm talking about. Hell, you've made more friends here this summer than you've ever had in your life."

"Everything you say is true," Bobby Lee says. "I won't argue with you. But I want to go home."

Forrest realizes that they've been waiting to have this conversation for a long time.

"That place is not home," he says. "It never was for people like us. It may be sometime, but I don't expect to live long enough to see it."

"That's one way of looking at it."

"Is there another way?"

Bobby Lee gazes over the railing. Forrest knows he's right and he knows Bobby Lee knows it, yet Bobby Lee's going to leave anyway. And beyond Bobby Lee's congenital pigheadedness, Forrest doesn't understand why. One thing Forrest knows for certain. No matter how many arguments he wins with Bobby Lee, he always manages to lose them anyway.

"Daddy's still trying to make a go of raising tobacco," Bobby Lee says. "Maybe with me there to help out. . ."

Forrest really never will understand.

"And I don't think he's ever forgiven himself for selling off the dairy herd when Bucky died. Maybe I'll use some of my savings to buy a new herd."

"Oh, Bobby Lee."

"You know, Forrest, we can't all just pick up and leave like our people were never there."

"What do you mean, our people? Look around you. The guys on this boat are our people. Oh, I know they're not related to us. But we have more in common with them than with our own family."

"You know what I mean," Bobby Lee says. "You do. You know exactly what I'm talking about."

Maybe Forrest does. But that doesn't mean he agrees. It doesn't mean Forrest doesn't think Bobby Lee's throwing his life away.

"She's eighty-nine years old and she's still got you buffaloed."

Bobby Lee shakes his head.

"She's not going to live forever."

"All the more reason," Bobby Lee says. "Once she's gone, somebody's got to keep it going."

"Keep what going? I don't understand you. What is there to keep going?"

"Why, the way it's always been."

This is Forrest's cue, of course. He could quote Bobby Lee chapter and verse about the prejudice against Jews and blacks and homosexuals and, yes, even science teachers. About the exploitation and abuse of women and children. About the ruthless suppression of anything and anybody the least bit different. All those things constitute the way it's always been. But he knows Bobby Lee would just listen until he runs out of steam and then nod and say, yes, there's all that. But he's going to go anyway, so what's the use? It's in Bobby's Lee blood in a way it really never was in Forrest's. And that's all there is to say.

"I'll be back."

Forrest thinks he's talking about coming for visits every now and then, but then he notices Morgan leaning against the rail about twenty feet away, looking at them. Bobby Lee gets up. Forrest refuses to watch him go over there.

* * *

Forrest buzzes Morgan in downstairs. He goes into the bathroom to check his hair a last time even though it's not supposed to matter. After all, this is Bobby Lee's party. A farewell dinner. Just the three of them. Forrest took off work this afternoon and came home and cooked and cleaned, and, he admits it, dressed up. Just a little bit. There's nothing wrong with wanting to look nice. It doesn't mean anything more than a wish to show proper respect for one's guests. It doesn't mean he has the least intention of seeing Morgan again after tonight.

Once Bobby Lee gets on that plane tomorrow, Forrest won't ever have to face Morgan again or listen to Bobby Lee singing his praises. Forrest will miss Bobby Lee right smart, but he won't miss that, nor Bobby Lee's tireless attempts to throw Morgan and him into each other's arms and then padlock them into position. Last weekend on the Island was the last straw. Forrest was truly embarrassed for Bobby Lee. Morgan, to his credit, gave no indication that he noticed, though he must have. A true gentleman. Everyone else Forrest knows noticed, and most of them razzed him. He's sure he hasn't heard the end of it.

There's a knock at the front door. Forrest realizes with more than a little chagrin that he's still staring himself in the mirror. He goes to answer it. Morgan smiles in. His Aegean blue eyes dance. He's wearing a loose fitting long sleeved shirt in what looks like raw muslin. It sets off his tan spectacularly and makes his upper body look too imposing for real life. He's got on breathtakingly tight jeans and topsiders with no socks. His thick shock of straw colored hair is freshly cut and perfectly combed. In one hand he's holding a bunch of daisies from the vendor down at the corner. Somebody, somewhere is dreaming of a boy just like this.

"Hi. Come on in."

"Thanks," Morgan says, smile never wavering. He holds out the flowers. "Bobby Lee said you like these."

Forrest doesn't especially. He smells a rat.

"Why, thank you," he says. "I'll just go find something to put them in. Make yourself at home."

In the kitchen he lays the daisies on the counter and opens the cupboard over the refrigerator where Phillip always kept the vases. He can't remember that last time he looked up there. The phone rings. He waits until the machine picks up and listens to Phillip's greeting message on the tape.

"Cous," Bobby's Lee voice comes into the room. "Pick up. I know you're there."

Forrest grabs the receiver.

"Where the hell are you? Young Mr. Mile Wide Shoulders and Pecs To Die For is out in the living room waiting to wish you *bon voyage*."

"Listen," Bobby Lee drawls, "I don't have much time."

"What are you talking about?"

"They're about to call my flight."

"You're crazy. Your flight isn't until tomorrow. I'm looking at your itinerary this very second, right here on the refrigerator door. 10:43 out of LaGuardia."

"Crazy like a fox," Bobby Lee cackles. "I changed my reservation Tuesday."

And that boy sitting in the living room is his parting shot.

"You bastard," Forrest fumes. "You motherfucking, shit sucking, no good snake in the grass. You get your ass into a taxi and back up here."

"Not on your life," Bobby Lee laughs again, obviously enjoying this a great deal. "Now get your tail into the dining room and remove the extra place setting of your great-grandmother's china from the table. And then you settle down and enjoy a nice evening with that gorgeous young hunk who's so crazy about you."

"You've gone too far this time, Bobby Lee Reynolds."

"Have I? Good."

"Now listen here."

"No, Forrest. You listen to me. For once in your life. And listen good. You and Morgan are perfect for each other. He is head over heels in love with you. And though I know you'd rather stick needles in your eyes than admit it, you're gaga over him. If Phillip could, he'd reach out and slap you clear into next week for even thinking about throwing away this chance. But he can't, so I have to do it for him. He's not coming back. Ever. It's time you got that straight and got on with the rest of your life. I know it's a little soon for you. But the universe operates on its own timeline. It always has and it always will. A boy like that only comes around once in a lifetime, if ever. And you can't afford to miss the opportunity. So go out there and throw yourself at Morgan and have a wonderful rest of your life."

"Bobby Lee, I can't."

"And whatever you do, don't fuck this up just because you can't stand it when I'm right about things."

* * *

The wind off the water is a knife to the heart, carrying with it a chill which feels like it come fresh off the polar ice cap. It plasters Morgan's hair to his skull. Clouds glower low and thick and lead colored over the dark, agitated waves. A Hollywood director couldn't have ordered up a more convincing day for this errand. Forrest hugs the urn close to his chest. He and Morgan walk side by side down the beach toward the water, into the gnashing teeth of that wind. There's no possibility of gently scattering ashes on a day like this. It will fling them back onto the shore. And into Forrest's face like a taunt. On the ferry earlier he was ready to turn back. But Morgan says he has an idea.

The tide is out. They walk a long way across wet, hard packed sand. Side by side. Without speaking. Their silence is a comfortable one. The wind and the whitecaps are enough racket. Five feet or so from where tattered remnants of waves are washing up, Morgan stops. He looks around. Forrest follows his gaze. Directly up the beach is the house. Closed for the season now, it could almost be mistaken for derelict. The windows are boarded up. Paint which was fresh last April is already fading and salt crusted. Sand has invaded the deck, which looks as if it hasn't been swept in decades rather than weeks.

Morgan nods. Not at Forrest, but simply as if he's found things to his satisfaction. He crouches with his back to the wind and water. He reaches up for the urn. Forrest hands it over. Morgan begins digging. Forrest watches him for a moment. Then he understands. He crouches next to Morgan. He follows Morgan's movements exactly, like a shadow. In seconds there is a shallow depression in the sand.

Morgan pries the lid off the urn and nods at Forrest.

Forrest takes a small handful of ashes. He pats them into the wet sand at the bottom of the hole they've dug together. The ashes change color slightly as they absorb moisture from the sand. Tears fall from Forrest's eyes onto the ashes. He blinks them back and looks at Morgan.

"Are you sure?"

Forrest nods.

They empty the urn by turns. The ashes almost fill the hole, leaving room only for a thin layer of sand on top. It's just enough to keep them from blowing away before the tide comes in. They crouch silent and motionless for a moment before Morgan begins gently smoothing wet sand over the spot. They huddle together there with the wind howling around them and the surf crashing. Morgan finally finishes smoothing sand over the temporary resting place. The next storm will disturb the sand of the beach enough that these remains will scatter without a trace. Forrest takes those two gritty hands and raises them to his lips.

Then he cries. Loud, heavy sobs. Like he can't remember ever crying before. It's like crying for the end of the world. He feels Morgan's arms tighten around him.

"I can't replace him, Forrest. I'd never think of trying."

The wind shrieks.

"I love you," he says, hugging Forrest still tighter. "I'll do my best. I promise."

Cooper and Griffin: November, 1979

Griffin stared at himself in the bathroom mirror. Cooper could see he was skeptical. Three days ago, Cooper had taken him to the salon where all his friends went to get their hair cut. Griffin sat tense and upright in the chair while Cooper supervised every snip. It cost more than Griffin used to pay for a week's groceries. This was the result.

"Relax," Cooper said, toweling himself off.

"I'm just not sure about this."

"It's perfect."

"It just seems—I don't know. Isn't it kind of unfashionable? Does anybody really wear their hair like this nowadays?"

"Of course it's unfashionable," Cooper said. "We don't believe in fashion around here."

"We don't?"

"Fashion is a trap other people fall into," Cooper explained. "Fashion is for losers. Fashion is for people who have no taste and no sense of identity. Fashion is accepting other people's notions of how you're supposed to look and ultimately who you're meant to be. So fashion has no relevance under this roof. It's a cardinal rule, if you will."

"O.K." Griffin said. "I get all that. But I'm still not sure about this haircut."

"What we do is find our best look and stick with it. With adjustments as needed, of course."

"Is this really my best look?"

"Trust me," Cooper said. "Anyway, it's not really that different from how you were already wearing it. Just shorter on the back and sides. And for everyday, you don't have to put stuff in it if you don't want to."

"It just reminds me of when I was a little kid."

Somehow Cooper didn't believe that was the whole story.

"Noted. Now get dressed."

Cooper had also selected Griffn's wardrobe for the evening. Black weejuns, white socks, a pair of vintage 501's, an argyle v-neck sweater in yellow and midnight blue. The sweater was a size larger than Griffin would have picked out for himself: Cooper believed he should wear his sweaters looser. The V-neck made him feel horribly self-conscious. His skin was milk white and totally hairless, and that neckline seemed to accentuate these defects. He hoped Cooper was right, but he was pretty sure he was going to end up going to the party looking like a clown.

If Griffin allowed himself to about it, Cooper's instructions for the evening might seem strange. He would probably have assumed, for instance, that when a couple attended a party together, they attended it *together*, instead of, as Cooper proposed, splitting up as soon as they got in the door. Of course it had to be granted that Griffin had no previous experience of couplehood, especially in its gay variety. And with reference to this evening, he had nothing more than his first hand observations of the habits of straights to go by—not that this could be considered helpful. Nor, for that matter, did he have much experience of the kind of social gathering they were on their way to. So any prior assumptions he might have were based on nothing more, really, than his imagination. Still, it seemed strange.

But the question was meaningless. Regardless of what Griffin might be thinking and feeling, what mattered was that Cooper had issued instructions. The specific nature of those instructions was of little or no intrinsic significance. And it wasn't Griffin's place to analyze, much less ask questions or challenge him. Cooper, Griffin's as yet nebulously defined whatever-he-was, had spoken. And that was enough. Because to all intents and purposes, Cooper was the handsomest man in the world. There were other handsome men in the world, certainly. There were men who were taller, men who had blond instead of raven hair, and brown, hazel, or gray eyes instead of blue. There were men who spoke like British aristocrats or truck drivers, French gigolos, or German airline pilots instead of New Yorkers. But these were differences of type rather than degree. They didn't make those men handsomer than Cooper, just different. And given his type—black haired, razor cheeked, unimaginably muscular—it wasn't possible to conceive how he could have been better looking than he was. Hence, the handsomest man in the world.

And Griffin knew, both from experience and instinct, what to do when the handsomest man in the world expressed an opinion or a preference or issued an instruction. Griffin was perfectly conditioned, so much so that hearing the *diktat* he immediately forgot he'd entertained any other notion.

New haircut?

New outfit?

When we get to the party we do this?

Or that?

Far easier, really, than figuring any of those things out for himself.

And on his own he'd never be on his way to this party in the first place.

*   *   *

The dual mandates of Cooper's Labradors and Big Steve Fabiani were unequivocal. The matter might have been definitively settled among those authorities. But Cooper, who didn't believe in intuition or received wisdom either as concepts or phenomena, required empirical evidence. His bedroom had yielded extensive data, but there was more to life than sex. He'd even gone so far as having Griffin move in with him. The results of this had been satisfactory so far. But you could live happily with a roommate without considering yourself married to him, though obviously they were more than just roommates. Perhaps they were more even than roommates who shared a bed. But how could Cooper know for certain? And if they were more than roommates who had lots of sex, what did it mean?

Indeed, did it have to mean anything? Couldn't it just be?

Cooper didn't like unanswered questions. He was no existentialist. He had no appreciation for metaphysics and no patience with ambiguity. You might think this made him a poor candidate for romance, and if you did, you'd be right. Romance was an illusion that other people suffered from, period.

As to what Griffin might be thinking or feeling about the situation— well, that was Griffin's business. Cooper had spent his life so far ignoring the opinions and feelings of other people and he wasn't inclined to change. But did that mean he wasn't capable of having a relationship? In the event he decided he actually wanted one?

The point of the gathering was introducing Griffin to Big Steve's crew. But the point also was doing that without making a production of it that might cause that purpose to be sufficiently obvious to spook Griffin and leave open the potential of major loss of face for Cooper should he decide to abort the mission somewhere down the road. The only way of achieving Cooper's objective was to make some other, apparently unrelated production. One that had as few of

Cooper's fingerprints on it as possible. And because another objective—since Cooper invariably killed as many birds as possible with one stone—was to observe Griffin in a social setting rather than an intimate one, the crowd had to consist of more than just the usual suspects. There had to be a scattering of twinkies to keep things suitably festive, though nobody currently active among the ranks of official go-go boys. There had to be the requisite quota of both opera and musical comedy queens, but carefully selected so as to avoid unfortunate collisions—as opposed to serendipitous ones—between the groups. There had to be a solid backdrop of suit gays, even though they might not dress that way for the occasion, but there also had to be a few interior designers and gallery owners to keep things sufficiently aesthetic. There had to be just enough bohemians in the crowd to establish the evening's authenticity both in gay and San Franciscan terms. And in order that the immediate world was left in no doubt that the affair had been classy beyond words, the gossip queens had to be represented. Cooper hit on the strategy of inviting Holly Montezuma and Marina del Rey to attend as their less colorful alter egos, Enrique "Henry" Sandoval and Bartolomeo Correa. Out of drag they'd be positively incognito, yet their testimony afterward wouldn't lack sparkle, authority, or impact.

Cooper hated asking Ned Westerleigh for favors. His account with Ned was already disastrously overdrawn. But Ned had a way of making favors he did you seem like favors you were doing him. And Ned was overdue to host a party anyway. His last one had been in early May, when Nick Romanovsky had debuted his new husband, Dario. Ned arranged the catering and beverage service, leaving only the guest list for Cooper to handle.

You could lie to a trick. In fact, lying to tricks was almost obligatory. But this situation didn't remotely qualify. Cooper might not yet have been able to classify Griffin with certainty, but Griffin absolutely wasn't a trick. Cooper knew he couldn't say "this isn't an audition". It wouldn't just be a lie, it would be ridiculous. So he didn't say anything except "Ned's hosting a party and we're invited." Everything followed from that.

"One more thing before we get there," Cooper said.

They were riding up on the elevator. In a few more seconds it would stop in Ned Westerleigh's foyer.

"What's that?" Griffin asked.

"Don't go anywhere near Ned's Bechstein," Cooper said. "I understand that it's one of the finest pianos in the Bay Area and you adore playing it. But you're not here as Harry Gordini's second string artiste tonight. Or as a graduate student in music. You're here tonight as a guy. That's your mission."

"Roger."

* * *

"Griffin, my boy," Ned Westerleigh said, "welcome."

"Thanks for having me, Ned."

"The pleasure is all mine, I assure you. Now, you've been here before. Please, make yourself at home."

This was easier said than done. "Home" was a concept so abstract in Griffin's current worldview as to be nearly meaningless. Still, he thought he knew what Ned intended. And Ned's apartment was the platonic ideal of a certain type of domesticity. When you read Forster, for instance, or perhaps Woolf, this was the kind of setting you imagined. Waugh's bright young things had relations with such establishments. For that matter, you could imagine Bertie Wooster embarrassing himself here. The difficulty for Griffin was imagining himself inhabiting such a place, even temporarily.

* * *

The man was almost exactly Cooper's size and shape, handsome, Viking blond, older by only a few years. His hair was short in back and on the sides, longer on top and in front, and was oiled into immobility. It featured a side part as straight as a ruler. It was outrageously unfashionable but at the same time absolutely the right look for him. Griffin recognized its significance instantaneously but couldn't begin to understand the underlying motivations.

Everything about the man was perfect, in fact. He was wearing 501s, penny loafers, and a sweater of the softest baby blue. The effeminacy of that sweater only emphasized his ruggedness. He was breathtaking, and if Griffin wasn't been attached to Cooper, he'd throw himself at this man so fast, this near perfect replica, albeit a couple of inches shorter, of someone whose name he still refused to speak even under his breath.

Addressing such a vision was about the last thing Griffin considered himself capable of, but a promise to your lord and master was a promise you kept.

"Excuse me," he said, "but would you happen to be Cooper's buddy, T.?"

"Hi, Griffin. Nice to finally meet you."

That accent: familiar as newly plowed soil or freshly mown hay. Cooper hadn't mentioned it.

"Same here."

"Having a good time?" T. asked.

"Let's say that's my assignment this evening."

"I'll just bet. Well, with no further ado, I need to introduce you to Big Steve. And Nick just got here. I know you've heard all about Nick."

"I have."

"Don't worry," T. grinned, "they won't eat you."

Nick, T., and Big Steve. Cooper's holy trinity. The men he most admired. The men he most desired to emulate. They shaped his opinions and tastes. Their approval or censure determined his choices. Cooper had never said any of this, but Griffin knew it as surely as he knew what day it was. He knew it from the tone of Cooper's voice and the expression on his face when he spoke of them. He knew it from the way Cooper quoted them: they were the law and the prophets. But as long as they were just names, Griffin only found them partly terrifying. Now that he'd met T. and Big Steve and Nick were imminent, it was all he could do not to run away. As he wove through the crowd in T.'s wake, he realized that since the moment he gave himself to Cooper this had been perhaps his deepest dread—meeting the friends. He steamed toward them like the *Titanic* steamed toward that iceberg. Long before he was prepared for it he was face to face with Big Steve and Nick. They were giants, and as terrifying as he'd expected.

"At long last," Nick said, gray eyes flashing, "the renowned Griffin MacDonald."

"And about damned time, too," Big Steve growled. "Ought to horsewhip that Cooper for keeping you under wraps."

"I'll be sure to tell him you said that," Griffin ventured.

"Oh, he knows," Big Steve smiled. "We've complained often enough, haven't we?"

"You said it." Nick tossed his amazing mane of blond hair. Griffin thought he couldn't look less like a prosecuting attorney. More like a soap opera doctor—Springfield's reigning surgeon and bad boy.

"So, youngster," Big Steve said, "is our boy Cooper treating you all right?"

"Like a prince," Griffin stammered.

"Glad to hear it. You have any trouble keeping him in line, you just let me know."

"He means it," T. murmured at Griffin's shoulder.

"That Cooper's a handful, all right," Big Steve mused, "but I bet you've got what it takes to tame him."

"I don't think I'd want to," Griffin said.

"That's exactly how you do it," Big Steve nodded.

"I don't understand."

"You will. Stick with him, boy. It'll be a bumpy ride most of the time, but God will it be worth it."

"You're in graduate school at State," Nick said, changing the subject.

"That's right."

"Who do you study piano with? We asked Cooper, but he couldn't remember your teacher's name."

"Michael Krakowiak."

"He's my cousin," Nick said. "My mom's first cousin, to be exact."

"Really?"

"Kind of surprised not to see him here tonight."

"I think he's got a performance with his string trio."

"Oh, God, was that tonight?" Nick asked.

"I believe so."

"Damn," Nick said. "I told him I'd be there. So, he behaving himself?"

"As far as I know," Griffin said, baffled.

"You mean he hasn't chased you around the piano yet? Because you're exactly his type."

Since Griffin couldn't imagine being anyone's type, this information didn't tell him much of value about his piano teacher.

"There you are, Cooper," Big Steve roared. "I was just telling my boy Griffin here that I'll tie you up and spank you sideways if I hear you're not doing right by him."

* * *

At the buffet table, Griffin ran into Elizabeth Montefiore, one of Cooper's business partners.

"I'm not supposed to talk to you tonight," he said.

"I know."

"We could cheat."

"Let's not," Elizabeth smiled. "Just this once let's do what Cooper wants."

"Just this once? I always do what Cooper wants."

"Good boy," Elizabeth laughed. "I, on the other hand, almost never do."

"Really."

"Of course, I have practically nothing at stake," Elizabeth said. "That's why I'm able to get away with it, but I wouldn't recommend trying it in your case."

* * *

"Griffin," Ned said. "Come over here. There are some people I want you to meet."

Ned always reminded Griffin of a veteran actor playing a retired general wintering on the Cote d'Azur in a Noel Coward play. Beside this splendor, Ned's companions were gray blurs.

"Great party, Ned," Griffin said, making a special effort to smile. Cooper had been particularly intent on that before they arrived. He mustn't forget to smile. Besides, Ned was always extremely nice to him. Ned invariably put him at ease.

"Griffin, this is Joe."

"Nice to meet you, Joe."

"And this is Ernie."

"Nice to meet you, Ernie."

"Griffin is Cooper's other half," Ned explained, "though some of us find it more accurate to think of him as Cooper's better half."

* * *

"Griffin, I'm Ashby."

He was Griffin's height and Griffin's shape. The similarities ended there. He was black haired, dark eyed, mustachioed, and handsome like an actor in an old black and white movie.

"You're the doctor," Griffin said.

"Third year resident in internal medicine," Ashby nodded.

That accent—not Griffin's but unusual enough. Was it Cajun?

"My husband is the gentleman over in the corner with Elizabeth Montefiore. She reminds him of his ex-wife."

"My God," Griffin said.

"Yes," Ashby grinned, "old enough to be my father."

"That's not what I meant."

"I know," Ashby said, "but it's true. He is old enough to be my father. What you meant was something along the lines of 'where do they all come from?'"

"The gym, obviously," Griffin said. "But yes."

"Believe me," Ashby said, "I know exactly how you feel."

"You do."

"Like a Whippet in a kennel full of Dobermans."

"You, Whippet, maybe," Griffin said. "Me mongrel. Runt of litter."

"Got to get over that attitude, *mon frere*," Ashby said. "I know they're all stupefying physical specimens, but you don't have to be a meathead to fit in with this crowd."

"No," Griffin said, "they also accept applications from underwear models."

"That's Trevor," Ashby said, "Buzz Montgomery's boyfriend. And he's no underwear model, just a sophomore at Berkeley. Anyway, we're not sure he's going to make the cut permanently. But you will."

"Will I?"

"Oh, boy, will you," Ashby said. "I've heard you play the piano."

"'Of all the gin joints. . .'," Griffin shrugged.

"Not referring to Harry Gordini's place," Ashby said, "estimable as it is. Though I've heard you perform there, too."

"Oh?"

"Attended your graduation recital at the conservatory last spring. A friend from med school dragged me along. He was trying to date some girl who plays violin. You see, the Glenn Gould recording of Beethoven's *Pathetique* pretty much got me through my first year of med school, and here was this kid—you—playing the living daylights out of it. In real life. I'd never heard it except on record, you know. And you were somebody I could imagine having gone to high school with. It impressed the hell out of me. If you can do that, you can swim with this school of sharks."

"I'm not sure I see your point," Griffin said.

"Simple," Ashby said. "You don't have to be remarkable looking for them to adopt you. Trevor's certainly remarkable in his way and they're turning up their noses at him, however subtly. The one thing they insist on is authenticity. And the way you played that Beethoven—if that wasn't authenticity live and in color, I don't know what is."

* * *

"Small world," Jared smiled.

"Practically microscopic," Scott nodded.

Less than a year ago, they'd been Griffin's upstairs neighbors at Millicent Peabody's place. He'd never spoken to either of them to amount to anything. Tall, broad shouldered, magnificent, they were far too intimidating. Now it turned out that they, too, were part of Cooper's gang.

"Great to see that Cooper's finally settled down," Scott said.

"Yes," Jared said. "It certainly was time."

It was astonishing how Cooper's friends all seemed pleased that he and Cooper were together. He would have expected some skepticism at least, if not outright disapproval. Surely at least one of them must think Cooper could have done better for himself.

* * *

"I'm Judah," the young man said, "and this is my boyfriend, Fausto."

Judah was so cute he hardly seemed humanly possible, while Fausto was nothing less than a deity. Generally, such types flummoxed Griffin into silence. But his orders from Cooper were clear.

"Nice to meet you," he said.

"My Cousin Bella thinks Cooper is about to propose to her," Judah grinned. "Please don't burst her bubble. Her show is better than anything on T.V."

* * *

"Cooper," Greg Yates said, "great party. Thanks for getting me on the guest list."

"My pleasure," Cooper said. "Mitch isn't with you tonight?"

"Who's Mitch?" Greg asked, his grin wavering microscopically.

"Like that, huh? What's the story?"

"He decided to go back to his wife," Greg said.

"I didn't know he was married," Cooper said. "I hope you realize I'd never have introduced the two of you if I had."

"I'm still not sure he is," Greg said. "I have a sneaking suspicion it was just a convenient story."

"Well," Cooper said, "I've got half a dozen excellent prospects here to-night. You know I'm always happy to introduce you to somebody nice. What kind of guy are you in the mood for?"

"This time?" Greg asked. "This time, I'd like a guy who won't dump me."

"I'll do my best," Cooper said.

"Speaking of which," Greg said, "who's that hottie over talking to Eliza-beth Montefiore?"

"You know Bart," Cooper said.

"Bart? No, I don't think so."

"Sure you do," Cooper insisted. "Bart Correa. Oh, wait. Maybe you don't recognize him out of uniform."

"Uniform?"

"He's incognito tonight," Cooper said. "Everybody knows him better as Marina del Rey."

"You're kidding."

"I know you don't approve of drag queens."

"It's not that I don't approve of them," Greg said. "It's that I don't grasp the whole phenomenon."

"You know what? Neither do I. But they exist. And Bart's a hell of a nice guy when he's being Bart. I should introduce you."

"I don't know," Greg said.

"Why not? Check out that hair."

"If I looked like that," Greg said, "I sure wouldn't go around in disguise."

* * *

"Cooper!"

"Hello, Esteban."

Cooper had sold Esteban his last condo, after which Esteban had passed him on to several of his friends, also real estate deprived. Cooper was in the process of remedying that status for several of them.

"I just met the most charming young man," Esteban said. "And do you know what he told me? He said you and he are living together."

"That'll be Griffin."

"Griffin? So it's true?"

* * *

"So what's it like?" Sean asked.

Cooper wasn't used to seeing him dressed like this. Usually he was either mostly naked or in waiter-at-an-expensive-restaurant drag. Cooper wouldn't have guessed Sean had either a polo shirt or a pair of khakis in his closet. Perhaps they were left over from Halloween.

"What's what like?"

"You're settling down," Sean said. "That's what this production is about, right?"

"Sssh," Cooper said. "Nobody's supposed to know."

"Everybody knows," Sean said. "Except your boyfriend, I'm guessing."

"Damn," Cooper laughed. "You always were smarter than people realized."

"That wouldn't be difficult," Sean said. "Speaking of settling down, who's that hot blond over there?"

"Name is Morgan Lundquist," Cooper said.

"Saw him working out at the gym the other day. Jesus."

"What were you doing there?"

"Sneaked in, didn't I?" Sean laughed. "I know when Big Steve's mafia aren't around to enforce the ban."

"You want to watch that," Cooper said. "He has spies everywhere."

"Do you really think he could disapprove of me more than he already does?"

"You wouldn't want to find out," Cooper said.

"I thought we were talking about Morgan Lundquist," Sean said.

"He's Lance Garrison's latest discovery," Cooper said.

"I thought that was Evan Powell," Sean said, "now that he put on all that size."

"Morgan's more recent."

"Jesus," Sean said. "What I wouldn't do. . ."

"Wouldn't get my hopes up if I were you," Cooper said. "He's a married man."

"Is he married?" Sean asked. "Or is he *married*? There's a difference."

"I know," Cooper said. "In this case, I couldn't say. I don't really know them. I only sold them a home."

"Where?"

"Pacific Heights."

"Not the. . ."

"That's right. Across from the wedding cake house."

* * *

"Cooper, dear, you know everyone here. Who is that stunning boy over there by the fake Picasso?"

"That's no fake, Terence."

"Are you sure?"

"Ned just acquired if from Foster Murchison."

"Well! What do you know about that! But now, don't change the subject on me: the boy, Cooper, the boy."

"That's Tristan Bentley. You've known him for years. You'd better make an appointment with your optometrist."

"No, no, not the muscleboy. The other one."

"Oh, you mean Griffin."

"Griffin," Terence crowed. "Griffin. He looks divine. That dark red hair. Such an unusual shade. Not quite Titian. Not quite auburn. Do you know if he's here with anyone?"

* * *

"Bella says hello," Yvette Grossman de Havilland said.

"How was Santorini?" Cooper asked.

"Lesbos, actually," Yvette said. "But don't go getting ideas. And she's bored there. But I'm not supposed to tell you that."

"I didn't hear a thing," Cooper laughed. Across the room he saw Yvette's husband, Kirk, Yvette's husband's best friend, Evan, and the best friend's husband, Will, an associate in Nick's office, standing in a tight knot. Something was a little off about the tableau, but Cooper wasn't sure what. He'd have to ask around.

"What I'm supposed to say is that this separation is for your own good," Yvette explained. "It's meant to give you time to think things through carefully."

"So far, it's working," Cooper told her.

"Yes," she nodded. "Everybody gets that. I'm not on her side, you understand."

"Sure," Cooper said. "With you Jewish girls it's always every man for himself."

"Right," Yvette nodded.

"How's the baby, by the way?"

"Flourishing," Yvette smiled. "More like his father every day."

"Which makes him a handful," Cooper said.

"Yes," Yvette nodded. "He runs nanny ragged. I should probably give her another raise. She had one just last month, but. . ."

* * *

"We love the house," Forrest said.

"Good," Cooper smiled. "That's what we realtors like to hear."

"Or at least I do," Forrest said. "Morgan's a little ambivalent."

"Oh?"

"He feels it's ostentatious," Forrest said. "Too much house for guys like us."

"Well, it is," Cooper said. "From any normal perspective, at least. I thought that was the point."

"I had no idea he'd find it so objectionable," Forrest said. "I believe the real problem is he has too much time on his hands. He needs something to occupy him."

"Like a job?"

"Ouch," Forrest laughed.

"I know it's none of my business," Cooper said, "but working is how most of us spend our time. And an idle boyfriend is the devil's playground. I have that on good authority."

"Noted," Forrest nodded. "The thing is, I've been thinking about buying a business for him to run. He says he's always wanted to own a gym."

"Really."

"Do you know if there's one in the area that might be available? I'm not sure I think he could handle a startup, but if there was an established one I could acquire, that would be ideal."

"That would certainly give him something to do," Cooper nodded.

"Even a partial interest in a gym might work for what I have in mind."

"I don't know of anything for certain," Cooper said. "That kind of transaction isn't really in my line. But I know the owner of the gym I'm a member of would like to retire."

"Really."

"He would have quit years ago, but there's never been anybody he'd consent to turn the business over to. And he wouldn't just lock the doors and leave the members in the lurch."

"You're familiar with my financials, Coop," Forrest said. "Do you think what he'd want for his business is within range of my resources?"

"Probably," Cooper said. "Let me do some asking around."

* * *

"You bad, bad boy," Richard grinned, wagging his finger at Cooper.

"What have I done now?"

"Keeping that one all to yourself. If I had a boyfriend like that, I'd show him off everywhere."

* * *

Even Ned Westerleigh's powder room was intimidating. Griffin stared into the mirror trying to recognize the guy with the unfashionable haircut and unfamiliar clothing. He couldn't reconcile that guy with the one he knew how to be. Give him a frosty morning and a barn full of cows to milk or a steaming afternoon and a vegetable patch to weed. Sit him down at a keyboard. Plonk him in a cluttered, musty studio with an aging, eccentric virtuoso to audition for. Hand him a musical score or a hoe. He'd know what to do. He'd pull it off. He'd barely have to think.

This new incarnation was more than he could get his head around.

Brock Van Der Jagt's demands of him had been simple and clear. *Worship me silently and from a culturally appropriate distance.* From infancy through early adulthood, Griffin practiced that vocation until it became second nature. Cooper Luxemberg was a completely different animal. He demanded devotion as abject and total as Griffin was capable of and notions like cultural appropriateness had little relevance. Worshipping him brought satisfactions Griffin had scarcly been able to imagine prior to experiencing them. But it entailed—well, unfashionable haircuts and unfamiliar clothing. And that was just for starters.

It entailed coming out of the barn whether the milk pails were full or not. It required stepping away from the piano. It insisted that he pull his nose out of that textbook or score and interact with living people instead of dead composers. The myriad demands involved overwhelmed him. He couldn't imagine living up to them long term. Yet he couldn't imagine what his life would become if he was forced to leave Eden again.

The farm belonged to a different family now. Those majestic heifers had gone on to their ultimate reward. Brock and Juliette were married and had a son. The past was a closed book.

Outside the powder room door, the next chapter was in progress.

* * *

"I told you so," Ned Westerleigh said. "But you wouldn't be you if you hadn't insisted on seeing it for yourself."

"Thanks for indulging me," Cooper said.

"My dear boy. Don't be silly. There's very little I wouldn't be willing to do for you, you know."

"And I hope you realize I'd never want to take advantage of you," Cooper said.

"My understanding of that is what makes our relationship possible," Ned said, "but in this case I had an additional incentive to make myself of assistance."

"Really? What's that?"

"You, my dear," Ned said, "were bent on making a certain kind of observation of your new whatever-he-is. And that provided me with an opportunity to observe you in a completely new way."

"Ouch."

"Fair is fair," Ned laughed.

"I think I know better than to ask you what you believe you learned."

"Quite right," Ned nodded. "The relevant question right now is what you believe you learned tonight."

"Not sure," Cooper said. "I need some time to think about it."

"Just so," Ned agreed.

* * *

"Your problem," T. said, "is you've always had too many choices."

"Except," Big Steve said, "all that was never real."

"Huh?" Cooper asked. "It felt pretty real to me."

"The sex was, sure," T. grinned.

"You've had the illusion of choice," Big Steve said, "when there's only ever been one."

"And you," Cooper said, turning to Nick. "Come on. Say it."

"Say what?"

"How should I know?" Cooper asked. "But you're always itching to add your two cents."

"I am, huh?"

"Damn right," Cooper said. "Tonight can't be any different."

"O.K." Nick said, grinning. "Well, in this case, I'd tell you to obey your elders."

* * *

Cooper had thought that observing Griffin in a social setting would clear matters up. And it did. Partially. But it raised as many questions as it answered. And it failed to answer the fundamental one. Further investigation would be required. He was convinced of one thing, however. He had been right to take Griffin off the market when he did. He might not yet know whether Griffin was the right choice of husband—though Big Steve was convinced of it—but Cooper wasn't giving anyone else a shot at him until he'd made up his own mind. And that, in its own way, was a major development. Or if not that, at least something he hadn't ever done before. And as much a creature of habit as he was, he knew what anyone he discussed it with would make of it.

* * *

Cooper steered the Jaguar through the foggy streets.

"You looked like you were having a good time tonight."

"Better than I expected," Griffin admitted.

"Big Steve was really impressed. He liked everything about you. When Big Steve's your friend, you've got a friend for life. T. and Nick, too. They're real solid guys."

"They were very nice to me. Scott and Jared were, too."

"Of course they were very nice to you. Don't sound so surprised."

"I am surprised. A little."

"Listen, you should never let people intimidate you. The ones who try to are assholes. They don't count. You don't need to impress anybody but yourself, O.K?"

"What about you?"

"You've got nothing to prove to me. I know you don't believe that, but it's the truth."

"All right," Griffin said after a long silence. "You know, I can't believe Big Steve and T. are policemen."

"No?"

"Well, maybe I can, but. . ."

"They're easy enough to picture as policemen. What you can't believe is that they're gay."

"Right."

"Don't let Big Steve let you hear him saying that."

"Why not?"

"You'll get this sermon about how they're the real gays."

"Yeah?"

"You see, he thinks that the drag queens and go-go boys and leathermen and hustlers are just the tip of the iceberg. The real gays are just regular guys who love other guys."

"I guess I can see that."

"That's why Big Steve liked you. He could tell that you get it."

"Oh," Griffin said. "Does that mean I'm a regular guy?"

"Oh, sweetie, you're about as regular as they come."

"I've never thought of myself that way."

"You wouldn't," Cooper laughed. "You're pretty hung up on what a freak you think you are."

"No kidding."

"Any other questions?"

"I can't imagine why a guy like Nick is single," Griffin said.

"I knew you'd catch that," Cooper said. "Fact is, he isn't single."

"So where was his boyfriend tonight?"

"Dario's parents are visiting from Europe," Cooper said. "They don't know about Nick. Dario's not actually out to them. So Nick was on his own tonight."

"Where in Europe?" Griffin asked.

"Geneva," Cooper said. "They're university professors there."

"Swiss," Griffin said. Cooper could hear the wheels turning as he tried to come up with a visual.

"Argentine," Cooper said. "They fled the country due to some political disagreement."

"I see."

"Dario never really lived there. He was very young when they left."

"What does he do?"

"Teaches comparative literature at Berkeley. I have no idea what that even is, but I'm sure you do."

"Somehow I don't see Nick with an egghead."

"In Dario's case, what you see is not what you get," Cooper said.

"I'll have to take your word on it."

"What else is bothering you?" Cooper asked. He hoped Griffin wouldn't embark on the obvious line of questioning. At least Cooper thought it was obvious, having to do with how long Nick and Dario had been a couple and what, if anything, that had to do with Cooper's own abandonment of bachelorhood. No, God, don't let it. . .

"Who says. . .?"

"Oh, please."

"Well in that case, why do I have the exact same haircut as Tristan?"

"Oh, that," Cooper laughed. The deflection had paid off. "Does it bother you?"

"I don't know. Should it?"

"Does he look good with that haircut?"

"Uh, yeah."

"Well, you have the same hair texture and growth pattern as he does. Your head and face are the same shape as his, too. It's a very flattering look for you. That's all it's about."

It wasn't the kind of lie you went to hell for. It wasn't even the kind of lie people broke up over. And it was only partially deceptive. The aesthetic assertion was as true as that night's moonlight. But nothing was ever as simple as the kind of explanation Cooper preferred to give.

* * *

There was nothing sexier, Cooper believed, than driving your car through the night streets with the guy in the bucket seat next to you half-terrified and half-crazy to have you inside him. Griffin was practically whimpering.

One thing Cooper knew for certain. Griffin was as insatiable as anyone Cooper had ever encountered. He might give no sign of it in normal circumstances, but once the door was closed and the clothing began to come off, the truth was inescapable. It might not be the whole truth, but the rest of it could wait for later.

The End

Also by Jackson Peoples-Rosenblatt

The Navigators
Lodestar
The Current
Intersections

Rococo, Chanel (aka Johnnie Miller): born, 1950. Graphic artist, painter, empress. (*The Current*)

Romanovsky, Nikolai "Nick" aka "Niko": born, 1940. Attorney. Big Steve Fabiani's second in command. Legendary Castro Street sexual athlete and bad boy. (*The Navigators; The Current*)

Sainte-Claire, Ashby: born, 1950. Medical student. (*The Navigators*)

Schein, Jean-Pierre: born, 1943. French-born professor of piano performance. Griffin MacDonald's teacher at the San Francisco Conservatory. (*The Current*)

Weitzmann, Trevor: born, 1960. High school athlete. University student. (*The Navigators; The Current*)

Westerleigh, Ned: born, 1918. Youngest son of a minor English aristocrat and a cousin of Czar Nicholas II. Attended Winchester College and Oxford. Served with MI6 during and after World War II. "Deactivated" from the intelligence service at an undisclosed point during the Sixties or Seventies. Resettled in the United States, were he began a career in real estate. Mentor of Elizabeth Montefiore and Cooper Luxemberg. Community benefactor. (*The Navigators; The Current; Intersections*)

Yates, Gregory: born, 1951. Cooper Luxemberg's freshman composition teaching assistant at San Francisco State. Subsequent career as a high school English teacher. (*The Current*)

www.ingramcontent.com/pod-product-compliance
Lightning Source LLC
Chambersburg PA
CBHW051431260626
47162CB00001B/42

Directory of Recurring Characters

Bailey, Scott: born, 1953. Son of an American professor and the daughter of a German Field Marshal executed for his role in Count von Stauffenberg's 1944 plot to assassintate Hitler. She survived the fall of Berlin in 1945, later marrying Scott's father and coming to the U.S. Scott has built a career translating literary works from German. (*The Navigators; The Current*)

Bartok, Jared "J.B.": born, 1950. Wounded during a tour in Viet Nam, nearly losing his left leg below the knee. This injury discouraged him from entering bodybuilding competitions, though his mentors, Big Steve Fabiani and Matthew Duckworth, insisted he try anyway. An architect specializing in Mid-Century Modern style. (*The Navigators; The Current*)

Bentley, Tristan: born, 1947. Graduated from NYU, where he was involved with a student radical cell. Served as a combat medic during one tour in Viet Nam. Joined the San Francisco Police Department subsequent to his military service. A competitive bodybuilder. (*The Navigators; Lodestar; The Current*)

Crawford, Will: born, 1952. Published poet. Attorney. Judge. (*The Navigators*)

de Havilland, Kirk: born, 1955. Trust fund baby. Bodybuilding competitor. (*The Navigators*)

Del Rey, Marina (aka Bartolomeo "Bart" Correa): born, 1951. Travel agent. Drag queen. Chanel Rococo's second-in-command. (*The Current*)

Duckworth, Matthew: born, 1933. Airline pilot, husband, father. Successful bodybuilding competitor. (*The Navigators; The Current*)

Eastman, Sean: born, 1952. Former CBC child star. Former member of the Royal Canadian Mounted Police. Former professional rugby player. Bodybuilder, waiter, sometime hustler. (*The Navigators*)

Fabiani, Stefano "Big Steve": born, 1935. Joined the military while under-aged. Served in Korea and Viet Nam. On retirement from the army, joined the San Francisco Police Department. A guru of local bodybuilders. (*The Navigators; Lodestar; The Current*)

Garrison, Lance: born, 1950. Collegiate and later Olympic wrestler. Physique photographer. (*The Navigators; The Current*)

Krakowiak, Michael: born, 1935. Professor of piano performance. Griffin MacDonald's teacher at San Francisco State. First cousin of Nick Romanovsky's mother. (*The Current*)

Lundquist, Morgan: born, 1956. Gym owner. (*The Navigators*)

Luxemberg, Cooper: born, 1955. Realtor; partner with Ned Westerleigh and Elizabeth Montefiore in the Luxemberg-Montefiore Realty. (*The Navigators; The Current; Intersections*)

MacDonald, Griffin: born, 1956. Graduate student in classical piano perfor-mance and local piano bar performer. (*The Navigators; The Current; Intersections*)

Montefiore, Elizabeth: born, 1940. An aspiring opera singer, she was dis-covered in the chorus at La Scala by fashion photographers. She modeled for Dior, Chanel, and others before returning to the U.S. A partner with Coo-per Luxemberg and Ned Westerleigh in the Luxemberg-Montefiore Realty. (*The Navigators; The Current*)

Montezuma, Holly (aka Enrique "Henry" Sandoval): born, 1953. Trav-el agent. Drag Queen. Chanel Rococo's court jester and enforcer. (*The Current*)

Montgomery, Burton "Buzz": born, 1947. Former high school English teacher. (*The Navigators; The Current*)

Norberg, Kent: born, 1958. The platonic ideal of the late-Seventies go-go boy and twinkie-about-town. (*The Current*)